Cherry Blossoms in Winter

A RIVETING SOLDIER'S STORY OF THE KOREAN WAR, FRIENDSHIP, AND LOVE IN POST-WAR JAPAN

MICHAEL J. SUMMERS

Black Rose Writing | Texas

ISBN: 978-1-68513-478-5
PUBLISHED BY BLACK ROSE WRITING
www.blackrosewriting.com

Printed in the United States of America
Suggested Retail Price (SRP) $21.95

Cherry Blossoms in Winter is printed in Minion Pro

I dedicate this work to the young men and women of this story who feared not to love, and the GIs, who bravely fought and died in Korea.

Special thanks to my wife, Aki, who made my life whole and for whom this work couldn't have been possible; our son William, a climber of grand heights; and my brother, John, with whom I've shared many amazing adventures, inspiring this novel.

Finally, a special thanks to combat veteran and author David Valley, who shared his incredible experiences in Occupation Japan and as an Infantry Rifleman in Korea for the 24th Infantry Division, 19th Infantry Regiment, arriving at the battle for Chinju during the fourth week of July 1950.

PRAISE FOR
Cherry
Blossoms
in
Winter

Five Star Review
"Author Michael J. Summers has written a superb and appealing novel that explores the enduring bond of love."
–Chicago Book Review

"*Cherry Blossoms in Winter* shines a light on the power of love and the chaos of war while captivating readers with catchy humor, action-packed scenes, and adorable love goals. Get ready for a very entertaining and educational experience."
–Los Angeles Book Review

"*Cherry Blossoms in Winter,* by Michael J. Summers, is a captivating blend of romance and historical events. While it contains strong language and adult themes, making it best suited for mature readers, it offers a deeply engaging experience for adults who will appreciate its nuanced storytelling and historical depth."
–Literary Titan

"*Cherry Blossoms in Winter* offers a stellar blend of falling in love from a soldier's perspective without overpowering the story with romance. The balance between common human experiences and those of young, enlisted men makes Cherry Blossoms in Winter a captivating ride that military and historical fiction enthusiasts will love."
–Independent Book Review

"A detailed exploration of Japanese culture following World War II, and the emotional journey of a unique American GI with an epic story to tell, *Cherry Blossoms in Winter* is a delicately crafted masterwork.

Honest, expressive, and thought-provoking, this layered book will resonate profoundly with readers looking for an accurate historical novel and with those hungry for an extraordinary love story.

Summers's pen allows feelings of exquisite nuance to bloom and ring true."
–*Self-Publishing Review*

"With wonderfully drawn characters, attention to setting details, and a great narrative voice, this book is a must-read for people interested in post-war Japan, the cross-cultural romantic relationships that often developed during the occupation, and the men who came of age while stationed in the Far East."
–Diane Hawley Nagatomo, author of *The Butterfly Café* and the forthcoming novel *Finding Naomi*

"*Cherry Blossoms in Winter* deftly evokes two very different worlds: the Korean conflict and the exhaustion, blood, and filth of soldiers at war, and the tenderness and passion of a redemptive love affair in postwar Japan. With his thorough research and familiarity with the settings of this novel, Michael Summers has written a complex tale that prompts reflection on risk, choice, and commitment."
–Carolyn Korsmeyer, author *of Little Follies: A Mystery at the Millennium* and the forthcoming novel *No Final Harbor*

"Michael Summers has written a novel about resilience, tragedy, love and redemption. It is a page-turner that grips the heart and fires the imagination with human drama interspersed with exciting battle scenes."
–Lea O'Harra, author of the *Inspector Inoue Mystery Series* and the forthcoming novel *Sayonara My Sweet*

My purpose in writing this novel is to illuminate through historical fiction the extraordinary events and experiences of thousands of young American soldiers who served in Japan during the occupation and then, without warning, were the first American troops sent to Korea to fight and die in the Korean War. For this purpose, I created a fictitious Army division, the 15th, allowing me to draw upon this notable historical period without being constrained to a specific military unit or engagement.

Of historical significance, the 1st Cavalry Division operated in and around Tokyo during its occupation duty, with its headquarters at Camp Drake. The 24th Division's outgunned and out-manned Task Force Smith was the first American unit to engage the invading Korean People's Army on July 5, 1950, near Osan. Subsequently, the 24th Division endured the brunt of the horrific fighting through the initial three weeks of the war before the 25th Division and the 1st Cavalry Division arrived at the front. The 7th Division, 24th Division, 25th Division, and 1st Cavalry Division were serving their occupation duty in mainland Japan at the outbreak of the Korean War on June 25, 1950. The 29th Regiment served in Okinawa.

Many young American men and Japanese women fell in love during the occupation, and over 45,000 married.

Cherry Blossoms in Winter

We cannot only live for ourselves.
A thousand fibers connect us with our fellow man.
–Herman Melville

CHAPTER ONE
The Americans

Time's passage from one generation to another, from father to son or mother to daughter, from dying civilizations to ascending ones, beckons the question: Is there any passage at all? What comes from continuing in the footsteps of those who came before? Etched in history, did their lives bear less significance than those now present or not yet lived? Love, hardship, beauty, passion, responsibility, death—aren't these the words that bind humanity together?

Such musings consumed me for hours, not knowing why he brought them to me. But, yes, he was unusual, his story important, and I didn't expect to meet him there. I traveled on assignment to Manila to interview Filipino veterans about the Second World War, where I met him, the American.

I live in Hanoi, Vietnam, in the city's Old Quarter, under the shadow of trees. I've lived here for four years, taking my room just after the millennium when the world was supposed to go silent but didn't, so I arrived on a chilly February morning in 2000. My room is small, twenty-by-twenty feet, with an aged wooden floor, desk, rusted steel fan, and a rosewood bed covered by gray mosquito netting.

There is a bathroom inside my room, a luxury. Also, glass-paned French doors open onto a small terrace overlooking busy Hang Ga Street. I chose the Hang Ga Guesthouse in the Old Quarter, close to Hoan Kiem Lake, the French Quarter, and my favorite drinking holes and cafes. I could have picked the quieter, more upscale French Quarter with the posh Sofitel Metropole Hotel and tree-lined boulevards. Still, I wanted the exotic busyness of the Old Quarter—the streaming, colorful Old Quarter.

I am thirty, and this number feels like a dangerous tipping point; my old man always warned me: *Get your career shit together by thirty.*

I push aside a heavily edited stack of two hundred sixty-five pages of unpaid labor that comprises my first novel. I separated it from a pile of papers, notes, and clippings for a paid assignment for *Men's Adventure.* My slender Vietnamese girlfriend, Lan, lounges on the bed with many books scattered about, heavy stuff with fancy lettering and smelling of research, the musty deep bowls of libraries and roaming minds. Her long black hair hangs lazily over her petite shoulders, covering a snug-fitting white cotton blouse that reveals a lovely figure. A pair of black high heels lay next to the old rosewood bed.

On the table is the American's sketchbook, one of the few objects he gave me, and the book is open to a drawing of a beautiful Asian woman dressed in a kimono before the bending red bow of a bridge. A creased letter, one of many his father had returned to him, dated June 25, 1950, from Kamakura, Japan, denotes the page; only now do I know this date marked the beginning of the Korean War. I pull the cap on a cold Tiger Beer, take a long, potent drink, and reach for the book.

There is no writing inside—notes, but no lengthy explanations. Instead, sketches fill the pages, many drawn hastily and others in meticulous detail, some in black and many in color. Places, faces, and scenes, and reflecting upon them now, after what he said, fill me with an odd sense of gratitude, sadness, and hope.

I am not so vain to say he did not change me. In one's adult life, few do materially. The change was subtle, reflective, and newfound maturity. I remember he once said a young man's life is like a meadow of wildflowers, and they should have the right to bloom and draw attention before the colors fade. The tragedy of war is that young men die and never bloom.

I had the chance to bloom, and I wondered whether this blossoming was of any great importance, that hollow feeling that somewhere there is a meaning to life more significant than one's self-indulgence.

Until now, life had always been like a station. You ride by rail to one, get off and enjoy it, and debark for the next—an endless Eurail pass. So, I did a three-year stint in Tokyo, teaching English and bumming Asia during my golden twenties. Then I returned to the States to *"get my career shit together."* But I found cubicle life intolerable—spoiled as I was by mystic temples, the sweet chorus of foreign tongues, and a desire to write—so I quit a Seattle public relations firm and headed for the next station.

I watch Lan lying on the bed, unaware my eyes are studying her. I've had others and observed them as well, and sometimes I recall them as one remembers a distant trip to Paris. We met at my favorite café in the French Quarter. Her crescent-shaped, deep-set oval eyes captured my imagination, and her face possessed an earthly beauty and powerful intelligence. I learned she was an international, and her grandmother, Marguerite, was French. Her grandmother fell in love with her grandfather following the Indochina war, and she remained in Vietnam. Lan giggled that morning at the café and said, "I suppose I'm one-quarter French. It's the vanilla cream inside my patisserie."

Lan graduated from the Paris School of Arts and Architecture and worked in Paris, relocating to Vietnam to lead the Hanoi office. "Why art and architecture?" I asked her.

She said she had loved painting since childhood, and her favorite subjects were the faces of children and elders. "A child's face reflects purity and an elder's face truth and wisdom," she'd said. She explained that developing countries require architects, and that she desired to inject humanism into Vietnam's community design.

She asked about my writing, and I explained a writer must have a tremendous passion for the craft and the story he desires to tell, since good writing requires multiple drafts. That thought leads to a sentence, a second, and a third. And then the writer goes back, like a potter to his wheel, revisiting the sentences repeatedly until the words capture his imagination.

She smiled and asked, "So, do you write like this?"

I returned her smile and said, "I write like I'm playing the piano."

Her face flushed the color of rose petals.

That is the woman she is, and I can't see a future without her, but then I can't see one with her. So, it's always been like that: one station and the next.

I take a drink of beer and return to the American's sketches.

•　　•　　•

It was March 2003, and the American seemed out of place in the cheap Manila pension. I'll never forget the first time I saw him. I walked down a short flight of creaky wooden stairs as he sat in the pension's street-level café. He was an older man, big and weathered with thick gray hair, a square jawline, and bluish-gray eyes, and was quite handsome in his mid-seventies. He wore a light buttoned-up flannel shirt with a stiffly starched collar, brown khaki pants, and well-worn leather sandals.

I carried a laptop, a thick bundle of notes, and newspaper clippings. I strolled to the waitress, Maria, and ordered a bottled San Miguel, taking a table across from the American. The man played solitaire and smoked from a pack of Camel cigarettes. He'd placed a glass-beaded ashtray to his left and a mug of black coffee atop a well-read paperback of Graham Greene's *Our Man in Havana*. The man looked at home in this cheap pension in Manila's gritty Ermita district.

Eventually, he turned and said, "Hey, kid, you going to sit there and play with yourself, or do you want a game of cards?"

His eyes possessed an unexplainable quality. The sound of his voice, too, like his eyes, grabbed one's attention. Command presence, I thought.

"Sure," I said, reaching out my right hand. "I'm Dane. I live in Hanoi, but I'm from Seattle."

"Well, son, it's a hell of a place to meet. The name's Jack Pierce," he replied, reaching out a big right hand and giving it a solid shake.

"The pleasure's mine," I said, and then with long arms and disproportionately long fingers, the man grabbed an empty chair and placed it next to his own.

"Put your shit here. So, tell me, kid, why are you in Ermita? If you didn't notice, the place is a little tired," he said, his eyes twinkling.

"Writers can't be choosy," I replied with a sheepish grin. "But I like it. The history and its convenience to Manila Bay and the Intramuros. It's the real Manila."

"Writer, huh?"

"I'm doing a story about Philippine guerrilla World War Two fighters for *Men's Adventure*."

"*Men's Adventure*? Well. I'll be a son of a bitch," he growled. "I've known some Filipino guerrillas and collaborated with them in other parts of the world."

Jack took a long puff on the Camel and placed the stub into the ashtray atop four others. I noticed how he neatly arranged the butts into the shape of a pyramid and pushed the ashes into a tidy pile. "A game of split?" he suggested, with eyes that sparkled.

"Never heard of it," I said, rubbing my own.

"Good gracious," he chuckled, "what did you do growing up?"

I laughed, feeling relaxed, sensing I'd enjoy the older man's stern, unencumbered home-spun company amid Ermita, Manila—Southeast Asia.

"Lots of video games—*Doom* and *Zelda*—and I played electric guitar in a grunge rock band, Smashing Pumpkins, Chili Peppers, Nirvana."

"Never heard of 'em," he said with a grin. "Elvis, did you play The King?"

"No," I chuckled, "but Elvis was The King."

Jack smiled and looked me in the eyes, studying them.

"And sports? Did you play ball?"

"Starting pitcher in high school but smoked too much weed to be any good. Pot and pitching don't mix," I said, chuckling.

"Ha, I feel sorry for the batters!" he bellowed. "I played football and never took a toke till the highlands, but I come from a fly-fishing family. So, my calling is the mountains and rivers. And, Dane," he growled, dangerously waving the angry-looking Camel, "what the hell is that fish tattoo with big green eyes on your forearm?"

"Body art."

"I see," he said, methodically shuffling the cards.

"Jack, if you don't mind my asking, what's the faded tattoo on your forearm?"

Jack brushed his fingers over the tattoo as one might do upon a stone memorial. He looked up, "Fifteenth Infantry Division, Korea, July '50 through '51. I'm damned lucky to be alive!"

Then, before I could pursue the matter further, he said, "Let's play split—I'll teach you how."

San Miguel bottles piled up that first afternoon, and a more massive mound of ashes emerged. We played for hours, and indeed, it never became dull. He talked about his life in intriguing but disorganized bits and pieces:

"One girl is nice, two even better, and no girl is damned unpleasant.

"I worked with the Montagnard, some wise sons of bitches, and by far the best with knives.

"You ever been chased by an Indian elephant, Dane?

"Love, never walk away from love."

And I noticed he studied me, or shall I say, tested. *Is the young man a bullshitter?*

"Tell me, Dane, do you believe in destiny? How close have you been to dying? Are you frightened of love?" And with each response, he sat with his cards, his bluish-gray eyes, studying me.

We played in that seedy little pension for hours that rolled into days and weeks. Outside, in the heat of tropical Manila, backpack travelers, sex tourists, hawkers, two-bit thieves, lowlifes, and highlifes occupied the gritty Ermita sidewalks.

I listened over games embellished by beer, coffee, mango juice, and burning cigarettes. This became our routine. We were dissimilar, of wildly different generations and paths, yet drawn together; an odd companionship is how I might explain it. And later, I would wonder why he chose me to be his messenger.

Reflecting upon this now, he recognized one must understand his place to understand a man. Comprehend his country, region, town, and neighborhood—his family, their social standing, and how they arrived at their position, education, and values. Perhaps he knew I would know these things. And he began his story here.

But while our paths were dissimilar, he must have seen something of himself in me. Perhaps a shared passion for the different, or more likely, an older man's compassion for a younger one's hubris. And inasmuch as we were Americans, we shared a common bond.

In the story I am to tell, I recognize that a young man tightly guarded these memories of the people, places, and events that follow. But for him to share it was for him to relinquish it. One evening, he told me, "The mark you leave behind is what others carry forward."

CHAPTER TWO
The Beginning

A fresh morning's calm bathed Arlington Heights with the loveliness of spring in May 1940. Hydrangeas created large splashing fountains of blues, whites, and pinks, and the pleasing scent of roses perfumed the air. On Spruce Avenue, a handsome American Revival looked across San Francisco Bay. The home stood awash in airy colors and smiled with an inviting, prosperous presence.

A twenty-foot-long cut-stone path led to the home's entrance through gardens swelling with butterflies. A sunroom with oversized windows, walls filled with fiction books, and large, comfortable reading chairs made the house cozy and intelligent. Beyond, in the grand living room with its Steinway piano, art, and oriental antiques, hung a well-done oil painting above a red-brick fireplace. It portrayed an elderly gentleman in a tweed suit resting comfortably in a wicker chair. The man looked reflectively across a vast open space, as if recounting the full measure of one's life. He sat straight, wiry, but not bony and resembled a long-distance runner. The artist had taken time to paint the details of the subject's face—sharp with a Mark Twain mustache and a healthy complexion. It was the face of a doer rather than a thinker.

Every family has a character that shapes its story. The man in the painting built the Pierce home with his own hands. He started country poor on the dry plains of Nebraska but made his money mining quartz in the Sierra Nevada. Later, he built a prosperous furniture business, Pierce Industries, and regularly played bridge among the San Francisco mercantile by his thirty-eighth birthday.

One Friday afternoon, a handsome boy of twelve sat stiffly at a wooden desk. He rolled his head forward, eyes focused upon a complicated addition of a pair of fractions. The boy had bushy blond hair and a wide-open, cheerful face. He'd finished the fifth problem of a set of twenty when Mrs. Walker, a stern disciplinarian with iron-like wrinkles, ordered him to the front of the class.

"You are a lucky boy, Jack Pierce! Your father is taking you fishing along the Upper Merced."

"Yes!" Jack hollered, looking at his watch. It said 1:00 p.m.

Jack loved fly-fishing the Upper Merced. Jake Pierce, his father, also loved to fly-fish the Upper Merced, and so did his grandfather, Rufus Pierce, the man in the oil painting above the red-brick fireplace.

The Upper Merced spilled from the Yosemite Valley, thick with trout. The Pierce men cherished the area like a second home. Jack thought it was magical.

"Hey, Dad, why didn't you tell me we were goin' fishin'?"

"So, you wouldn't dream of rainbows instead of your studies."

"Is Grandpa Rufus coming?"

"Saturday night."

"Awesome!" Jack said, looking out the window at the big Sierra Nevada. "Dad, will I ever fish as well as you and Grandpa?"

"Nobody will fish as well as Grandpa and me," he said, playfully rubbing Jack's thick blond hair. "Jack, you will fish better than the both of us with practice!"

They rode along the dusty country roads and drank Coca-Cola from long-necked bottles.

"Dad, what do you remember about Grandpa when you were twelve?"

"He worked like hell, but always made time for the mountains and family. Your grandfather took everything seriously, even his fun!"

"Was he always kinda crazy, like now?"

"The life of the party, a great entertainer."

"Will we catch a lot of fish?"

"Sure, a hell of a lot of fish," his father said, grinning.

That evening, they fished for two hours and caught a hell of a lot of fish. Jack knelt by the river, cleaned the catch, and watched his father build a fire. His father smoked a cutty-shaped pipe after he fished, and it drooped lazily from his cracked lips, above which golden-colored whiskers colored his cheeks. Jack thought his father looked tough, with a face covered in stubble, smoking a pipe.

"Hey, Jack Pierce, are those damned fish cleaned?"

"I'll bring 'em right over, Pa."

That night, they listened to the movement of the river and the crackling of burning wood. A billion stars danced on a moonless night above the tops of a jagged line of granite mountains.

"Dad, did you always work with Grandpa?"

"I have, but I once wanted to be a Merchant Marine."

"What's that?"

"A man that works his way around the world on a freighter."

"Well, why didn't you become one?"

Jack's father pulled a shiny whiskey flask from his back pocket and sipped. "It's a long story, Jack. I'd set up a job on Dollar Lines, the freighter departing for Singapore, and packed my bags."

"And you didn't board the ship?" Jack asked, watching the wood crackle.

"Nope, your grandfather needed me. Running Pierce Industries put him in the hospital."

Jack observed his father's face. His eyes looked incredibly alive in the mountains—pure joy—and he didn't always see this at home.

"Jack, the day I'd decided, I'd gone to the Embarcadero to clear my mind. I still remember looking at Alcatraz Island that morning. Fog shrouded the prison."

"Did you see prisoners?"

"Nope, but I remember thinking of the caged men inside; trapped is how I felt."

"And you still didn't board the freighter?"

"Jack, family is more important than freighters in this life. So that day, I walked from the Embarcadero to the Presidio, through the Golden Gate Park and Chinatown, collapsing on Nob Hill, wondering what the hell I'd do."

"And what made you decide?"

"When I was a year older than you, your grandfather made me hike for three days straight through forests, above the tree line, and across snowfields until we finally reached a magnificent granite precipice, dropping thousands of feet. I remembered standing at its edge with towering formations in all directions. At that moment, lying under a giant Live Oak on Nob Hill, remembering making your grandfather proud, I decided not to join the Merchant Marine."

"Jack, now you understand why I take you to the Embarcadero to see the freighters."

"Because you still wanna ride one, right?"

His father chuckled. "Your grandfather sparked my interest in the Merchant Marine by taking me to watch those ships. Watching them come and go, I'd always dream of what it was like on the other end of that journey."

Jack sat quietly and listened to his father's story, feeding sticks into the fire. And finally, he spoke, "So you chose Grandpa Rufus over the freighters?"

His father grinned, removing a piece of paper from his wallet and reading it: "I signed and dated this note November 16, 1924. It says, *help father for two years and then jump ship to Asia.* And below, I wrote a favorite quote by Mark Twain: *I am an old man, and I have known many troubles, but most of them never happened."*

His father smiled and patted Jack on the shoulders with big, manly hands. "Yes, I chose your grandfather over those freighters, and later I married your beautiful mother over the same damned boats, and for that, I got you, my best fishing buddy."

•   •   •

Jack chuckled, taking a closing drag on the Camel. "Dane, when I joined the Army, my father gave me that note. I carried it through Korea until the paper finally wore out. My father was a good man and a fine outdoorsman."

Jack took a drink of coffee, and I noticed his eyes looked wet.

"Kid, I think I'll get rested before dinner."

He carefully placed the butt into its proper place and grabbed the Graham Greene. "How about poker tomorrow after breakfast?"

"Sure, I'd like that," I said.

I finished my San Miguel, pondering that you meet some damned interesting people on the road, and then ascended the creaky wooden stairs to my room. I switched on the overhead fan, removed my clothes, and observed my naked self in the mirror. In March, the heat and humidity in Manila hug you tightly, and thick misty sweat lay on my brow.

I stood in front of the mirror and observed my face. My hair had grown shabby since Hanoi, hanging well below my ears, and my mustache became fuller, so I gave each end a nice tight twist—*Ahh, the Imperial Style*, I thought. I liked my face. Everybody liked my look, and I suppose my mother adored it the most. It had changed little in the last several years, but a significant change quickly appeared when I returned to the States from Tokyo; it inherited a more stressed and fated look.

I grabbed soap and shampoo and proceeded to a communal bathroom shared by three second-floor guestrooms. I locked the door and turned on the shower's chilly water. My skin turned to goose bumps, and the refreshing water flowed through my bushy brown hair, over my mustache, tumbled down my shoulders, over my flat hard stomach, and finally to the white-tiled floor. I quickly toweled and returned to my room, where a message waited: "Dano, old boy, this is Bryant. I'll meet you in the lobby of the Manila Hotel at seven. Hanoi Johnny arrived this morning."

The sun would set at the Baywalk in thirty minutes, and I didn't want to miss it. So, I donned a pair of blue jeans, a Kahala button-up aloha shirt, my trusty Ecuadorian hat, and a book of poetry by Don Blanding.

•　　•　　•

Anytime you walk in Ermita, be on the lookout. The topography is a patchwork of uneven or nonexistent concrete with elephant-sized potholes the height of the Grand Canyon. As a result, the unsuspecting traveler may catch a foot, launch himself into traffic, and die under the savage wheels of a Jeepney. Yes, the Jeepney, a brightly colored dinosaur of a multi-passenger vehicle, hippie buses before there were hippies, and the public transportation choice of metro Manila. Big and rumbling, these dressed-up gas-guzzling beasts shine brightly with colored paints, glowing chromes, and tooting horns, genetically related orphans of American Army jeeps.

Shifty-eyed pickpockets lurk on Ermita's sidewalks, and I carry little cash, anything important, I strap tightly to my waist. Nevertheless, a stroll through Ermita hits one harder than a double cappuccino. You are the prey, the weakest element in the food chain, the dim-witted cash-laden foreign tourist. Your eyes search the landscape, on guard for cracked and uneven sidewalks, high voltage utility lines that lie untethered, ready to snatch your life, and the snarky thief prowling for a careless wallet.

I walked the more direct route to the Baywalk, along Adriatico Street to Pedro Gil, and then west, taking me by once-legendary go-go bars. Intimidating guards dressed like Star Wars stormtroopers pack loaded weapons before the money changers, banks, and gold dealers.

At the corner of Adriatico and Gen Malvar Streets, the ubiquitous 7-Eleven advertised Coke Slurpees. Distant memories elicited by powerful American branding—the big orange-red seven and Coca-Cola drew me inside. I purchased a good cold beer, Asahi Dry.

Manila Bay appeared postcard-perfect, like no other harbor in Southeast Asia. I sat on a bench admiring the modern steel-hulled freighters, well-worn traders, and bangka boats cutting soft, clean lines through turquoise waters. I thought of Jack's father and imagined him dreaming of sailing from San Francisco to Singapore during the booming twenties.

The sun dropped large and brilliantly into the horizon, burning itself into the memory, somehow different and more potent than the lifetime of sunsets that came before it. I popped the cap on the bottle that separated me from my cold beer. The Asahi Dry tasted refreshingly bitter and better than I expected. Cold beer always tastes perfect in places like this. I pulled the Blanding book of poetry and opened it to "Today is Here." The poetry wrapped itself tightly around me, speaking of this day, this moment, this "urgent hour." Yes, by God, be alive, and do not waste the treasure of this day! Feeling inspired and in love with Manila and the taste of a good cold beer fronting a famous sunset, I retrieved a notebook and pencil and improvised a poem:

The splendid fragrant colors of the Manila sun, like rich Spanish treasures of the 14th century, impatiently hovering upon a timeless horizon, bougainvillea purples, oranges, and reds, shimmering in the evening twilight, burnt cinnamon across a billowy sky, dull orange glaze lit a fire by the gods, timeless through the ages …., like a good cold beer.

I laughed aloud and surveyed the colored horizon and the unfolding scene. A dozen small children scurried here and there, their feet and faces painted muddy brown. "Hey, Joe, you got pesos?" they asked with outstretched palms.

"No, something better." And I passed about a handful of postcards and a couple of George Washington-faced American quarters for each, and they ran off chattering happily.

A pair of anxious-looking middle-aged German tourists nervously held hands far away. I watched as a long-armed beggar descended upon them in tattered clothes, and I suspected they wished for a twentieth anniversary in Hawaii.

Meanwhile, a pair of fashionable young lovers entwined their hands, excited for an evening of dancing in Makati and the prospect of lovemaking. And to my left, a half dozen Korean businessmen in stiff blue suits huddled together, chain-smoking. I imagined them strategizing over their next grand waterfront real estate deal.

I pulled hard on the Asahi Dry and felt a tap on my shoulder. I expected a panhandler, but she had long, deeply tanned fingers and a chiseled bar girl's face. She offered, "I make you happy, baby."

"No, not tonight, but thanks for asking."

•　　•　　•

The more I knew Jack, the more I admired him. He possessed an odd collection of unique sensitivities for a man of his kind. The following morning, I awoke early, finding him alone in the café. He wore white cotton pajamas and black rubber slippers. His gray hair hung disheveled over his ears. He hadn't shaved, and the stubble of his whiskers made him appear old and manic. He sat hunched over the table, and all I could see from the creaky wooden stairs was the bulk of his body and a familiar cup of black coffee. As I descended, I observed him working furiously; his knobby right hand held a graphite sketching pencil, and his face peered into the pages of a nine-by-twelve-inch leather-bound sketchbook. Suddenly, like the unexpected movement of a gecko, the pencil darted north, south, east, and west, and a form quickly took shape. *I'll be damned*, I thought. *He's an artist!*

Jack abruptly looked up, pencil in midair, and refocused his steely, bluish-gray eyes upon my bemused expression. "I've been sitting here since 4 a.m.," were the first words from his mouth.

"Then I assume you've had breakfast," I said.

"I'm well taken care of, thank you."

"I'm hungover, myself," I replied with one of those obnoxious, cotton candy guts that follows a night of binge drinking.

"Maria makes my breakfast," he said. "This morning, a delicious tomato omelet, the sweetest mango ever plucked from a tree, and fresh-baked pandesal filled with coconut jam. Hooo-weee, she's a good woman, Dane! So, Maria, get this lad a double straight black Americano and your famous breakfast," Jack hollered. "Now, what got you so hungover?"

"Burgos Street with buddies from Hanoi."

Jack chuckled. "I've romped through them all, from Wan Chai to Kabukicho, and been drunker than a skunk more than I can count, but the odd splashes of paint make life interesting! I am impressed, young man, that you pulled yourself from bed. It's youth, sweet youth!"

"Yeah, and a lack of common sense. Anyway, what are you working on?" I asked as the black coffee hit my pipes.

"A memory of the Himalaya," he said, turning the sketchbook so I could see the drawing.

"It's impressive," I said, "like a scene from James Hilton's *Lost Horizon*."

"For me, at that time, I discovered Shangri-La. The mountains and the Tibetans made me whole again. I want to show you something," he said, rising from the table.

I followed him down a narrow hallway to the rear of the pension and entered a darkened room. He switched on the light, and rich Philippine mahogany reminded me that the inn dated from the Spanish occupation. I noticed books lined one wall, filled with the classics, history, economics, languages, and philosophy.

"You like good books," I said.

"I've read them all and some of them twice."

Two caught my attention, the *Ugly American* by William J. Lederer and Eugene Burdick, and Will and Arial Durant's nine-volume series, The Story of Civilization.

"Did you read the entire series?"

"Twice. Dane, I learned early in life that brawn and bravery are no substitute for knowledge."

A half-dozen sketches and a pair of Japanese woodblock prints decorated the opposite wall of the otherwise spartan quarters. I immediately recognized Asakusa's Sensoji Temple's five-storied pagoda in winter from my previous life in Tokyo.

He led me to the sketches, and I stood before them, admiring their emotion, beauty, and sense of place. Two were portraits of a beautiful Japanese woman with flowing black hair, moonlike eyes, and delicate, angel-like facial features. Another showed a river with jagged peaks and a pair of fly-fishers. A black and white landscape hung next to the fisherman, depicting a dozen sampans alongside a steamship in the harbor of Saigon. And a portrait of a man's face hung next to this. The face appeared confident and handsome, with sharp blue eyes. "This is my father, as I remember him from my youth," Jack said.

"But I wanted to show you this one." And he pointed to a colored sketch of a half-dozen soldiers resting solidly against oversized olive-green packs, formidable rifles lying across their laps, with dirty, ragged, tired faces—but very much alive and smiling at the world. I studied each of the young men's faces and imagined their personalities. The one with curly red hair, a big wry smile, and eyes that said he sliced right through life's bullshit. Another, with mahogany-colored hair, deep brown eyes, and a happy-go-lucky smile, implied a big, gentle heart. A tall, lanky big man with an equally generous smile sat next to the redhead as if he had just cracked the biggest joke of the night.

"Each of these young men has a story," Jack finally said. "I remember them well; they were friends of mine. And some died soon after I sketched this. Their hands went cold in mine."

"Jesus, it must be hard to live with those memories," I said.

"At one time, but now I only remember their lives. And each day, I cherish my own because of the men in that sketch."

We returned to the café just as Maria placed her famous omelet before me. Breakfast rolled into the second day of card playing, and after several rounds of split, spades, and many hands of poker, a fresh writing project sat in my lap.

One night, Jack insisted we eat out. As he explained where we were going, I could feel a childlike excitement in his eyes.

"This place is on a small side street just off United Nations Avenue and makes the best tempura and gyoza in this whole sprawling city."

At dinner, Jack told me about Michiko.

"You ever had a woman you truly loved?" he asked.

"I'm seeing a girl in Hanoi."

"What's her name?"

"Lan."

"Is she beautiful?"

"She is," I replied with a mischievous smile.

"You never forget their eyes, Dane."

And I noticed that his own eyes searched through time.

"I suppose you don't."

He said sternly, "Goddamn, she had the most beautiful eyes. When you are in love, their eyes look different. I learned that too late."

"What was her name?" I asked him.

"Michiko."

"Was she the subject of those sketches on your wall?"

He looked at me, not saying a word, and ate another gyoza.

"By the way," I said, "I've extended my stay in Manila. I've found a new writing project."

"You have, have you?" Jack chuckled. "Wonderful! Then I'll tell you about Michiko, this damned tattoo, and those men on the wall."

CHAPTER THREE
Occupation Japan

An autumn morning's chill permeated the Kinugawa Spa near the ancient village of Nikko on the fifth day of November 1949. Her hair lay thick across his muscled chest, and her naked body warmed his bare skin. Outside, a dog barked unremittingly, like one does when its world is in peril. He pondered that a cat, mouse, or rooster had troubled the animal. Dozens of cranky black crows nested in this ancient village. Their eerie cawing mixed oddly with the crowing of village roosters, the dogs' barking, and the laughing children walking to school alongside the edge of rice fields turned golden by the approaching winter.

Frigid air seeped between the inn's wooden beams and paper-thin windows, turning everything cold inside. And burning rice fields brought the musky scent of autumn, reminding Jack of the fall leaves his grandmother burned in a stone fireplace in the rear yard of her Arlington Heights home. From the high peaks of the Japanese Alps, a stream, the color of glass marbles, rolled through the village. It sang a soothing melody, making Jack's body heavy and comfortable next to Michiko's.

Inside the futon, she warmed him, and he dreaded disturbing the moment. Jack closed his eyes and recalled their evening's lovemaking. They did it gently, with passion, and without haste, and her body shone in the warm glow of lanterns. He closed his eyes and reminisced over her glorious black hair spilling upon his face and her oval eyes alight with desire. The memory of her creamy soft skin, the taut brown nipples of her breasts, her narrow hips, and her legs wrapped around his own the moment they became one, the heavy panting, the release, and tranquility that followed. He pondered on its oddity, the anticipation, the buildup, and the waiting for that moment—that eerily steady buildup that makes a man edgy and strained. Then, it all drains away and begins its unremitting cycle again. *Yes,* he thought, *that persistent force of nature kept the entire system running.*

He loved Michiko. He loved her in a way he didn't recognize, and these newfound emotions startled him. Her being was as earthy and whole as the soil of Japan. She wasn't his first; Suzanne, a big-breasted seventeen-year-old redhead, took his virginity. But he didn't love her or the blonde he'd run around with in Honolulu or the handful of Hotel Street hookers the first couple of drunken months at Schofield. The whores meant nothing; instead, he remembered the hollowness inside him after he'd given them their money. But come payday, they went anyway, stupid, reckless, and laughing, exchanging cash for a quickie.

This girl beside him possessed a naturalness, a tenderness, and a fierceness in her being. He'd never connected to a woman like this before. Sure, he'd had that drive that makes a man crazy with desire. Until now, at twenty-one years old, he'd invested as much as any other, but never had he fallen in love, whatever that love might be.

But love existed with this girl named Michiko, whose name took him several tries to pronounce correctly. She was a twenty-four-year-old Japanese woman born in the mountainous village of Kakunodate, of a generation that was America's enemy. But for Jack, her long black hair and moonlike eyes fascinated him, and her hair and eyes bore the same earthly color as an Indian woman, as he recalled from the Western movies as a boy. So why, he pondered, did these new feelings overwhelm him? That she, among them all, had become as much of a spiritual release as she was a physical release.

Damn it, he thought, disgusted by these feelings; perhaps he'd spent too much time with her, and that was all there was to it, like being pulled in by a good Tennessee whiskey. For two months, she'd been his steady, and his time with her made him feel good and whole, and that feeling of wholeness had an addictive quality to it. *Yes,* he thought, *that was it,* and it depressed him to consider losing her, so he determined in his mind to marry her.

Then Michiko placed the tip of her delicate finger upon his belly and traced *kanji,* Chinese characters. "What are you writing?" he asked.

"Michiko wants to eat you," she replied, and they laughed.

He took her into his arms and quickly rolled her over. Afterward, Jack donned a dark blue *yukata*—bathrobe—tying it securely around his waist with a cotton *obi* belt. Michiko stood naked from the bed and placed a light blue *yukata* with a delicate pattern of white chrysanthemum flowers around her shoulders. She moved gracefully to the *shoji* door, sliding it open to expose the inn's rustic wood-beamed interior hallway that led to an outside natural stone path through a bamboo grove to the ancient baths below.

The hot spring pools sat alongside the stream, and bright fall-colored maple and ginkgo trees rose high above and then sprawled out, over, and across the gushing waters. They walked wearing wooden *geta* sandals that made a rhythmic *clop, clop, clop* as they meandered over the centuries-old stone steps to the baths. In midweek, the baths were empty. They washed each other with hot piping water flowing from a thick cut of green-stripe bamboo. Michiko unwrapped herself from the *yukata* to expose her beautifully firm breasts, curvy hips, and petite bottom. He took the sponge and washed her body and hair, and she did his hair and scrubbed his back. They moved from one pool to the next, some scalding hot and others tepidly warm. Their favorite sat alongside the fast-flowing stream, and when they dripped with sweat, they sat at the stream's edge and dipped their feet into the frigid mountain water.

After bathing, they retreated to their room and then to the dining hall for a breakfast of hot miso soup, fluffy white rice, freshly picked mountain vegetables, and trout caught that morning from the same stream. Jack and Michiko sipped green tea, and they laughed, telling childhood stories. He sat in the traditional style, his legs tucked tight under his buttocks and the weight of his body bearing upon the tops of his feet.

"Baby, I can't feel my feet; I need to stretch."

"It's okay," she giggled, "you're a *gaijin*, foreigner," and she pulled Jack's legs straight. "Today, we explore Nikko. But first, I will show you the great Ieyasu Tokugawa's tomb," she said.

That night, a banana moon hung lazily over the centuries-old Japanese inn, and Jack and Michiko enjoyed the pools late into the evening.

•   •   •

Two years before Michiko, Jack completed his first year of college at Berkley, uninspired and looking for a change. Like his father, he dreamt of wayward adventures upon untamed continents, but three years seemed a lifetime away. Africa, Asia, and the faraway islands of the South Pacific, with odd-sounding names like Bora Bora, Darjeeling, and Timbuktu, captured his imagination. Jack read Herman Melville and Jack London voraciously and was a dreamer. As a boy, he received immense pleasure from his mother's nightly readings of Rudyard Kipling, and in high school, he read Ernest Hemingway's *The Sun Also Rises* three times.

He'd decided when laying down his pencil after the semester's final exam. Jack wrote a note telling his parents he would return in three weeks, stuffed his pack full of gear, grabbed his fishing rod and rifle, and headed for the Sierra. He fished the high alpine lakes for twenty-one days, trekked a hundred miles over three mountain passes, and read *The Sound and the Fury*, *Nineteen Eighty-Four*, and *A Farewell to Arms*. Then, on his final morning, he awoke early, packed his tent, hiked to within two miles of his truck, shot a midsize white-tailed buck, leaving the guts for the bears, and packed the meat and his remaining gear well before nightfall.

The old Ford rumbled into Arlington Heights with Jack smelling of fish and smoky campfires, his face burned by the sun, bloodstained clothes, and bleached hair. "Dad!" he hollered, "I've got a quartered buck in the truck! I'll trim the fat after my run!" He jogged five miles through Berkley's golden foothills at dusk, and with the fifty pounds of venison and gear he'd rucked that morning, the day's effort satisfied him.

The summer days fell like dominos—cutting cabinetry at Pierce Industries, kissing with a sexy brunette at the movies on Friday nights, long evening runs with a dying sun at his back, and hooking up with college and old high school buddies. But he knew he wasn't going back. The renowned university of life would teach him lessons he'd never learn behind a desk.

"Dad, I'm joining the Army," Jack said, eating his mother's meatloaf and mashed potatoes one summer evening in '48.

"Well, why in the hell do that? You're in a fraternity and getting good grades. So, graduate and get a well-paying job or join as an officer?"

"Because I don't want to!"

"But enlisting makes no sense! You've got a high-salaried job at Pierce if you want it. Get your degree first, Jack, or you risk never finishing!"

"For God's sake, Dad. You should have caught that damned freighter for Asia when you had your chance!"

"Sometimes you do what's right in your heart. So, I made the best decision at the time."

"You did, but what's right in my heart is to enlist, and I've decided. I'll serve like Uncle Winston did in Italy and France during World War Two."

Jack's mother, Francine, looked up nervously, barely touching her meatloaf. "Uncle Winston died in France, Jack. Please say it's not the infantry!"

"Don't be anxious, Mom—there aren't any wars. It's just somethin' I want to do, volunteer, while I have the chance. Afterward, I'll make normal plans and finish college, but I will make my way in this world."

"Jack, do you remember the four words?"

"Sure—honesty, kindness, hard work, and common sense."

"So, does joining the infantry make common sense, Jack?"

"Dad, what kind of life will I have if every decision requires common sense? That kind of life doesn't excite me!"

"Okay, picture folks talking at the pool hall or even your damned funeral. *That Jack Pierce was a dishonest son of a bitch* or *the most honest guy you'd ever meet but always afraid of a day's work. The man worked hard but felt nothin' for stabbing a colleague in the back.* You get the point, don't you? You don't want folks remembering you as a man without common sense."

"Dad, I don't see the relationship between common sense and me joining the Army. It makes perfect sense. Besides, common sense is a matter of interpretation, isn't it?"

"It is, but if you weigh your decisions, you'll make the right choices. So then, where will the Army station you?" Jack's father asked.

"Europe, Japan, or Hawaii, don't know."

"Alaska?" And his father played like he was reeling in a sockeye salmon, surrendering to his son's wishes.

"Best fishing in the world, Dad!"

"You best prepare for Georgia or Mississippi. The big infantry bases are in the south."

"I'll go wherever."

Three months later, surrounded by prickly-faced pineapple plantations, Jack fired M1 rifles at firing ranges on the glorious island of Oahu, two thousand three hundred thirty-nine miles southwest of San Francisco. Then, in June 1949, he rotated to Camp Drake, Japan, for duty with the 15th Infantry Division. Life in 1949 tasted good. He carried a winning hand—four of a kind, all jacks, and controlled his destiny, and that's how he liked it.

•   •   •

Occupation duty at Camp Drake, Tokyo, was first-rate — "Good duty," the soldiers said with a grin. Jack stood sweating in the early morning humidity on the sprawling base's grassed parade grounds. He released his seventy-pound pack, and it fell with a thud. That big green pack, shaped like a monstrous Hawaiian sea turtle, burned its straps into his shoulders during the early morning's fresh, five-mile march. He didn't care about that, and he took his large right hand and wiped a mountain of sweat from his forehead.

The young man bent forward and removed a heavy canteen, a tall and particularly handsome young GI in his tight, camel-colored T-shirt and matching khaki shorts.

"Goddamn, Pierce, how do you move so fast? I ain't seen nobody march like that," said Tyrone Henderson, one of the company's newly integrated Black soldiers.

Jack grinned. "I've carried packs my whole life, Henderson. Besides, I like it," and he stood up, exposing a pair of long fast legs, designed like an alpinist's, and constructed with the same finely tuned mechanics as his grandfather Rufus and father Jake's.

"You got plans for the weekend, Henderson?"

"Heck yeah. I'm goin' into Tokyo. How 'bout you?"

The men talked about three things, mostly. Girls, sports, and weekends. And weekends meant trying to meet women if they didn't already have a girl lined up.

"I'm driving to the Alps with Abbott and Simons," Jack said.

"Oh, sure, I hear it's pretty up there. But I'll take the Ginza. Anyway, I'll see you around, Pierce."

"Alright, Henderson, see you next week."

Jack showered and walked across the parade grounds to the mess hall. Breakfast marked the beginning of a new day, and a new day was good because it was crisp and not yet lived. He pushed himself through two big swinging doors into the cafeteria, where high-pitched cheery sounds of joking soldiers, forks, spoons, plates clanking together, and chair legs screeching madly across tiled floors greeted his ears. Half-starved, he piled a hefty portion of scrambled eggs onto a big white breakfast plate with an equally sized mound of hashed brown potatoes, an orange, and two pink slabs of honey-fried ham.

A wrinkly-faced Japanese mama-san stood behind the counter smiling and said, "*Wa sugoi gochiso*, wow, wonderful feast! You beri beri hungly!"

Jack winked and rubbed his stomach. Grinning, he said: "*Onaka ga suita*, I'm hungry!"

At a table, four years before occupied by Japanese military officers, Perkins was smoking a Chesterfield. Perkins sat next to Robert and Robert next to Eugene, who also smoked a Chesterfield. They all appeared exaggerated, making big talk, jostling, excited; not wrapped tightly around the world's grand problems, they were in the thick of it. Jack sipped his charcoal-colored coffee, lit a cigarette, and listened to the conversation dart back and forth. June 22, Comiskey Park, Chicago, Jersey Joe Walcott versus Ezzard Charles for the World Heavyweight Championship. A brand spanking new Canon camera was purchased in Ginza at half the cost of a Kodak! *Twelve O'clock High*, starring Gregory Peck, showing on Friday night. Jack listened quietly, rolling the tobacco's smokiness around his tongue, mingling with the taste of hot coffee. He took a heavy bite of scrambled eggs, savoring their deliciousness and the deep happiness in his chest.

"Gentlemen," he interrupted, "this breakfast is the best. Wouldn't you agree, Eugene?"

Eugene lifted his head from a plate laden with scrambled eggs bathed in melted cheese. The young red-haired soldier had long baseball pitcher arms and resembled a lanky ostrich, the type of long-limbed critter seen in the underbrush of an African savanna.

"Charles will knock out Walcot in the fifth; Abbott and I got money on it!" he said. Then he swung himself violently to confront Jack. "Not bad, Pierce, but not the best. You must spend a week fishing on my Old Man's thirty-six-foot rattletrap. He mixes 'em with freshly caught salmon, and the eggs are something! Besides, Pierce, how is it that every mornin' you're telling us it's the greatest breakfast you've had?"

Jack laughed and took a double-sized bite of ketchup-stained hash browns. "I don't think about yesterday, and this is a fine breakfast!"

Perkins looked up, grinning but serious. "Pierce, I can cook a helluva tasty breakfast too! Mix the eggs with steak and add crispy brown fried quartered potatoes, ranch style. Hooo-weee—now that's a tasty breakfast!"

Sitting at an adjacent table, four tough-looking veterans worked through their own breakfasts. These old-timers fought in the Pacific campaign, thirty-year men.

"I heard Mel Chambers and Frank Johnson killed plenty of Japs in New Guinea," Eugene whispered, lofting smoke rings from his outstretched lips.

"They all killed plenty," Perkins said.

"Yeah, well, Chambers got two Silver Stars," Eugene said.

"What did he do?" Robert asked.

"Don't know, but he got two Silvers for doin' it."

"Whyn't you just ask Chambers what he did?" Perkins challenged.

"You crazy? I'm not pokin' my nose in those boys business!" Eugene countered.

"Why, you got mice in your trousers?" Robert teased.

Jack studied the four soldiers' faces at the opposite table. And he saw it in their eyes, but couldn't see what they'd seen. Nobody could unless you'd been there in the dirty Pacific jungles and done it as they did. And some younger boys wanted it too. Big Bill Burns did, and so did Russell Simmons. They talked about wanting it, a manly desire to prove themselves. But Jack wasn't looking, didn't feel he needed it, but then he wouldn't walk away either.

"Enough about breakfast and war heroes," Robert said. "Shall we spend the weekend in Tokyo?"

"You're right; we should," Eugene said with a big knowing grin.

Perkins looked up from his eggs and grunted in the affirmative, cowboy talk for "heck yes!"

"You're too quiet, Pierce!" Robert said.

"I heard rumors about your last trip to Ginza."

"Rumors? Pierce, you know I don't trade in fiction!"

"Give him the score," Eugene quipped. "Besides, to heck with Snakey Frank's reputation! The little redheaded shit likes it; the more notorious, the better!"

"Spill it," Jack said impatiently, knowing it wouldn't be pretty.

Robert explained they were upstairs at the infamous Club A, stinking drunk about midnight, chasing last-call beers with three Ojo-san lookers. Two gals had sandwiched Snakey Frank against Eugene's right shoulder in a big, smoky stall. The third, a curvy beauty with a throaty laugh and painted red swords for fingernails, dropped below the table and tied the soldier's boot laces together.

"Tied Snakey's boots? For what?" Jack laughed.

"So, he couldn't move his damned feet!" Eugene squawked.

Robert continued. He explained the three Ojo-sans started jabbering in Japanese, barking orders to one another, and before he could react, they had stretched the Snake flat as a pancake, one girl's bottom weighing down his chest, the other his knees, and the third securing his arms.

"He couldn't move an inch; you should've been there, Jack, seen the crazy look on Snakey Frank's son of a bitch ugly face, thrashin' like an eel in quicksand!"

The sight of Snakey Frank Connors big, coffee-stained bucked teeth and beady brown eyes running wild with terror was too much.

"So, what's the punchline?" Jack finally asked.

"We ordered the girls to pull Conner's trousers. And Snakey Frank's screamin', bouncing up and down, and the Ojo-sans are hollerin' '*Moto, moto, moto*'—more, more, more.

"And?" Jack said with a guffaw.

"The pretty one on his chest reaches under his underwear and starts …, and the Snake…" Robert paused.

"No!"

"You're damned right!" Eugene hollered; his face was so red Jack thought it might explode. "The sinister fuck popped a boner!"

The whole table broke into hysteria, even the thirty-year men, chuckling. Finally, gaining his composure, Jack said: "And I'm damned glad I missed it and went cruising after all!"

Finally, Jack took a big puff off the Chesterfield. "Anyway, I'd like to try my luck fly-fishing, and Abbott made some big dough on the black-market hawking cigarettes and whiskey and picked up a Buick."

"Come on, man, you blew us off land weekend!" Robert countered.

"And saw some magnificent streams."

"Isn't driving for men who have girls! And a Buick isn't all Abbott's got. I hear he's shacking up with a girl named Yuki!"

"He is, and Simmons is bringing his girlfriend, Miyuki. Miyuki's a friend of Yuki's."

"Names all sound the same!" Perkins said, chuckling.

"So whyn't you tell Abbott and Simmons you're invited to an orgy? I'm sure they'd understand then! Besides, once we hook-up, we'll pitch our money and buy our own ride!"

"Listen, before I got to Drake, I had a handful at Schofield. A crazy intelligent blonde with a pretty smile that would light up your heart. But I swear she rolled my ass over a cliff whenever I wanted to get away. So, I figure, in Japan, maybe I'll travel light, see more terrain."

Everybody laughed heartily, finishing their hot coffee.

"So, your mind's made?" Robert asked.

"Let me sleep on it."

•　　　•　　　•

The Tsukiji Fish Market welcomed the four green Americans to a strange new world. It bustled with orderly disorderliness, moving, stopping, and moving again. "*Irasshaimase*, welcome! *Irasshaimase*, welcome!" the sellers hollered. And the yen traded faster than lightning.

Fat-faced fish, small slimy octopus, live thrashing eels, oddly colored fish eggs, bony-looking crustaceans, and flat-backed crabs filled the market's stalls with strange sounds and stranger smells— yappity yap faces, and everywhere hustle and bustle.

They meandered wide-eyed through the tightly packed market, sticking out like towering Yankee thumbs, pushed along by a giant Japanese, black-haired mop, all fantastic. Through the fish, vegetables, sweets, and gift quarters. And a cheap, spanking-new Canon camera slung across Eugene's shoulders—*click, click, click*.

Catching a charcoal-burning bus to Asakusa, they stood in the aisle, and the city bounced by. Patches still lay in rubble, and despite four years of hasty rebuilding, some concrete structures still bore the ugly black scars of March 10, 1945. Eugene leaned forward, one lanky arm poking out the window—*click, click-click*.

"Fifty percent of Tokyo scorched to the ground," Jack said, reading a guidebook.

"The poor son of a bitches," Perkins replied, looking at the cityscape from the window, dumbfounded by the prospect of such widespread devastation.

"Tokyo was a tinderbox, especially Asakusa and Shitamachi, burned like kindling," Eugene said. "LeMay ordered the Superfortress to fly low under darkness and drop incendiary cluster bombs, thirty-eight per five-hundred pounder. The bombs spread out and hit the ground, and five seconds later, kaboom, napalm burning everywhere. The fires killed a hundred thousand and left a million homeless."

"More deadly than Hiroshima," Robert added.

"So, you'd think they'd hate us," Perkins said.

"Many do, but they hide their true feelings," said Eugene.

"Sure, but more are simply relieved and better yanks than Russians. They say *shikataganai*," Jack said.

"And what does *shikataganai* mean?"

"It can't be helped."

The bus abruptly stopped, creating a giant lung-crushing plume of smog. "Sensoji Temple!" the driver hollered, waving the soldiers from the bus onto a crowded street of pushcarts, bicycles, and rickshaws.

"Okay, Jack, why are we here?" Robert asked, testing him like a teacher.

"It's the oldest and most famous temple in Tokyo, founded in 628, over one thousand three hundred years ago. This, Robert, is one of the most sacred Bodhisattvas in Japan, famous for relieving human suffering."

"Correct," said Robert, adding that a fisherman snagged the Bodhisattva in his net, and with it, the village headsman founded the Sensoji Temple.

"Sounds like a moneymaker to me!" Eugene sneered cynically.

Click, click, click.

They meandered wide-eyed along the centuries-old Wakamise Shopping Street, leading to the sacred temple gates.

"How much are the teacups?" Perkins asked at one of the dozens of souvenir shops.

"I'll take a samurai mask," Eugene said.

Jack noticed a striking Ukiyo-e woodblock print of the five-storied Sensoji Temple's pagoda blanketed by crisp winter snow. "That's the one I want," he said to a wrinkly-faced shopkeeper.

The gray-haired man proudly reached for the beautiful art.

"No mo, no mo," he said, smiling with yellow, acorn-shaped teeth and pointing to the print's five-storied orange and gold pagoda and the majestic Kannon Main Hall. "*Hi, Hi*, Fire, Fire," he said, raising his hands and motioning for airplanes overhead.

"*Wakarimashita, I* understand," Jack acknowledged.

"*Shikataganai*," the old merchant replied, smiling.

The ancient temple grounds delighted Jack's imagination, making him dream of distant and unfamiliar worlds, so foreign to life back home—everything, the smells, sounds, tastes, and sights. But the old merchant's face stuck in his mind as he meandered through the temple grounds. That smiling old man had been under those B29s.

At the Sumida River, they drank bottled beer and snacked on chicken yakitori, watching the ebb and flow of the riverside junks, barges, sampans, and ferries. And all about them were hastily erected souvenir shops selling curiosities to greenback-toting soldiers. The occupied and the occupiers. Pushcarts, rickshaws, roaming gangs of kids, and the rebuilding of war-devastated Tokyo one slab at a time.

"You know why I'm here?" Jack said, enjoying a cold beer.

"Because you ate the fancy red apple, a true believer," Robert said, chuckling.

"Speak for yourself," Jack grinned. "I wanted days like this, where you wake up not knowing your destiny."

"You mean before marriage," Robert said.

"I suppose before every day becomes predictable."

"And today," Eugene interrupted, "geishas and dancing." He toasted his beer.

"So, Perkins, what brings you here?" Jack asked.

"My family's got this ranch; I expect I'll die on it. It ain't much; it barely keeps us alive. Still, it's all I know—fences, irrigation lines, the damned coyotes, and broken-down barns, and yet despite that, you try to keep it going."

"Sounds like a handful," Jack said.

"And you've got the icy winters, drought, cattle, and hogs—the land you're workin' twelve hours a day, and mountains, streams, and forests all around you."

And Jack, watching how Perkins explained it, understood he loved it. It was who he was.

"So, why did you leave it?"

"Same as you. How does a man know what he's got if he doesn't try somethin' different? So, I figured the Army was better than ridin' boxcars."

A street kid suddenly broke the silence. "Hey, GI, Yankee GI!" A burning cigarette hung from his right hand.

"How old do you think the boy is?" Eugene asked.

"Eleven, twelve," Jack said. "The others are younger. All over Ueno Station, living in the tunnels with the whores and boozing Jap soldiers. But it's better than in 47. A few old-timers said it was bad, homeless kids everywhere."

"And we're enjoyin' beer and chicken sticks," Perkins said disdainfully, sliding the last bite into his mouth. "It ain't right!"

"Sure, it's right; it doesn't bother me a bit," said Robert. "We're building their economy, aren't we? Spending millions of taxpayers' dollars teaching them democracy. So anyway, screw 'em!"

"Pretty callous, Robert! Where's your compassion?" said Eugene.

"Look at 'em, what do you see?"

"Homeless kids. Anyway, what's your fuggin point?"

"You're lookin' at somebody else's problem, Eugene. And why should a soldier care if their government doesn't clean it up?"

Meanwhile, a barefooted girl shaped like a pencil with shiny black curls, grimy feet, and a dirty blue dress joined the barefooted boys, stealing a cigarette from an older boy's lips.

"Wow," said Perkins.

"A future whore," Eugene said, disgusted.

"Look, nobody asked us to be here, did they?" Robert said.

"We forced it, didn't we?" Eugene said. "We're part of this mess. The Air Force burned half their city!"

"That's not the way I see it!" said Robert.

Perkins scowled. "I don't care how you see it, Robert. It's morals. And it ain't right, kids scroungin', and us livin' it up."

"Well, life isn't fair; it's a son of a bitch, Perkins. So, get used to it," Robert said. "We've got the same morality where I come from, the rich and everybody else; it's society. Besides, they got what they had comin', didn't they?"

"They're kids!" Perkins barked, pulling two dollars of scrip from his wallet and removing the prettiest teacup from his newly bought set. "My mom won't miss this one bit!"

"I'll go with you," Eugene offered.

"I'm in," Jack said, standing up.

"Alright, you gullible bleedin' hearts, tryin' to save this broken world. If it makes you feel better, take two bucks, but I'm drinkin' your share," Robert laughed.

The kids circled the GIs like prowling little wolves—the young girl with pretty hair and begging brown eyes, not smiling, just pleading. *Give me money.* And a burning cigarette between her dirty, cracked lips.

"*Onamae wa*, what's your name?" Jack said, speaking to the girl.

"Yukiko," she said shyly, holding out her palm.

"*Nan-sai desu ka*, how old are you?" he asked.

"*Ju-sai desu*, ten."

"*Okasan to Otosan wa*, your mother and father?"

She just stared, not hearing the foreigner's Japanese.

"*Kutsu*, shoes," Jack said, pointing to her charcoal brown feet and then to his polished black oxfords.

"You buy *kutsu*, shoes!" he said, showing her the money.

With this, she nodded obediently, smiling for the first time, a girl's shy smile, eyes understanding.

"My name's Eugene. What's your name?" Eugene said, pointing at the boy who hollered, 'Yankee GI.'

"Ryota," he said, trying to sound macho. "You Army?" the boy asked in a tough boy voice.

Kneeling, Eugene winked and began shadow boxing. "American Army strong!" Eugene grinned.

The macho boy giggled, smiling at the red-haired shadow boxer, and began a karate chop performance, dancing on the street.

And Perkins took four dollars of the scrip, two of his and the two Robert had offered, fanning the air. "For y'all to share!" Then he took the teacup and placed it in one of the boy's hands, a skinny kid wearing dirty shorts and no shirt, and watched his face blush with excitement.

"Well, you did good!" Robert said, grinning as they returned triumphantly. "Your money is safely deposited in First Yakuza Bank. Looky, looky."

Three teenage toughs arrived from nowhere, stuffing the American scrip into their front pockets and snatching the teacup, the kids watching submissively.

Perkins scowled and turned to give chase, but before he'd started, the pack disappeared into a mess of shanties along the river. The last one to flee—the pencil-thin girl with curly black hair—stared for a never-ending second at Jack, forever wanting to remember his face.

•   •   •

The men drank more beer and planned the evening, finally flagging down a taxi to the Geisha District at six o'clock.

"They've been selling pussy in the Yoshiwara since the 1600s," said Robert excitedly.

"I'm not payin' when I can get it for free!" Eugene said savagely.

Robert laughed. "You payin' one way or another, aren't you?"

"Not me, maybe you! I keep a ledger, fifty-fifty."

"Oh, great!" Jack said. "That'll make you popular, Eugene."

Walking through the narrow quarters of the Geisha District, Jack resembled his father when his old man gazed into the fog from the Fisherman's Wharf. His strongly built frame measured six feet precisely, and his fine-looking face featured a square jawline and a prominent chin dimple. Sandy-colored blond hair lay thick to just above his ears, and he possessed the cutting bluish-gray eyes of his father and a charming soft smile from his mother.

Perkins walked alongside Jack in his Class A uniform, cockily wearing his overseas cap at an edgy tilt, covering wavy brown hair and matching chocolate-colored eyes. Perkins's father, Benjamin Franklin Bigley, staked the family's rugged two-hundred-sixty-acre spread at the foothills of the Wind River Range in eastern Wyoming. The smallish ranch kept food on the table with grit. A young man who rode horses from the age of four, Perkins boasted his love for cold beer and whores—but he'd never slept with a woman, not a single kiss.

Yoshiwara's tightly knit streets simmered with energy. Hastily rebuilt two-story shiplap structures beckoned in the early evening twilight, decorated by fancy new lighting. Amorous pan-pan girls dressed in kimono huddled at each brothel and called out from dark alleyways. Bordellos, hole-in-the-wall sake bars, bathhouses, and other manly amusements reached out to snare them.

They walked the streets feeling jumpy, nervous excitement in their loins, the whores, the brothels, the darkened little amusements selling six centuries of pussy. Past the waving arms, womanly hips, and beckoning powdered faces, luring them into dark cavernous holes of dimly lit corridors, tatami mats, and barren futons, where strangers' bodies lay together in sweat and semen. They waited for permission, one to surrender to the pull of a woman's soft hand or the enticing glint from a doorway. Robert led the pack, Jack closely behind and Perkins and Eugene in the rear, snaking through the jungle on a mission.

Finally, Robert broke the silence, like he was hustling used cars. "Did you see anything you liked?"

"This place creeps me out," Eugene said.

"Why, sure, it creeps you out, Eugene! It creeps me out, too. But that's the whole point, isn't it? When else will you have a real geisha, where they've been selling it for centuries? Fellas, this is a story for the grandkids."

"Yeah, around a bonfire, Aunt Gertrude pourin' the Scotch!" Jack laughed.

"You know my position—I'm not wastin' my money," snarled Eugene.

"Well, how about you, Perkins? You claim you like whores. So, are you game to try one? There are plenty of options!" Robert suggested.

Perkins appeared visibly shaken, the experience turning his stomach in circles.

"I'm too hungry to think about it," Perkins said, wanting to change the topic. "Isn't there American food around here?" He moaned.

"Not in Yoshiwara, there isn't," Robert said.

"You know I can't eat Japanese food!" Perkins bitched.

"Well, you sure ate the chicken sticks at the river!" Jack reminded him.

Eugene growled, "Let him starve," and entered a hole-in-the-wall with strange odors exiting the door.

Inside, a short, fat bartender with a white knotted towel wrapped tightly around his forehead welcomed the men with a loud, "*Irasshaimase*, welcome!" The four soldiers sat at a dimly lit table, ordered Kirin beer, and lit up Chesterfields. Then, a tall, bony man wearing a white chef's apron, spectacles, and a crisp mustache appeared from the kitchen carrying a dozen hand-colored sketches.

Jack spread the pictures on the table and ordered fried squid, skewered chicken kabobs, prawn *tempura, maguro sashimi, ikura, yaki onigiri,* and white rice. He raised two fingers and said, "Two of everything!"

"*Ie, Ie*, no, no," the waiter said, shaking three fingers. "*Zenbu mittsu zutsu!*"

"Okay, three of everything!"

The dishes spilled across the table, sparking a bitter protest from Perkins. "I told you I can't eat raw fish and trout bait, for shit's sake!"

"Here," Eugene said, sliding over his plate of chicken kabobs and *onigiri* rice balls sprinkled with sesame. "Anything to keep you from bitchin' about food. But it's gonna cost you your trout bait—pass 'em over."

"Fair trade!" Perkins grinned.

"Watch me, Perkins, you drown the little red buggers in soy sauce like this. It's *takusan oishi*, delicious!"

A pair of pan-pan girls watched the Americans from a nearby table, admiring their good looks and giggling at Perkins's uneasiness about the food. Both were dressed in tight-fitting kimonos, one sitting high in her chair, skinny as a grasshopper, with long black eyelashes and too much lipstick. The other had a face like a plumb, cute and curvy, with stubby eyelashes and not enough lipstick. Both smoked cigarettes and sipped hot tea.

Eugene took a big gulp of beer. "Perkins, you'd like these fish eggs if you were brave enough to try 'em!"

"No fuggin way!"

"You mean you can't even try a single one, for heaven's sake?"

"Nope!"

Eugene lifted a single red egg between his thumb and forefinger, careful not to drop it on his lap. "Perkins, let me put the son of a bitch on your tongue and swallow it like a pill!"

"Nope!"

"Okay, Perkins, since you can't eat a single frickin' fish egg, then I imagine you can't satisfy a woman with your tongue. Would you?" Eugene chuckled.

"Go to hell!" Perkins snarled.

That's when Perkins noticed the smiling, plumb-faced pan-pan girl with too little lipstick.

"Look at those *Ojo-sans*!" he mumbled, tipping his service cap and sparking a giggling outburst. Then, finally, the cackling girls were too much; Perkins gagged savagely, his large triangular Adam's apple crushing his larynx, and the woman's pretty face spun in circles.

"See her—isn't she beautiful? Look at her," Perkins babbled, pointing.

"Perkins, they're right before us; please quit pointing!" Robert whispered.

"She wants him bad!" Jack chuckled.

"Sure, if he's got dough," Robert quipped.

"No, she's not a whore!"

"Of course she is, Perkins," Robert laughed. "This is the Geisha District! But, since you like her, why don't we take 'em for a ride? And I'll make you a deal: If the *Ojo-sans* are whores, you buy me the skinny one. If not, I'll give you five bucks. Deal?"

Perkins pulled his swarthy, bronco-riding nineteen-year-old frame from the table, pleading to the boys with coffee-colored eyes, terrified, in the fading minutes of his virginity.

•   •   •

Robert Galinski, a muscular, Brooklyn-born five-foot-ten-inch street-smart Jewish kid, joined the Army for the money. Fresh off the boat from Poland, his parents worked a vegetable stall in an industrious Manhattan market.

Robert possessed plush brown hair, big brown eyes, and a smallish mouth with full red lips. Raised by a doting mother and three elder sisters, he lived without the crippling insecurities afflicting men like Eugene and Perkins. Instead, girls adored him like a slumber party pal, one of their own, and Robert loved their attention.

Meanwhile, Eugene, a roguishly Irish soul, could turn from happy-go-lucky to ill-tempered stiff on the turn of a nickel. He'd plotted his life on a five-page Gantt chart from birth to death, proudly promoting his future in the barracks. So, Eugene would leverage the GI Bill, study aeronautical engineering, and build Boeing jet aircraft. Then, at twenty-five, according to the Gantt chart, he'd marry a blonde, buy a fancier Chris-Craft than his old man's rattletrap, and produce a couple of boys and one girl by thirty. The boys would play ball, and the girl, well, hell, she'd be a ballerina.

Eugene grew up in a working-class Puget Sound neighborhood called Alki, a Native American word meaning "by and by" that evolved to mean "into the future," which is perhaps why Eugene obsessed so feverishly over his own.

Eugene's father, Frank, a big-browed Boeing sheet-metal fabricator, carried rough hands and scarred knuckles. Frank liked to box, taught Eugene good defense, and to throw blistering-fast straight punches and counter hooks with deadly accuracy. Frank's brother, Eugene's Uncle Bill, worked the Boeing line with a chip on his shoulder. Uncle Bill possessed an extraordinarily salty mouth from a four-year South Pacific stint in the Navy, and his cruiser torpedoed to the bottom of the Coral Sea. The brothers shared the thirty-six-foot Chris-Craft rattletrap, which they fished between the Puget Sound and Ketchikan, Alaska. These "boys' trips" degenerated into nighttime poker, Scotch whisky, blood and guts, dozens of cigars, and language so foul the whales swam for cover.

"I'm savin' every nickel. But you watch, Jack Pierce, once the bread's in the oven, I'm buyin' stock! Money on the money! I'll have that Chris-Craft, a martini in one hand and a blonde in the other."

"Okay, your future's wonderful, Eugene. I've heard it all before. But how about we start living today? Let's catch a cab to the Ginza."

Jack retrieved a May '49 *Preview* magazine and pointed to the following advertisement:

Club Florida, the Best Beer and Dance Hall in Town
A New Partner Awaits You!! 200 Top Beauties of Japan
Or your Japanese partner is admitted with you
At Ginza's Most Famous Night Spa

The cab dropped Jack and Eugene on Ginza Avenue. Live orchestras played Benny Goodman, Nat King Cole, and Glenn Miller. The songs danced from amplifiers onto the busy Ginza sidewalks, past Baccus Club, Grand Palace, Club Cococabana, Oasis, and Club South Pacific.

"There it is, Club Florida, and her big red torii gate. She's the glitziest one of all!" Eugene said, and they pushed themselves inside, where the floor swayed back and forth with jitterbugging.

"Eugene, over there," Jack said. "That's Big Bill Burns and Snakey Frank Connors dancin' with a couple of lookers."

"Holy mackerel, look at ole Big Bill go!"

The platoon's six-foot four-inch machine gunner, Big Bill, jerked spastically back and forth, red beaky face and sweat flying across the polished hardscape. His Japanese taxi dancer, nicknamed "Bouncing Betty" Murakami, viciously swiveled her hips to the beat of Woodchopper's Ball.

"Goddamn!" Jack said in amazement. And they watched Big Bill throw himself forward, arms extended like an extra-large umbrella, his eight-inch smile showing perfect rows of pearly white teeth and Bouncing Betty's breasts thumping furiously against his swollen crotch.

"Holy crickets, no wonder he's smiling like a madman!" Eugene hollered.

The men pushed themselves through a horde of soldiers to the bar. The Japanese bartender stood tall and skinny with sharp, clearly focused eyes that gave away a man's life in a second. *Woodchopper's Ball* blared loudly and then abruptly ended, and the orchestra slid into a swanky rendition of Sidney Bechet's *Blues My Naughty Sweetie Gives to Me.*

The slender bartender spoke with an impressive English vocabulary. Still, the words dripped from his mouth in choppy little bursts, the English consonants painfully stitched together. Those damned Ls and Rs, and no Ms and Ps! But his heart welcomed the challenge, its rewards, and his eyes sparkled when he spoke.

"Goo eviningu, za drinku spesharu izu Kirin biru."

Jack and Eugene ordered two charcoal brown bottles of Kirin biru.

The bartender wore a sleek black suit with matching black polished shoes. A Rudolph Valentino-style mustache rested upon well-formed lips, his slicked black hair reflected brilliantly from the overhead lights, and he was exceptionally handsome.

"Udu you like a smoke?" The man offered, pulling a box of cigarettes from his front shirt pocket.

Jack and Eugene saw that the man's right hand had just three fingers and a thick, grisly layer of scar tissue beneath the middle one. The deformity produced the appearance of a forty-five-caliber pistol.

"Thank you," Eugene said, shaking the bartender's mutilated hand.

"I'm Eugene. It's nice to meet you."

"Itsu nice to meet you as well. I'm Kenichi, but please call me Ken."

"Thanks for the smoke," Jack said, extending his hand.

"Itsu nice to meet you, too."

Jack looked at the deformed hand. "If you don't mind me asking, what happened…?"

Kenichi straightened up, nervously looked at it, and struck a match to a cigarette, drawing the smoke so deeply the tobacco might have exploded.

"Ito was hell," he drawled.

Jack and Eugene glanced at each other. They wondered if they should leave the man to himself. But Jack persisted. "What was hell?"

"Guadalcanal was hell. War is no good; it's beri, beri bado!"

"Fuck," Eugene said. "So, you fought on Guadalcanal?" Eugene lit another cigarette, looking excited but mostly terrified.

"Yes," Kenichi said. "A machine gunner hit me in the right hand and shoulder. It was zaa American Army, 15th Division, January 13, 1943."

"I'll be damned," said Jack. "That's our division!"

Kenichi slowly unbuttoned his shirt and pulled the collar over his bony right shoulder. Two perfectly round bullet holes lay below his collarbone, an inch from a kill shot. The holes, the size of a quarter, looked grotesquely like goat cheese. Psychotic tiny wounds, they stared back savagely, mad at the world. "*So why the hell are we here?*" they screamed.

"Son of a bitch," Jack said.

Kenichi continued, "We Japanese held the ridges called the *Gifu*. We waited and observed from the hills. The American Army below moved about the battlefield like toy soldiers, but they didn't come until later."

Kenichi took a stiff drink of *shochu*, potato whiskey.

"So, what happened?" Eugene asked.

"They attacked. Kaboom! Kaboom! Kaboom!" Kenichi shouted. "Zaa smell and zaa rotting flesh, maggots, screams, and fires. I hear the cries at night—*okasan, otosan, tasukette, mother, father, help!* Every day fires burned, the smoke scorched our eyes, and the smell of shit, the dead, and the spread of flies like locusts."

The crazed man stopped, gathering his thoughts. "Waru is bado—beri, beri bado—no fucking good!"

Nauseous, Jack and Eugene looked sideways at each other. Kenichi smiled exhaustedly, and two solid gold front teeth broke the appeal of his Valentino face, which now looked a decade older.

Kenichi continued, "Love izu better than war; war no damned good."

Then, pointing his pistol-looking hand, he said, "See those beautiful Japanese girls? I love all women, but Japanese are *ichiban,* number one."

Jack and Eugene looked at the row of young Japanese beauties. They were in their early to mid-twenties and were taxi dancers.

"Well, Ken," Jack said. "Do you suggest we introduce ourselves?"

"Yes!" said Kenichi. "Those are Akita girls. They are famous for their great beauty."

"They are stunning," Eugene suggested.

"Yes, and they have the softest and most beautiful skin of all Japanese women. It comes from zaa snowy mountains and hot springs above Kakunodate in northern Japan."

"Who is the tall one in the middle?" Jack asked.

"Her name is Michiko. She has the prettiest eyes. She is the most popular dancer but will not go with anyone. She married her sweetheart in the war's final year, a very handsome young soldier, but he died in Okinawa."

Kenichi smiled, and his two gold teeth shone like lost Inca treasure. "I taught Michiko to dance. English officers taught me my steps at the Sham Shui Po prisoner of war camp, where I served as a guard after my recovery."

Jack and Eugene liked Kenichi; his war experience made him even more respected, like the Pacific veterans in their division.

Jack said, "We're going to introduce ourselves. How 'bout you come and join us for a drink?"

Kenichi smiled, his gold teeth reflected expensively from the ceiling lights, "I woodo riku to beri beri muchi, but I must keep working." Then he leaned forward and said, "Remember, her name izu Michiko."

•   •   •

Everything rests in its proper place: the rosewood billiard pipe inside a red tin can, the bottle of Kentucky bourbon in the cupboard to the left of the refrigerator, the French cognac next to the bottle of bourbon, and the leather tobacco pouch with the initials T.O. 1891 in the reading room, next to the eighteenth-century Imari vase. As she washed a tub of soapy dishes, Michiko reflected upon two of her mother's favorite proverbs: *don't judge the tree, till you see the fruit,* and *you can learn ten things by learning one.* She recalled how often her mother had repeated these sayings, encouraging her to try the unexpected and be open-minded.

Michiko looked at the clock, and her mind turned to Thurston and then to the summer kimono she would wear to Club Florida. She doesn't have much time, just an hour between the conversation she and Thurston had each evening, and then she must catch the 7:20 to Yurakucho station, a short walk to Ginza. The year following March 1945 was the most terrible of her life. Only time and a powerful desire to keep moving seemed to heal her overwhelming sadness. With her husband dead, her mother and father killed by the fires, and Tokyo in rubble, there seemed nowhere to go. But she knew she couldn't stay; Kakunodate stood still, and to survive, she needed motion. It frightened her to leave her hometown; at least Kakunodate had food, but more than the food, she needed a reason to be alive.

Her big break came from a small advertisement printed in English. It read: *Housemaid wanted for an American engineer. Must have a basic command of English.* The salary promised room and board in a rambling Japanese home and a monthly stipend. A towering figure with gray hair and bluish-green eyes, her first impression of Mr. Thurston Ogilvie, the fifty-eight-year-old regional director of infrastructure reconstruction for the Supreme Commander of Allied Powers, was awe. His eyes reminded her of a bright, cloudless sky on a frosty February morning. She had never seen such colored eyes before, and he stood six foot three, a whole foot above her, with a dapper gray mustache and a half-bent billiard pipe.

Knowing he was a civil engineering man, Michiko learned Thurston had a zealous eye for detail and a penchant for nightly conversation. She slipped into a light blue country dress and brushed her long black hair. She thought: *Thurston will be home in minutes,* and she pulled the bottle of bourbon from the cupboard, fetched his pipe and *The New York Times,* and placed them by his reading chair next to the Imari vase.

When Etuyo and Mayu introduced Michiko to Club Florida, she politely refused, imagining the tears flowing from her deceased parents. She'd lived until her twelfth year in the mountainous village of Kakunodate, famous for its hot springs, snowy mountains, and rice fields. This life in the countryside, where gossip traveled liberally, instilled a traditional Japanese view of a woman's place in society. But Etsuyo and Mayu insisted that the work paid well, and she would meet young men and improve her English at Club Florida.

Following dinner, Michiko returned to the reading room carrying a fluffy chocolate cake she'd baked and a tumbler of cognac. She enjoyed these nightly chats with Thurston, who she trusted like a scholarly old uncle. Sometimes, perhaps once a week, he peppered her with questions: "Can you tell me about your hometown? Why is it you enjoy dancing? What was your mother like?" And he always took the time to correct her English and introduce new vocabulary. She found these evenings delightful and became proud of becoming Club Florida's most proficient English speaker.

After lounging with Thurston through a second pipe, Michiko returned to her quarters. The small, three *tatami* mat room had a *tansu,* a wooden dresser, and a built-in closet for her bedding and kimonos. A large window opposite the closet, where the sun would set each evening, overlooked a delightful Japanese garden. Michiko went to the *tansu* and turned on the radio, filling the room with a beautiful love song. A delicate *Hakata* doll of a white-skinned geisha, an English dictionary, and a family portrait rested atop the chest. A pretty schoolgirl in braids wore a two-piece winter uniform with copper buttons, polished black leather shoes, and white woolen socks in the black-and-white photograph. In the picture, Michiko is twelve years old, and a smile is noticeable from an upturned lip and a dimple on her right cheek. Standing to her left are her mother and father, killed when the fires spread through Asakusa, near the famous Sensoji temple. Michiko's grandmother and her deceased brother stand to her right. And her elder sister, Kimiko, is behind her brother, wearing a formal winter kimono.

It is Saturday evening, which is a kimono night. Michiko wore her prettiest white silk dress and black stiletto dance shoes the night before. All the girls flock to the Shibuya markets to buy fabrics and sew their favorite Western gowns. And Michiko loves fashioning her hair, and wearing Western dresses allows her to replicate popular styles. Gene Tierney is her favorite Hollywood actor, and she feels an uncanny bond with the glamorous star. A black-and-white photograph of the actress smiling for the cameras sits on her vanity.

Michiko selected a darling summer kimono with delicate dark blue chrysanthemums and a wrap-around matching blue *obi*, belt. She smiled at the kimono and took it into her hands to enjoy the touch of its soft silk, removed her blue cotton dress, powdered her naked body, and it became buttery smooth and fragrant. Then, at the vanity, Michiko applied makeup, accentuating her dimpled cheeks, mahogany brown eyes, and crescent-shaped lips. She is a beautiful twenty-four-year-old Japanese woman, and in the mirror, she sees a slight resemblance to Gene Tierney, who smiles back approvingly.

•　　•　　•

Inside Club Florida, Michiko walked hastily to the dressing room. There, dozens of young women busily prepared for an evening of hosting and dancing. The girls giggled, gossiped, smoked cigarettes, and a handful browsed through a heavy spring edition of a 1949 Sears Roebuck catalog.

From her mirror's reflection, Michiko watched Mayu fasten intricate costume glass earrings to her buttercup earlobes. She admired her friend's beautiful facial features, especially her opal-shaped eyes, girlish cheekbones, and playful red lips.

"*Wa Sugoi*, that's great, Mayu-chan. I love your earrings!" Michiko said. "They are striking on you!"

Mayu giggled. "I bought them in Shibuya this morning. So, let's go some time, Michiko-chan."

"Sounds fun, Mayu-chan! Let's have coffee and dessert too. How about Saturday?"

"*Hai, issho ni ikou*, yes, let's go!"

Mayu raised her hands and slapped them hard upon her thighs. "It's time to work!" she said, taking one final peek in the mirror.

"*Ganbatte ne*, do your best!" Michiko said, smiling.

The girls entered the dance hall, cute and sure-footed. Inside, young men filed impatiently through the doors, eager to kick things off.

Mayu, Michiko, and another talented hostess, Etsuko, waited to escort a group of soldiers to a table. Then, with humor, they observed the young, large-eyed Americans coalesced around the entry doors, nervously playing with their dancing scrip. And the shiny floor swayed back and forth to the rhythm of jitterbugging couples.

"*Wa bikkuri*, how surprising, look at Hitomi-chan dance! She's quite the spectacle, isn't she?" Etsuko said. "I can't bear to watch her shake her *oppai*, breasts, like that."

"She's pounding *mochi*!" Mayu giggled.

With a wry smile, Etsuko whispered, "I hear the soldiers call her Bouncing Betty!"

"Why Bouncing Betty?" asked Mayu.

Etsuko giggled. "It's a bomb that bounces before it blows up."

"Well, I don't think Hitomi cares one way or another about what we think," said Michiko. "Look at the American's big smile. He loves it!"

"*So desu ne*, that's true!" said Etsuko. "I wish I had bigger *oppai* like Hitomi's; if I did, I would pound *mochi*, too." Etsuko giggled.

"You girls are silly," Michiko smiled and rolled her eyes.

Abruptly, Etsuko became focused on movement across the room. "*Mite, mite*, look, look," she said. "Kenichi-san is introducing us to those two Americans."

"*Waa Sugoi, honto ne,*" Mayu said excitedly. "The American with the blond hair is so handsome. He's looking at you, Michiko!"

Michiko could sense the American's keen attention on her.

"Well, Kenichi-san does like to promote my dancing. He's a darling, isn't he?"

Etsuko and Mayu nodded. "And a gentleman and nice-looking, too," Etsuko said.

Jack and Eugene stood from their stools and thanked Kenichi for the cigarettes.

•　　•　　•

Michiko moved gracefully across the dance floor in her beautiful summer kimono to the beat of *Sing, Sing, Sing* by Glenn Miller. Her work and naturally flowing figure made her a skillful dancer, a much better one than Jack. She danced like a bright shooting star, whereas he danced raw and irregularly—but he smiled when he danced; a big happy grin and a passion for life, and his presence made her feel warm, secure, and bubbly inside.

In many of her partners, the hungry lustfulness of men who expect too much oppressed her. She sometimes wondered if these men even knew she existed. However, she didn't feel such oppressive lust from Jack. Instead, he danced for the freedom of movement, the simple pleasure it brought him, unguarded by the watchful eyes of others.

They danced to *Sing, Sing, Sing, Rust Rusty Blues,* and *Jumpin' Jive.* She observed that a natural, carefree beauty filled his demeanor, all that is good and pure in the world, reminding her of the fresh spring mornings of her youth before the terrible war when her family was alive and happy.

She, her sister, and her father would awaken early and stroll beneath the cherry blossom trees along the Sumida River to see the old iron bridges, the rushed movement of sampans, and ferries burgeoning with passengers. Her father, Yuto, bought them plum tea and their favorite Sunday sweets. Michiko liked *kushi dango,* which is three *mochi* balls skewered and covered in sweet, green tea sauce. The kindly faced father and his teenage daughters, Michiko and Kimiko, sat on the cast-iron benches and watched the river. Michiko preferred to sit quietly and savor every small moment on these special occasions. She ate her *kushi dango* slowly and smiled, tasting each small piece of sweet rice, relishing its chewy texture, the warmth of the green tea sauce, and its savory deliciousness.

And like savoring *kushi dango*, she smiled while dancing with Jack, relishing every moment; her smiling wouldn't stop, and she realized happiness had evaded her for a very long time.

Her steps were faster than his, always a stride ahead of him. *But he appeared so content*, she thought. He looked relaxed, safe, and buoyant, yet his dancing was choppy and not as beautiful as hers. Nevertheless, he beamed when he danced. His cheeks were pink, and his eyes were so clear she couldn't see to their brilliant, bluish-gray depths. She acknowledged his eyes with her own. She peered into them, fascinated, helpless, drawn in, and falling. And he into hers, transported through time, place, generations, and tribes, to that common origin of man's humanity, the making of its soul.

They danced to a dozen songs. Time and place didn't matter any longer. *String of Pearls, One for my Baby and One for the Road*, and *In the Mood*; and as they danced, she didn't think about the past; she relaxed while they danced, and for the first time in a very long time, happiness swept over her like the welcoming warmth of spring.

They said goodbye, agreeing that they wanted to see each other again.

"I had a wonderful time. I sure hope I didn't embarrass you," Jack said.

"No, I enjoyed it. We danced the entire evening, didn't we?" She giggled.

"I forgot about time, too. But, if possible, I would like to see you again."

She smiled. "I work Wednesday, Thursday, Friday, and Saturday from eight to eleven. Please come anytime." Then she offered a card with her name—Michiko Okura—and Club Florida's telephone number and address in Japanese and English.

"It's a deal," Jack said, smiling brightly. "I promise you'll see me next Saturday night. And I always keep my word."

She took a slight bow.

Jack and Eugene said goodbye to Kenichi while a couple of sailors from Yokosuka ordered beer.

"Michiko enjoyed dancing tonight," he said over the two sailors. "You had fun together!"

Jack smiled. "I had all the fun. You're right—she is a lovely girl!"

Kenichi gave two thumbs up and grinned, exposing the gold that became his two front teeth, starvation and infection on Guadalcanal eating away the ivory-white originals.

Outside Club Florida, the evening felt sultry. A usual mixture of drunkards, black-market hucksters, sailors, and soldiers bustled about Ginza, debating their next moves. Then, finally, Jack and Eugene flagged a taxi for Camp Drake. The cab sped through traffic, navigating between big charcoal-polluting buses, hundreds of rickshaws, motorcycles, bicycles, and pedestrians. While the taxi bounced along, Jack's mind and body became heavy.

In his dream, he saw his father's face. The sun had turned his father's complexion dark reddish-brown, like the dying seconds of sunset when the summer's hayfields burn at midday. Whiskers formed across his cheeks, making him look like the rail yard hobos of his youth, but masculine to his son. His father wore a hand-knit woolen sweater and matching cap, garments his grandmother gave his father on his twenty-fifth birthday, which was the year of Jack's birth. And Jack could smell the smokiness of the evening's campfire upon the wool sweater, always present during their frequent trips into the wilderness. A pack full of gear hung across his father's back, and a backcountry shovel protruded from its top.

His father carried a Winchester Model 70 rifle in his right hand. Its two-toned red mahogany stock supported a steel gray barrel, the same color as the arched back of wild steelhead, and in the skillful hands of his father, it was deadly.

In his dream, a frigid wind blew across father and son that early morning in late September. The brisk breeze burned their faces red and forced them to squint from a high mountain ridge, offering cover from a herd of unsuspecting elk in a draw far below. His father motioned for Jack to unharness his rifle to take the shot from two hundred yards. Jack lay on his stomach, resting the weight of his rifle on his left forearm, and then brought the butt to his right cheek.

"Okay, son, nice and easy. Let him have it below the shoulder, through the heart and lungs."

The elk looked magnificent through his sights in its natural habitat of high mountain ridges, old-growth forests, and green fern meadows dotted with autumn reds and golds. Finally, Jack found his mark, took a deep breath, held it calmly, and slowly released the air through his lips—*crack!*

Jack awoke suddenly to the high-pitched sound of rifle fire in the rear of the taxi, and it startled him to be buzzing by lighted signs of *kanji* characters with Eugene snoring next to him. He shook himself to regain his bearings and thought of Michiko.

His body became heavy again, warm, and slightly intoxicated. He saw Michiko's face, and its contours, beginning with her eyes and then her forehead, thick black hair, and milky white complexion. He studied her eyes again, seeing their intriguing moon-like beauty, pear-shaped elegance, deep brown and mysterious, exotic, lovely—life's energy—drawing him to her like he had drawn her to him.

Jack wanted to see those eyes again, confirm he had remembered them correctly, and assure himself of the feelings he experienced that evening. So, he studied Michiko's delicate red lips, raised Asian cheekbones, and slender shoulders. He recalled the contours of her chest, its soft peaks and valleys, and these thoughts made him feel restless. So, he replayed the soothing sway of her hips, the wholeness of her bottom, and her irresistibly long legs until his crotch swelled, and when he awoke, the taxi had arrived at Camp Drake.

CHAPTER FOUR
Amaterasu

The week began as the prior weeks had for Easy Company. They marched in the morning before sunrise, ate at the mess hall, conducted routine drills, performed other trivial duties, and schemed over weekend plans. That is why on Thursday morning, before PT, the notification that Captain Carlson would address the company about an upcoming operation caught the men by surprise. At 0700, the captain stood before the formation. As a stern and professional officer with combat experience fighting the Third Reich through France and Germany, the young soldiers feared and idolized the no-nonsense Captain Carlson.

"Men, this company will move out tomorrow morning at 0400 to participate in live-fire exercises with the 24th Division at Camp Fuji. So, pack for twenty-one days in the field. Your commanding officers will address you after morning drills. That is all."

The bitching erupted at breakfast.

"Fuggin live-fire exercises. Nobody told me that a damn war was going on," Walter Abbott savagely protested.

Big Bill Burns raised his head. "Heck, Snakey Frank, Russell Simmons, and I had plans with the Buick this weekend. We were going to drive up the coast to Shonan. They've got a black sand beach and good waves up there. I've never seen a black sand beach; we could have gone body surfin'. And live-fire exercises stole our weekend. Fuggin Army!"

"Son of a bitch," Perkins spat, beads of saliva departing his mouth, fanning across Robert's pretty face and nearly hitting Jack. "I told Naoka we would go to Red River's final showing. John Wayne is the best, and I wanna show her how we American men are."

From across the table, Robert wiped away Perkins spittle. "You silly cowboy, your girl's name isn't Naoka; it's Naoko. And don't you forget she's a pan-pan girl. She's probably sleeping with a cherry-faced sailor right now; you should remember who you're sleeping with."

"Screw you," Perkins said. "Naoka's taking care of her family. And I don't care if she's usin' the money that way. She cried tellin' me her story, and I damned near cried myself, you son of a bitch!"

"That's what all workin' girls say, so they can squeeze you for more. You remember she isn't your girl!"

For Jack, the thought of not seeing Michiko on Saturday night made his stomach churn like a load of wet cement. But how could he message her? And then he remembered Kenichi. *Yes*, he thought, *that crazy grenade-throwing gold-toothed bartender*. He interrupted Eugene mid-sentence, lecturing the men that they were all a bunch of pussies because proper soldiers welcomed live-fire exercises. "Walter, I've got an emergency. Can you help me sort it out?"

Walter sneered at Jack. "That depends; what kind of pickle are you in that needs my help to sort you out of?"

The table went quiet, and the six men of Easy Company, 1st Platoon, 5th Squad, focused their eyes on Jack.

"You see, I met this *Ojo-san* at Club Florida. And I promised we would dance this Saturday evening."

"Oh, for heaven's sake!" squelched Walter Abbott, and the other men laughed. And Robert goaded Jack: "I think I'll travel light, so I can see more terrain," to the men's delight.

Eugene interrupted the chuckling soldiers, his lanky neck bending halfway across the table, robotically swiveling this way and that, and his Popeye "*the sailor man*" face beamed wildly. "Boys, you should've seen her, this *Ojo-san*, Michiko, my gosh, is she a looker! Prettiest *Ojo-san* dame I've seen on this whole fuggin island. The two of them danced the entire night. Popped a boner just watchin' 'em!"

"Okay, that's enough, so how do I fit into this love story, Jack?" Walter Abbott asked.

"I want you to speak to Russel Simmons and see if his shack job, Yuki, will pass a message to the club's bartender, Kenichi. The bartender will remember who I am. He's a good man who fought the 15th on Guadalcanal. So, I can trust him to give the message to Michiko."

"Sure, I can do that. The problem is that Simmons is in Charlie Company, and they are headin' to Camp Fuji today at 1600, so Simmons has to get to Yuki before. So, I can't promise nothin'."

The conversation broke off, and the men finished their coffee, not speaking more of the weekend. There would be no more bitching about live-fire exercises. Instead, the soldiers looked forward to rejoining the field again—marching, firing their weapons, and practicing large battalion-sized maneuvers in Camp Fuji's heavy, unforgiving terrain. Once the realization was that nothing would save their weekend liberty, their disappointment faded, and the men thought only of the twenty-one days of soldiering ahead of them.

Jack scrounged a pen and paper and wrote to Russell Simons: *Russell, I have a big favor. I met a girl at Club Florida, and I need to tell her I can't meet her this Saturday evening as promised. Her name is Michiko Okura. She is a dancer at the club. Can you ask Yuki to pass a note on my behalf to the bartender, Kenichi? Please have him give the following message to Michiko:*

Dear Michiko,

I was looking forward to seeing you again this Saturday evening! I enjoyed our dancing and desire to meet you again. It was a perfect night, and I've thought about you since. Unfortunately, our company is shipping to Camp Fuji for twenty-one days of maneuvers. Nevertheless, I hope to see you again upon my return.

Yours truly,
Jack Pierce

•　　•　　•

At 0400, a long green line of two-and-one-half-ton deuces departed Camp Drake with a noisy belch. The men sat on hard wooden benches, eight men on each side. They placed their field packs directly to their front—sixteen total, and each stuffed full of the standard equipment of the infantry rifleman, totaling one thousand two hundred eighty pounds.

The men were glad to go. They sat facing each other, consumed by the morning's darkness, not speaking, and tired after three hours' sleep. They waited impatiently for the half-darkness to lift and the opening gentle rays of the morning sun to light the city. Jack sat intermittently rigid with his back pressed against the open wood slats, then he slumped forward as if trying to relieve himself from a cramp nestled into the hollow of his back. But he suffered no pain and felt relieved to be going. Jack studied the men's faces, hard, tough-looking infantry riflemen's faces. Being among them made him proud, a collage of miens of differing shapes, angles, and fenestrations from cities and towns as dissimilar as Gary, Indiana; Little Rock, Arkansas; Boise, Idaho; Macon, Georgia; New York, New York; and Seattle, Washington.

He observed the gear they had. Each pack looked the same. Rugged round olive-green backpacks expertly stuffed with infantrymen's equipment. Field jacket, poncho, two pairs of trousers, two pairs of woolen socks, two pairs of underwear, extra shirt, woolen blanket, maps, compass, two grenades, ammunition belts, flashlight, ten clips of eight-round thirty-caliber cartridges, trenching shovel, ten-inch serrated knife, and bayonet. Their turtle-like steel-green pots weighed five pounds, carefully fastened to an eighty-pound pack. Alongside each soldier was the M1 Garand, a polished steel killing machine from the fading battles of Leyte, Iwo Jima, and Okinawa.

The beastly column rumbled through the predawn twilight of Tokyo's early morning hours. The streets were mostly empty except for an occasional stray cat, shifty-eyed dog, and the sporadically disheveled Japanese war veteran. Men draped in depressingly tattered uniforms, rudderless outcasts, brushed aside like cigarette butts by a society desiring to forget.

Predawn Tokyo bustled with wholesalers and retailers filling their stores with the wares of six million residents. But, like the men beside him, Jack lost himself in his thoughts.

The morning sun brought forth a soft, penetrating warmth, which also evaporated the evening's dew from the asphaltic roadway, producing a willowy white haze that hovered about the base of the vehicles. The men became more active as the sun rose. They moved about, jostled one another, and observed their surroundings. As the trucks rolled southward from the outskirts of Tokyo and the energetic port city of Yokohama, they returned the waves and smiles of delighted children dressed in freshly pressed blue and black uniforms. "Hey, GI, GI; America number one." And they watched eighty-year-old hunched-over toothless shopkeepers scurry about tidying up their shops, and some would grin, with deeply creased eyes and leathery skin. They observed attractive young mothers wearing dark gray kimonos with their hair tied into perfectly shaped buns and their babies strapped loosely to their backs by braided rope knapsacks. And the young mothers surveyed the young foreign conquerors of their generation, and some bowed and shared a shy smile of respect for the Americans.

The journey continued like this for several hours until they left the tightly packed city of Yokohama for the sprawling Kanto plain, a flat agricultural basin of rice and vegetable farms and rolling forests, low-lying hills, and verdant valleys. The scenery became more rugged as they approached the base of Mount Fuji and beyond the line of peaks known as the Southern Japan Alps.

Leaving the city's sights and sounds, the men became more energetic as the mountain air and earthy smell of the countryside filled their lungs, engulfing their bodies. The landscape became awash with working agricultural landscapes, creating a vibrancy of greens, golds, reds, yellows, and browns. Some men stood and pointed out the sights; others took photographs and hooted and hollered, overcome by the first unobstructed views of Mount Fuji's dominance of the checkerboard landscape. Still, other men remarked it reminded them of the delightful rural landscapes in Georgia, California, Iowa, and Louisiana.

Jack peered across the rolling countryside, feeling free, excited, and blessed to be alive. He felt more joyful than he had in a long time, and he'd mostly felt this way during his twenty-one years. He stood with the other men and joined them, pointing, hooting, and hollering upon the first views of Mount Fuji's cylindrical cone-shaped summit, rising godlike to 12,397 feet. But he was equally excited by the enchanting landscape of small working farms, rustic villages of red- and blue-tiled roofs, grasslands, riverine valleys, crystal blue lakes, and dark green forests.

"I promise you," he said to Eugene, who grasped the truck's wooden slats alongside him. "I'm going to climb that mountain!"

"Yeah, how in the hell will you do that?" Eugene asked.

"I don't know, but when I stand on Fuji's summit, I will look above this beautiful landscape and see the whole of Japan. What do you say?"

"Sure, I'll go with you. You tell me how and when, and I'll go," Eugene promised. They laughed and shook hands.

Jack sat on the hard wooden bench, not speaking to Eugene or the other men during the trip's last leg. Instead, he quietly watched Japan's toughened farmers work their fields, wide-brimmed conical hats sheltering their faces from the late summer sun. These fibrous people, operating modern tractors alongside ancient water buffalo, created sleek lines in the dark brown loamy soil to feed the millions. The ripened fields mesmerized him. Long lines of golden-colored bushels of freshly harvested rice draped over bamboo poles, shedding their grain. He witnessed small, tightly clustered villages surrounded by a puzzle of green and orange landscapes and laughing children frolicking under the watchful eyes of a more traditional generation soon to disappear. And he took in the ragged-looking dogs, the wailing red roosters, and the tightly strung cream-colored onions and white braids of garlic that hung like pearls from the rafters of ancient wooden houses built by the hands of their ancestors hundreds of years before.

He sat on the hard wooden bench with a sketchbook and recalled one of his father's favorite sayings: *Jack, you've got to search for beauty. It doesn't just appear on its own.* And so he worked furiously to capture the scenes that inspired his imagination—a little boy eating from a red, dripping wet snow cone in the hands of his mother—a line of elderly farmers harvesting bushels of rice across the open sweep of a bone-dry field. And the splendor of Lake Ashi with Mount Fuji as a backdrop. The drawings weren't refined or highly detailed sketches. Instead, they were a collection of lazy loose strokes to memorialize the experiences and stir the artist's imagination that would return to these sketches throughout his life.

At 1600, the convoy rumbled into Camp Fuji. The men tumbled from the vehicle and stood in formation facing the famous mountain, the stars and stripes slumping large, motionless, and miserable looking atop a seventy-foot flagpole.

The heat beat down unpleasantly now that the vehicles had stopped, and clouds of chalky dust fell upon the men's sweaty faces, while they stood at attention, some fearing heatstroke. A few unfortunate men hadn't urinated since leaving Camp Drake. These miserable soldiers gritted their teeth, promising the Holy Spirit redemption for amnesty to not soil their pants. So, they stood at attention for thirty miserable minutes before Lieutenant Colonel Sam Jones finally addressed them.

The colonel, a short, stocky man of thirty-eight years with a bulging chest and powerful arms, boxed at West Point before Pearl Harbor, and he had a reputation for toughness and for being a hell of a gunfighter. He'd fought in Italy and France in General George Patton's 7th Army, cementing his reputation with a Silver Star and Purple Heart for gallantry during the battle of the Troina in Sicily's Caronie Mountains.

Army legend described the story this way: Captain Jones watched through binoculars as the battle of Troina unfolded, and the Germans initiated an envelopment of his 1st and 3rd Platoons in the hills near Monte Basilio. Fearing a massacre, he swore violently, grabbed a Browning Automatic Rifle, grenades, and a bazooka, and commandeered a jeep to intercept his men before an ambush. Then, according to eyewitness accounts, he drove high-speed over exceedingly dangerous terrain to his platoons' front-line positions, repositioned the men to the southwest, and single-handedly led a devastating counteroffensive before a German sniper shot him through the ass.

The men stood in awe as the colonel approached the formation, nearly fainting from the oppressive Japanese heat. His face appeared round, his cheekbones out of proportion with his other facial features, partly attributable to a prickly heat rash that levied its ugliness across his cheeks. The colonel's lips were parched and puffy, his chin recessed inwards, and he had a mighty outcrop created by a cabbage-shaped forehead. A perfectly trimmed, thick black mustache topped a pair of puffy red lips. He was ugly, and the soldiers were insightful enough to know that the colonel had made the rank through action alone.

"Gentlemen, welcome to Camp Fuji. I'm Lieutenant Colonel Jones. I'll be directing the battalion's activities over the three weeks. You are dismissed for five minutes to piss. That is all."

The men quickly broke formation and fled to the restrooms and the protective shade of a Quonset hut. Several middle-aged farmers' wives bustled about serving iced water, green bottles of cold 7-Up, caramel-colored Coca-Cola, and miscellaneous cookie and peanut snacks. Eugene took water, and a bottled Coca-Cola. The Coca-Cola he drank first, tipping the base of the bottle skywards. "My God, that tasted good," he said, and then he belched so furiously that some men jumped, and the four-foot eight-inch cola-serving farmer's wife let out a short, startled scream: "*Wa sugoi*, that's incredible!"

"That son of a bitch colonel scares the shit out of me," Perkins quietly drawled so the men outside the tight circle couldn't hear. "He's ugly and nasty-lookin' and scarier than a rattlesnake in your underwear."

"I'm just happy there isn't a war going on," Robert said.

"Colonel Jones looks the type that's itchin' for a fight, and I sure as hell like to avoid em' when I see em," said Walter Abbott. "I had enough scrappin' with wops and paddys over turf and broads. It's all about turf and broads, fellas. Mark my words. And if any dumbasses should get the idea to scrap with me, you better think twice—never once did I ever get a scratch from a wop."

"Aaaah, go screw yourself, tough guy," Eugene said to Walter. "You're just fast at runnin' your mouth. I bet I could whoop your ass from here to eternity and back again."

"Alright, that's enough hot air, fellas; you'd best shut your traps before I bury the both of you here at Camp Fuji," Jack said. "Anyway, I have a good feeling about the colonel. You saw how he gave us a break from formation. So, let's form up before we get ourselves in trouble."

The men quickly made their way into formation just seconds before the colonel returned to address the company.

"Men, you are at Camp Fuji. Today, you are here because of the fearless sacrifice of sailors, soldiers, Marines, and airmen between December 7, 1941, and August 15, 1945, to return peace and freedom to the world. Your purpose is to maintain that freedom for the men who died fighting for it. This mission is a responsibility that I, as your battalion commander, take with unflinching seriousness—as so must you.

"This sacred ground where you will conduct operations over the next twenty-one days has a history of training soldiers for combat dating back seven hundred years. The Kamakura Feudal Government trained thirty thousand samurai warriors here, in this hallowed camp, at the base of Mount Fuji in 1198. The Japanese Imperial Army used these facilities to wage its fascist war of aggression through Asia and the Pacific.

"Now, the United States Army controls these facilities to protect democracy and freedom for all humanity. To support this effort, your commanding officers will lead you through live-fire exercises with supporting armor and artillery during the next three weeks. Men, we are training you for combat. You are the tip of a deadly spear and members of the most powerful fighting force assembled in Asia— soldiers of the United States 15th Infantry Division. Now, Captain Carlson, address your men."

Captain Carlson stepped forward.

"Men, we will load up and move to South Camp. Training will commence immediately upon our arrival. Proceed to your assigned vehicles."

The men reloaded and sped toward South Camp, through more farms and wide-open landscapes, and into the vast southeast maneuver area. The terrain comprised thousands of chewed-up acres, pancake-like flat lands, and rough mountainous topography. Driving to South Camp on the narrow dirt road, the vehicles crawled alongside a convoy of deuces returning to Camp Fuji McNair. The passing soldiers wore their division's insignia proudly. The yellow Norman shield, with a solid black band cutting diagonally from left to right across the midsection. A black thoroughbred horse's head proudly rested in the upper right corner of the shield, the 1st Cavalry Division's insignia. After three weeks of training, the soldiers were dirty and unmistakably tired from lack of sleep. But their faces were excited—as beaten-down faces get after an unpleasant ordeal where the pain and suffering become a badge of honor. As the 1st Cavalry's two-and-a-half-ton deuces swept by, the soldiers faced each other, hooting, hollering, and goading the other side.

"Hey, coconut heads, I hear the Fifteenth couldn't hit a mountain's ass from a hundred yards with a Browning Automatic Rifle!" one of the 1st Cavalry Division's soldiers shouted to the delight of his comrades.

"Oh, yeah, rumor is the 1st Cavalry is a bunch of pussies. So now we know the rumors are true!" Eugene sneered back, to the delight of the soldiers in his truck.

Jack sat on the wooden bench next to the yakking soldiers, the outside air blowing nice and fresh against his face. He hunched himself over, half-listening to the men's jabber, greatly amused, working away on another sketch. A cartoonish caricature of his two friends' faces— each man's expression he made to look oversized, features distorted, waggish. For an unknown reason, he wanted to record this moment that way.

•   •   •

The deuces pulled into a spartan camp of hundreds of primitive green tents, degraded steel Quonset huts, a sizeable haggard mess tent, and a tired, former Imperial Japanese Army command post. "Fuck me, this place is a dump," were the first words from Robert's mouth.

The vehicles disgorged their cargo, and the soldiers stood again in formation under the hellish heat of the summer's suffocating humidity.

The 2nd Platoon's commanding officer, First Lieutenant Clarence Somerset, a brilliant man of twenty-six, stepped forward to address his platoon. In his right hand, he carried a sixteen-inch balsa swagger stick. His grandfather, who'd spent countless hours recounting to young Clarence Somerset stories of the Spanish-American War—and continuously tapping that damned stick—passed it along to Clarence after his death. And now the lieutenant brazenly carried the stick wherever he went and waved it around just as fanatically, addressing the men like a grand composer of armies. The men knew that someday the first lieutenant would make general; he was just that good at the profession.

Observing the lieutenant, Jack imagined the man directing British armor during the desert battle of Tunisia—a Lawrence of Arabia with deep blue eyes, opal blond hair, ivory white teeth, and a leanly structured face with a finely tailored, rusty red mustache. A sporty look and one that brought forth rose-colored emotions of entitlement and jingoistic pride for the Anglo-Saxon race, whereas Lieutenant Colonel Jones, the bigwig battalion commander, produced quite the opposite effect.

Every soldier in Easy Company liked First Lieutenant Somerset. He commanded 2nd Platoon, and he had a way with his men so that they trusted and confided in him. Born in Peoria, Illinois, and educated at the University of Chicago, with a degree in political science, he was a bright, well-mannered Midwesterner.

During World War Two, he fought as a private on the cold, desolate island of Attu. Then he island-hopped across the Marshalls, fighting alongside the 4th Marine Division at Kwajalein and Eniwetok atoll. Somerset's war ended on Leyte in a puff of smoke and shrapnel when a deadly barrage of Japanese artillery blew his eardrums and lacerated his neck, requiring a hundred stitches. But, to the chagrin of his well-connected parents, the freshly degreed intellectual volunteered for a second stint in green.

That evening, the men ate their last fresh meal. They piled extra portions of sweet Nippon rice with boiled cabbage, chicken, thinly sliced red peppers, onions, and potatoes onto plates they wouldn't see again for three weeks. The men ate like lions and bitched like soldiers. "The lieutenant says we're sleepin' in foxholes, marchin' sixty miles all the fuggin ways to North Camp. They must think a stinkin' war's goin' on," Russell Simmons bitterly complained.

"The Chinese Communists are cozyin' up to the Russians. Lieutenant said we'll get in heavy with China. But how I see it, they owe us—big time!" Walter Abbott sneered, visibly irritated he wasn't alongside Yuki and her manicured bush, a treat he'd devolved into a topic of incessant boasting to his jealous comrades.

"I've told you trench monkeys, it's dirt and broads; it boils down to D and B, nothin' more, nothin' less. Men fighting for the world's treasure."

"And how do you figure?" Simmons asked.

"It's motivation, pullin' yourself from bed, the fuel for the damned system to keep churnin'. I dare you to give me a better motivator than sex!"

"Perkins, why you mopin'? Something burnin' your mind?"

"Nothin'."

"Bull shit, somethin'?"

"Yeah, Somethin'."

"I got it. The little geisha, Naoko-chan, right?"

No response.

Big Bill Burns pushed his jowls forward, shoving aside an empty plate. "You boys think we'll get liberty? I hear the girls are sporty in Fujioka."

Walter banged his fists on the table. "D and B, I rest my fuggin case!"

"See, it's how the world wants to be, not how it should be," Robert growled.

"What the fuck, Robert?"

"Just sayin'."

"I'd sure like a cold beer before bed," Perkins complained.

"Ain't nothin' like cold beer and whores," Abbott chuckled.

"You're all burnin' in hell!" Jack grinned. "Let's hit the sack. We've got work to do tomorrow."

•   •   •

At 0400, Easy Company's platoon sergeants rushed the men out of sleep with loud whistles and deep-throated hollering, "Rise and shine, dumb turds—move, move!" The troopers quickly donned their fatigues, combat boots, helmets, and eighty-pound packs and boarded the trucks. The vehicles sped rapidly northward, kicking up vast clouds of choking red dust. Meanwhile, Mount Fuji's hulking lower mass still lay hidden by darkness, an hour before the sun's wispy orange rays would illuminate the rugged terrain.

Lieutenant Colonel Jones ordered Easy Company to march for three days to a series of steep ridgelines. Once there, the company would set a defensive perimeter and conduct simulated operations against Able and Charlie Companies, which were tasked with locating and destroying them. Meanwhile, Able and Charlie proceeded to firing ranges for work on the M1 Garand, thirty- and fifty-caliber machine guns, two-point-eight-inch rockets, fifty- and eighty-one-millimeter mortars, and hand grenades. Finally, after dark on the fifth night, Jones ordered Able and Charlie to march within five miles of Easy Company's position and initiate a simulated frontal attack. An armored squadron would engage heavy weapons to cover the attack upon Easy Company's entrenchments.

Easy's men disembarked from their vehicles just as the sun's first rays broke the horizon. The topography was now more varied, becoming rugged, rawer, and wilder than before, with a row of low-lying hills beyond their current position. And in the distance between them and their final objective, the men faced a series of daunting ridgelines, valleys, jagged gulches, and forests. Fuji-san loomed ominously above—so large the men could reach out and touch it.

As the sun emerged above the hills to the east, it cast a blanket of deep purples, reds, and translucent yellows across the Kanto Plain. Lieutenant Somerset maneuvered his platoon into formation and explained to the men that their squad leaders would take direct control for the next four days. First, the lieutenant ordered the squad leaders to carry a topographic map and compass and to rendezvous at an area where the platoon would bivouac each night. Then he ordered the five eight-man squads to march a sixty-mile route over three days and reserve sufficient time each evening to dig foxholes, create listening posts, and establish defensive perimeters before sunset.

At 0530, the men hoisted their packs, and the weight bit deeply into their shoulders. They adjusted their feet to spread the unnatural bulk across the totality of their bodies. Jack ordered his squad to hike for an hour and then break for chow.

The trail started gently through a patch of forest and then broke into more rugged terrain toward Fuji-san's towering cylindrical cone. A rush of excitement swelled through Jack's veins. Then sweat emerged and rolled over his forehead while the muscles in his legs loosened, allowing his strides to become rhythmical, and his confidence swelled. He listened to the men behind him breathe in and out and in and out, and he stole glances at their faces and saw they were flushed and awkwardly serious.

Marching in the early morning dawn, Mount Fuji loomed overhead, majestic and godlike, and Jack understood its divinity to the Japanese people. In late summer, the mountain exposed all its rugged imperfections. And as it drew him closer to its splendor, like a magnet—not that he desired to conquer it; he wanted to become one with it, to learn from its secrets.

As he marched onward, his back and chest moist with sweat and the sun now becoming more of a burden, he thought it strange how, when he considered the mountain, Michiko came to mind. He recalled her beautiful round face and hair, long and wild, flowing freely, tumbling out of control, rushing through a furrowed gorge. He thought again of her lush black hair, the explosive movement of her hips, and the reflective light upon her skin that mingled with a fine sheen of sweat. Her penetrating dark brown eyes captured the depths of his imagination, and these thoughts swirled around wispy and light. And then they disappeared as abruptly as they came, and once more, he focused upon the trail and the rhythmical breathing of the men behind him.

The route bent sharply to the right and then dropped precipitously through a deciduous forest and beyond to a mountain-fed stream two hundred feet below. The stream cut through a gully twenty feet wide and, once crossed, they would begin a more arduous trek through dark, reddish-brown foothills into Fuji-san's lower-lying mountains. A string of tall maple trees shaded the stream bank with leafy green leaves that would become bright red in fall, and there was sufficient space between the trees for the squad to rest and eat their morning chow.

Each man packed enough rations for the six-day mission, carefully separating breakfasts from lunches and dinners. Finally, Perkins reached into his pack and hollered, "I got 'em, I got 'em!" His long hairy fingers latched onto the three gold-colored tin cans comprising his morning's ration. "What the hell do we have here?" he bellowed. Some of the men mingled about watching. Others relieved themselves upon nearby trees, smoked cigarettes, or stood motionless, watching the stream meander on its downhill journey to Lake Ashi.

"Uncle Sam is feedin' us well today! Eggs, hot dogs, pound cake, and a tin of peaches. Hooo weee!" Perkins hollered.

"Let me see your tins," Eugene said.

"You've got your own!" Perkins snarled back.

"Just want to look—I'm not goin' to steal 'em," Eugene said.

"Peaches," Perkins said, tossing the can to Eugene.

Meanwhile, the men dropped their packs, removed their C-rations, and made themselves comfortable under the shade of the maple trees to enjoy a twenty-minute hiatus.

"Well, son of a bitch," Eugene hollered. "Date stamped February 1943! Leftovers from the Big One."

"Yuck, seven-year-old peaches—mine is 1942! I just lost my fuggin appetite!" Robert growled.

"Okay, enough bitchin'. The rations won't kill a soldier. Just eat. Besides, in three weeks, we'll feast on steak and beer," Jack reminded them.

The men rested beneath the leafy maples, while a dark blue sky's stillness was pleasant in the early morning but promising hellish heat in the afternoon. The stream meandered by them, and a row of waist-high reeds grew in thick round bundles on its opposite embankment. An enormous school of yellow butterflies sailed in the wind, their papery wings moving bright and angel-like against the barren, volcanic backdrop. The glimmering stream, the yellow butterflies, and the rough landscape created a scene from an impressionist painting—perhaps a Van Gogh—inspiring one's imagination.

Jack recognized all this, quietly eating his morning rations and allowing the natural beauty, like an opiate, to calm his being. Then he took the sketchbook from his pack and began to work furiously, drawing the slender green reeds bending towards the sun, seeking to embrace creation as a newborn gropes for its mother's breast. Jack then added the swooshing movement of the yellow butterflies swarming low upon the water's surface and then high above the reeds and down again, creating a wispy fog of dazzling yellow against the cobalt sky. And he sketched the silvery-gray color of the stream, its surface smiling brightly, and high above loose herds of cream-colored clouds floating seductively, and the starkness of the volcanic terrain dominating the foreground.

At a moment when his fingers lay motionless, his attention fixated solely upon the alignment of the reeds rising upwards from the muddy stream bank, movement caught his attention. It was a motion Jack had seen hundreds of times before. It is a scene blessed by its beauty and as predictable as it is inevitable, whose signs fathers teach to their sons, and then it travels from one generation to another.

"Quit your yappin' and look by the reeds. See the movement in the water?" Jack said.

"Been watchin' it, too," Perkins whispered.

The other men stopped talking, and it became blessedly quiet, with just a few birds chirping and the sound that water makes when it rolls downhill. Then the stream suddenly cracked wide open, and a great brown trout leaped high into the sky; its broad mouth and fan-shaped tailfin swung violently from east to west. The men watched in awe, not thinking it could go any higher. Still, its energy propelled itself further skyward, up towards the butterflies, where it winked at the pearly gates of heaven, and then it fell headfirst with a thunderous splash.

"Oh, man! I've never seen such a beautiful trout!" Walter Abbott hollered.

"What do ya say we stay here and screw the sixty-mile march?" Snakey Frank Connors suggested.

"If I had my fly-fishin' pole," Perkins said.

"Who needs fishing?" Robert laughed. "I'd lounge and skinny dip all day."

"Skinny dippin', why the hell didn't I think of that?" Eugene hollered. And he leaped from his trousers and stood stark naked, just combat boots laced to his feet.

"Holy shit!" Robert yelled. "Look at that pink-faced pecker swing back and forth. Do you hit fly balls with that thing, Eugene?"

"Screw you, Robert!" Eugene yelled back, running like a madman into the stream.

"Let's go!" Big Bill Burns hollered, and he jumped out of his clothes and charged Eugene with the savagery of an Indian water buffalo, grabbing the smaller man by his horns and tossing him high into the middle of the stream. By now, the rest of the men also stood naked, including Jack, and they encircled Big Bill Burns like a pack of wolves. The first to make a charge was Robert, head lowered like a bull, but Big Bill moved deftly, grabbed him under the shoulder, and lobbed him onto Eugene, who gleefully watched the action unfold.

Snakey Frank Connors charged next. He juked right but moved left, avoiding Big Bill's massive defenses. His five-foot-ten-inch frame slammed squarely into Big Bill's fleshy midsection. The force did little to drive Big Bill's hulking body backward, but it buckled Snakey Frank's skinny legs, and Big Bill, now enraged, grabbed Snakey Frank and tossed him onto Robert and Eugene.

The remaining men fully encircled Big Bill Burns, faking thrusts, and backing off to reorganize for the attack. "Abbott, stay at his rear; Perkins, hold his left flank; Simmons, hold the right flank; Parker, join me at his front!" Jack hollered savagely. "Okay, *banzai* on three! One, two, three—*Banzai!*"

The men smashed into Big Bill Burns, causing the stream to explode. Loose peckers and bleached white asses rolled about like dolphins. But Big Bill Burns went down quickly. The wild screams could be heard miles away, upon the summit of Mount Fuji.

•   •   •

On the third night, the men dug a line of foxholes atop a ridgeline that offered unobstructed, panoramic views of the low-lying terrain. To the south, a full moon dangled low in the sky, and it cast soft beams of vanilla-colored contentment across the dark, reddish-brown landscape and the men's foxholes. Mount Fuji's elegant silhouette posed before the men, and it seemed even larger and more sacrosanct than at midday when it exposed its entirety. And the moon, enigmatic and candle-like, possessed an oddly erotic effect. It rested just below the heavens, suspended, held in place by the earth's gravitational pull, shining brightly for the men to ponder.

Jack lay in his dirt hole with the broadside of his body against the cool, chalky soil. He kicked his booted feet forward, rested his ruck behind the hollow of his back, and gazed up leisurely at the moon. Jack observed its lighted surface and slowly scanned it from top to bottom, looking for irregularities like he'd done so many times before. Then he visualized its ruggedly beautiful face scarred by a million years of meteors. Some of them mammoth craters the size of the Great Lakes— and they appeared dark and metallic, while others seemed almost brownish and fertile in his imagination. He saw the vast lunar mountain ranges, steeply cut gorges, and massive flows of barren lava. He reflected upon how God dangled such jewelry from the heavens— the moon, the stars, the Milky Way. How blessed, he thought, to have it so visible and all about them: Mount Fuji's silhouette against the evening's sky, the moonlit magic of the Kanto Plain sprawling southward to the lighted city of Yokohama, the emptiness of the Pacific Ocean far away and nestled into the horizon, fluttering yellow butterflies among the green reeds during the morning's twilight, and the splendor of a brown trout thrusting its naked body from the water to feed itself upon a butterfly.

Life, creation, and balance appeared so manifestly all about them. Generations of solid concrete and cast-iron bars had detached man from nature. The clearing of its forests, grubbing of its land, and diversion of its waters created the great cities, but at what cost? It had taken its toll upon man's morality and had imprisoned humanity's capacity for understanding and compassion for the basis of its existence. But here upon this sacred high ground, nature was abundant to nourish the men's youthful souls—the fantastic honey-sweetened scent carried northward with the wind from the late summer's flowers blanketing the Japan Alps, the blackness of the evening's sky, the vast open space unobstructed by civilization, the brightness of the moon. Jack felt his mind drifting peacefully and more deeply into introspection. There was so much to be grateful for and much more to look forward to in his life. The world appeared measureless, unexplored, and wide open to his appeals. He was young and strong, and his body delivered upon his command. It took him through deserts, across rivers, and over mountains, and the pain this caused brought more satisfaction than if it had been dormant, like a volcano that is no longer sufficiently masculine to shake the earth at its core.

The following morning, the soldiers awoke well before sunrise to an acrid, salty, pungent stink from a series of Snakey Frank Connors's celebrated stink-bombs. The pernicious smell passed over the men slowly and hung like a thick gray morning's fog, burned their eyes, and made breathing difficult. Snakey Frank's beady, cobra-colored eyes smiled back at the nasty sneers—delighted because he had caused such significant unpleasantness and supremely tickled by the attention it garnered. "Good morning, men," he said, chuckling. "I hope ya'll enjoyin' the fresh alpine air."

"Go fuck yourself," Robert yelled, coughing violently as he quickly lit a cigarette to mute the stink.

"So, what, where are your mornin' manners, Robert?" Snakey Frank innocently replied. Here, have some more," he said, and slowly and with great precision, he swiveled himself like a battleship's turret, bent his lanky frame forward, and took the three-point position of a Green Bay Packer's lineman.

"You'd better back down—I'm warning you, Connors!" Robert yelled.

"Eat this!" Snaky Frank hollered.

"You son of a bitch, I'm going to kill you!" Robert screamed.

This was too much for Snakey Frank, and he broke into a hysterical fit of laughter and tried to evade Robert's wrath with a quick left juke. The tackle was square, just below Snakey Frank's sternum—a cigarette burning brightly between Robert's smiling lips. The momentum lifted Snaky Frank and threw him several feet backward, dumping his skinny ass hard upon the dirt, with Robert resting solidly upon his stomach. "Serves you right for stinkin' up the place, you ratbag of a bitch," Robert hollered.

"Nice fuckin' tackle!" Eugene chimed in.

"Yeah, you stuck the skunk good," Walter Abbott added.

The rest of the men laughed hysterically.

"Okay, okay, I quit!" Snaky Frank squealed as he tried to avoid a deluge of heavy stale smoke that Robert blew into his terrified face.

"No more, Snakey Frank!"

"Okay, let me up, for heaven's sake, I'm dyin'."

"No, you're not getting off that easy," Robert said harshly.

"Hey, Big Bill, decommission this man," Robert ordered.

"No, no, for God's sake, no!" Snakey Frank screamed.

Big Bill Burns, the platoon's other notorious farter, gallantly strolled forward, rubbing his lower abdomen. "Where do you want it placed?" he asked.

"Broadside and fire for effect," Robert ordered.

Big Bill eased his two hundred ten pounds onto Snakey Frank's chest, squeezing the remaining oxygen from the man's depleted lungs. "Free yourself," Big Bill ordered, and Robert sprinted for safety.

Just as Snakey Frank's face lost color, Big Bill released his payload.

"Hooo weee, isn't that a sight to see!" Walter Abbott stammered as Snakey Frank slithered in the dirt like a morning's nightcrawler, grasping wildly for air.

"Serves the man right for stinkin' up camp," Russell Simons added.

"Well, I'll be a son of a bitch!" was all Eugene could say.

•   •   •

On the fifth day, the squad arrived at its final bivouac in the concluding hours of a spitefully hot late summer afternoon. They dug in along the narrow spine of another ridgeline and waited for the others to arrive. Here, too, Mount Fuji beckoned, looking down upon the men, laughing at their pitiful faces—dusty, drained faces—faces streaked and stained with olive-colored sweat; faces intensely orange, red, and tanned from the unrelenting summer sun.

A thick matt of coffee-colored stubble covered Jack's face. And dirt, sweat, and grime clung to his fatigues like bloody scabs from five, sixteen-hour days of marching and trenching among the volcanic soils. The sweat, dirt, and oily muck blanketed the men so wholly they didn't care anymore; it became invisible, comfortable, protective, and almost uplifting since it no longer mattered.

Jack sat atop his foxhole with his boots dangling, sore, and fatigued deep inside. The sun now rested more comfortably to his rear, lighting the mountain with a warm glow. It was a big and grandeur mountain, now bathed by the late afternoon's shimmering rays. He dug his hole deeply into the forgiving soil and sat atop its precipice, his legs hanging lazily into the cool, chalky blackness. Before evening, there wasn't much more to do, and his body and mind slowly relaxed, becoming fixated upon the beauty of the mountain.

Eugene and Perkins completed their foxholes, and both men sat inside their finished architecture, smoking cigarettes.

"Hey, how 'bout a sip of bourbon?" Eugene hollered above his newfound home.

"I'll be damned—you packed whiskey!"

"Yours truly," Eugene said, smiling like a savior.

"Well, bring the bottle here," Jack hollered back affirmatively. And Eugene leaped from his hole like an Australian Kangaroo and walked long-legged and monkey-like, proudly swinging bottle and cigarette back and forth the one hundred feet to Jack's foxhole.

"Ya got space in your mansion?" Eugene asked.

Jack grinned. "Yeah, but it'll cost ya; give me that fifth." He grabbed for the Early Times. Jack swooshed the whiskey around in the bottle, making his body and mind more relaxed. Then, leisurely, he read the label: "*This is the Whiskey that made Kentucky Whiskeys Famous,*" uncorked the bottle and took a deep, stomach-fulfilling whiff.

The *kabuki* was too much for Eugene's waning patience. "For shit's sake, Jack, are you goin' to fuck it or drink it?"

Jack grinned and moistened his drought-stricken lips, tilted the bottle back, and let the honey-colored bourbon flow unhindered so that it would wrap itself around his alcohol-starved tongue before he discharged the hot liquor deep into his gut. "Hoo wee, that was the best drink of bourbon I've ever had," he said, a warm glow spreading across his dirty face, which still admired Mount Fuji's cone-shaped beauty.

Greedily, Eugene snatched the bottle from Jack and discharged a prolonged drink into his needy gut. He then tossed the booze to Perkins, who arrived moments before, towering above them like a Midwestern sheriff's deputy intent on ticketing each man for driving under the influence.

"You know," Jack said to the two men. "Have you seen such a beautiful sight in your life?"

"It's different," Perkins replied. "But it's the type that reminds me of Wyoming in early fall. Every year, durin' the first week of September, the leaves turn from yellow to the color of roses—as Ma says. Pa and I'd pack the horses deep into the Wind River Range to hunt and fish. On my fourteenth birthday, we made camp at the head of a lake surrounded by those mountains. A stream connects this lake to a smaller one higher up and offers some good fly-fishin'. We'd ride up there and fish that stream in the early evenin' when the sun went crazy on those mountains; 'Indian colors,' my pa used to call them wild oranges, purples, and reds, and the fish always bit like hell during those beautiful colors. The Wind River Range is like cliffs—jagged and granite, and the peaks are big, sharp, and dangerous. There is a hole in that stream where a fisherman can see both lakes—the big and the small—and the granite peaks reflect from the water, lit up crazy in those Indian colors. When I was a boy, I didn't think there was nothin' so beautiful in this world where we camped that summer. But this mountain is different. It ain't exactly dangerous lookin' in the way my mountains are, but it has just as much beauty."

"It reminds me of Mount Rainier," said Eugene, dangling his feet into the hole. "Rainer is also volcanic, more massive, and covered by glaciers and snow. But this mountain feels perfect, as if a sculptor chiseled it. It makes you feel like you're in Japan."

"You're in Japan," Jack reminded him.

"Sure. But there's somethin' Japanese about it," Eugene said.

"Maybe it's the other way around," Jack responded. "There is something about the Japanese that is Mount Fuji. This mountain's been here for thousands of years, with the Japanese in its shadow. Perhaps Fuji-san's perfection shaped the Japanese culture."

"You're an odd son of a bitch, Jack," Perkins said, laughing.

"But consider the great Meiji gardens, Japanese Ukiyo-e, the tea ceremony, and the delightful kimono—simple, exact, and earthly art. Living in the shadow of that perfectly shaped mountain for thousands of years is why it seems so Japanese, but it's the other way around—the Japanese reflect Mount Fuji."

"Well, I never thought of it that way, but how you explain it makes sense. By God, Perkins, we've got a philosopher on our hands!"

"He's a nutty son of a bitch," Perkins said as he squashed his cigarette into the chalky soil. "I never met a man that marches like him, shoots a rifle straighter, draws fancy pictures, and philosophizes. You're a quirky son of a bitch, Jack Pierce!" Perkins said almost disgustedly.

"You can thank my old man and Grandpa Rufus," Jack laughed. "Boys, what do you say? Shall we climb it tonight? See the sunrise from the top of Mount Fuji!"

"Sure, I'd go with you, but I don't see how you'd climb it without getting spotted," Eugene said skeptically.

"It's a damned stupid idea!" Perkins grunted. "Colonel Jones will throw us in the brig if he catches us doin' something donkey-ass retarded like that!"

"But how is the colonel going to know?" Jack asked.

"How in the hell is he not?" Perkins replied.

"Because we'll climb it at night. And be back in our foxholes before the battalion's frontal maneuver tomorrow afternoon. Nobody, especially not the lieutenant or the captain, will think their men are so cracked-up that they'd climb Mount Fuji—especially as worn as we are after five days marchin'. Anyway, we are 'bout halfway up the mountain, and I can see a perfect line to the top. We would make the summit before sunrise, for sure!"

"So, you propose we leave after the rest of the platoon is sleepin' and hike like Billy Goats through the night to make the sunrise?" Eugene asked.

"I propose we leave even earlier while the men are playin' poker," Jack said. "And then hike like Billy Goats through the night and run like mountain lions back to the line in the morning."

"Well, how in hell are you gonna keep from bein' seen running down the mountain in the mornin'?" Perkins inquired cynically, spitting a gluey brown blob of tobacco juice next to Eugene's booted feet.

"Easy, Jack said excitedly. We take a different route down, further to the south, which will put us a mile to the rear of the platoon. We can link up with the men in the morning. Nobody will see us descend, and it won't cross anybody's mind that we just came off the mountain."

"You know, it might just work," Eugene said as he took a second swig of Early Times. "You see, Lieutenant Somerset is hikin' down to the command post to consult with Captain Carlson and Colonel Jones 'bout tomorrow's maneuvers. So, the lieutenant won't be back on the line until 1400. And until tomorrow afternoon's maneuvers, nobody in the platoon will be doin' shit anyway but playin' poker and writin' letters home. They won't think much about anybody else's business."

"So, are you in, Eugene?" Jack asked with great seriousness, letting them know the matter could produce dire consequences.

"Yeah, I'm in!" Eugene said.

"My God, you boys are some foolish sons of bitches," Perkins said, shaking his head and spitting another blob of tobacco juice into the volcanic soil. "Y'all goin' to do it, aren't ya? It's a crazy idea, a cracked idea! But fuck it, I'm goin', too," he said unexpectedly. "Hell yeah, I'm in!" he stammered. Then Perkins broke into a fit of laughter, and the hysterical laughter infected them all—but deep in their minds, they knew it was a damn silly idea, but they didn't care about that.

•   •   •

Jack pulled the squad into a tight circle just after dark when the moon hung fat and lazily above the mountain. "Listen, men—we gotta let you in on something big and secretive you can't say anything about."

"What the hell is it? Are there a bunch of dollies up here or somethin'?" Big Bill Burns chuckled.

Jack sneered back, his expression saying, *how in the hell are we going to get girls up here?*

"Listen—me, Eugene, and Perkins will climb Mount Fuji tonight."

"You gonna do what?" Walter Abbott asked in disbelief.

"You heard me; we are going to climb Mount Fuji tonight—and we need you in on the plan."

"That's nuts! How in the hell are you not going to be seen?" Robert said in disbelief.

"It's figured out, but we need your help," Jack said.

"It's gonna cost ya!" Snakey Frank Connors shot back instinctively, licking his parched, apricot-colored lips.

"Shut up, Snakey Frank, before I crack your skinny neck. Listen to the fuggin plan," Eugene said.

"Okay, this is how it works," Jack said. "It will be the three of us—me, Eugene, and Perkins. But everybody in the squad must know the plan to cover if we're spotted. So, we will bed now, slip off the line at 2100, and make straight for the summit. A full moon is at our backs to illuminate the mountain, so we will use just one light and wrap ourselves in blankets to provide camouflage when we leave. We will travel light, just rations, an extra shirt, and four canteens for each of us. If we go straight for seven hours, we make the summit by 0400. Sunrise starts at 0530, giving plenty of time for rest."

"And what's the plan for the trip down?" Russel Simmons asked.

"We stay at the summit until 0630 and return south of our accent, so we link up a mile behind our positions," Jack said. "Our line of descent will keep us out of sight of the company in the morning. We'll be back on the line by 1130, giving us three hours' rest before afternoon's maneuvers."

"And us?" Abbott asked.

"Walk the line and stoke up poker among the squads," Perkins said. That way, everybody will be focused on their cards, tryin' not to get cheated."

"And try to keep the games goin' late. That way, the men will sleep late. There ain't nothin' goin' anyway until the lieutenant returns to the line in the afternoon," Eugene said.

"You sure you don't want to stay put and play cards with the rest of us?" Big Bill Burns suggested.

"Big Bill, I've had my eyes on that mountain the whole time I've been here," replied Jack. "It's been bothering me, like I might have regrets, being so close to a mountain that's so damn perfect and not trying to climb it. But Perkins and I, well, hell, we live for the mountains—they're in our blood, and I've been climbing them my whole fuggin life, and we have this opportunity to climb Mount Fuji tonight, right now, and we'll remember it for the rest of our lives! When a man's got a chance to make memories, he's a fool not to grab it."

•   •   •

That night, poker games roared back and forth all along the lines. Thousands of miles from America, atop a rugged ridgeline on the eastern flank of Mount Fuji, in the cold dead stillness of a full moon night, the men played cards, smoked cigarettes, told dirty jokes, reminisced of high school proms, and bragged about girls they'd never even had the courage to talk to.

Meanwhile, Jack, Eugene, and Perkins quietly slipped away at 2100. They walked like cats, swiftly, low to the dirt, intensely focused, and draped in their olive-green blankets, they blended into the foreground like a master painter's stroke. They walked for only a few minutes, perhaps five at the most, and not more than a football field, before a corporal from the third squad noticed a small beam of light and the appearance of a ghostly shadow moving snakelike up the mountain. *Must be a man with a bad case of diarrhea*, the corporal thought to himself, and he turned his attention back to a pair of tens and jacks.

The men walked thirty straight minutes and then stopped just as sweat formed heavy upon their brows, and they gazed back at the line. From high above, they saw tiny flashlights and the burning orange embers that came and went with each draw of a cigarette — flickering like fireflies up and down the line—and featureless men bobbed here and there—and all silhouetted by a pale, moonlit blackness—small, insignificant, unnoticed in this world.

"Ain't it strange, seein' them from up here?" Perkins said in a whisper.

"Yeah, it makes you feel small and unimportant," Eugene said.

"They are a good group of men, aren't they?" Jack said with unflinching gratitude. "It's almost lonely to see them from here, but we better go; we've got a tall order ahead of us."

So, the men continued steadfastly towards the summit. The climb became more challenging, reckless, and dangerous than they thought. What appeared to be a mountain of undeviating pitch and terrain in the comfort of daylight was a devious brute under the cover of darkness. It lashed out at the three haughty intruders, throwing them down upon its steep slopes. It watched with pure pleasure as they struck hard upon its bladed shale. In its jingoistic cruelty, the mountain forced the soldiers to bear the suffering of its birth, as it had arisen thousands of years before from the bowels of the ocean in fire and fury, expunged from the earth's molten core by an angry outburst of his master's temper. The mountain slashed savagely through the soldier's leggings, slicing their skin, and drawing blood. It forced them to scamper into unseen ravines, scramble over burly boulders, and maneuver across dodgy gulches. It ripped at the soles of their boots, tore at their courage, and forced each man to question his wisdom. Finally, after five hours of straight-up slogging, they were shattered, bruised, thirsty, and hungry. "Listen, men, I've had enough already. Just leave me here, and

I'll enjoy the sunrise from where I am. Heck, I'll just sip on the remaining whiskey and then meet up in the morning and we can walk down together," Eugene suggested, now happily convinced his misery was over.

Jack sat next to Eugene and didn't say a word, like he hadn't heard what he'd said. It was just shy of 0200, and they'd hiked for five hours, and the breaks were just long enough to loosen their boots and drink warm water. Jack understood Perkins was worn thin, too, and that spirit alone separated the men from the summit and the summit from their lines.

"I figure we are three-quarters there, and this is a good place to rest," Jack said. "How 'bout we break out our C-rations? The peaches and pears sound delicious, as does the pound cake and a little milk chocolate."

"Think I'll have a smoke," Perkins said, and he removed a Chesterfield from a half-filled pack, expertly sheltered it from the choppy wind, and then lay down in luxury, resting his head upon his green pack. "My gosh, look at that full moon. It sure feels closer from up here, doesn't it?"

"It does!" Jack said. "It makes you wonder what it would be like to look at the earth from up there. From its surface, the earth would be somethin' special—the oceans, the mountains, the forests."

"Yeah, it would be something!" Eugene said, slowly emerging from his weakened spirit.

"I wonder if one could see the lights of New York City?" Perkins asked, feeling new life flowing fresh and unencumbered into his tired limbs.

"Or the snow and ice of the North Pole," Jack said.

"Or even the red sands of the Sahara," Eugene said, feeling happier and more confident now that he wasn't moving uphill. "My uncle Bill works at Boeing and says someday we'll travel to space. It's only a matter of time, and it is top-secret stuff. So, when I'm out of the service, I'll get my aeronautical engineering degree and work for Boeing. I want to be a part of projects like that—that will change the world."

"Not me," Perkins said. "I just wanna go home and run my family's ranch. It ain't much of a spread, and ya always livin' in the moment—mendin' fences, shoein' horses, deliverin' calves on a Christmas Eve. You just prepare for what nature is givin'. But it's nice being close to the good earth, and everybody helps everybody. 'Bout you, Jack? Got plans?"

"Yup, I'm going to marry Michiko," he said, gazing at the moon and not thinking twice about what he had said.

"My god, Jack, have you told her your plans?" Eugene asked, chuckling.

"Nope," Jack said. "But I knew I would marry her the moment I saw her."

"How in the hell does a guy know somethin' like that?"

"I don't know. But I think Michiko knows it, too; maybe not like I know it, but I think she knows it, too."

"But haven't you thought about her being Japanese?" Eugene said. "The Army strongly discourages these types of marriages, and what would your folks and neighbors back home say?"

"I don't much care about what others think," Jack said without emotion.

"Well, what the hell are you gonna do if the gal doesn't wanna move to America?" Perkins asked.

"I'll stay in Japan," he said.

•　　　•　　　•

The men summited Mount Fuji at 0400. They stood in disbelief, shocked by their remarkable unguided scramble to its summit. Jack arrived first, well ahead of Eugene and Perkins. Charcoal-colored dust blanketed his face in a thick layer that resembled the mountain's hard, porous surface. And like the other two men, multiple holes scarred his trousers, and pink patches of dried crusty blood created thick, painful lacerations over his knees, hips, and elbows where the shale slashed through his skin.

With the sun's lazy march to the horizon, the earth brightened, the sky transformed from midnight blue to the color of hazelnuts, and the moon still hovered milky white above the Kanto Plain, but now it was an afterthought. Jack's life became full of boundless opportunities from the top of Mount Fuji. The entire world lay below him, and nothing seemed to matter so high above its folly. Only now—the irreplaceable moment—did anything matter. Time held still. It became unbreakable and eternal in the way that it was.

Only after the passing of the initial euphoria did the mountainous wind become bitterly cold. It slapped itself wickedly against the men's sweat-drenched bodies, so they sought warmth within their woolen blankets. Dirt, sweat, and grime colored each man's face, running from their hairlines in muddy little torrents to the backs of their necks and cheeks and into their distended eyes, which protruded from hollow, windblown sockets. From within the shelter of their blankets, they peered like bats over the swollen, misty forms of the awakening hills below—and far beyond the Japanese hills, they looked through an endless horizon, eagerly anticipating sunrise from the summit of Mount Fuji.

The new day's first visible appearance was the color of rust, deeply scratched across the horizon. Then marmalade, sandstone, fire, and apricot were stitched together upon a ream of the highest quality Japanese silk. Jack lay upon his stomach and envisioned a stage master supervising the hoisting of her majesty's curtain and the servants pulling gently upon the glorious embroidery to draw her subjects into tempestuous anticipation. And he dreamt of the beautiful *Amaterasu*, her majesty, the Japanese sun goddess, presenting herself upon a hallowed stage, the grand composer beating his drums more furiously and the crowd becoming more and more frenzied. He observed that bronze and fire formed the bridge of its head, the body of a tiger more intense, powerful, and alive than the silken embroidery of celebrated colors in the foreground. The sun rose slowly before him, steadily. And he counted a tenth of its surface, a quarter, a half, until a tremendous white light burst from its apex, and she burned brighter and brighter and more and more potent until she overpowered his senses. Then, finally, *Amaterasu* thrust herself upon the tiger's back. There, she danced wildly, her hands moving in tight circles, forging the great bronze legs of an Olympian. Fire, marigolds, and ginger burned fiercely, and she knelt and placed its glory on a pedestal. Its great belly turned white, its muscular legs straddled the ocean's depths, and its brawny arms stretched with immense confidence across the heavens to form the perfect star.

The men's bodies became heavier as the earth warmed and the chill receded from their weary bones. Finally, they abandoned their tired bodies beneath their woolen blankets and fell asleep.

Perkins dreamt of Gypsy, his favorite horse, a well-mannered brown and white Appaloosa his father gave him on a snow-white Christmas in 1939. He felt himself riding him—the childhood smells, sounds, and colors of the natural earth all about—falling into and out of sleep, his body rising and falling with the horse's movements. Daniel Boone, his English Spaniel, ran well ahead, fast, and as natural as a red fox along a narrow horse trail, which cut the vast open range into two great continents. The familiar warmth, smell, and rocking of his horse's muscled body and Daniel Boone's companionship drew him further away from the mountain and into a blissful sleep.

Eugene snored savagely next to Perkins. And his sleep excited him, the kind that a man desires not to waste. The leaves of the old oak, plum, and maple trees lining 65th Avenue had turned a golden yellow, and Eugene wore the Senior Letterman's jacket he'd earned from baseball. How he ended up in the back seat of his father's Ford Super DeLuxe pressed tightly against Jenny Fisher, he did not know; the dream didn't divulge these crucial details, and it didn't really matter.

In twelfth-grade chemistry, Jenny sat in the same row as Eugene, two seats to his left. She had a beautiful round face, russet-colored eyes, and a thick mane of golden blonde hair rolled over her well-formed shoulders like a waterfall. Eugene developed a deep adolescent love for her, and during his senior year, her womanly figure had often been a topic of his nightly orgasm. Still, his love was a secret, and he had never broached the subject of his attraction to her, and by the time they graduated, she had found somebody else.

In the back seat of his father's car, Jenny's perfume invaded his senses, and the warmth of her heavy breathing, lips pressed firmly against his own, made him crazy with desire. Subconsciously, he knew it wasn't real, that disagreeably, he lay atop Mount Fuji with only men, but he pressed himself forward. He drew his sneaky fingers beneath her sweater, unclipped her brassiere, and crept the palm of his greedy hand to the fullness of her breasts. His mind swirled in chaotic little circles, so he focused his attention—tried to master the dream—knowing it wasn't real, but it *was* real. Then he slid his free hand beneath her waistline and felt the tight wrap of silk atop his fingers and the soft brush of her pubic hairs—*Oh man, this is the best dream I've ever had,* he thought hungrily. And she raised her hips so slightly to offer more space for his industrious fingers to browse the soft underbrush he'd never touched before, but before he could unearth it, this little treasure box of Jenny Fisher's, Jack Pierce's boot struck him in the ass.

"Come on, men, it's already 0700; we're wastin' precious time and had better return to the lines!" he yelled above the howling wind.

Eugene looked up bewildered and tried to focus his tired eyes. Then he remembered where he had been, what he was doing, and how Jack so selfishly stole it from him. "For shit's sake, Jack," he yelled, "I was just about to lay Jenny Fisher!"

"Sorry for stealing your girl, Eugene, but you boys were about to sleep clean through the day. Tell us about this girl, Jenny, and your dream as we get off the mountain!"

The men packed their rucks quickly. But before descending, they stood at the edge of the earth and peered across the caldera. "I've seen nothing like it," Perkins uttered.

"It's like a great lake—only it's dry and hellishly scary-lookin'," Eugene said.

"Yeah, it's hard to imagine this mountain blowing its top thousands of years ago," Jack said. "It must have been something to see from Tokyo—all lit up in a fire, smoking, and throwing lava, rock, and ash for hundreds of miles."

"Hey, guys," Jack continued, "if we look east, we can see over the Sea of Japan towards Korea, China, and Russia."

Eugene added, "And if we turn west, we are looking across the Japan Alps and over the Pacific Ocean to California."

"How about if we turn north, Perkins? What are we looking at?" Jack said.

Perkins said happily, "Heck, if I know; it sure is a sight to see!"

"Let me tell ya," Jack said, "if we look north, we are looking over Tokyo, Hokkaido, and toward the North Pole."

"That's right," Eugene said, "and if we turn south, we are lookin' towards Hiroshima and over the islands of Kyushu and Okinawa towards Taiwan and the Philippines."

"What a beautiful earth it is! 'God's Country,' ain't it?" Perkins said.

"God's Country," they all agreed.

It was now 0730, an hour past their planned descent, and the sun lay well above the horizon, the summit alive with light, and they knew the line was awash with activity.

"How do ya think the boys are doing?" Perkins wondered.

"They're probably wonderin' how in the hell we're doin'," Eugene said.

"Do ya think they will cover us?" Perkins asked.

"I've got a lot of confidence in Robert, Simmons, Abbott, and Big Bill Burns. It's that fuckin' Snakey Frank Connors that's got me worried," Eugene mumbled.

"Snakey Frank doesn't worry me," Jack said. "He's not one to trust in a tight spot, but he is intelligent. Smart people like Snakey Frank know how to play their cards—they're always lookin' for the angle that gets them ahead. The problem with guys like Snakey is that you don't know they've taken you until after they've eatin' your lunch. Snakey knows well enough that his best hand, the one that works best for Snakey, is to go along with the plan, but he might try to get something at the back end and cash out his chips. So, we must keep an eye on him, so he doesn't pull a fast one."

Descending from the summit, the men were lighthearted and happy. But then it was all downhill to the line—a few hours of sleep, the battalion's maneuvers, and they would return to Camp Drake in a few weeks. "The first thing I'm gonna do at Drake is drink a cold beer, eat a T-bone, and stuff a baked potato with butter, rosemary, and chives," Perkins said.

"Not me; I'm going to drink a thick chocolate milkshake, eat a cheeseburger, and then have a cold beer, a T-bone, and a baked potato," Eugene said.

"It's a chocolate sundae for me, then a cold beer, a New York steak, French fries, a big mound of coleslaw, and a shot of bourbon," Jack said. "Then I'll take a hot shower, sleep eight hours on a soft mattress, eat eggs and bacon, drink black coffee, conduct drills, and dance the night away with Michiko."

"You are a lovesick dog," Eugene laughed.

And they rambled happily down the mountain this way. They talked about anything that came to their minds. Eugene bragged about his dream with Jenny Fisher. Perkins recounted his dream about Gypsy and his English Spaniel, Daniel Boone. Jack told them about his father, grandfather, and their fly-fishing trips to the Upper Merced. Eugene talked about boxing, baseball, and the sleekest new jet fighters. Perkins about ranching and horses, and Jack summarized the story of a book he'd recently finished, *The Razor's Edge* by Somerset Maugham. And the lyrics of the American West floated through the pages of time for nobody's pleasure but their own, and the witty Japanese gods rolled with laughter, beamed with big red faces, and danced away happily in the heavens:

Oh I've got no sugar baby now
All I can do is to seek peace with you
And I can't get along this a-way
Can't get along this a-way
All I can do, I've said all I can say
I'll send it to your mama next payday
Send you to your mama next payday
I got no use for the red rockin' chair
I've got no honey baby now
Got no sugar baby now
Who'll rock the cradle, who'll sing the song

Who'll rock the cradle when I'm gone
Who'll rock the cradle when I'm gone?

And then they broke into a popular little ditty, laughing hysterically, singing it to only themselves, again and again, so glorious to be alive.

On top of old Smokey all covered with snow.
I lost my koibito, sweetheart, cause I pom-pom too slow.
She said Sayonara, I'll see you again.
I'll see you on payday when you have takusan, much, yen.

•   •   •

I looked outside at the hustle and bustle in Manila in mid-morning. My coffee was nice and hot, and then I sank my teeth into a fresh-baked pandesal, warm, fluffy, and filled with coconut jam. Jack sat with his big burly arms folded across the tablecloth. His division's tattoo colored his forearm, with its single lightning bolt slicing diagonally across a mountain. The glass-beaded ashtray was in its usual location, and his weather-beaten face was so alive with memories.

I asked him, "So what happened when you returned to the line?"

"They made us climb it again," Jack chuckled. "When we got back, our officers were waiting for us: Colonel Jones, Captain Carlson, and Lieutenant Somerset, the three of them standing there with crossed arms. The sons of bitches had seen us at the mountain's caldera from a telescope at the 2nd Battalion's position. The lieutenant told me years later, at one of those reunions where too many cheeseburgers and Budweiser are involved, that we created one hell of a commotion at the command post."

"I'm sure you did, Jack," I said. "What was the fallout?"

"According to the lieutenant, Captain Carlson flew into a rage, became bright red and madder than a cobra—hollered at the lieutenant for not establishing sufficient discipline. And he then stormed into the

CP and pulled Lieutenant Colonel Jones from a breakfast of bacon and eggs to take stock of the situation for himself."

"Sir," Captain Carlson said punitively, "we've got men from Easy Company on the summit of Mount Fuji! I can't tell you how these men got there or who they are, but they are our men. You'd better have a look."

"For shit's sake," the colonel growled, storming from his half-eaten plate of lukewarm eggs.

Jack continued his story. "The colonel arrived at the telescope just as we dropped off the caldera and traversed to the east, and then he lost sight of us. We would have made it unseen if we had stuck to our original plan and gotten off the summit just thirty minutes earlier."

"Oh, shit," I said, half-laughing. "So why didn't the officers throw you in the brig?"

"According to the lieutenant," Jack said, chuckling, "the colonel stormed from his quarters—still carrying coffee—and grabbed the telescope. He stood there watching us for about a minute, digging away furiously at overcooked bacon embedded between his gums and molars—with, according to the lieutenant, an enormous shit-eating grin spread across the entirety of his wolfish face."

"Why, those crazy sons of bitches," the colonel finally growled to Carlson and Somerset. "Those silly bastards must have hiked through the night to see the sunrise! Goddamn, I wouldn't have even thought of that myself!"

"So, what do you want to do about it?" Captain Carlson asked the colonel, anticipating the sharp edge of a sword decapitating the soldiers from the Army.

"I will not court-martial them," the lieutenant colonel said, rebuking Carlson. "The infantry needs soldiers like these men, crazy high-strung bastards that are tough as nails. So let us greet them at the line," he said.

Jack chuckled as he relived the memory. "The colonel thought the whole affair quite admirable, but he sure scared the hell out of us!"

Jack struck a match to a cigarette, his third of the morning, and continued.

"As we approached the line from its eastern flank, we saw Easy Company moving about quickly and with purpose, and we sensed uneasiness in the air. So, we walked in formation, ragged, weak-kneed, and bleeding, stomachs sitting in our throats, feeling like we were marching to our hanging. And I'll never forget the contorted look upon Perkins's face like a five-pound mango rolled up his ass," Jack growled.

"That would fuckin' hurt," I cackled, not knowing what else to say.

Jack smiled and set his coffee down. "So, there we were, marching into the officers' hands for a court-martial, and Perkins five-pound mango up his ass."

"Colonel Jones was in the lead, and Captain Carlson and Lieutenant Somerset stood just behind him. Somerset held his balsa swagger stick, striking the palm of his left hand hard and methodically, sending shivers down our spines. I recall the colonel's face like it was yesterday. His nose wrinkled upward like a German Shepherd ready to bite, his chin jammed down, and his bottom teeth positioned slightly over his front. And he smiled the psychotic smile of a madman, pasty black mustache glued beneath his wrinkled nose—sinister, condemning, evil-looking."

The colonel barked at Jack, "Well, I'll be a son of a bitch! Looky here, Captain Carlson and Lieutenant Somerset, we've got tourists in Easy Company. So, how was the tour, gentlemen? Did you get to the summit? Did you take a couple of wonderful photos for friends and family? Is the bus waiting to pick you up and take you to your hotel? I must say you look like shit!"

"Sir," Jack said, "we hiked through the evening to reach the summit for the sunrise intending to reach the lines before the battalion's maneuvers would begin. With all due respect, sir, we thought the hike would be a once-in-a-lifetime opportunity—sir."

"Did you hear that Captain Carlson and Lieutenant Somerset, a once-in-a-lifetime opportunity! Did you get permission from the lieutenant for this once-in-a-lifetime opportunity, Corporal Pierce?"

"No, sir, we did not, sir."

"Did you get permission from the captain to carry out this once-in-a-lifetime opportunity, Corporal Pierce?"

"No, sir, we did not, sir."

"Did you get permission from me—your goddamned lieutenant colonel—for this once-in-a-lifetime opportunity, Corporal Pierce?" And a thick misty spray of the colonel's spittle painted the three soldiers' faces.

"No, sir, we did not, sir."

"Goddammit!" Colonel Jones yelled. "So, you're telling me the three of you abandoned your positions without orders to take a self-guided tour of Mount Fuji so you could have for yourselves—a once-in-a-lifetime opportunity. Is my understanding of the situation correct, Corporal Pierce?"

"Yes, sir. I'm sorry, sir, but your understanding is correct."

"Goddammit!" the colonel yelled again.

"Corporal Pierce, are you a combat veteran?"

"No, sir, I am not, sir."

"Corporal Pierce, am I a combat veteran?"

"Yes, sir, you are, sir."

"How about Captain Carlson and Lieutenant Somerset? Are they combat veterans, Corporal Pierce?"

"Yes, sir, they are, sir."

"And do you think Captain Carlson, Lieutenant Somerset, or I would abandon our positions for a once-in-a-lifetime opportunity, Corporal Pierce?"

"No, sir, I do not think you would, sir."

"Well, how in the hell do I know that when bullets are flying, you three tourists won't abandon your goddamned positions for a once-in-a-lifetime opportunity—Corporal Pierce?"

"Sir, we would never abandon our positions in a situation like that, sir—never!"

Lieutenant Colonel Jones stood staring down each of the men like a prizefighter sizing up his opponent, and he stomped his boots into the volcano's red dirt.

"You know, I could court-martial you men and have you thrown into the brig, but I'm not going to do that, not this time, goddammit!" he yelled. "I'm going to give you three soldiers a once-in-a-lifetime opportunity! Do you hear that, Corporal Pierce?" he said, pointing his stubby finger into Jack's terrified face.

"Yes, sir, thank you, sir."

"The battalion's maneuvers will begin at 1500 sharp and cease at 2000," the colonel shouted. "Once we complete the maneuvers, you three tourists will depart immediately for a once-in-a-lifetime opportunity. You men will hike once again through the night without sleep to the summit of Mount Fuji. The captain, lieutenant, and I will meet you there at exactly 0700. Moreover, there will be no special cafeteria privileges upon your return to Camp Drake—no steak, no beer, no soda, no ice cream, no nothing! Furthermore, the three of you will be restricted to base, without weekend liberty, for one month, and assigned cafeteria and latrine duties. Corporal Jack Pierce, Private Perkins Bigley, and Private Eugene Trevor, do you now understand the stupidity of your once-in-a-lifetime opportunity?"

"Yes, sir, we do, sir!" the men hollered.

"Good, you men are dismissed."

"My gosh!" I said to Jack, grinning. "It sounds like a once-in-a-lifetime opportunity."

"It was," Jack said with a twinkle in his eye.

The next morning, clouds covered the summit, and we couldn't see the sunrise.

CHAPTER FIVE
The Return

When the men finally returned to Camp Drake, it seemed a year had passed. The Camp looked the same, smelled the same, served the same food, and the same civilian and non-civilian employees mowed the same green grass, trimmed the same plum trees, and serviced the same enlisted and NCO clubs. But to the men, Camp Drake had somehow changed. They were the upperclassmen now. They were no longer strangers within the Camp's walls; its grounds were familiar and welcoming to them. By now, they knew the Japanese workers' names and could pronounce them in the native language—Hitoshi, Goro, Eiko, and Kaori.

Beyond the Camp's north and east gates, they commanded the streets, the soldiers of Easy Company. "Soldier habitat," they called this world beyond, a collection of bars, pool halls, and souvenir shops; tattoo parlors, late-night eateries, and barbershops that included lathered shaves, hot towels slapped across the face, and powerful shoulder rubs. And for the men's amusement, lighted cabarets, short-time hotels, and streetwalkers painted with heavy red lipstick and powdered faces. They knew by heart the fastest route to the station, the platform for the train to Ikebukuro, and how to transit to Ginza, the center of Tokyo's shopping and entertainment district. They learned when the first train departed from Camp Drake and when the last train returned. They became experts in their habitat.

But the communal camp shower was one aspect of barracks life that never became comfortable. In packs, naked peckers are sickly, dehydrated creatures, extraterrestrial lookalikes, and there is nothing less likable to showering among a large herd of beastly little peckers.

Easy Company's communal showers had heads for fifty men, and by the time Jack, Perkins, and Eugene stripped naked, forty-three dirty grunts from 2nd and 3rd Platoons had taken forty-three. The water from the cast-iron showerheads smacked hard against the filthy platoon and darted in all directions, flinging soapy gray water upon the men. Volcanic residue from the forty-three sweating male bodies streaked the white tiles brown from their three weeks at Camp Fuji.

Eugene turned towards Perkins and Jack and bitched, "Three weeks in the bush, and I've gotta stare at dick while I shower."

"Yeah, hard to beat the meat when you're starin' at peckers," Perkins chuckled.

"No ladies for us," Jack said in dismay. "Captain Carlson spotting us at the top of Fuji-san was damned bad luck. And who would've thought they'd have a telescope at the CP? I sure wanted to see Michiko at Club Florida tomorrow tonight. Anyway, some swabbie's probably already copped her."

"And I'm sick and tired of havin' Snakey Frank Connors and Big Bill Burns rubbin' our bad luck in our faces," Eugene said. "If I hear Snakey Frank brag one more time 'bout his weekend plans for Tokyo and our weekend duties cleaning the toilets, I'm gonna bust him."

"The first thing the son of a bitch said to me when we jumped the deuce was how he's gonna dance at Club Florida with Michiko," Jack said bitterly. "He says that since I'm stuck on base and won't enjoy her company anyway, I oughtn't to mind allowing him to have fun with her."

As they sized up the forty-three swinging Charlies in 2nd and 3rd Platoons, Eugene joked to Perkins and Jack, "Why is a man like a snowstorm?"

"Why?" Eugene asked, chuckling.

"Because you don't know when he's coming, how many inches you'll get, or how long it'll stay."

The men doubled over in laughter. "Isn't that the truth?"

The showers were piping hot, and the steam was suffocating when Jack, Eugene, and Perkins finally washed the accumulated grime from three weeks of maneuvers. Robert, Russell Simmons, and Walter Abbott talked up their weekend passes.

"I've got a room in Shinjuku for the three of us," Robert said as Jack took an empty showerhead within spitting distance of the three soldiers.

"Are you boys staying in Tokyo for the weekend?" Jack asked.

"We sure are," Walter Abbott replied. "I've got a room for the three of us. It's too bad you can't join us. We've got tickets to watch the Yomiuri Giants on Saturday, and then we'll dance in Ginza."

"That sure sounds great! Do you think you will go to Club Florida?" Jack asked.

"We're going to the eight o'clock at Cabaret Mimatsu and then dancing at Club New Yorker. It's a shame you're grounded."

"Aaah, it's alright; it was worth it," Jack said.

"It doesn't sound worth it to me," Russell Simmons replied. "What you, Perkins, and Eugene had done up there was the craziest thing I'd ever seen. But when we heard that you three boys made it to the summit for sunrise, we were dammed proud."

"Hard to believe," Jack grinned.

"It's true," Robert said. "Even that skunk Snaky Frank was running about talking up what badasses we are in Easy Company."

"That makes it even harder to believe," Jack replied. "But I'm glad I did it. My old man used to tell me he had many things he wanted to do, but not the time to do them. That night on the ridgeline, we were so close to Mount Fuji that you could reach out and touch it. The moon was full, and the whole damned mountain lit up in light; we had the time, so we just did it. I appreciate you boys doing your best to keep it under wraps. And I'll tell you what, I'm awfully proud of Perkins and

Eugene; those are some tough troopers—some of the best in the company."

"Anyway, Jack, you boys gained the respect of Easy Company," Walter Abbott said.

"I just want you boys to know I don't have any regrets. Colonel Jones was rough, but he could have been rougher, thrown us in the brig, and busted us down in rank if he'd wanted."

"He could have kicked you out of the Army!" Walter Abbott said. "But the colonel's got good sense; he knows when he sees good soldiers, and he ain't gonna waste good men when all they've got are stallion hairs up their asses."

"Good infantry soldiers always have stallion hairs up their asses, or they wouldn't be in the infantry in the first place," Russell Simmons added.

"We had a hell of a three weeks, didn't we, boys?" Jack said.

"The best three I've ever had," said Robert.

•   •   •

During summer, the Ikebukuro market bustles with heat-wracked shoppers on Friday afternoons. In winter, they bundle themselves in heavy jackets and soft hats. However, the temperatures are perfect during fall and spring, and the market is happy, resourceful, and busy with smiling sellers and buyers.

Michiko wound her way through the stalls wearing a light blue sundress with a wispy flower print. It was a happy dress that went well with her sandals and matched her mood, which was cheerful and dreamy. She hadn't seen Jack since they danced that evening almost five weeks before. Still, she received a half-dozen letters—some scribbled on postcards, some on neatly folded scratch paper, and the most recent on beautiful *washi* paper with an imprint of Fuji-san's reflection from Lake Ashi.

Kenichi passed Jack's most recent note to her the night before at the club's close, and she tucked it inside her purse until she returned to her room, bathed, and lay down upon her futon. She waited to open it until she cleared her mind and peeled back the envelope like a child separating gold foil from a piece of milk chocolate. She tugged the paper gently from its soft white cocoon and noticed it neatly folded into three crisp sections. It took just a moment for her eyes to adjust to the light, the flatness of the paper, and the imprint of Fuji-san's reflection. Then, finally, she noticed a small, wallet-sized photograph tucked inside the letter—a picture of Jack wearing an Army service cap in his green dress uniform. He did not smile in the photo, and his sharp bluish-gray eyes cut through the picture and took her breath away.

On the paper, he had sketched her. Nobody had ever done so before. He drew the picture in the upper right-hand corner of the letter. He used a pencil, the same one he used to write her letter. She could tell he'd taken his time to draw her face. The woman's face on the note was beautiful. It was her face, Michiko's face, especially around the eyes, nose, forehead, and cheekbones. She could tell he'd taken liberties, the type a man might take in his imagination when he lusts for a woman. That evening, she tied her hair into a bun. He had drawn it long and flowing, dark and wild. And he made her lips a little fuller than they were, but she could tell they were her lips, lips he drew more sensuous and desirous of a man's attention. He had also taken liberty with her eyes, but not in their proportions, shape, or placement below her brow, but she could see he had taken time to make them more moon-like than they were—deeper, darker, more mysterious, and sexual.

She then read his note. It wasn't much of a letter. He'd informed her again that he desired to see her and could do so in another two weeks, and apologized for the long delay he had caused. He said he was doing well and offered a few quirky recollections of events during the week.

The letter made her heart flutter and feel warm and flushed inside. She turned off the light, and the room became dark and still. She heard the birds chirping and the sound of crickets in the pine trees planted in a lovely bonsai garden just outside her window.

When she closed her eyes, she saw his drawing, not moving but perfectly motionless, and felt his desire, lust, his wanting in the strokes of the pencil—making love to her, and his forceful bluish-gray eyes staring back at her from the photograph. She desperately desired to pull him inside, wrap her arms around him, and kiss him all over. But her body began to feel lighter and even more flushed. It wasn't something she planned; her movements had no premeditation. Her hands simply moved unconsciously, instinctively, over her chest, then to the needy area between her legs. All the while, she felt his desire, his lust, his wanting until her body suddenly shuddered with pleasure, and she quietly fell asleep.

Now Michiko glided through the market feeling happy, relaxed, and seeking a pound of *shiitake* mushrooms, a batch of *shungiku* leafy greens, a head of green cabbage, a round sweet onion, carrots, *daikon*, and long green razor-sharp *negi*, green onions. She meandered from the vegetable stalls through the market's tightly woven network of capillaries, veins, and arteries to the noodle sellers. Noodles made of rice, wheat, and barley; long, skinny, short, and fat noodles; hard and soft, wide, and narrow noodles—like the bodies of the early fall shoppers in the tightly packed Ikebukuro market.

Michiko took a heavy handful of long and skinny rice noodles and passed them along to the noodle seller—a heavy-set, round-faced man who never stopped smiling and yapping for customers — "*Irasshaimase, Irasshaimase; Saikō no men o hanbai shite orimasu. Men o zehi okaiage kudasai! Irasshaimase, Irashaimase!*" A copper-colored ten-yen coin exchanged hands, and he bundled the noodles together by a ruby-red rubber band and placed them into a small brown paper bag. "*Domo arigato*, thank you very much," Michiko said, smiling at the noodle seller.

Next, she needed *yaki tofu*, thinly sliced *wagyu* beef, *dashi*, *mirin*, *shoyu*, and a small amount of Okinawan brown sugar to complete her *sukiyaki* recipe. But first, she wanted to buy fresh shelled Chiba prefecture peanuts, famous for their sweetness, and Thurston Ogilvie's favorite crispy Japanese *Senbei* rice wafers—salty, crunchy, and flavored with *shoyu*, or red pepper, or hot *wasabi* powder, shrimp, or *nori*.

Michiko enjoyed making Thurston happy. His happiness made her happy, and his displeasure made her sad, but he was generally a cheerful man, albeit having a most serious and meticulous personality. The *sukiyaki* broth was hot and fragrant, and she'd set out vegetables, tofu, and sliced beef she'd cook at the table. Thurston arrived home from a busy day of meetings with the Japanese Ministry of Public Works. He opened the door to the sweet, mouthwatering anticipation of *sukiyaki* and hollered, "*Tadaima*, I'm home!"

Michiko prepared a double Suntory whiskey on the rocks and filled a bowl of sweet Chiba peanuts.

"Here, Michiko-chan, please take my hat, will you?" Thurston said as he passed her his Stetson.

"*Okaerinasai*, welcome home," she said, bowing deeply. "Let me show you the house. I have your whiskey waiting for you in the reading room."

They walked through the house, admiring the fresh flower arrangements she'd cut that morning. He observed the dining room table prepared for dinner—all the while Michiko gliding gracefully across the tatami mats and Thurston shuffling along in his tight black socks enjoying life in occupied Japan.

"You are such a sweet young lady for buying me my favorite peanuts," Thurston said, sipping whiskey.

"*Arigato gozaimashita*, thank you very much," she said, admiring the older man's refined manners and stately good looks, which included a broad, intelligently shaped brow, neatly trimmed silver hair, rose-colored cheeks, and crisp blue eyes.

Thurston's bubbly mood pleased her, and she swiveled happily from the reading room, her long black hair tied into a bun and the rhythm of her young sexy hips swaying back and forth. Thurston watched, admiring her movements full of purpose, life, and a future. He enjoyed her beauty like he appreciated the extraordinary artistry of the woodblock prints that adorned the reading room's walls. It was a splendor to indulge oneself, enjoy, and venerate in the manner of flowers following a long gray winter. So, he allowed her infectious beauty to warm him, take hold, and enliven his kindred soul. Then he took another sip of whiskey and shook loose the front section of *The New York Times*.

•   •   •

"I am in love with an American soldier," Michiko said.

"You are…" he responded, looking up from the paper, the twinkle in his eyes refocusing upon her pretty face, becoming more amused by the innocence of her candid admission.

"Tell me about this American, you fancy, Michiko," he said, taking a sip of whiskey and placing the ice-filled glass on the cherry wood table.

"He's tall, handsome, very polite, and has beautiful eyes," she said, her eyes dancing with the stirring emotions that lingered from his letters and their brief encounter five weeks before.

She continued, staring dreamily into the puffy white clouds of her love. "I've never seen eyes like his before. They made me dizzy," she giggled. "When I saw them, I didn't know if they were real. They're beautiful, like a glassmaker's marble, blue and gray, and I could see inside of them, not like our chocolate eyes."

"Is he an officer or an enlisted man?" he asked her gently.

"Enlisted," she said, smiling shyly. "His name is Jack Pierce," and she spoke his name like she'd revealed a great secret. "He recently returned from training at Camp Fuji." She then giggled and removed his photograph from her purse. "Do you want to see his picture?" she asked Thurston enthusiastically.

"Surely," he said.

Thurston observed the man's face. He saw a young, handsome American face, like Michiko was young, beautiful, and Japanese. But, from the man's expression, Thurston immediately sensed Jack was serious-minded and bright, but different somehow, and he couldn't place his fingers on this difference. Thurston studied the soldier's face a little longer, and then he realized: The eyes were different—they had that expression—the expression that forms in a daredevil's eyes. He had seen this expression before in China and then in Burma during the war, in the eyes of the young fighter pilots who flew with Claire Chennault's Flying Tigers, where he supervised the construction and operation of Chennault's airfields.

"He's very handsome," Thurston said, returning the picture to Michiko. "When do you expect to see this young American again?" he asked her.

"In two weeks," she said, her cheeks becoming the flushed color of a Belgian strawberry truffle—creamy white, pink, and chocolate brown all melted together.

"Why not sooner?" he asked her.

She paused and looked at her feet, no longer perched in the clouds. "His commanding officer confined him to base," she said, ashamed she had revealed this.

Thurston's eyes squinted. "For what reason?" he asked her.

"He climbed Mount Fuji."

"He climbed Mount Fuji…? But I thought he was training," he said, bewildered.

"He was," she said, still flushed, her hands pressed tightly upon her thighs, still looking down at the tops of her feet.

"He climbed it without orders?" Thurston asked.

"Yes."

"Well, I'll be damned," was all he could say.

Thurston and Michiko did not speak of Jack after that until two weeks later, on a sultry late-September evening. Thurston rested in the reading room, reclining deeply into his favorite leather armchair. He'd finished his evening's glass of French cognac, and the ice cubes were slowly losing their shape, becoming amorphous as an early evening becomes after a glass of cognac. A porcelain dessert plate lay beside the glass with chocolate cake crumbs and streaks of rich fudge meandering aimlessly across its white surface. Outside, it was a moonless evening, and he stared blankly into the sky, searching for stars.

"In June, I love to sit here and watch the fireflies emerge," he said unexpectedly. "Do you remember how they dart back and forth across the garden and the beautiful orange glow of their bodies streaking across the night sky?"

"Yes," she said. "In Japan, we believe fireflies are the spirits of soldiers who died in battle. So, on those evenings, I sometimes think of my brother when the fireflies are visible—the Sunday mornings we spent together as a family along the Sumida River, holding hands, watching the boats, and eating mochi together. I imagine he is one of those fireflies and has come to say hello."

"I'm sure he does, Michiko. The lives of so many were lost in the war," he said.

"*So desu ne*, that is true," Michiko replied sorrowfully to Thurston.

"I'm reading the ancient poetry of the *Man'yōshū*, the *Collection of Ten Thousand Leaves*, in English. They write in these eighth-century poems that the firefly's mystical light signifies love's burning passion. Do you believe this, Michiko?"

"Yes, in June, it is the season that the fireflies are searching for their mates."

"And tonight is the night you will see Jack again, isn't it, my child?"

"How did you know?"

"You are happy; it shows across your face and eyes. Your mood is as bright as a firefly's warm glow."

Michiko giggled and smiled cheerfully.

•   •   •

The train to Ikebukuro took ten times longer than he remembered. He sat feeling nervous, thick cement in the gut, unlike Robert, Eugene, Perkins, and Water Abbott. They chatted excitedly, jostling one another, driven by a strong desire to drink and maybe get laid. He, too, lusted for sex, so horny that it made him nauseous, ready to vomit. The difference between his and theirs and his reaction was that he and Michiko would meet tonight. The others embarked upon a safari, predictable because of its unpredictability—no predetermined outcomes and nothing to lose. In contrast, Jack had a catch, and there was something dreadful of all he had built up around it over the seven weeks since he'd seen her.

Jack pressed himself against the back of the seat and tried to recall her face. He thought how much easier it would be if he'd returned to the club when the experience was fresh, but nearly two solid months had passed. Earlier in the day, he wasn't nervous at all. Oddly, he felt like he did when he sang himself down the slopes of Mount Fuji, with the entirety of Japan below him. At breakfast, he talked more than usual. "Oh, these eggs and pancakes are tasty—the best I've eaten. Tonight is the night, boys. Third Squad will take Tokyo by force!" he hollered happily.

"Hooah!" his friends howled back.

That night, just after the sun fell below the horizon, he jogged around the base's perimeter to let off steam. He took a cold shower, shaved, dashed himself with Old Spice, and donned a fresh-pressed Class A Army uniform. The creased, three-piece green looked sharp and manly, and he laced up a pair of polished black oxfords. Then, standing before the mirror, he sized himself up; this is whom she would see, and he practiced an expression or two. And he didn't want to come off too hungry—best to look well-fed.

They disembarked at Ikebukuro and quickly boarded a connecting train to Yurakucho Station, a quick jaunt to Ginza. This trip took another twenty-five minutes; by now, a surge of excitement overcame the dread affecting him earlier. He tapped his oxfords impatiently and imagined dancing the night away with Michiko, her guiding him through the steps. However, his imagination did not dwell solely upon her dancing; he envisioned her when he'd arrive. She'd smile, and he would stride confidently, presenting her with a box of chocolate and a single red rose he'd purchased that morning. Before they'd dance, he'd insist upon a drink, and they'd reacquaint themselves and then dance until closing, feeling the joy they experienced that first night. He stuffed his Army scrip and ten crisp, one-dollar bills into his wallet, enough for dinner, some Ginza trinkets if he desired, and to purchase tickets from Club Florida for dancing, drinks, and snacks.

At the Yurakucho Station, the five men leaped from the train. The big, glitzy district preyed upon the service members' hard-earned greenbacks. A collection of rowdy revelers and yakuza sharks filled the streets, nothing like the small dusty towns and brick-and-mortar establishments from back home—soldiers, sailors, airmen, hostesses, whores, hucksters, politicians, salarymen, and gangsters.

"Hey, guys, I'm starvin'! How 'bout *yakitori* at Nobunaga's before dancin'?" Walter Abbott suggested.

"I'm game; I could eat a friggin' horse!" Eugene said.

"Literally, they serve horse's ass at Nobunaga's," Robert laughed.

"I ain't eatin' no horse's ass," Perkins said.

"How's eatin' horse any different from beef? They're both ranch animals, aren't they?" Eugene argued.

"Sure, but a rancher gets personal with his horse. We talk to 'em like they are our wives, best friends, or dogs—tell 'em our troubles. You damned well don't eat your wife…! Do you?"

"Some men do," Walter Abbott said with a chuckle.

Jack looked impatient. "Let's hurry. I promised Michiko I'd be at Club Florida by eight and wouldn't be late!"

They entered Nobunaga's to the crack of a *Taiko* drum and a hearty shout of "*Irasshaimase*, welcome" from a line of strong-looking men behind burning *hibachis*. The restaurant smelled like sweet smoked meat—barbequed skewers of chicken, pork, beef, horse, and various vegetables and seafood—eel, squid, octopus, and fish crackled over orange charcoal.

A cute Japanese waitress with pink dimples greeted the group, dressed in the traditional costume of the *Oharame* village firewood peddler, a white towel wrapped about her forehead, white leggings, and zori slippers. She bowed and led the five hungry soldiers through clouds of smoke and blaring *enka* music to a large circular table near the restaurant's center.

The men ordered big brown bottles of cold Kirin beer. A table of muscled sailors dressed in navy blue skivvies with tattooed forearms and rough-looking faces sat nearby. A dozen twenty-four-ounce bottles, already empty, were atop their table, and packs of Lucky Strike cigarettes. One sailor, a meaty-looking brute with a blockish green face, receding hairline, and a sinister smile, mumbled to his friends, "A bunch of dog-faced wops and kikes," and he wobbled drunkenly to the soldiers' table.

"Y'all from Camp Drake?" he asked the men, flexing his meaty biceps as he spoke—his bulging black eyes sneering at Eugene.

"What's it to you, swabbie?" Eugene spat back.

"Y'all look like a bunch of Hollywood's in y'ur fancy uniforms, Fifteenth dog faces, eh," the sailor said, still flexing his meaty biceps and cracking the knuckles on his oversized, calloused hands.

"I can see you want it up the ass, don't you, sailor boy? Well, don't waste your time flirtin' with us—you've got four willin' peckers at your table," Eugene snarled back, pointing to the sailors at the adjacent table. The sailors' shipmates pushed themselves back, preparing for a fight.

"Alright, enough poppycock!" Jack said, and he reached over and took the beady-eyed brute by the shoulder with the friendliness of a childhood buddy from the same small town.

"You sailors gotta go to the Yoshiwara on a Friday night! They've got the finest-looking ladies in Tokyo and more pan-pan girls than bars. A cab will get you there in twenty."

Happy for an out, the four drunken shipmates scurried from the *yakitori* and flagged a taxi. And Jack tied his arms around the ugly brute, pushing him from the restaurant. "You boys have fun in the Yoshiwara!" he said with a grin, noticing the big brute's wallet lying in the gutter. The cab sped away with the five sailors packed like sardines. And Jack stood patiently, waving goodbye to the blockish-faced bully, who smiled back like a big drunken kid, and Jack knew he'd be too hungover the following morning to remember where he'd lost his wallet.

"Hey, boys, dinner and beers are on the United States Navy," Jack said, slapping the sailor's Navy identification onto the wooden table.

"Hoo wee, there's two ten-dollar bills of scrip inside," Perkins said as he helped himself to the yen.

"That dumb swabbie deserved a good ass whooping," Eugene said, still upset by the sailor's unhinged drunkenness.

"Would you rather be fighting or fuggin?" Jack said.

"Fuggin," Eugene grinned.

"Good, then let's eat and get out of here. I told Michiko I'd be at the club thirty minutes ago."

Heavy September clouds had gathered above Ginza, and golf-ball-sized missiles fell from thousands of feet, flooding Ginza Avenue with oil-laden runoff. The torrent meandered along the gutters like a fat gray python topped with gasoline, cigarette butts, and drunken soldier piss.

"Damn, we better buy umbrellas," Robert suggested.

"How far is Club Florida?" Perkins asked.

"About three blocks to Z Street and Ginza Avenue," Jack replied.

"I see a couple of cabs a block up—let's run for it," Walter Abbott suggested.

"I'm going," Eugene hollered, and he sprinted for the taxis, followed by Walter Abbott, Robert, and Perkins close behind. Jack followed, but didn't get far before seeing a blue bus loaded with sailors bearing down upon him. The big belching vehicle sped up Ginza Avenue, and as it became closer, a white-capped Navy driver flashed Jack a buck-toothed grin, turning the heavily ribbed tires into the shit-water. Then, before Jack could react, a tsunami flew from the roadway and crashed over his thighs.

"You motherfucker!" Jack hollered, kneeling, plucking a soggy cigarette from his shiny black oxfords.

"Fuck it, I'm out—I'm not going to the damned club!"

"Get the fuck in the cab," Robert hollered.

Jack paused, and he thought of Michiko waiting for him.

"Okay, screw it; I'll take the second cab with Perkins!" he hollered.

During the short drive to Club Florida, Jack devised a plan to sneak into the restroom to clean himself up. But standing at the club's grand red *torii* entrance brought memories—bongos, horns blaring furiously, Big Bill Burn's swollen pecker, the crazy bartender Kenichi, and Michiko's beautiful, chocolate-brown eyes.

Adrenalin pumped through his veins, and, because of his excitement, he temporarily forgot the unpleasant sensation of his wet feet. Instead, he peeked inside, located the bar, and saw Kenichi. But he didn't see Michiko, so he slipped inside the bathroom and removed his socks and shoes. Both smelled like green toads. And he lathered them with soap, worked on his pants, washed up, and waited ten minutes.

I'm going to restart tonight, he thought to himself. *I'll leave the club, smoke a cigarette, walk through the torii gate once more, and have a fresh beginning. I'll give Michiko the rose and chocolate and have a cocktail and dance.* The plan overwhelmed him, and he became excited and couldn't wait to start. "It's been seven long weeks of waiting," he said aloud, finishing his Chesterfield, visualizing her receiving the rose.

Back inside, the club hopped with a surprising number of dancers. They jostled shoulder to shoulder, and navy-blue trousers and white-capped sailor uniforms were everywhere—*a friggin' carrier group is docked in Yokosuka!* he thought to himself. He pushed through the crowd and found Perkins, Walter Abbott, and Robert milling about, drinking beers with a couple of Japanese hostesses.

"Hey, Perkins, have you seen Eugene?"

"He's sittin' at the bar drinking a beer with the bartender," Perkins said.

Jack turned and saw Eugene conversing with Kenichi, and even from two hundred feet away, the bartender's gold front teeth reflected from the lights.

"That man's two front teeth must be twenty-four-karat gold," Perkins said, pointing to Kenichi. "Is he the Guadalcanal man?"

"He sure is," Jack said proudly.

"It's too damned bad that our Pacific vets aren't here; they'd wanna compare notes," Perkins said.

Jack jostled his way to the other side of the club, where the orchestra played a song by Benny Goodman. There, the music was louder and the energy more frenetic. He pushed himself through more revelers until he noticed a group of tables occupied by sailors and girls. The sailors wore their crisp whites, their sailor caps plopped on their heads like an upside-down bowl, and all had naval chief insignia on their shoulders. Michiko sat next to one of these sailors, a handsome man in his mid-twenties with a bright, college-educated face and a finely trimmed mustache. Michiko wore an elegant, tight-wasted red and white striped party dress, black stiletto-heeled shoes, and rose-colored rouge, and he thought her prettier than the prettiest Hollywood actress. He watched her unnoticed for several minutes. She sat beside the sailor, rubbing elbows, refilling the man's glass each time it became low, seemingly enjoying herself immensely.

Plates covered their table, filled with steak bites, fried shrimp, French fries, hamburgers, chicken wings, and several twenty-four-ounce beers. Jack stood silently, dumbly watching the party unfold, feeling childish. He held the box of chocolates and a red rose, his skin feeling sticky and damp under a wet uniform. But then Mayumi noticed the tall, good-looking soldier standing alone and motionless. She smiled and waved to Jack, covering her mouth with her palm, and whispered in Michiko's ear.

Michiko briskly stood, took her purse, and walked to the restroom like she had practiced this routine before. Mayumi glanced at Jack and signaled with her eyes that he should follow.

"Jack-san, I waited thirty minutes, and you didn't come. So, I thought you'd changed plans," she said, looking into his eyes.

"I'm sorry, but the guys wanted dinner, and then we had a problem with some sailors, and then the rain, and I got splashed by a truck, and it took so long to get here!" he said, holding her by the hips.

"The management watches us, Jack. We must attend to the customers. I couldn't wait. I'm sorry!"

"No, don't be. It's my fault!"

"Jack-san, I loved your letters and the picture you drew. I missed you!" And then she hugged him. "I'm sorry, but I must go. They're waiting."

"But can't you take a different girl to your table? It would be nice if we could dance, and I bought chocolate, and a rose for you," he said, holding up the rose.

"I'm sorry, Jack-san. Please wait, and I'll join you later," she said, then darted away.

Jack felt light-headed, flushed, cheerful, and depressed. He worked his way to the bar and sat beside Eugene, angry at himself for being late. *I blew it for the two of us*, he bemoaned. *I waited seven weeks for this moment!*

Jack ordered a double whiskey on the rocks.

Kenichi reached below the table, retrieved a whiskey glass, and filled it half-full of heavy rectangular ice cubes. The bourbon meandered between the cubes and ponded into an intoxicating desert.

"Wrong time, no see," Kenichi said, handing Jack the half-filled glass.

"Thank you for passing my messages to Michiko," Jack said, extending his hand to shake Kenichi's mutilated forty-five.

"No problem! She comes every day to check for messages. You should see her face—so sad when no retter comes and so happy when it arrives! She reary rikes you beri beri muchi. She is rike a happy child! So why don't you dance with her now?"

"I arrived late. She's tied up with a table of navy officers," Jack said, looking dismayed.

"That's too badu! Why don't you dance with a different girl? Michiko won't mind," he suggested.

"Nah, I'll wait for Michiko to break from those sailors. I don't suppose it will be much longer."

Jack reached inside his front right breast pocket and retrieved a solid brass Zippo and a pack of Chesterfields. He bent over the lighter and allowed the flame to dance seductively in the dim light. "It was a shitty stunt that fuggin swabbie played, splashing me with water. I've never seen such a disrespectful asshole in my life!" Jack grumbled to Eugene.

"I figure you got *bachi*," Eugene said, smiling, his burning stub hanging loosely from the corner of his mouth.

"Got *bachi*...? What the hell is *bachi*?" Jack growled.

"I was tellin' Kenichi about what happened at the *yakitori*. How the drunk swabbie came for a fight, and how you settled it down, took the dumb sailors outside, and put 'em on their way, but not before you lifted the swabbie's wallet from the gutter."

"Yeah, so what?"

"Well, I then told Kenichi that you got whitewashed by that swabbie bus, and Kenichi said you got *bachi* for not returning the sailor's wallet. So, it means 'what goes around comes around'—like karma."

"Son of a bitch, I guess you're right. I am *bachied*, for fuck's sake! Here, take the sailor's wallet. I don't want the damned thing anymore."

"Heck no, keep the fuggin thing away from me—I don't want no *bachi*!"

"Screw it. I'm gonna throw the damned thing away, but I'm keeping the man's money. I deserve it for all this *bachi* nonsense. Kenichi-san, *Kirin, biru i-ppon kudasai*," Jack said, ordering a bottle of beer in Japanese.

"*Hai, dozo*," Kenichi said, popping the cap from a big bottle and pouring the first glass.

"*Arigato, thank you*," Jack said, feeling proud of his expanding use of the local language.

Eugene and Jack drank a couple more beers, and the conversation meandered from pleasure boating in Seattle's Puget Sound to fly-fishing the upper and lower forks of the Owens River to boasting to Kenichi about their nighttime ascent of Mount Fuji. Jack's misery over arriving late became duller and duller with each drink until he almost forgot about Michiko by the fourth bottle of beer.

Perkins, Robert, and Walter Abbott vanished, consumed by taxi dancers and a table stacked with bottles, courtesy of the US Navy. The men talked happily, flushed from two hours of drinking and hot-blooded dancing.

Finally, at ten, Eugene and Jack joined the others. The men were having a splendid time, beaming like ninety-watt bulbs. Even Perkins, the shy meat and potato eater, held sushi in one hand, and a skinny Ojo-san taxi dancer sat on his lap. "Goddamned kings," Jack said, sitting next to Robert. "To the victors, go the spoils!" he mumbled.

The music paused briefly so the orchestra could nourish their toad-dry throats, and the dancehall erupted into a loud conversation, laughter, and chairs screeching across the dance floor. Then the music roared to life, first the drums, bass guitar, and horns, and into Tommy Dorsey & Charlie Shavers's "The Hucklebuck."

Robert rose first, grabbed his taxi dancer by the hand, and hollered for the guys to join him. Then the rest jumped in, even the awkward Eugene grabbing a girl. But Jack remained alone, just him and another beer. He recalled the purpose of his evening and wandered to the far end of the club, hoping to see Michiko. When he spotted her, she was among a crowd of dancers, still in the arms of the handsome naval chief, smiling and having a wonderful time. Jack stood limp-legged, watching them dance, feeling even stupider than before. Finally, he returned to the table, uncapped another beer, and finished it in one growly drink to the beat of a new love song, Dick Hames, "Maybe It's Because," which became too much to bear. *Goddamned bachi!* he fumed, storming from the club, thoroughly sozzled and miserable.

Jack walked hunched over alongside the gutter. He passed a couple of glassy-eyed Japanese war dead and meandered through the busy Ginza side streets and its glitzy clubs—New Yorker, Club South Pacific, Bacchus Club, and Cabaret Mimatsu. Each was stuffed with sailors, reminding him a carrier task force group had docked in Yokosuka. "Too many swabbies—fuggin *bachi*," he grumbled drunkenly. But, of course, he'd had these drunken walks before, especially during his posting at Schofield, when they'd carry a bottle to Hotel Street and then indulge in more drinking at the bars and whorehouses.

As drunken walks go, it passed quickly, only half-conscious of his surroundings and everything moving faster except for sound. Honking, bellowing, crooning, reveling—background noise—trapped by his drunkenness and the city's hardened surfaces. As he meandered by the famous Imperial Hotel, he briefly stopped to observe the crowd leaving the ornate, Frank Lloyd Wright-designed building. It was a crowd of suits and ties that evening, officer dress uniforms, ladies wearing expensive evening gowns, gold rings, pearls, and diamonds—captains, majors, colonels, businessmen and their lackey politicians, and the American administrators of Occupied Japan.

At twenty-one, a corporal, an infantry rifleman, the best marksman in the platoon, a hunter and angler, surfer, and trekker—this world, the Imperial Hotel world, seemed distant, foreign, and remote   like black and white photographs of the incredible Athenian Acropolis. Jack knew it existed and had experienced its inner workings within his family's circles. However, it was an inaccessible club for the enlisted man and required an admittance fee; its subjects had their own set of etiquette, standards, rules, and protocols.

At Yurakucho Station, he purchased a ticket for Ikebukuro. He didn't feel like a tourist—a *gaijin*, but not a tourist—not a North American or European visitor, a fresh off-the-boater. The trip would take twenty minutes to Ikebukuro and another thirty to Camp Drake. So, he took a window seat at the train's rear, where he wouldn't be bothered.

What a fool I am, he thought to himself. He didn't even know this girl he had met just once, danced with a single night, yet he wrote her letters, took her far too seriously, and allowed his heart and imagination to run wild with her beauty. *She was a damn taxi dancer, for heaven's sake*, he thought. Every night was a dance night, probably receiving letters from dozens of GIs like himself—playing him like a fool until the fun wore out. "Fuggin gullible fool," he said aloud, shaking his head in disgust.

But when he closed his eyes, he couldn't see anything but her striking eyes. Her pretty face hung low, like a fog overwhelming his needy imagination. She'd met him at the bathroom, hugged him, and told him to wait for her. She said she'd waited thirty minutes but had to care for the arriving customers to please the management. Kenichi told him she'd asked each night if a letter had arrived. Of course, she wouldn't bother if she didn't want him. But why abandon him at the club for two hours? She stuck to that naval petty officer like cement, patting his hands, fawning over his every need, perfuming his skin with her own; the two were all smiles! Besides, why not choose a naval chief over a lowly corporal? He had to admit the petty officer was a better catch than a ground pounder like himself.

The train sped through a jumble of tired cityscape to the Ikebukuro Station. He jumped from the train and quickly caught a connection to Camp Drake. Other soldiers, some from Easy Company, milled about, returning from liberty. Many had girls, arms and hands braided together, looking giddy by the prospect of an evening's lovemaking.

Jack sat alone, watching the September rain turn everything dreary, making the telephone poles inexorable. Still, colorful umbrellas carried by fashionably dressed bar girls shimmered under the glow of the streetlights. And suddenly, it occurred to him. *We are alive now, and then we all die*, and he thought it again and again. *Is there any purpose to my feeling this way—brooding over a girl I don't even know?*

The main street leading to East Gate had once been typical of a Tokyo suburb, without the perversions that had spread like the clap beyond the gates of Occupied Japan's American bases. Kokusai Dori Street was no exception, and the three-block walk to East Gate sold almost anything a man might crave. Soldiers still packed the streets, and Jack had no desire to return to the barracks. The Black Cat Bar had pool tables, a solid drink menu, American food, a dance floor with attractive girls, and short-time hotels nearby.

Jack followed a group of three inside, flashing neon above them— *MEOW, MEOW, MEOW. Must be a hell of a litter inside waiting to be stroked*, he chuckled. He didn't waste any time and ordered a whiskey and Coke. The Black Cat was busy at half past ten, and Jack recognized some from the company. But, following twenty-one days at Camp Fuji and four weeks restricted to base, he lusted for a woman. The accumulated tension and loneliness had a breaking point, and its corrosive edginess had become far worse than before the debacle at Club Florida.

The first whiskey and Coke went down fast, like water. The second brought back the drunkenness he'd felt at Club Florida, and the lump in his stomach reappeared. He remembered Michiko's smiling face, the happiness in her eyes upon seeing him by the restroom, and her saying, "I missed you so much!" And finally, he recalled her departing words: "Please wait, and I'll join you later."

He ordered a third whiskey and Coke. "Screw it!" he said. "I'm gonna catch the friggin' train back to Ginza. She's probably finished with those damned sailors by now." Each additional drink made the feelings worse, his disappointment and frustration even more depressing. These emotions brewed inside until they finally exploded with her fussing over the damned swabbie petty officer, probably an E-7, and now they reached their breaking point.

He rolled the remaining whiskey around his glass and watched the ice swirl in circles—and it unexpectedly brought back a memory of him with his father riding the merry-go-round—what a distant, long-removed world it seemed. And this distant childhood memory and his present loneliness made it insufferable. "Fuck it, I'm going back to the club," he grumbled. But before he could stand, two firm hands pushed down commandingly upon his shoulders, and a woman's warm body and her seductive scent made him dizzy and weak-kneed.

The girl sat next to him and smiled, and she introduced herself as Reiko.

The Black Cat hostess had observed Jack and watched him quietly drink his whiskey and Coke without so much as a turn of his head or even a change in facial expression, just staring numbly into the glass. From experience, she knew that this handsome young lion was brooding over a girl. She wondered if she was an American back home or a Japanese toying with his heart. Perhaps he had even received a Dear John letter. She had slept with many who received such letters, and she grinned at the recollection of their lovemaking. Sometimes, they acted out furiously and with overheated passion, administering their revenge upon her womanhood with painfully sharp nips, powerful thrusts, and harsh slaps across her buttocks. Still, others were as gentle as kittens and would lie curled up beside her like a helpless child. Some of these men even wept, trying to make sense of their loss until her nakedness awakened their beastly cravings, and they made passionate love with swollen, tear-stricken eyes accompanied by screams of pain. She'd found very few men that landed somewhere in the middle.

She'd watched Jack closely and admired his tall frame and handsome Western face. She thought it looked rugged but graceful and neither too sharp nor square in its architecture. His ears were pink like roses—perfectly selected for his skin tone, and she recalled how different his ears were from those of her first love, whose rose petals became deformed by years in the dojo. Then, the Russians killed him during the war's final week.

She decided to approach him and make the first move. She'd been through the game before, was already twenty-seven, and nobody knew it better. So, she walked the length of the bar, surveying him from his rear as he stared into his drink, and when he stood to leave to find his way back to the Ginza and Michiko, she pushed firmly upon the tops of his shoulders. He turned and met her eyes, and the seduction that met him made his crotch quiver, and it briefly stood erect.

"I can't take a back seat to anybody," she whispered in his ear, "at least not for the time we share a bed. How bad is your grief, soldier?" she asked, playing with the idea of how he might respond in the cradle—would he be the avenger or the pussycat?

"Aren't I supposed to be the one asking the questions?" he said, polishing off his third whiskey and Coke.

"Sure, ask me anything you like, soldier," she said.

"Can I buy you a drink?" he asked her.

"Same, same," she said.

Jack snapped his finger and ordered two more.

"I'm going to catch a train to Ginza and Club Florida," he said, taking a long, stiff drink.

"Why are you going to do that? Club Florida will be closed when you get there. It's already half-past eleven," she said.

"Damn, I didn't figure it was that late. I've had a hell of a case of *bachi*," he said, as if he were reporting scores from Sunday morning ball games.

"*Bachi*," she laughed. "How did you get *bachi*, soldier?"

"I stole a man's wallet…well, kind of stole it. The man dropped it, and I didn't return it. Afterward, I went to Club Florida to meet up with a girl I had waited a long time to see, but things blew up getting there. When I finally arrived, a naval chief petty officer had her tied up."

"There are a lot of pretty girls in Japan besides this girl at Club Florida. Maybe you should tie yourself up with somebody else. How about the girl sitting next to you?" she said, looking into his eyes and placing her left hand on his thigh.

Jack could feel the strain of the whiskey pulling hard at his common sense. He hungered for this girl. She smelled good, and she looked even better than she smelled, and she spoke sexy, and it made him want to make love so this *bachi* affair with Michiko would be done and forgotten. But he wasn't a damned quitter—and there were too many unanswered questions, and the Navy man only made him more determined to see her again and get it figured out.

"Not tonight. I'm going back to my room. If things don't work out, I'll know where to find you."

"You are determined, aren't you?" she said.

He stared back at her. She was pretty—the short black hair in a bob, the well-formed breasts, the solid womanly body with its hidden crevasses.

"I've got to go now," he said, taking her right hand and gently squeezing it.

"I'll walk you to the gate," she said, believing he might change his mind.

"I'm not going to the barracks," he said. "I'll get a room at the Rex Hotel."

"Then I'll walk you to the Rex, and maybe between here and there, you will change your mind," she said.

"Sure, but my mind's made up."

•　　•　　•

She didn't know he was watching until she knew it was too late. While she danced with the naval chief, she saw him for a fleeting moment, but a moment is all it takes.

She wished she'd reached out and hugged him, told him he had misunderstood her, that she felt nothing for this dance partner; it was her job. But how can a man with love in his heart understand? His complexion changed from pink to the dull color of a shark's belly, and his eyes bore feelings of disbelief, hurt, and jealousy in that split second, all the time in the world, to fracture a future. *She must have looked like a harlot*, she thought—smiling, fumbling, and fawning—and how could he understand her inattention? She feared he couldn't help but think she was trivial, that a professional had played him. She watched when he abruptly turned and left, quickly winding through the crowded club. *When will this wretched evening end?* She asked herself in dismay.

She poured another beer while smiling brightly at the naval petty officer. Still, before he drank it, he grabbed her by the arm and pulled her to the dance floor again—*boom, boom, boom*—Jonny Mercer's "Sweet Georgia Brown" carried her into a heap of loose-legged couples.

She couldn't remember a more miserable dance. Her heart ached, yet she forced herself to jitterbug with attention—pretend fun, something she rarely did at the club. She enjoyed dancing and socializing with the Americans. She practiced her English with young foreign men of her generation. These Americans were exciting—once feared terribly, but now accepted and respected for their integrity and childish good manners. But for the longest time, she couldn't feel passion and was devoid of emotion; her feelings were bombed away in 1945, and the deep weltering scars were raw and painful.

The music paused, and before it could resume, she excused herself from the young petty officer's grasp. "I'm sorry, but my shift's ended." And before the young officer could protest, she pushed herself away and disappeared into the dressing room. Inside the tiny space, she observed herself in the mirror. She was twenty-four years old and noticed how her face had changed since she said goodbye to Hideo four years earlier, before her husband shipped to Okinawa for the island's fatal defense. She'd placed a small picture of them on her dressing room table, and picked it up, examining the photograph. They both looked young and innocent, first-love smiles on blushing faces, consumed by their newfound emotions towards another human being. They'd married just three days before and were honeymooning at a small onsen resort in Beppu. He shipped out one week later. In the three months that passed, she received six letters, but in March 1945, the American offensive began, and she never heard from him again.

She looked at her face in the picture and then into the mirror. Tears welled up in her eyes and rolled unchecked upon her cheeks, creating little swales in her makeup. She hadn't cried like this for a long time, so freely and unencumbered, and she couldn't determine if the tears came from sorrow, joy, or a merging of the two.

She took several tissues and wiped away the tears. Now that she had stopped crying, she found herself alone, deserted, drifting towards an unknowing horizon. And rather than allowing these feelings to overwhelm her, she realized she must now let go, that she couldn't turn back. She washed her face, reapplied her makeup, and brushed her long black hair until it danced in the light. She looked once again in the mirror. The past and the present were there for her to see, but now she saw a future. She picked up the picture of the young husband and wife. Unrecognizable to her now, this prior life would forever remain suspended without a string to retrieve it. It would live for eternity, a memory, a place in her history, a dream that experience and circumstance would dim. She held the picture to let her lips kiss it.

"*Sayōnara, Hideo-san. Watashi wa, anata o itsumo aishiteiruwa. Anata o wasurenai*, Goodbye, Hideo. I will always love you, and I will always remember you." She then wrapped the photograph in paper and placed it inside the drawer.

Her heart suddenly fluttered, a nervous excitement overtaking her, and she hoped he would understand. She first went to the bar and spoke to Kenichi.

"Kenichi-san, have you seen Jack?"

"For most of the evening, he waited for you at the bar," he said. "But he and Eugene went to join their friends at a table, maybe an hour ago."

"He didn't come back here?" she asked him.

"No."

"Did you see him leave?"

"Too busy."

She made her way among the tables until she spotted Eugene, Robert, and the rest of the men.

"Excuse me, Eugene-san, have you seen Jack?"

"He was here, but he's left. Did you check the bar?" Eugene asked.

"I can't find him anywhere," Michiko said.

"It's possible he returned to Camp Drake. He was disappointed you were busy with the sailors. Jack is odd; he reads books and draws pictures. Guys like that see the world differently, take things more seriously."

"I suppose you're right. Jack must not think much of me anymore, believing it was just a game. I don't expect he would understand."

"Jack's funny, but there is no more loyal guy in the company."

Michiko left Eugene feeling sad and depressed. She, too, dreamed of this evening for weeks, built it up in her mind with each letter, and placed him upon a pedestal. How thoughtless she'd been to allow him to sit alone while she groveled over another man, even if it was her job.

She walked quickly through Ginza, wondering where he might have retreated. She tried Club South Pacific, Bacchus Club, and Club New Yorker; a Ginza steak house, and an Italian restaurant popular with

American servicemen, and looked inside Lyon's beer hall. When she arrived at the station, she purchased a ticket to Camp Drake.

• • •

Rain fell in heavy drops outside Camp Drake. She had never seen the sprawling military encampment, and the sheer volume of American soldiers and the enormity of the seedy nightlife persuasions surprised her. Like thick black tar, they seemed to hold Kokusai Dori Street together all the way to the East Gate, where four armed MPs searched visitors entering the camp.

The rain-soaked street reflected yellows, reds, greens, and whites, and between these colors, soldiers walked in packs, meandering between bars, restaurants, and Turkish bathhouses. Michiko looked up the street at the odd mixture of signs in Japanese and English, with names like Venus Bar, Hime Bar, Café Snack Bongo, Bar Lunar, Club Alibi, The Sunrise Restaurant, and The Black Cat.

She didn't expect to find him; she knew how improbable that would be. Her shoulders, waist, and legs were heavy, feeling weighted to the earth, standing alone in the rain. And her mind cried out, gravity pulling at her feet, tugging her through the earth's thick crust where loneliness promised to consume her. After the war, she'd become depleted, numb, and desperate for a return to her humanity. She wanted to discover and be swept away by a renewed passion for life. She'd finally known it within herself for Jack, despite how odd and impractical that might be, and isn't it possible, she thought, that the *Shinto* god of love, *Musubi-No-Kami*, delivered him to her for that simple purpose?

She checked her watch. The final return train to Washington Heights would depart in thirty minutes. The rain fell in a steady stream, rolling off her hair and face like little waterfalls, cutting fresh swales in her makeup and dropping to the ground, contributing to a large puddle inside her black stiletto dance shoes. She stood, feeling naked in the rain for thirty minutes. It was her way of paying retribution for her inattentiveness, knowing she would never see him again, but standing patiently, in vain, nonetheless.

She decided to wait another five minutes and then return to the station for the last departure. She surveyed the street once more, but this time, she saw a tall American escorting a Japanese woman beneath the cover of an oversized umbrella. Their faces weren't visible, but as they got closer, she sensed it was him—the shape of his body, the tip of his hat, his sway—and her heart pounded furiously, almost leaping from her chest. She stood silently and watched the couple become closer until the fullness of their features came into view. She saw that the woman with the man was likely a hostess, a pan-pan girl from the nearby bars. They stopped at the Rex Hotel, not over two hundred feet from where she stood in the rain. She still couldn't see the man's face beneath the umbrella's cover, and she stood feeling paralyzed, watching them talk for what seemed like an eternity. Finally, the American tilted the umbrella skyward, and she saw Jack and the woman laughing huskily. They shared an umbrella, a Japanese symbol of love, courtship, and intimacy.

Her heart squeezed viciously, and her stomach rolled in circles. Still, she couldn't stop watching, torturing herself with unbearable emotions, needing the pain to penetrate her heart, hoping a surgeon's scalpel might finally take it away. And just as quickly as it started, it was over, and he returned the woman's umbrella and disappeared into the hotel.

She stood in the rain and watched the woman walk to the Black Cat and recede within its dirty bowels, and she trembled, feeling the dampness of the moisture chill her skin. She stood alone, not seeing the street, the gawking passersby, or flashing neon lights, but only Jack's face as he had said goodbye to the woman moments before. Dreadful insecurities flooded her mind like quicksand, threatening to steal her happiness, surrendering herself to the life of a castaway.

She allowed the summer rain to drop freely upon her face, wetting her hair, bosoms, and the soft skin beneath her red dress. The wetness renewed her desire, which only moments before had abandoned her. So, she walked towards the hotel, determined to confront her heartbreak, loss, and fear of the unknown, wanting to expose her insecurities, loneliness, and desires.

A bespectacled Japanese man with oversized black eyes glued to a mouse-like face worked at the reception. He looked incredulously at Michiko, amused by her wet hair and water-filled shoes, and enjoying the outlines of her heavy, wet breasts.

"May I help you, madam?" he said, his pointy, rodent-like nose twitching back and forth, moving a patch of gray whiskers like an old maid's broomstick.

"I would like Jack Pierce's room number, please."

"Yes, just a moment. It's 206," he said, smiling coyly.

She walked to the stairs and climbed the first flight, feeling the wet dress grope her body like an octopus's tentacles, her legs limp and rubbery, and her mind dizzy with anxiety. Then, finally, she stopped, grabbed the rail, and thought about what she was about to do. Something was terrifying about it all. The next step was letting go of Hideo, abandoning the security of the fortress she'd constructed. But she pressed forward, upon a rocky shore, an undiscovered continent; through a fog, she continued, not knowing if salvation or more loneliness awaited. Yet she could no longer stop; the next step and the next steps were easier.

Jack was lying naked on the bed when he heard three knocks. He'd been reflecting upon the disappointing evening, his childish behavior, and the foolishness of leaving Club Florida before Michiko's shift had ended. The knocking jolted him from his melancholy, and immediately, Jack concluded that Reiko, the sexy pan-pan girl from The Black Cat, had given him a second try. He slipped into his pants and shirt and walked to the door. He turned the knob slowly, opening the door to find a wet red dress standing before him and the most beautiful eyes he had ever seen.

CHAPTER SIX
Cherry Blossoms in Spring

That night in Nikko at the Kinugawa Spa, on November 5, 1949, they bathed in the hot springs under a banana moon and loved each other during the new morning. When they finished, a sharp chill permeated the ryokan, and the stream below greeted them with a delightful chorus of harmonious melodies. His body lay heavily upon the futon, and his right leg spread across her bottom. He luxuriated in its softness and felt content in this relationship with a Japanese woman.

She stared back at him, lost in his bluish-gray eyes. She measured the angle of his Western nose, burned his prominent brows, perfected jawline, and rose-colored cheeks into her memory. Since their reunion two months before, she had still seen him that way, every day in amazement. And she rolled her body so the taunt flowering tips of her breasts brushed his chest, and her hair fell like a silk waterfall, and all he could see were her dancing brown eyes.

"Tomorrow, you will meet my sister and grandparents," she giggled.

"Do they know we are coming?"

"I mailed Kimiko-chan a letter a week ago."

"Did you tell them about your American?"

"You were the topic of my letter," she said, still smothering his face in soft black hair.

"Did your sister respond?"

She lifted herself and looked earnestly into his eyes. "I didn't receive a response."

"It's a seven-hour train ride to Kakunodate. Shall we see the shrines and forests before we go?"

"*Hai*," Michiko said, her eyes still dancing. "But after, we'll buy *omiyage* and gifts for *Ojiichan*, Grandfather, and *Obaachan*, Grandmother!" And she bounced to her feet, naked as a butterfly, goosebumps covering her backside.

Jack lit a Chesterfield and watched Michiko slip into snow-white undergarments and wrap herself in *komon*, kimono fabric, awash with white and turquoise spoonflowers. She tied a warm blue *obi* about her waist and knelt before the mirror, piling her hair into a bun and inserting a single lacquered chopstick through its center.

"*Ikimashyo*, let's go!" she said.

They left the inn to cool mountain air that brushed their faces, turning their cheeks pink. Earthy colors dripped from the trees in broad-brushed strokes of dangling yellows, browns, and reds. And they walked hand in hand alongside the Daiya River, following the mountainside road towards the village center.

At the bending red bow of the famous Shinkyo Bridge, "Sacred Bridge," they paused at its apex and watched the river frolic madly beneath them through its historic beams. A complex of centuries-old Buddhist shrines and temples nestled themselves into the forest, a short walk upslope from where they stood.

"I want to sketch you here," Jack said excitedly, "with this beautiful red bridge, the autumn leaves, and the Buddhist temples in the background."

"Hai," she said, smiling brightly. Michiko blended naturally into the sense of place—so picturesque, Japanese, and complimentary, wearing her autumn kimono. He worked quickly with his colors as a prodigy does with extraordinary prowess. He envisioned this sketch as an evolving piece he'd play with and refine over time. Michiko, in delicate spoonflowers, her playful brown eyes, hair rolled into a bun, and a single lacquered *ohashi*, chopstick, through its center. And he drew her standing upon the ancient red bridge and beyond, in the background, the hazy outlines of Buddhist temples, centuries-old spruce trees, and delicate golds, reds, and yellows.

"An aesthetic monk, Shodo Shonin, introduced Buddhism to Nikko and built the Futarasan *Jinja*, Shrine, and Rinnoji Temple across the river in the seventh century," Michiko said.

"Why did he choose Nikko?"

"Because he fell in love with its beauty and wanted to bless these sacred mountains," she pointed to three of them, saying their names, "Nantai, Nyoho, and Taro," for whom the shrines were honored.

"It's incredible to imagine," Jack said. "Robed monks, samurais, and shoguns walking across this bridge to the temples."

"*Hai*, they made their pilgrimage to Nikko to seek nirvana among nature. Hundreds of years before the shoguns, Shodo Shonin and his students built many of the shrines here today."

Jack felt oddly disconnected from the Buddha, but strangely at peace around it, especially in the presence of Nikko's forested hills.

"These shrines are over a thousand years old," Michiko said proudly.

And when she spoke, wearing a kimono and hair rolled into a bun, he imagined how fitting she'd be hanging upon the wall on a woodblock print in that small shop at the Sensoji Temple, where, five months earlier, he'd purchased his artwork the day he'd first met her at Club Florida.

Looking across the river, she explained the history of the Genpei War and how members of the Taira clan fled to Nikko in 1185, establishing a unique culture and dialect in the surrounding mountains. "In 1616," she continued, "they interred shogun Ieyasu Tokugawa at the Rinnoji Temple. Later, his grandson, Iemitsu Tokugawa, planted a hundred thousand cedar trees in these mountains as a tribute to his grandfather."

"You love your history, don't you?" Jack said, putting the finishing touches on his work.

"It helps me dream and forget," she said. And for the first time, when she said this, Jack fully recognized the depth of her sorrow, so deep he'd never known such sadness could exist.

"Here," he said, showing her his sketch, and the sadness disappeared.

She looked at herself on the page and giggled. "I wasn't standing on the bridge, Jack."

"I know, I just wanted you up there. I improvised."

"*Suteki*, wonderful!" she said, her cheeks flushed.

"You just wait," he said excitedly. "It's not finished yet!"

They walked amongst the brilliance of the sacred forest dotted with the shrines and temples of Michiko's heritage. "It's all so incredible; I've experienced nothing comparable," Jack said, relishing in its tranquility and beauty. With his words, Michiko's face brightened with pride and happiness for Japan, emotions seldom felt in the years since the war's violent conclusion.

At the Tosho-gu pagoda, where they entombed the founder of the Tokugawa shogunate, Ieyasu Tokugawa, Michiko explained that each level of the pagoda represents an element of existence beginning with earth, water, fire, wind, and void. "How do you know all this?" Jack said, bewildered by her depth of knowledge.

"*Benkyo shita,* I studied," she said with a coy smile. "Now, I'll show you the *three wise monkeys*. This is the first depiction of the *Sanzaru* in Japan!" Michiko took his hand and walked him to the Sacred Horse's Stable, where the ancient priests displayed the famous carving. The seventeenth-century carver had masterfully tucked the three wise monkeys into an elaborate carving of painted greens, golds, blues, and pink flowers where they playfully stared back at Jack. "Wow, those monkeys are awfully cute, aren't they! I've gotta take a picture," and he quickly snapped a shot.

"So why is one covering his eyes, the other his nose, and the third his eyes?"

"The *Sanzaru*, three wise monkeys, is a Japanese symbol of morality. It teaches us to hear no evil, see no evil, and speak no evil."

Indeed, Jack later discovered the *Sanzaru* sprinkled all over Japan–along mountainside trails, displayed at Buddhist temples, and sold at *Omiyage* shops–*hear no evil, see no evil, speak no evil.*

Following the temples, they continued along the river and across a concrete bridge to Nikko's historic *omiyage* quarter. Wooden shop fronts lined the narrow streets, selling snacks, curious religious offerings, and handicrafts. Jack watched Michiko go from one shop to another, buying trinkets and sweets. He purchased *sake* for Michiko's grandparents, locally made candies, and a sandalwood figurine of the Japanese deity Ebisu, a god with a cheerful round face carrying a fishing pole in his right hand and a fat carp in his left. Michiko took the deity into her hands and giggled. "Do you know who this is, Jack?"

"I think he's a very happy fisherman!"

She smiled, holding the miniature figurine in her left hand for him to see. "Let me introduce you to Ebisu, our god of fishing and good harvests, and one of Japan's Seven Gods of Fortune, *shichifukujin*. Ebisu gives luck and prosperity to Japan's fishermen and farmers, and honesty is his virtue."

"Then he's my favorite. And Michiko, which of the Seven Gods of Fortune is your favorite?"

Michiko smiled, looking at each of the seven sandalwood figurines on the display shelf, and then picked up the beautiful goddess, Benzaiten, playing the lute. "Of course, I adore all *shichifukujin*, but especially Benzaiten. She is our goddess of art and knowledge, and her virtue is joy. Yes, she is my favorite."

"Well, she fits you perfectly," Jack said. "I want to buy Benzaiten for you, so you can remember this wonderful day."

"Then, Jack, I want to buy Ebisu for you, so you will always remember this day."

Waiting for Michiko outside the shop, Jack watched a tall American in his late twenties walk arm-in-arm with a Japanese from the far end of the street. Jack thought the man's movements possessed a buoyancy, and he guessed him a captain from his demeanor. The Army strongly discouraged fraternization with local girls, but the man's swagger said *stuff it.* Everybody knew the officers had girlfriends, and this officer enjoyed displaying his.

•　　•　　•

From a speeding train, Jack surveyed northern Japan from plate-glass windows.

He witnessed the nation's farmers planting every morsel of tillable land with rice, turning Nippon into a giant grain basket. Dressed in the indigo attire of their ancestors, they wore baggy *mompei* pants, stuffed overcoats, and *tenugui*, traditionally patterned headscarves. Jack pondered the common threads that bound peoples of the land together, the mindfulness of their selfless humanity and a farmer's subservience to the whims of divinity.

During their morning in Nikko, they explored Shinto shrines, Buddhist temples, and purchased gifts. Afterward, they returned to the ryokan and hiked along the river through enchanting pine forests to a seventh-century shrine by a waterfall. Finally, they boarded the train in the late afternoon, snacking on sweet Nikko *mochi* and watching the countryside pass by.

At dawn, they awoke an hour from Kakunodate Station. Three years earlier, when Michiko said goodbye from this same train, she did so as a young widow. Then she departed with little money and no definitive plans, but she knew her happiness depended upon her leaving—that staying was far more dangerous.

Now, an anxious lump swelled in her stomach. She looked uneasily upon the familiar landscapes of her childhood, overcome by unsettling insecurity. *Perhaps it would be too much?*

"Do you feel okay?" Jack asked, sensing her uneasiness. "You look tired."

Michiko stared blankly from the window, and Jack offered her a hot cup of green tea.

"*Arigato*," she said, turning away.

"What's the matter? You're not feeling well?"

"I've decided I don't want to meet them."

"Why not? Yesterday, you were so excited to see Kimiko and your grandparents!"

"I didn't consider their feelings. They won't want you there," Michiko said sharply.

Her words cut like a knife. And then Jack said, "It's the world we have chosen, isn't it?"

"Hai," she said.

"Then, I'll return to Tokyo."

From the window's reflection, he saw her tears.

Jack took her hand and held it gently.

"I'm scared," she said. "I know these feelings are cowardly, but I fear the shame I might bring to them, and they are all that is left. Please forgive me."

He didn't have to guess what she meant; it was a shame he would administer like an inflamed dose of syphilis. She'd fallen in love with a man whose kind killed her mother and father—her grandparent's only son; how does one forgive such deeds? Shame for entertaining and sharing a bed with an American, a gaijin—disgraceful, soiled, un-Japanese. And he knew why he hadn't written home about her, that deep inside, he carried these same insecurities, that there were boundaries even within his own family.

"It's the world we live in," he sighed again. "Don't worry about my feelings and enjoy your family's company."

"I was just thinking of Mayumi-chan and Reiko-chan," she said. "Their families have disowned them, and the neighbors call them pan-pan girls. My grandparents probably think I am a whore, too."

"You know it's just a stereotype, and besides, even if you were a pan-pan girl, I'd still love you."

"There are a lot of terrible stories from the war," Michiko said.

"I know. Perkins's girl, Naoko, has burn scars across her back from Hiroshima. The atom bomb wiped out her entire family. Who may question how Naoko-chan must now survive? Or to question Perkins's love for her? Did I tell you Naoko is Perkins *onrii*, only?"

Michiko giggled. "Perkins is a funny guy."

"He's the biggest-hearted person I've ever met," Jack said.

"You are kind, too, Jack."

"I just try to keep an open mind, that's all."

"Then let's go to Kakunodate together," she said, wiping her tears away.

•   •   •

Michiko's face regained a pinkish hue, and she became chirpy as a mockingbird, less burdened, set free by her decision to return with Jack.

The train emerged from a ring of forested hills into a great plain of golden rice fields interspersed with tiny hamlets. "We are almost to Kakunodate, Jack-san! Over there is the Hinokinai River. In springtime, you must see it. The *sakura* are *kirei ne*, beautiful!"

He looked into her bright eyes, visualizing a young schoolgirl with ponytails playing in fallow fields among friends, chasing butterflies and dragonflies, catching frogs, and eating ripe summer melons, the sweet juice dripping from her chin.

Then suddenly, the train braked hard, screamed hysterically, and chugged into an old town of a few thousand residents. Jack and Michiko grabbed their bags and leaped from the car, the station greeting them with a hot tin roof, a rickety newspaper stand, and an old-fashioned snack shop staffed by an antiquated gentleman with crooked yellow teeth and a sporty straw hat.

Outside the station, the locals stared with rubbernecks. The stares didn't bother Jack, but some were long, jaw-dropping gawks that greatly irritated Michiko. And the giggling, too. "*Hora, hora,* look, look, *America-Jin yo ne.*" And more rarely, a sneer or contemptuous head turn.

Michiko flagged a taxi for a five-minute drive to her grandparents' home. The trip wound through the old Merchant District and nearby Samurai Quarter. "Tomorrow, I'll show you the samurai houses, and we will eat at my favorite ramen shop," she said.

The taxi turned right away from the river and onto a narrow lane. "My grandparents' house is at the end of the street." And beyond the last home, a forested hill carpeted in rich fall colors rose sharply. Jack noticed many small gardens associated with each *minka,* traditional farmhouse—thick wasted spruce, apple, and citrus trees interspersed among them, the countryside smelling of sweet turned soil.

The taxi stopped aside a two-story wood-beamed home, leaving Jack and Michiko alone, except for a wrinkly-faced neighbor holding a basketful of bright orange persimmons. "*Ohayogozaimasu, Okamotso-san. Ogenki desu ka?*" Michiko said.

Stunned by the abrupt appearance of the American, the old lady stood agape before erupting into a toothy grin.

"*Un, Genki datta yo. Okaerinasai,* Michiko-chan."

"*Arigato gozaimasu,* thank you very much."

She knocked at the entrance to her grandparents' home, the family *washi, a* traditional paper shop. Muffled talking, hurrying feet, and rattling teacups snapped back. Again, Michiko knocked, and then again, she struck the door even harder, and this time, it finally opened cautiously until two brown eyes stared back.

"Michiko-chan, you didn't receive my letter?" her elder sister Kimiko said with dismay.

"No, but we left Tokyo early for Nikko."

"*A soo desu ka,*" her sister said, pondering the predicament.

"Sister, grandmother and grandfather do not want to see me?"

"*Shikataganai,* it can't be helped," her sister said. "It's the American."

Michiko's beautiful elder sister, Kimiko, looked at Jack, and her face flushed bright red. She whispered, "He looks like a Hollywood actor!"

"*Ja, Onee-san,* older sister, we will return to Tokyo. I'm sorry to trouble grandmother and grandfather," Michiko said.

Michiko's harsh words caught her sister's attention. "*Ne chotto matte,* well, wait a moment, please stay the night; perhaps grandmother and grandfather will change their minds," she implored, tugging at her little sister's hand.

"*Ja O ne-san*, then we will stay one night."

Jack followed Michiko inside, studying the tiny *washi* shop. Like everything else in rural Japan, it seemed centuries-old, a dozen generations of Okura family proprietors. Nevertheless, the shop's delightful handmaid papers brightened the room with an assortment of motifs, colors, designs, and textures. He acquired several pieces to recreate his work of Michiko at the Shinkyo Bridge.

Kimiko led them into the main house, along an exterior wood-floored hallway with big picture frame windows that looked outside upon gardens and into a sizeable *tatami*-matted room. In the room's center, a small fire burned in a sand-filled fire pit, an *irori*, and a cast-iron pot from a meaty steel hook hung above it. Cushions lie around the *irori*, smoke twirling from the embers into the rafters like a long Indian cobra.

Kimiko prepared green tea. And Jack sat cross-legged and watched the fire burn, rural Japan seeping all about him—its colors, smells, and antiquities. *How extraordinarily different were the bright city lights of Ginza*, he thought to himself. At that moment, Michiko's rustic Kakunodate childhood seemed remote, and suddenly, for reasons he couldn't understand, loneliness overtook him, crawling along his spine and leaving a frigid chill, and he longed for the familiarity of his own family's home.

A wooden cabinet held several incense sticks and framed photographs in the room's corner. "That is my family altar or *butsudan*," Michiko said. "Would you like to see it?" They stood before the altar, and Michiko lit an incense stick and then said a prayer. Jack studied the photographs of Michiko's ancestors. Their lives gave her life, and they would be honored at the *butsudan* until time erased all memories.

"This is my mother, Shiori, and father, Yuto."

The man wore a traditional black yukata, and the woman wore a kimono.

"You look like your father," Jack said.

Michiko giggled. "I have my father's face and my mother's figure. But my father always told me I inherited my grandmother's eyes."

Jack considered that the handsome young couple in the photograph could not have foretold the disaster that would befall them by the pernicious rise of Japan's fascism.

"This is my elder brother, Ryota. He died in Burma. And he mailed this last letter to Kimiko and me," she said, lifting the dirt-stained envelope.

"What did he write about?"

"He mostly spoke of hunger and how much he longed for Japan. He also wrote about his pride in his service to the emperor."

"He must have been a brave soldier."

"I only remember him as my dear elder brother."

"I think he resembles your mother."

"*So desu ne!*" Michiko giggled.

"And these are my grandparents."

"What are their names?"

"Mieko and Yoshitaro," Michiko said. "Is it true that my eyes look like my grandmother's?"

Jack studied the photograph of her grandmother, Mieko. Michiko's eyes looked like her grandmother's—giant, stunning, moonlike opals, and his heart thudded at the close resemblance.

"Good gracious, your grandmother's eyes are beautiful!" he said.

"My grandmother was one of the most beautiful girls in Akita," Michiko said proudly.

"You never told me why your father left Kakunodate," Jack said.

"My father was a big dreamer! He often traveled to Tokyo with my grandfather to buy and sell paper. He loved the idea of city life and starting the Okura *washi* shop in Ginza. But when the war started, conditions in Tokyo became unbearable."

"And so you returned to Kakunodate to escape the bombings?"

"Yes, when I was seventeen."

"So, you lived in Tokyo for just five years?"

"Yes, and I finished my final year of high school in Kakunodate."

Outside, a shrill November wind traveled south from northern Hokkaido, and Jack placed additional wood upon the fire.

"Tell me about your childhood, Kimiko," Jack said.

Kimiko spoke in Japanese, and Michiko translated, "In winter, we stayed in this room all day. It was the only room in the house that wasn't icy cold. We played games, read books, did homework, and had family meals together. My grandfather, Yoshitaro, is a wonderful storyteller. He recounted many historical stories of feudal Japan."

"So that is another reason you love Japanese history. Isn't it, Michiko?"

"Yes," Michiko giggled.

Michiko continued, "We also played *Jan-Ken-Pon*, rock-scissors-paper. The loser had to retrieve snacks from the kitchen. Nobody wanted to leave this warm room in winter!"

"Can you show me how to play *Jan-Ken-Pon*?"

The room filled with laughter and the familiar swell of happiness Michiko knew as a child swept over her.

"Kimiko wants to know about your childhood, Jack," Michiko said.

"I'm a city boy, growing up on the outskirts of San Francisco, but my family loved the outdoors. My fondest childhood memories are fishing, hunting, and hiking with my father and grandfather."

"Our father and grandfather fished together, too," said Kimiko. "But following the death of my parents in the firebombing, my grandfather never fished again."

At the mention of the firebombing, an awkward silence crept over the room like an incurable malignancy.

"I'm terribly sorry about your parents. My Uncle Winston died fighting the Nazis in Europe." Jack then recalled the words of the bartender Kenichi: "War is very bad; love is better than war," he said.

"*So desu ne!*" Michiko and Kimiko agreed, bowing their heads to emphasize the gravity of his words.

After tea, Michiko showed Jack her childhood room, where she slept before returning to Tokyo. Inside the closet was a heavy silk *futon*, some garments from her past, and a handful of letters, which lay atop a man's neatly folded clothing.

"We will sleep here tonight," she said.

They removed the bedding and rolled it out onto the *tatami* mats.

"I must prepare dinner with Kimiko. So, this afternoon, let's go to the market and buy ingredients."

"A walk would be nice," Jack said.

Michiko left the room, and Jack surveyed the closet, placing his hand on the young man's neatly folded clothing and opening one of his letters to Michiko. Jack imagined Michiko reading the note several years before, longing for her first love to return from the war. An indescribable loneliness suddenly crept over him again, sending shivers through his spine, so he returned the letter and lay on the futon. From upstairs, Jack could hear muted voices speaking in Japanese. The voices sounded old and raspy, and he also heard shuffling footsteps. He knew Michiko's grandparents, Mieko and Yoshitaro, were discussing the *gaijin*, foreigner, wishing he wasn't defiling their home.

Son of a bitch, he suddenly thought. *I sure wish I were in Tokyo with the boys.* And all this strangeness made the lump in his stomach grow larger and more uncomfortable. Michiko returned, and she immediately sensed his uneasiness. "Are you feeling sick?"

"Yeah, it's my stomach, that's all."

They left the house, walking toward the river. Being outside in the cold autumn air refreshed his mind as they passed through the quaint Samurai Quarter. The old estates, gardens, and rich fall colors seemed the perfect spot for an impressionist painting. First, he imagined the strangeness of a bearded Claude Monet in his top hat—canvas, brushes, and oil paints to his side—surrounded by a crowd of samurai onlookers. Then they walked beneath the reds, yellows, and browns of leafy maple trees at the river. "This is the first time I've missed home since I left America," Jack said.

"Is it because you don't like Kakunodate?" Michiko asked.

"No, it's not that; it's all very different from where I come from."

"Which means you don't like it."

"I didn't say I didn't like it. It's just different."

"That sounds like you don't like it to me."

"Dammit, Michiko, I didn't say that! I like it, and it's beautiful and interesting, but it's different from home. That's all."

They didn't speak for the rest of the walk, and Michiko didn't look at him either.

They purchased bottles of beer, shrimp, fish, vegetables, tofu, and eggplant for *tempura* at the market. Everybody stared at Jack, and he counted six times that shoppers mumbled, "*Hora, hora, gaijin desu ne!* Look, look at the foreigner!"

By the time they returned, the sun had laid just above the horizon, so he'd wrapped himself in a heavy sweater, wishing he could drink a beer and sleep.

"I'd like to stay in the room and rest," he said.

"Hmm," was all Michiko could say before she slipped into the kitchen to assist Kimiko.

That evening, a fire crackled in the *irori*. Jack sat near the flame wearing warm woolen socks and a heavy gray *yukata*. The nauseating pit in his stomach disappeared with a restful nap and a hot Japanese bath. Instead, he focused on his sketchbook, recreating a scene from earlier in the day when Michiko and Kimiko sipped tea at the *irori*. One six years older than the other, both women possessed such refined beauty that his mind swam with possibilities.

He toyed with their expressions, how he would display their eyes, and the messages he'd convey in one still image. Jack sat alone in the big room beside the *irori*, warmed by its heat and a cup of green tea. He didn't notice the old man watching him; instead, he relived the morning scene just as a novelist dwells within his characters' minds.

Moments later, the shrimp arrived, lightly salted. Michiko poured a glass of beer before returning to the kitchen.

•   •   •

Yoshitaro couldn't take it any longer. He and his wife, Mieko, barricaded themselves in their room after the *gaijin* arrived. They played *hanafuda* until their backs protested in pain, reread old newspapers, and finally, the old man sat stone-faced and cross-legged, draping himself in a heavy autumn *yukata*, smoking hand-rolled cigarettes.

A fifth neatly rolled stick poked from his lips when Michiko announced herself.

"Grandfather, it's Michiko. May I come inside?"

"Yes," he said, delighted by his granddaughter's voice.

"Grandfather, why are you scowling? Aren't you happy to see me?"

The old man fought to conceal his happiness at the sight of his granddaughter. But rather, he forced a miserable-looking pout on his wrinkled face and grumbled miserably.

"Grandmother, aren't you pleased I'm here?" Michiko asked.

The old lady studied her granddaughter. She felt the young woman beaming with sunshine, an early spring flower bending into a fresh new beginning.

"Welcome home, Michiko-chan," her grandmother said.

"*Arigato gozaimasu,* thank you very much, Grandmother." Her grandmother's kind words brought tears to her eyes. "I hope I see you both later," she said, returning to the kitchen.

"Foolish old man!" Mieko complained to her husband.

Yoshitaro Okura stood, the tenth generation of a long list of proprietors, stretched his body straight as an arrow, and then waved his skinny arms back and forth to draw blood into his arthritic fingers.

"You're always so excited to see Michiko. But, unfortunately, now all you can muster is a dour pout. Poor Michiko-chan!"

The old man grumbled again. He cherished his granddaughters, perhaps with greater reverence than Michiko's father, his own deceased son. But for some queer reason, the *gaijin* excited him.

"Mieko-chan, the smell of Kimiko's cooking is delicious, isn't it?" he finally muttered.

"*So ne!* Yes, it is!"

The sweet fragrance of seasoned shrimp and marinated beef grilling over hot coals wafted throughout the house.

Old Man Yoshitaro held his cigarette nervously and began pacing the room. Then, oddly, like an unexpected magnet, this young man downstairs tugged at him; with each tug, he grumbled a little louder.

"Son of a bitch, I'm tired of being stuck in this room. I'm going to have a look at that *gaijin*."

"*Jiji*, don't embarrass your granddaughter!"

The old man tiptoed to the *irori* room and peeked inside. It was empty, aside from the *gaijin*, sitting next to the *irori*. He could see the young American's face frozen, deep in concentration, holding a pencil above a sketch pad. He stood still, invisible, studying Jack for several minutes until the kitchen door slid open, so he stealthily slipped away into an empty room.

The old man listened as Michiko delivered several plates to the *irori*, and after she left, he returned and watched the *gaijin* again from a crack in the door.

Jack plopped a second fat shrimp in his mouth, savoring its salty ocean texture, and reached for his beer, suddenly noticing the old man's eyes, and then they disappeared.

Interesting. He chuckled. He took a long slug of beer, snatched a third fat shrimp, and dropped it into his mouth.

Kimiko and Michiko returned a few minutes later, carrying plates overflowing with crispy vegetable *tempura*. They removed their slippers before the crackling fire and sat in autumn *yukatas*. Their faces looked delightful, and their bangs hung flirtatiously over cream-colored cheeks.

Good gracious, these gals are fine-looking, Jack observed.

Michiko opened a fresh bottle of beer, refilling Jack's glass. She then poured a glass for herself and Kimiko.

"Your grandfather peeped at me from the door," Jack said.

Michiko shrugged her shoulders and translated to her sister.

"My grandfather must be curious about you," Kimiko said. "He is a kind man, but stubborn and old-fashioned, too. Grandmother still walks five feet behind him in public, but five feet ahead at home!"

Meanwhile, Yoshitaro returned to his wife and rolled another cigarette, but his jumpy fingers dropped the burning match on the *futon*.

"Be careful, or you'll burn the house down!" Mieko-chan grumbled.

"I saw him," Yoshitaro said, striking another match.

"Well, what did he look like?"

"A *gaijin!*"

"Of course, he looked like a *gaijin.*"

"It's difficult to explain, but his eyes are glass blue. They're strange, like I saw a ghost!"

"*A soo desu ka. Me ga aoi desu ka…,*" Mieko said. "I've seen eyes like that in English dolls."

"*So dana,* that's right! Also, you won't believe this, but the *gaijin's* an artist."

"An artist?"

"Yes, he sketches pictures."

"What else did you see?"

"He likes beer and shrimp."

Knowing her husband's fancy for socializing, his wife said, "It must be fun at the *irori.* It's too bad we are stuck in our room. We are too old for such foolishness!"

"I'd better make sure it's safe with that *gaijin* in the house. I'll bring a good bottle of *sake.* Do you think the *gaijin* likes *sake*?"

"I don't know, but you better hurry, or you'll miss the shrimp!"

The old man brushed his heavy white hair and wrapped a fine autumn *yukata* about his waist. Mieko-chan powdered her face and colored her eyelashes black, making herself as pretty as the eight prior decades would allow.

"*Ja,* I'll see you at the *irori*, then."

"*Hai!*"

The shoji door opened unexpectedly, and there Yoshitaro Okura stood.

"*Ojiichan!*" Michiko said, wide-eyed. And Kimiko leaped to her feet and arranged pillows at the head of the table. "Let me get you a plate of *tempura*, Grandfather," Michiko said, hopping about to retrieve another plate.

"And here is your beer," Kimiko said.

"*Iya, sake da*, no, I want sake!" the old man ordered harshly. And he placed the sake on the table.

"A *guinomi*, sake cup, for myself, one for the *gaijin*, and two for you," he ordered.

Kimiko poured the sake into a long-nosed *tokkuri, sake* bottle, and placed it into a pot of hot water. Meanwhile, the table fell more silent than a snowy winter night. Then, finally, everyone focused their attention on the proprietor, Yoshitaro Okura.

Michiko filled each cup carefully with warm sake. "*Hai, dozo*," she said.

The old man raised his cup, and then Jack and the girls followed.

"*Kanpai*! Cheers!" the old man hollered.

•   •   •

The train sped south towards Tokyo. In those few days at Kakunodate, something significant had changed: a seismic shift in their relationship, its passion, trust, and respect.

Michiko slumped sideways like a rag doll, resting her head upon his shoulder, sleeping. Jack wondered if she was dreaming, perhaps visiting her mother or father, her elder brother Ryota, or maybe her late husband. Was she telling them of the love she had discovered and that what they left behind was now secure?

What a burden for a lover to be disowned for whom they love. What a relief to know it was safe. She slept heavily on the return train to Tokyo. After the first cup of sake and several more, a jubilant Yoshitaro Okura spread his retired fishing hardware across the *tatami* mats. He and Jack surveyed the treasure, four slender handmade rods and a collection of flies, lines, spooners, hooks, and nets. They smiled and spoke rapidly in tongues, understanding only the unspoken language of fishermen.

That evening, as Jack slept, the house black, ice forming upon the inside of the windows, not even the sound of a chirping bird, Michiko rolled herself upon him. The love that followed came with such fire that it was transcendent, and when he awoke, he asked if it was a dream.

At dawn, the old man and Jack left for a secret hole in the river where Yoshitaro had once fished with Michiko's father and elder brother. The early morning sun's playful rays dancing upon the water's surface reminded Jack of the Upper Merced in spring. He plied the river with the old man's flies, and they laughed, drank tea, ate *ume onigiri*, plum-flavored rice balls, and caught a basketful for dinner. In the late afternoon, Michiko took him to the samurai houses and along the river, visiting her childhood memories. They walked through rice fields, alongside thatched farmhouses and a bamboo forest, to a stream where a Shinto shrine had stood for five centuries. They sat by the stream's cold water, shaking the centuries-old bell, and prayed for their future.

That evening, her grandmother and Kimiko prepared a feast. The neighbors arrived at sunset wearing indigo *yukatas* and *geta* sandals. They were Meiji people, a generation of farmers born before the tractor when Japan sought to emulate the West. Their faces told the story of a country's transformation, and they carried big glass bottles of shochu and pouches of sticky tobacco. Most had never seen a *gaijin*, and their wide eyes shifted nervously. Nevertheless, the spectacle of dining with a foreigner excited them.

The men occupied pillows encircling the *irori,* firepit, and the women sat behind them. Michiko and Kimiko attended to the guests. Plates filled and emptied quickly; stories, laughter, and songs filled the room; the presence of Yoshitaro Okura's two beautiful granddaughters and the handsome young gaijin with bluish-gray eyes added to the merriment.

Jack didn't understand, but he didn't need to. He laughed, waved his arms in agreement, used sign language, drank his fair share of *shochu,* and made himself a legend.

•   •   •

February 1950 came and went, and so did a year pass of occupation duty in Japan. Jack reenlisted. Michiko quit Club Florida, continued her work for Thurston Ogilvie, and took a part-time secretarial job for Headquarters Company at Camp Drake. Raucous Ginza drunks lost ground to beer and sukiyaki parties. The weekends they spent having dinners and movies in Ginza and cultural and scenic outings away from Tokyo, sometimes driving a shiny black Buick.

Green fields of spring rice and a checkerboard of tiny truck farms surrounded a flat Jack rented. It was a simply furnished hideaway they shared three days a week when Jack wasn't garrisoning. He paid twenty dollars a month, less than other soldiers spent womanizing in Ginza.

They made love to a chorus of frogs, tractors, and yappity-yap neighbors in the early mornings and again in the evenings. This routine was as natural as the coming of tulips in spring. They commuted everywhere by bicycle, and Jack, dressed in full military uniform, waved lightheartedly to the school children and farmers along the way. And on her own bike, Michiko giggled hysterically, especially when he'd pop a long, happy-go-lucky wheelie to the delightful squeal of children on their way to school. So alive, so brazen, so unencumbered, she thought the American.

During the second week of March, Michiko awoke early to visit Asakusa's Sensoji Temple.

"Today is the fifth anniversary of my parent's death," she declared.

"And so you want to visit the temple?"

"*Hai*, to pray for their souls."

"I've never known the loss you've experienced," he said.

"Many Japanese understand—we are a sad generation."

"But your parents would only want their daughter to be happy. And they now live within you."

"Do you believe that?"

"I do."

And Jack believed this. It was the way he perceived life as one long continuum.

On the few occasions that Michiko raised the issue of her loss during the war, he never lectured her about its cause or became defensive about the suffering of the Japanese people. The Japanese, he felt, had adequately owned up to their past. The bruised, the battered, the vanquished, and the poor plodded forward. The nation suffered in great silence, discarded militaristic machinations, and sought only to rebuild, move forward in peace, and forget the terrible trauma, *shikataganai.*

Rebuilding continued at the Sensoji Temple, yet thousands of others like Michiko returned to pray for the souls of their loved ones. The fiery hell that fell from the sky on March 10, 1945, killed a hundred thousand and left a million homeless.

Jack meandered among the mourners. They didn't strike him with clubs or berate him with insults. They simply prayed for their dead and wished for eternal happiness, *shikataganai.*

Afterward, they walked to the Sumida River, crossing the Azuma Bridge to the old Shitamachi District. Giant bulldozers, trucks, and other equipment rebuilt large swatches, and larger areas remained razed, a city devoid of buildings, overgrown with weeds, interspersed by vegetable gardens and scrappy shanty encampments as far as the eye could see.

"We lived over there," Michiko said, pointing to an indistinguishable blob somewhere in the distance.

"How long does it take to walk there?" Jack asked.

"Five minutes."

"It was full of homes, shops, and family businesses, like my father's *washi* shop. But after the war began, many started making war materials. My school was over there." She pointed to another indistinguishable area.

"My best friend, Tomiko, lived next door. We often slept at each other's houses and played games together. She saw my mother and father on the night they died. My friend saved herself by jumping from the Ryogoku Bridge into the river. A boat rescued her."

"What happened to her family?"

"Her father survived the fires, but her mother drowned in the river. Her brother returned from Korea after the war.

"Tomiko told me she saw my parents that night frantically packing their best *washi* paper, rice, and blankets into a cart before fleeing. Then, a terrible wind blew through Shitamachi, and flames engulfed the streets as everyone ran toward the river. Then, finally, she witnessed my father's cart catch fire, the last she saw of my parents.

"During her escape to the bridge, Tomiko saw many people catching fire. One young mother had her baby tied to her back. Her baby caught fire, but the woman didn't notice until her own kimono burned. Tomiko said she'd never heard such horrible screaming like that. Before my friend leaped from the bridge, she said her hair caught fire, and smelled it burning when she fell into the water."

Michiko cupped her hands over her face and began to sob. "I just pray my mother and father didn't burn like that."

"Jesus," was all Jack could mutter. And he wrapped his hands around her, buried her face in his chest, and whispered that he loved her.

After crying herself dry, she told him she'd never spoken of what Tomiko had told her to anybody, not even her elder sister, Kimiko. "I kept it a secret and tried to believe it wasn't real," she said. "But I couldn't remove the pain. It just stuck inside my heart. So, I wanted to share this with you."

• • •

They arrived before the evening crowds and their friends and laid blankets beneath the crooked brown arms of the ancient *sakura*. The cherry blossom branches spread upwards and clawed wildly at the heavens. With the coming of the first week of April, the *sakura* had blossomed into a magical carpet ride of puffy whites, pinks, and imaginary hints of blues. The blossoms danced in the wind and slowly fell in twos, fives, and tens until the earth became pink.

"It's incredible to watch them float across the sky like snowflakes," Jack said, lying on the blanket with his head cradled in her lap.

She ran her delicate fingers through his hair and toyed with it playfully, admiring his handsome face.

"Each spring, the cherry blossoms arrive—indifferent to peace, war, sorrow, and happiness. And the trees offer their beauty; sometimes we rejoice, and sometimes we don't. I couldn't enjoy these blossoms for several years, but they are more beautiful this year than I ever imagined. For we Japanese, the *sakura* symbolizes life's ephemeral nature."

"When we are young, we only see our lives as eternal," Jack said.

She looked into his eyes. "Not until one observes the coming and going of the *sakura* does one understand."

"Then we are the delicate blossoms, and the tree is eternal life, isn't it?"

"Yes," she said. "Following the war, when so many lives were lost, time moved on without those that died."

He studied Michiko's face, and it suddenly occurred to him she was the only woman in Japan, the others he hadn't truly seen, not since that first night at Club Florida.

The spell became broken with the arrival of the evening's *Hanami* celebration crowds and pent-up festivity. Eugene and his date, Samantha, an American Army nurse with big red lips, broad shoulders, and salacious breasts, arrived first, and they spread their blanket alongside Jack and Michiko's. Next came Big Bill Burns and his Ojo-san looker. Walter Abbott and his girl, Yuki, arrived shortly after that. Then came Russell Simmons and his girlfriend, Hanako, with Snakey Frank Connors walking alongside single. Unlike the others, Snakey Frank stubbornly preferred whores to girlfriends, and in his right hand, he carried a big bottle of shochu and a fifth of whiskey in his left. Finally, Perkins arrived, sauntering through Ueno Park in a cowboy hat and boots, looking like a giraffe among zebras. His curvy little pan-pan girl, Naoko-san, whom he still called Naoka, smiled sheepishly alongside him, agreeing to be his *onrii* after weeks of incessant begging, and Perkins agreeing to rent a little room for her in Asakusa.

Blonde-haired Samantha lay pressed against Eugene. "I'd rather be in Europe than Japan, and I thought I might go crazy until I met Eugene," she said, giving him a rowdy stare. "I guess I just needed somebody to be a tourist with."

"Baby, I'll be a tourist with you any day of the week!" Eugene said, admiring the super-sumptuous breasts tumbling from her red blouse.

Samantha squealed with delight, rolling herself upon him, kicking off her shoes, and smothering his face with dazzling blonde hair and kisses.

Laughter and giggles erupted. "Yee-haw!" Big Bill Burns hollered.

The blossoms danced above the couples, illuminated by a clear night with a full moon.

The blankets looked larger as the evening wore on, and the couples moved closer together. More sake, sushi, and laughter traveled in circles, and songs of Woody Guthrie and Misora Hibari floated across the sky like dandelion seeds. All the while, they basked in the delicious fragrance of their youth. Finally, the evening's crowd dispersed. The couples held hands, dripping with anticipation for what lay ahead. And the *sakura* still fell like snow, turning everything pink.

Meanwhile, Snakey Frank Connors lay passed out drunk, and Big Bill Burns placed him on the last train to Camp Drake. That night, Jack and Michiko cuddled at their hideaway, surrounded by rice paddies. And the crickets and toads sang in chorus with not a care in the world.

•   •   •

During the third week of June, before the rush of the summer crowds, they took a holiday to the historic seaside village of Kamakura. The town was quiet, and they had its shrines, temples, and beaches to themselves. They were long lazy days filled with unhurried morning walks, swimming in the ocean, and sunbathing, and during the evening, they dined on seafood at portside cafés. The rainy season brought showers once or twice a day in heavy warm bursts, and they escaped to their room, wrapped themselves in a *futon*, and made their bodies hot and sweaty, tighten with pleasure, and quickly melt away. Afterward, they read books, drank beer and tea, and dreamt of the future.

He wrote a letter home dated June 25, 1950. He had written it under the spell of Kamakura's summer rains, and decades later, he would describe it as the *final one*. The words dripped from the pages, boundless and eternal, and this letter became a significant demarcation, but he didn't realize this until much later. The last paragraphs read:

I walked along the beach this morning, and in one direction, the ocean's horizon stretched as far as I could see, and in the opposite direction, a splendid inland view of Mount Fuji. It's a beautiful, almost perfect mountain. I looked at its summit and recalled having stood there—twice. Ha!

By the way, I'm dating a Japanese girl. Some guys keep this from their parents. But I want you to know. She is more intelligent than I am, very nice-looking, is rather outdoorsy, and has good values. She is my kind of girl! Her name is Michiko, which means child of beauty, wisdom, or knowledge in Japanese.

Hey, I'm going native, and you should hear my language ability. Life is good!

I miss you both.

Love,

Jack

They walked to the post office, depositing the letter in the late afternoon. A steady breeze rolled in from the Pacific, carrying with it the sweet scent of the ocean and making the humidity more bearable. They continued through the town center and walked below a big red *torii* gate, which marked the entrance to Komachi Dori, Kamakura's famous shopping street. A corner grocer sold them soft drinks and snacks, and the tobacco shop next door sold American cigarettes. They walked along the busy roadway until it ended, where a narrow lane took them to the Tsurugaoka Shrine.

Inside the sprawling temple grounds, a centuries-old tree offered some shelter from the sun. And under its branches, Jack and Michiko enjoyed the enchanting temple and delightful ponds. Jack released the cap on a bottle of ice-cold Coca-Cola, took a long refreshing drink, and passed it to Michiko. Michiko took a swig; the carbonated drink forced her nose and eyes into tight wrinkles, and then she belched loudly.

They both cracked up and Michiko, laughing hard, lay on her side, holding her stomach.

"I don't think there is anything so amusing as when you drink Coca-Cola," Jack chuckled.

"It's *oishi*, delicious, but so strong!" she said, and then she had another drink, which wrinkled her eyes and nose again.

They sat under the tree, enjoying the sense of place. They didn't speak, just watched the visitors mill about—an older man and his wife in *hakata* and kimono, a bundle of children in crisp black uniforms and their pretty teacher pushing them along like a mother hen, and a few tourists from Yokohama and Tokyo. Beneath the tree, they listened to the big cranky caws of black crows, the temple's ancient guardians, and flocks of doves, thrushes, and wagtails chirping in various frequencies.

"I love these green sanctuaries from the busy city streets. I could stay for hours and read," Jack said.

"Yasunari Kawabata lives in Kamakura. He wrote *Snow Country* here in 1937," Michiko said.

"Then I suppose he comes here often and sits beneath this same tree!"

"Yes," she giggled, "and to the same coffee shops and seaside cafés we've visited. Kamakura is popular with Japanese artists."

"Perhaps we should live here someday, just the two of us."

"I would like that, and you can become a famous painter, and I can start a *washi* shop, study for my teaching license, and teach children English," Michiko giggled.

She took his hands and looked into his eyes. His eyes told her he was sincere; he wanted it to be that way.

They left the temple just as the night lights began to flicker along Komachi Dori and then they hailed a taxi to Sagami Bay for the sea view of Mount Fuji at dusk. The mountain stood in silhouette, with tiny bands of clouds about its peak. Jack thought it strangely resembled a giant samurai warrior standing guard over Japan in full body armor. At a popular seaside café, they ordered beer, calamari, oysters, and *harusame* noodles with pork and vegetables.

Jack noticed two tough-looking sailors drinking beer at a small table by a window. The men saw Jack, and the bigger of the two stood and stared through the plate glass.

What the hell do these sailors want? Jack thought, planning for the worst.

The meaty man walked outside and stood before them. "Did you hear the news?" he asked, with a heavy Brooklyn accent.

"Nah, what news?"

"The North Koreans attacked South Korea. The damned reds are overrunning the entire country, heading straight for Seoul."

"You've gotta be kidding!" Jack said. "Are the Russians involved?"

"Probably, the North Koreans have got their tanks. So, you best get back to your unit."

Soft yellow light bathed their sidewalk table; the samurai had gone home, and the sailors returned to their beer. Moving towards the horizon, the fishing fleet bobbed up and down, like sparklers, for an evening of fishing.

Michiko and Jack sat silently eating, unsettling anxiety settling over the table.

"Do you think you will go to war?" Michiko asked nervously.

"No, and even if we do, the reds will run at first sight of American soldiers."

"So, what do you think will happen?" she asked.

"I don't know, but it will blow over soon. Anyway, I'd best get back to the company. We'll pack tonight."

The following morning, the train carried them to Camp Drake.

CHAPTER SEVEN
The "Rat"

Even in the evening, the mountain was dreadfully humid; it smelled of squalor and death, and the only relief from the heat and stink was to crawl beneath it. All along the line, the men peered into the darkness, pitch-black on a moonless Korean evening, and the company's assault would begin in four hours. This would be the third attack of the week, and already a third of the company was wounded, sick, KIA, or missing in action. The men didn't believe they'd get killed, but they knew some of them would.

Jack gave Perkins four twelve-round magazines, thirty-caliber ammunition, which he stuffed into his bandoleers, and two extra hand grenades. Perkins took some ammo and carefully laid it next to the Browning Automatic Rifle, which rested atop a small foot-high berm built to protect the foxhole. Jack watched Perkins adjust the BAR, securing its steel, twenty-four-inch barrel upon the ledge.

"The damned gooks better think twice about assaultin' our position," Perkins said savagely to Jack. His bloodshot eyes were the only feature Jack could see on his face, which was tattooed orange by sweat, blood, and mud from two weeks of killing on the Rat. Filth covered both men, even more obscenely than during their descent from Mount Fuji, and their hair revolted in protest. Some men grew beards, and those that couldn't didn't.

"They ain't goin' to hit us tonight, not tonight they won't," Perkins said.

"Don't be so damned sure. Gooks overran Russell Simmons's foxhole on a night just like this and stabbed him in the stomach," Jack reminded Perkins.

"He's a lucky bastard! He's probably shacked up with a pretty, stateside nurse 'bout now," Perkins said disgustedly.

The two-person foxhole measured six feet wide and four feet deep. They spent the entire day digging it using nine-inch entrenching shovels. Deep inside, they found it cooler than standing up. In early September, the Korean Peninsula's humidity smothered the men, and sickly brown mold grew on everything with frequent rain and the threat of typhoons. The pungent smell of mildew added to the stink of white phosphorous, sweating male bodies, excrement, and dead men rotting on the mountain, which created a giant magnet that drew millions of lazy black flies, maggots, and rats to feast on the stink. Koreans called the mountain *Ganghan-san*, Strong Mountain. Army brass called it Hill 257. The generals called it essential because of its vantage point over the North Korean's main line of attack along the Pusan Perimeter. The soldiers of the 15th called it Rat Mountain, and the bloody campaign became known as the Battle for Rat Mountain.

Jack drew himself deep into the foxhole. Even inside, his body sweated profusely and ached for proper food, untainted water, and a woman's soft body. Moreover, a sharp-bladed, uncomfortable irritation hung over him from the constant killing and lack of sleep. He tried to lie on his side with his back pressed firmly against the damp earth, attempting to escape the humidity, but the sweat still clung to his face, even in the eerie darkness of the hole.

He closed his eyes to sleep, but his mind wandered back to Michiko. He prized his twelve months of memories with her like treasured souvenirs. When not soldiering, he removed the memories individually, like postcards, to recall the stirring emotions, engrossing his mind with the happiness they shared, easing the goddamned suffering in Korea. He focused his memory again upon the first night they made love, on that rainy summer evening at the Rex Hotel in September 1949.

Jack closed his mind to all the wretchedness about him. Instead, he peered more deeply into the memories of that evening, playing them back like a vinyl recording, wanting to recall every detail. He remembered the rousing waves of emotions seeing her dripping wet in the hallway, the frightened look upon her eyes, her wetted shapely contours in the tight red dress. And he recalled the relief upon her face when he smiled, took her hand, and drew her inside.

It took him a moment to register her presence; he recalled questioning the scene's authenticity and felt content to play it out. She gazed upon the floor, not meeting his stare, self-conscious of her vulnerability, wondering if she'd have enough strength to accept love for another human being again.

"Let me dry your hair. It's wet. You'll catch a cold," Jack said.

"Hai," she replied obediently.

He gently dried her raven-black hair, beginning at the front, then the sides, the back, and to her swan-like neck, her shoulders, back, legs, and down to her feet, being careful not to rub too vigorously.

"I'm sorry I didn't dance with you tonight. I wanted to more than you would understand and thank you for your letters."

"It was my mistake for being late to the club. I should've waited until closing. But, Michiko, I can't believe you came here to find me! I'm sorry for the trouble I've caused you."

"It was a big misunderstanding, Jack-san. I didn't want to ignore you. I was just doing my job."

Michiko stood quietly, staring into his solid chest. She had already surrendered her sorrow for happiness, loneliness for love, a past for a future. She reached out, placing her hands upon his hips, and he reciprocated by wrapping his arms around her slender waist.

He recalled how they stood this way for a long time, staring into each other's faces and trying to match what they'd seen seven weeks before with the details their imaginations had constructed since they'd danced that first night at Club Florida. He thought her face looked a little rounder and her cheekbones fuller than he remembered. She felt his eyes were a little less blue and a little grayer and his nose a little higher and more exaggerated than she'd seen in her dreams. This continued for several minutes until what they saw before and now was the same and no longer distinguishable by time, place, circumstance, or the lonely trickery of one's imagination.

When they were satisfied that their memories were secure, they danced. They danced to Jack's gentle humming of Frank Sinatra's "Almost Like Being in Love." They danced like they were at Club Florida, like the evening had started again just for them. They danced without the worry of *bachi*, without the interference of the Naval Petty Officer's amorous flirtations, without the smokiness of the sultry Black Cat bar, or the seductive pan-pan girl that moments before had walked her man to the hotel.

He remembered her body when her dress fell to the floor, coiling about her ankles. He recalled how he reached behind her shoulders and unclipped her bra, and her vanilla-colored cones became visible for the first time. In his memory of this, powerful manly forces of sexual desire built within his loins like they had when he first undressed her. He remembered how her breasts looked ripe and budding, soft, swollen, and crème brûlée delicious with two oddly shaped rose petals begging for his affection. His heart pounded as his hands rolled down her buttery smooth back to the bridge of her small, foreign, Asiatic pillow and beyond to the silky black curtain nestled between her legs.

He closed his eyes tightly at the bottom of the deep dark depression of war-torn soil. He saw Michiko naked, no longer noticing the heat or the stench of the battlefield, or dwelling upon the killing, or considering that a gook might take his life tomorrow or in the coming weeks. Instead, his mind moved carefully over the rugged terrain before him, studying every detail, watching his step, pondering the movement of his fingers, and he drew in the sights, smells, sounds, touches, tastes, vestibular, and proprioception.

They were both naked now on the bed's soft white sheets. He recalled her slow and submissive nature at first, but then her motions became more frantic, and she panted with pleasure, lightly at first, and she reached for him and began slowly and rhythmically and then with force.

He opened his eyes, and all about him was the darkness of war. The heat returned, and so did the stink, retaking hold of him, and he felt the knife-edged restlessness renew its discomfort; the irritation and anxiety had unfolded all about him once more in the darkness of Korea.

"Fuck it," he said aloud and reached over and grabbed a roll of toilet paper.

"I gotta take a shit, and I can't sleep," he told Perkins.

"Alright, but don't go too far out, and be fuggin careful comin' in," Perkins warned.

Jack lifted himself from the hole and grabbed his rifle, a big wad of toilet paper, and a single pineapple grenade. He leaped from the foxhole and bounced into the darkness, scrambling to a draw a hundred feet down the slope where a tree burst toppled a pine tree earlier in the week. Jack rested against the tree and placed the M1 rifle, toilet paper, and grenade at his side. He lay against its broken trunk, deliberately thinking of Michiko, pulling his pants down, tightly closing his eyes, and reopening them. His hands were chalky, dirty, and crusty, and he took a little water from his canteen and wiped away as much as he could. Then, on his side with his boots still laced and rifle nearby, he dreamed of Michiko again. He pumped it hard with her hand, then she gently rolled him over, and she slid him inside for the first time like she had done that evening.

He lay on his side like a worm in the dirt, feeling himself within her, and it didn't take long for him to shutter, and his lust exploded fiercely all over Rat Mountain. Afterward, he wiped himself up and left the tissue for a horde of hungry black flies, retrieving his weapons and cautiously working his way back to the hole. Deep inside, a few precious hours of sleep awaited, and he became keenly aware of the great booming and flashing of artillery prepping the head of the Rat for the assault. Finally, he fell asleep, and it was more restful, and when Perkins awoke him a few hours later, he couldn't remember having had any dreams or even having slipped from the hole to seek relief against the pine tree.

•   •   •

When Jack left his foxhole that evening, Colonel Jones was at battalion headquarters crafting plans for Operation Red Thunder, the division's code name for the assault of Hill 257. The lieutenant colonel arrived at Rat Mountain just a few hours before and felt tired and grumpy after a dangerous armed jeep escort from Masan.

At Masan, Lieutenant General Walton Walker, the Commander of the 8th Army, flew in from Tokyo, demanding the Pusan Perimeter's buttoning up and more aggressive action against the North Koreans. Among the generals, Hill 257 was a topic of dissatisfaction. They were infuriated that the North Koreans still commanded the high ground despite weeks of costly attacks and aerial bombardment. General Walker informed Colonel Jones that a significant amphibious assault at Inchon was in the works, which could change the war's outcome, but Hill 257 was critical to the mission's success. Because of the battalion's lack of progress at 257, the generals ordered Colonel Jones to take operational control from Lieutenant Colonel Sean Pinkerton and report immediately to the battle lines.

The apish, five-foot-nine-inch lieutenant colonel stood in the center of the command bunker, his famously knotted right hand, the deadly hand that knocked out the welterweight champion in thirty-nine, clutched a burning Cuban cigar. The cigar turned the bunker into an inferno, making the air stiff and dead like the Black Sea. Captains Carlson, Murphy, Hennessey, Morrison, and Major Johnson sat in a circle on sandbags, crouched below the smoke line, waiting for the colonel to speak.

"Captain Carlson, how many of the 3rd Battalion have died trying to conquer this son of a bitch?"

"A hundred twenty killed and three times as many casualties, sir."

"Do you think it's worth it, captain? I mean, the one hundred twenty killed to own this son of a bitch? Should we get more men killed tomorrow, captain?"

"I don't know that we have a choice, do we, sir?"

"Gentlemen, the army that controls Hill 257 can observe the whole southern sector to Pusan. The gooks atop that hill see our lines, troop movements, heavy weapons emplacements, and fucking destroyers in Pusan Harbor! Their 6th Army is giving the division an ass-whooping because of their dominance of the goddamned high ground!"

"They are dug in deep, sir, and well-supplied and outnumber us ten to one on the battlefield. So even if we make it to the summit, they'll throw us right back off," Captain Hennessey warned.

"Sir," Captain Murphy interjected, "the mountain's northern side is cut with roads wide enough for deuces, whereas our side is steep, strewn with boulders, gullies, and gulches, making it too damned rugged for our vehicles to maneuver and resupply."

"That's right, sir," Captain Morrison confirmed. "The North Koreans can walk a well-equipped battalion to the summit. During our last push, sir, Lieutenant Somerset got Easy Company's 2nd Platoon into the Goose's Neck and threw the Reds from their holes all along the ridgeline in close-quarters fighting. He reported a goddamned enemy anthill on the northern flank, gooks everywhere and well supplied."

"It was a real son of a bitch keeping the gooks off our backs," Captain Carlson informed the colonel. "They counter-attacked Lieutenant Somerset's 2nd Platoon during the evening, throwing them off the ridge. They lost a quarter of 2nd Platoon killed and another quarter missing in action, probably captured by the gooks and executed."

"Somerset is a smart and tough-as-nails first lieutenant. He'll be a goddamned general someday," the colonel said, smoking a cigar.

"He's got the goods, sir."

"How about Corporal Pierce, the crazy son of a bitch that climbed Fuji-san? Isn't he in Somerset's platoon?"

"He is, sir. He's a damn fine squad leader, promoted to sergeant."

"Goddamned crazy sons of bitches!" the colonel said, taking a deep draw on his Cuban cigar. "So, he made it off the Goose's Neck alive?"

"Yes, sir, wasn't on the casualty or MIA reports."

"Well, captains, the lieutenant will get a second chance at that summit. And I'm aware of what we're up against, and Colonel Pinkerton raised your concerns with the generals at Masan, but the big pipe-smokin' Five-Star in Tokyo wants the gooks off that mountain. So, they ordered me to Hill 257 to take over the operation from Pinkerton, who has remained in Masan, awaiting reassignment to the 27th Regiment."

"Sir, when will we begin the attack?" Major Johnson asked.

"Tomorrow at 0500."

"Sir, we've just lost half of Easy Company's 2nd Platoon at the Goose's Neck, and the companies suffered thirty percent casualties. Perhaps we should wait for reinforcements," Johnson suggested.

The lieutenant colonel stared at the battle-weary officers huddled below the smoke line and gave each a stare, making their asses pucker and drop like an elevator.

"Negative! We won't delay this fight, gentlemen. The attack will commence at 0500. However, fresh troops will arrive from Sasebo and reinforce the lines during the assault."

"Then why not wait the extra couple of days for reinforcements? It would give the men a chance to recover and put additional boots on the mountain," Captain Hennessey suggested.

"Now listen, the meteorologists promise three days of damned fine weather. Yes, hotter than a son of a bitch, but fine for an attack and perfect for the B-29s and Mustangs. However, a fat-assed typhoon called Samantha will brush our positions on day four. If we can push to the summit in three days, the gook vehicles will bog down, depriving their resupply! Meanwhile, we'll fortify our positions, and reinforcements will take over the battlespace once the rains clear."

"We have a hell of an advantage in artillery and airpower, sir."

"That's right, Captain Murphy. And now that you know the backstory, let's get to work. Gentlemen, how in the hell do you propose to conduct this attack? Captain Morrison, any ideas?"

The men lay their maps across the dirt floor, ragged edges worn and marked with notes and highlights from weeks of similar meetings with the prior commander. Again, they huddled together, reliving the mortar bombardments, nasty little firefights, and hand-to-hand combat that had already occurred across the topographic map showing Rat Mountain. And again, they studied the narrow valleys, spiny ridgelines, knobs, and gulches forming a spider web of death to the mountain's summit.

"Sir, there are three routes up this mountain where our infantry can maneuver with the support of recoilless rifles and mortar squads," Captain Hennessey suggested. "For three weeks, we have penetrated each route at tremendous cost. As Captain Murphy explained, Easy Company's 2nd Platoon breached the Goose's Neck within two hundred feet of the summit. Still, the reds threw them off the ridge during a counterattack that evening."

"There is a fourth route, sir, which we've not yet exploited," Captain Carlson interrupted. "It's here, and then here on an aerial photograph taken in early August. It would take a platoon a full day to march twelve miles to the foot of this valley, then another four hours into its belly. Neither Army has entered this sector of 257; it remains in its natural condition. You can see that the eastern flank obscures this route from the enemy's positions. As it gets closer to their lines, it becomes narrow and heavily forested, providing excellent cover from the enemy during a flanking attack," Captain Carlson explained.

"Well, how in God's name do you propose to get to the summit from the valley floor?" the colonel asked incredulously.

"Sir, from the topographic map, the ridgeline running parallel to the valley's eastern side is impossible to climb from the south because of its steep, unstable terrain. However, four miles into the valley, a draw ties into a narrow spiny ridgeline. This ridge rises to about seven hundred feet, linking into the main ridgeline above those cliffs you can see in the photograph."

"From that aerial, captain, the spine looks damned narrow," the colonel said.

"It's treacherous in areas, perhaps just two to six feet wide, with a sheer drop of several hundred feet or more," Captain Carlson said.

"Well, captain, how in hell will you get your men and gear across this spine?"

"Damned carefully—crawl, if necessary—but it's our only hope, sir."

"Alright, and once the men are across, how do you maneuver to the summit, captain?"

"The main ridgeline is steep but appears to be maneuverable. And here," the captain said, pointing to a wave of tightly bunched topographic lines slithering upwards to the summit, "the ridge snakes back toward our main line's assault."

The colonel brushed the men aside and grabbed the map with both hands. His meaty body and ugly face stared into its contours; the tip of his burning cigar so close to the linen that Captain Carlson feared Rat Mountain would burst into flames.

"Yes, I see your point, Carlson."

"This plan sounds dangerous, almost reckless. What are the risks of committing two platoons to this fourth route, Captain?"

"Sir, if the frontal attack through the Goose's Neck can't breach the summit, it would cut the 1st and 2nd Platoons off from our line. The gooks will counterattack with overwhelming force as our men attempt a retreat down the ridgeline in the typhoon. The heavy rains will make crossing the gulches impossible from flash floods, and the men will be drowned, overrun by the enemy, killed, or captured. Even if they can cross the gulches, they could never retreat across the spine under those conditions. And we know what gooks do with captured GIs," Captain Carlson warned.

"Yes, I can see from the note-taking that you've spent some time consulting this route. But, Captain Hennessey, what does this note say at the spine? I can't read the man's shitty writing!"

"It's Lieutenant Colonel Pinkerton's writing, sir. It says, 'Point of No Return.'"

"Well, I can see why! Men, we have three days to fight to the top of Hill 257 and hold it. After that, we've got one shot at our objective, and then the rains will come—filling the bellies of those gulches with raging rivers. Do you need this flanking attack to be successful?"

"Sir, this will be our fourth frontal attack against the summit. We've only made it to the Goose's Neck once, and the North Koreans overwhelmingly counterattacked. Therefore, a surprise flanking attack will give us a tremendous advantage against their defensive positions. Still, I can't be certain we will secure the summit even with a flanking attack," Captain Carlson said.

"And if we don't execute the flanking attack?" the colonel asked.

"Then we won't hold the summit, sir."

"Okay, gentlemen, we will launch a frontal attack up routes two and three with Baker, Charlie, Alpha, and the three remaining platoons from Easy Company.

"Major Johnson. Your artillery will support the attack with close-in barrages.

"Meanwhile, the regiment's 155s will pound the enemy's northern flank. Captains, you will have seventy-five-millimeter recoilless rifle squads with your companies. There will be a two-hour heavy bombardment of the enemy's line positions by combined air, naval, and artillery assets beginning at 0700 on the morning of the third day of the assault. Once the bombardment ceases, you will attack the summit in force.

"Captain Carlson. You will lead Easy Company's 1st and 2nd Platoons in a flanking attack up Point of No Return. Your remaining platoons will form up with Alpha, Baker, and Charlie Companies for the main assault."

"Yes, sir."

"Captain Carlson, I want your men across Point of No Return by 1300 of day two. You will encamp within two miles of the summit by 1600. You will then proceed up the ridgeline and begin your flanking attack. Once Baker, Charlie, and Alpha push through the Goose, you will flank the gook lines from the west and fight your way into their positions."

The lieutenant colonel raised himself, thrusting out his chest. The former title holder's muscles were thick and powerful, and, at forty-six years old, he remained a danger to any man, even to soldiers half his age who were reckless enough to challenge him to a fight.

"Gentlemen, Operation Red Thunder begins tomorrow morning at 0500 sharp," the colonel growled, pushing the butt of his cigar from his lips with his heavy tongue. The men watched in silence, the butt hitting the bony ledge of the colonel's chin and then tumbling to the dirt floor like a hard-brown turd.

"Captain Morrison, do me the favor of squashing that butt."

"Yes, sir," the captain said, standing from the table and grinding it into the dirt.

"Gentlemen, I want you to know there will be a lot of media attention surrounding this campaign. Following the disastrous results at Hadong Pass, Taejon, Chinju, and Masan, Tokyo wants good news from Korea. They want to assure the American people we are winning this conflict, not in a stalemate against a horde of Russian-equipped North Koreans. Furthermore, they want the country to have confidence that the United States Army is the best-damned army in the world! That is all."

·   ·   ·

It was well past midnight when Captain Carlson left battalion headquarters for Easy Company's positions. Sweat rolled from his forehead, and his fatigues smelled of the colonel's Cuban cigar and days-old body odor, creating the putrid scent of spoiled mayonnaise, and but for the stench of the Rat, he would be disgusted.

His right leg hurt like hell. It had nearly been separated from his body when the 2nd Platoon pushed into the Goose's Neck. The enemy mortar killed his radioman and pummeled his thigh with a boulder fragment the size of a bowling ball. Nevertheless, the half-dozen stitches and ugly-looking bruise awarded him a Purple Heart, his first of the Korean War, and it shocked the medics that his femur hadn't snapped.

As he hobbled closer to the lines, beady fluorescent eyeballs bounced across the landscape like a Thanksgiving Day parade. *Only fuggin rats love war,* he grumbled in his mind. And he considered if the war hadn't started, he'd be driving his bright red convertible between Key West and Camden, Maine. Instead, the men snored in their foxholes, returning memories of the Siegfried Line in '44. During the Big One, working against panzers, nobody in the company expected to survive. The shelling at the Hurtgen Forest was terrifying, and then they fought it out at the Bulge, and he got a Silver Star and two bronze ones.

I'd better be damned careful coming into the lines, he thought. The men were edgy—trigger-happy fingers. When the company boarded the transport from Sasebo to Pusan in mid-July, they expected the "police action" to be over by August. Instead, a third of the company was dead, missing in action, or casualties by September. There was no end in sight, and the soldiers were worn thin. He knelt to relieve the worst damned Charley horse he'd ever experienced and considered his bad luck; no man deserved a war, and much less two, but he'd signed up for the shit and would damn well do his job.

Inside the bunker, it smelled of mold and all the other Rat Mountain obscenities. Lieutenant Somerset lay on his blanket in laced boots and evil-smelling fatigues on the dirt floor. His pistol and rifle were ready. "Welcome back, captain," he said, putting down a novel by Dostoyevsky. "Would you like a little bourbon?"

"Yes, thank you. And I think you'd better have one for yourself."

Lieutenant Somerset reached into his pack and produced a silver shot glass. "It's nice, isn't it, captain?" he said, brandishing the expensive Ginza trinket.

"You like fine things, don't you, lieutenant?"

"I do," the lieutenant said brightly. "You watch—the whiskey will taste better this way." He pulled a matching flask from his pack.

"Thank you, lieutenant. Cheers to life once this dirty little affair is over!"

"I take it the colonel accepted our recommendation."

"He did, and he damned near burned the map up with his cigar."

"Where does that leave us?"

"Murphy, Hennessey, and Morrison will attack through the Goose. We've got the Point of No Return."

•   •   •

Jack stood straight-legged in the foxhole, clutching the BAR. The deadly steel barrel pointed directly north at the summit of Rat Mountain. His grenades and an extra twelve-round magazine were within easy reach. He'd been on guard for two hours, subjected to a steady growl of Perkins snoring. He could never get used to it, that motor-like snoring crawling up his neck like cockroaches, but you couldn't shake them off. The flashing and thudding of artillery eased his annoyance but didn't exclude it. On guard duty, especially at night, the steady rhythm of a man's breathing was comforting. He found it better to hear a man breathe than to stand in silence. Silence and darkness can instill sinister anxieties when one should be sleeping. But Jack still preferred silence and darkness over the throaty growl of Perkins ghastly snoring.

He adjusted the gun atop the berm and readied himself for an attack. The enemy sought to maneuver using the advantage of darkness, cover, and surprise to kill its unsuspecting victim. And somewhere in the blackness, a gook wanted him dead. A week earlier, Russel Simmons received a knife in one such attack through the belly. The North Korean received Russel Simmons's bayonet through his chest. But such brazen attacks were rare, and the man on guard typically looked for rifle fire and grenades.

During the long, lonely evenings, Jack mastered using both sides of his brain with equal acumen. He performed his duty using the right side, which required peering into the darkness, seeing, smelling, and listening for the enemy. The left side he used to protect his sanity. When Lieutenant Clarence Somerset announced himself at 0400 with a *click, click, click* of his swagger stick, Jack's left side roamed meticulously over his Mount Fuji climb. The sneaking away with Perkins and Eugene, peering down upon the men smoking cigarettes, the arduous ascent under a full moon, and the early morning's blissful sunrise over the Sea of Japan.

"Sir, is that you, Lieutenant Somerset?"

"Good morning, Sergeant Pierce."

"Top of the morning to you, lieutenant."

"That's a hell of a snore down there, Pierce!"

"I try to shut my mind to it, but it irritates the shit out of me."

"I can see why," the lieutenant chuckled.

"Pierce, I want you to wake your squad. Tell the men to pack enough gear for a five-day assault against the summit. Where we are going, there'll be no resupply! So have them eat their C-rations and be ready to move out to battalion headquarters at 0500."

"Yes, sir."

"And Pierce."

"Yes, sir."

"Give the BAR to Carter. I need you walking light."

Jack watched the lieutenant proceed up the line and disappear into the early morning darkness, snapping his balsa swagger stick against his green steel pot. Then, finally, he dropped to the bottom of the foxhole and awakened Perkins.

"Perkins, the lieutenant says we're moving out."

"Holy shit, what time is it?"

"It's 0400. Pack your gear for a five-day assault with no resupply. And we're passin' the BAR to Carter and Thunderbolt."

"Heck, ya!"

•   •   •

At 0500, Easy Company's five beleaguered platoons, one hundred fifty battle-bloodied grunts, stood in a half-circle enclosing Colonel Jones and Captain Carlson. Even in the still of the morning's grayness, an hour before the sun would break the horizon, the uncomfortable heat and humidity of the Korean summer exhausted the men. They stood at attention in a half-circle, anxious. The men looked rangy and tired, dressed in muddied green fatigues masked as clothing, hanging from their bodies like a dead man's cloak. And all that distinguished these men from the loggers, pickers, steelworkers, nail pounders, and college kids back home were the grenades, knives, bullets, rifles, and machine guns adorning their short, tall, skinny, muscled, and chunky framed bodies.

Lieutenant Colonel Jones thrust his stocky frame before Easy Company. He dug his boots deep into the loamy North Asian soil, lurching forward, ready for a fight, looking over his one hundred fifty men. They were in their late teens and early twenties with a handful of weathered World War Two veterans, and instinctively, he knew some would not walk down Rat Mountain alive. The Colonel had fought enough gunfights to appreciate those younger men who couldn't envision their mortality. Still, he was sure as Sunday morning football that many would die before he'd see the company again.

The one hundred fifty still fit for fighting—the weak, strong, awkward, and scared; the confident and insecure; the Bible worshippers and whoremongers, and the whoremongers that Bible worshipped— stared into the colonel's ugly face. But they didn't see an ugly man's face. The colonel was too ugly to be ugly. They trusted his face because it wasn't the face of a charlatan, a masked face, the face of a disingenuous politician who would happily trade their lives for a gold star. The face staring back was one of their own, a battle-hardened soldier's face, a straight shooter's face, a face that once stood terrified, excited, confident, and exhausted in that exact half-circle awaiting his orders. The men trusted Lieutenant Colonel Jones, knowing he played the sport well, to win, and even if death awaited, they'd die fighting on a damned good team.

"Good morning, men," the colonel said, staring at the soldiers with unsmiling eyes like it was just another title game on the gridiron.

"Good morning, sir!" they hollered back.

"I don't have a big fancy speech. It's too damned humid for fancy speeches, and anyway, you all know what we must do. And I don't need to remind you that the last several months have been rough in Korea, as difficult as any battles fought during the Big One—indeed, very costly fighting! We've had our hard knocks and lost a lot of fine men, soldiers who fought bravely and died for their country under terrible odds. We all know about the losses at Hadong Pass, Taejon, Masan, Chinju, and the many other bloody fistfights all along the Pusan Perimeter, and right here on Hill 257, 'Rat Mountain,' as I understand you call this shithole."

"Hooah, hooah!" the men hollered.

"Today, we will launch Operation Red Thunder to take away the enemy's high ground, and the North Koreans will not relinquish their advantage without a fight. But for the next three days, the 8th Army will bomb the stuffing out of these no-good reds. After that, there wouldn't be a North Korean on this mountain who would not wish he were back in Pyongyang. For the enemy that survives our artillery and napalm, they will meet your bullets on the battlefield. Those that survive your carbines will become the property of the United States Army."

"Hooah, hooah!" the men hollered in approval.

"Do we have questions?"

"No, sir!" the men hollered back to their commander.

"Good. Easy's 1st and 2nd Platoons will be under Captain Carlson and Lieutenant Somerset's leadership. Captain Carlson, address your men."

Captain Carlson stood before his soldiers. Another fit of high-pitched echoing besieged his ears, becoming a recurring nightmare from the mortar attack that cut his radioman in half just one week earlier. His right thigh also throbbed; it was not a crippling soreness like it had been after the boulder fragment had nearly broken his femur. Instead, the discomfort doled a constant reminder of the tragedy in overlapping waves of misery. Standing before his men, he wretchedly wished he'd mixed some shots of Somerset's bourbon with his morning's black coffee.

"Gentlemen," he said, masking his pain, "you all look damned fine this morning, and you smell even worse than you look." He grinned coyly, trying to test the sound of his voice over the ringing and thudding of the North Korean mortar blast that played in his mind.

The men laughed nervously.

"The weather will be hot, humid, and without rain for the next two days. However, by day three, we will experience the effects of Typhoon Samantha, which will become windy with bands of heavy showers. It will be wetter than a green frog's ass by day four, the mountain becoming knee-deep in mud. Nevertheless, Easy Company must attain the summit and dig in when the rain strikes. Once the rains have passed, reinforcements will relieve your positions, giving you much-needed R&R."

The captain took a swig from his canteen. The warm water tasted of halazone tablets, poisoning typhoid, cholera, encephalitis, giardia, leptospirosis, worms, and everything else in the miserable-tasting liquid.

"Remember, gentlemen. You are vital to the success of this operation. Third, 4th, and 5th Platoons are reassigned to Alpha, Baker, and Charlie Companies and will attack through the Goose's Neck. Meanwhile, the 1st and 2nd Platoons will conduct a flanking attack from the west. Lieutenant Somerset and I will initiate a two-day march where we will tie into the line for the final offensive. Men, we need that summit by 1800 on day three. There will be absolutely no bugging out! Any order to retreat will come from your company and platoon commander. Your bayonets are to be ready and expect to use them!"

Upon hearing the word *bayonets*, the men's stomachs rolled. Nobody liked the prospect of bayonet fighting. It terrified them all.

Lieutenant Colonel Jones again approached the soldiers with a stony face. He looked like a German pit bull but meaner in the face of an attack. Lieutenant Somerset stood closely behind the colonel and captain, twirling his swagger stick, anxiously looking forward to the fighting.

"Men, this is our Mount Suribachi, our Normandy, our time to take it to the enemy and make him pay for what he did to our boys at Hadong Pass! We didn't ask for this war, but we hit back twice as hard as we got it. When it's tough on the mountain boys, I want you to remember what they did to Task Force Smith. I want you to remember how they shot up our unarmed medics, the chaplains, and the injured at the Pass and Taejon. I want you to make them pay for it," he said, swinging his famous right in a cross, ready to crush every rickety bone in his opponent's face. He continued, "When it gets tough, boys, I want you to remember who you are and who's at your side—United States infantry soldiers! Now let's get those goddamned sons of bitches!"

The jacked-up soldiers lifted their raggedy faces and raised their rifles decisively, ready for revenge. But just as fast, the adrenaline was gone. Instead, anxiety took hold, their stomachs crawling with fear and weakening their legs as it always did before the beginning of a brutal campaign.

The men said goodbye, wishing each platoon success with their assignment, patting the others on their shoulders, giving gregarious hugs and firm, manly handshakes. Jack said goodbye to Robert, Big Bill Burns, and Walter Abbott. They were assigned to the 3rd Platoon under Lieutenant King and would assault through the Goose's Neck.

As each man said farewell, they were fraught with the insecurity of not knowing, their eyes darting about, unsure if they'd see each other again, fearing to leer too deeply into the other man's anxiety. Anxiety that hung in clusters of white vines from their youthful faces, a feature of men thrice their age and long burdened by the responsibility of wives and children. It was noticeable in the awkward movements and forced conversations as they waited for the operation to begin. *It was best just to get going and not dwell upon it;* they thought to themselves.

Jack's six-man squad was assigned to the 1st Platoon under Lieutenant Somerset's command. Eugene and Perkins were in Jack's squad. The other squad members included a twenty-year-old black farmer named Lysander Carter. Twenty-year-old Pfc. Carter had sweat buckets working for pennies on a haggard pig farm near Macon, Georgia. The fifth squad member, Pfc. Willie Johnson, or Thunderbolt Willie, an always smiling nineteen-year-old wiry black man from New Orleans's slummy west side, played the trumpet like a prodigy. At eight years old, he'd learned jazz, carrying the shiny instrument wherever he went. Nobody from the neighborhood would have guessed he'd eventually haul the damned thing across a godforsaken shithole like Rat Mountain. While Pfc. Carter, the pig farmer, volunteered for the Army to better his chances, the always smiling Thunderbolt begged for mercy, requesting an assignment to Germany. Still, the unlucky draftee became Russell Simmons's replacement in the first wave rushed to the Pusan Perimeter.

The final man in the squad, a bitter, mean-spirited Kentuckian named Pfc. Alfred Carson III still held a grudge over the Civil War. Nevertheless, he volunteered for the infantry and used a seven-inch switchblade knife with precision, possessing a heinous dislike towards Negroes, and not much caring for "no-good" Yankees, either. Carson's only friend in the platoon was Snakey Frank Connors. Snakey Frank, not discriminating in whom he befriended, mostly liked everybody in the company, despite their general annoyance with him.

The first mile went quickly, the sun below the horizon making a wispy orange serenade from the east. The men were glad to be going, relieved that the goodbyes were over, and welcoming a cessation of their weeklong battle against a million-man army of lazy black flies and yellow-toothed rats. Being on the march would occupy their minds, and unoccupied minds dwelled on dark insecurities.

Before sunrise and after dusk, life moved about in relative comfort. A mile out of camp, the Korean countryside erupted into unexpected greenery, with large airy swathes of yellow daffodils and brightly colored eruptions of splendid wildflowers. Miraculously spared from the bitter months-long fighting, elevated dikes rose above an ocean of abandoned rice terraces. The fields created havens for birds, grasshoppers, frogs, butterflies, and many other critters, which roamed about unmindful of the war's terror and destruction.

The soldiers feasted upon the peacefulness of the morning's glory, enjoying it for a whisper, and then it disappeared. With each slow minute of the sun's rising towards noon, the heat became increasingly hellish, furnace-like, and it didn't let go. They bubbled like pancakes on a hot iron griddle, their bodily fluids wetting the Korean summer's soil, and their eighty-pound packs—loaded with ammo, C-rations, water, and misery—became the dreaded enemy.

At 1400, Pfc. Stephen Manley, an always chatty twenty-one-year-old baseball fanatic from Providence, Rhode Island, became the first casualty. His springy, six-foot-two-inch frame moved briskly in the early morning hours. But by 1430, with one-hundred-degree heat hanging off his shoulders like a dead elephant, the always chatty Manley went silent, his body reviling in protest. First, it refused to drain itself of fluids; a grapefruit-sized headache crawled from the base of his skull to his pear-shaped forehead. Next, his calves, back, and thigh muscles stiffened. But Pfc. Manley was damned if he would not keep up with the rest of the boys, and he soldiered on, drawing his steel canteen and taking a swig of warm water.

By 1500, Pfc. Manley no longer knew he was in Korea. It was late spring 1942, and he walked alongside his younger sister, father, mother, and grandfather to Sunday morning's service. The cathedral's beautiful brass bell spoke to its congregation in comforting melodies. Its timeless white spires of old European glory—solid, round, and tall—rose skyward above the city, offering passage to love and salvation.

The spires were easily noticeable from four blocks away, and between them and his home, tree-lined boulevards framed by big wrap-around porches, white picket fences, and stately gardens pregnant with red roses led the way.

By 1530, Pfc. Stephen Manley's field of vision narrowed, the spires becoming more prominent, and he reached out to touch them, his body departing the earth, no longer bound by gravity. By 1540, he lay coiled in the dirt, dry, one hundred four degrees hot, without sweat, stiff in seizure, his swollen tongue hanging from bleeding lips. Five minutes later, twenty-one-year-old Pfc. Stephen Manley of Providence, Rhode Island, was dead.

The 1st and 2nd Platoons stood dumbfounded around the body in disbelief. Next, Captain Carlson removed Manley's dog tags, placing them among eighteen other steel tags in the bottom of his pack. Lieutenant Somerset drew the man's rations and canteen and offered the water to the soldiers. He then distributed the tins of canned peaches, pound cake, instant coffee, corned beef, chicken stew, mashed potatoes, and meatloaf. Finally, the lieutenant took the dead man's cigarettes and doled them out in equal quantities to the squad leaders.

A big, unsmiling corporal named Mike Hesse spoke first. "Captain, it's hotter than a skunk's ass, and a man just died of heatstroke. Don't you reckon we should find shade and wait for evenin' to continue this march?"

Captain Carlson pushed himself up from the dead private's belongings. His body languished under the crushing effects of the summer's heat, and the big muscle of his right thigh twisted tight into an eight-figure knot, contorting his face into an impatient scowl. "Hesse, many more soldiers will die if we don't keep moving. We've got the whole battalion depending on this flanking attack."

"But Captain, if we die durin' the march, there won't be a flankin' attack to support the battalion," Hesse said, taking his big hairy forearm and pushing the sweat and grime from one side of his face to the other. He continued, "For heaven's sake, captain, we saw a man drop dead from overheatin', and you expect us to just keep marchin' right through the sun till we all end up dead like him?"

"Listen, corporal, if I want your goddamned opinion about this operation, I sure as hell will be the first to ask," Captain Carlson growled before wincing from the thud of another mortar round echoing deep within the chambers of his inner eardrums. "Now, if any man with a headache is feeling sick to his stomach or is suffering severe leg cramps, move to the shady side of the berm, lie down, and get yourself cleared by the medics. Meanwhile, we will head out in thirty minutes," he hollered above the infuriating bombardment, driving him mad.

Fifteen beaten-down bodies shuffled to the protected side of the berm and lay exhausted against the shaded slope. The medics busily went from one to another, asking each the same questions. *Do you have a headache? How bad is it? How long have you had it? How much water did you drink? Are you experiencing muscle cramps? Is your body sweating? Can you urinate? Are you having trouble concentrating?* Any man, especially hot and dry, had his temperature immediately taken. The medics determined five men were too severely dehydrated to move on, and two of these showed early signs of heatstroke. They established a bivouac, and two healthy soldiers stayed to care for the heat-stricken men until they could all return to the lines and reintegrate with the battalion. The remaining fatigued men moved out, intending to bivouac six hours later at the entrance to the valley that would take them to the Point of No Return.

"How much more do ya think we gotta be marchin' to this place they call Point of No Return?" Pfc. Lysander Carter asked Pfc. Thunderbolt Willie.

"Hell if I know, but I'm guessin' we're 'bout halfway there."

"Another six more fuggin hours of dis shit, and then we all gotta do it again tomorrow. This fuggin Army is cracked up, Thunderbolt. If it doesn't get your black ass shot 'n' kilt, the Army is going to kill you just going to get kilt!" Lysander chuckled.

"Any place the damned Army call Point of No Return is a place I don't wanna be goin'," Thunderbolt Willie complained. "I reckon they got evil spirits in that valley. And all this senseless killin' has got them spirits worked up and angry and stuck in a pot a peppered stew! Some of them spirits got devilish powers—I saw 'em myself. Spirits can make a man lose the only mind he's got. But, you see, colored folks don't take to all this killin' as white folks do. Never did take to it. Oh, yeah, no, sir, colored folks saw plenty of dyin' when the Yankees burned down

Georgia, and all the folks, white and black, be starvin'. Slave folks couldn't speak a word about that sufferin' to anyone except for those who saw it for themselves—no, sir, they saw too damned much killin' to make 'em crazy just talkin' 'bout it."

"I reckon every man gets himself thrown to the wolves, and he either gonna make it or he ain't," Lysander said.

"Yes, sir, this life is like walkin' in a minefield through a wall of fog, and you don't know when you gonna step on somethin' that gets you all blown to hell. Growin' up, I never, never heard of no fuggin place called Korea—and here I am in Korea—watchin' good men gettin' shot and blown up, dyin' by all kinds of diseases. We saw poor Manley die by sunstroke, his tongue hangin' from his damned mouth and them big blue eyes rollin' into the back of his head. I never would've believed this shit!"

"Yes, sir, I never heard of no Korea, and here we are gonna die in that minefield you talkin' 'bout."

"Willie, my granddaddy taught me that life's full of counterpunches, and that's why you wanna live it by your terms and not let it control you. But, Willie, I sure as hell don't feel no control in this Army, and it scares the hell out of me!"

"It sure is different back home in New Orleans. Ain't nobody gonna believe what we doin' down here."

Just then, cutting their sentence in half, roaring sixteen-inch naval artillery shells slammed into the pockmarked face of the Rat, throwing sediment, boulders, trees, Russian-made rifles, and North Korean soldiers hundreds of feet into the scalding hot air.

"Goddamn," Perkins said to Jack, walking five feet behind him. "How in the hell can a man live through a naval bombardment? Do you think the gooks will leave the summit before we get there?"

"No, we will have to fight them, probably with bayonets."

"Why do you say that? We're hittin' them good—harder than before. Maybe they've scattered."

"Scattered? Have you seen the bastards run yet?"

"You've gotta point."

"Everybody said the commies would turn tail and the hell they did! The sons of bitches ran their T-34 tanks right over us. All the talk in Tokyo was that this would blow over in thirty days, and now it's ninety. It'll get worse before it gets better."

"Goddamned Rat Mountain!" Perkins said in disgust.

Plodding along twenty feet behind Carter and Thunderbolt Willie were Carson and Eugene.

"I have a problem with you calling them coons; it just doesn't feel right. No man deserves to be called names like that," Eugene said.

"Okay, I'll call them niggers then, if that's what makes ya feel better," Carson growled.

"Why don't you just call them by their names—Carter and Johnson—as we all do in this squad? They're both good, honest men, and you know it's true," Eugene said.

"I can call them what the hell I please. It's a free country, ain't it? Ain't that what we supposed to be fightin' for? Free speech, you damned Yankee," Carson spat.

"I'm from Seattle, you dumb turd," Eugene said, becoming increasingly disgusted.

"You northerners are all the same, a bunch of damned Yankees."

"I was born in the west, not in the north, you dumb ass," Eugene growled.

"You're still a damned Yankee."

"There are plenty of Southerners in this army that don't think the way you do," Eugene said.

"And there are plenty that do," Carson growled back.

"Why are you such a bitter redneck, Carson? All that damned hate brewing in you! What the hell did they ever do to you anyway?" Eugene said.

"I just don't like niggers," Carson said, spitting a big fat one into the dusty landscape.

"I suppose some folks need somebody to hate; it makes them feel better about their stinkin' lives. But it must be hard livin' like that—I mean that sickness burning in your heart, Carson," Eugene said, giving up on the man.

"You'd better watch yo' mouth, Eugene," Carson growled, sneering nastily.

"Are you threatening me?" Eugene said with disgust.

"Just watch yourself," Carson said, moving his right hand over his switchblade knife.

"Go fuck yourself, Carson," Eugene growled, wishing he could smash the man's head with a baseball bat.

The two looked at each other in mutual disgust.

Meanwhile, the sun dispensed an unescapable misery upon the rucking soldiers while the rats sought comfort in the shade of subterranean burrows. First and 2nd Platoons marched through the insufferable blaze, only stopping for water and checking for heat exhaustion. This pattern of the soldiers' movement—marching, halting, checking, and marching—continued until sundown, two miles short of the head of the valley. Six more men succumbed to heat exhaustion, and two more were left behind to tend to their injuries. Thus, thirty-eight healthy ones remained of the forty-eight troopers that started before daylight. The exhausted marched on in silence for two more hours, and then bivouacked under a somber-faced, Northeast Asian moon's blanket of milk-colored contentment.

At 0200, Lieutenant Somerset crawled from under a fetid poncho into the abandoned early morning darkness. The sky appeared heavy and silent, except for a tribe of croaking brown frogs and a choir of prong-faced crickets. Like every evening in the bush, the snorers sang their distasteful Shakespearean hymns, infecting the lieutenant's mood with a melancholic disgust. Upsetting the cacophony of frogs, crickets, and snorers were well-placed salvos from Major Johnson's battery of one-hundred-five-millimeter howitzers. The thirty-five pounders ripped through the silence every hour, tearing the sky apart as the shells thudded violently into Rat Mountain's summit.

Lieutenant Somerset walked several hundred feet along the top of a mounded fourteenth-century agricultural berm to escape the men's dreadful snoring. He plopped his eighty-pound rucksack on the ground, where a bend in the berm opened upon a large expanse of rice terraces. Beyond the terraces was a shawl of rolling foothills that encircled the base of Rat Mountain, creating a seductive backdrop to the meandering topography. He squatted upon the dewy earth facing the moon's warm glow, listening contentedly to the nocturnal world until its biological rhythms subdued him into a restful sleep. At 0300, he awoke to more rounds of thudding artillery and a moon retreating towards the horizon. He noticed the formation of dark, muscular storm clouds far away over the Pacific, signaling increasing atmospheric turbulence from the approaching typhoon. The artillery methodically pounded the summit several miles away for ten minutes. Still, the flashing explosions felt oddly detached from the small slice of moonlit paradise that engulfed his depleted senses with peace, serenity, and calmness.

Lieutenant Clarence Somerset of Peoria, Illinois, a fair-haired veteran of the Second World War, scuttled from Japan to Korea to block the communists; block the communists, the army ordered him; obsolescent two-point-five-eight-inch rockets were no match for Russian T-34 tanks; stop the communists; stop the goddamned communists the army ordered him; fought and died at Taegu; fought and died at the Hadong Pass; fought and died at Chinju, Pohan-dong, and all along the Naktong; stop the communists, the generals ordered; stop the goddamned communists!

Lieutenant Clarence Somerset of Peoria, Illinois, sat atop a fourteenth-century agricultural berm overlooking seven-hundred-year-old Joseon dynasty rice terraces and the pockmarked backdrop of a smoking Rat Mountain. He reached greedily for coffee and a fresh pack of cigarettes, prizing these treasures, taking them decadently into his hands, the anticipation of a junkie's rapture flooding him with wellbeing. He thought, *if only peace, serenity, and solitude may last thirty minutes.*

He positioned the eighty-pound pack to conceal a small fire. It exploded into a dozen smiling-faced revelers. He watched in awe as they moved across the dance floor, consuming everything in their path until they became just a brightly burning mound of charcoal. He placed the metal cup alongside the embers and slowly stirred the grounded coffee beans until gently rising bubbles signaled the beverage was ready.

Oh, yes, he groaned as the bubbles swam drunkenly to the surface. He removed the coffee from the fire, squashing the embers with his right foot. He lay back against his heavy canvas pack and lit himself a Chesterfield, taking a deep draw of the sweet American tobacco and lifting the hot cup of Joe to his lips.

Oh, that's a good girl; you're still too hot, aren't you, baby? He said into the darkness.

Again, he tested the surface of the coffee with his deprived tongue, and again it nipped back, burning it.

Oh, you're playing hard to get—trying to drive me fucking crazy, aren't you? Well, I'll fix that—you watch me! And in the darkness where no restless eyes could observe his oddly deprived perversions, the lieutenant blew again and again against the hot coffee—*hoow, hoow, hoow.* Finally, he brought the joe to his nose and inhaled deeply, enjoying the rich, earthy smell of home. "Oh, baby, you smell good— so damned good," he said aloud, bringing the cup to his lips again. "Oh, you are so splendidly tasty, better than I thought you'd be," he moaned, taking a second sip.

"Is that you, Lieutenant Somerset, sitting behind the pack?" a soldier called out from the darkness.

"Shit," the lieutenant hollered, and he spun to his left, spilling the hot cup of coffee on his fatigues. "Who the fuck goes there?" he barked at the unrecognizable figure.

"I'm sorry, sir. It's Sergeant Pierce. I had to take a leak and saw you walking atop the berm with your pack, so I made hot coffee for you and the boys. I brought you a cup, sir."

"Son of a bitch, Pierce, don't you know to knock when you open a door? You made me spill my coffee, dammit!"

"I'm very sorry, sir. Please have another cup. Shall I get you something to dry your pants?"

"To hell with my pants, Pierce! Anyway, I want to talk to you about the operation. Go fetch a cup for yourself and be back here pronto."

Jack departed for the bivouac. Meanwhile, Major Johnson's final thirty-five-pounder left its cannon at 0400, and a split second later, the shell crashed into Rat Mountain. Little orange fires burned in the distance, and once the thunderous explosions abated, serenity again settled comfortably over the berm. The lieutenant lit another Chesterfield and sipped the fresh cup of coffee, watching little orange fires burn in disorganized clusters all over the Rat.

Jack returned with his own hot cup and sat next to Lieutenant Somerset. Neither man talked. The lieutenant intended to draw out the silence, while Jack wanted the lieutenant to break it. Finally, halfway through his coffee, the lieutenant spoke.

"You see those fires burning?" he said, pointing at the summit. "It's beautiful, isn't it? Sitting here and watching the little red fires dance across the mountainside."

"I suppose it is the way you describe it, sir."

"Well, underneath those fires, Pierce, there are a thousand pissed-off, bloodthirsty gooks wanting to kill you."

"Do you expect it'll be bad?"

"Major Johnson's artillery has killed more than a handful, but there are just as many filling into their lines, protected by trenches, bunkers, and underground fortifications like the Japs constructed on Peleliu and Iwo Jima."

"I expect so, but down here, watching the mountain burn, it's hard to imagine," Jack said.

"It is, and that's what we thought fighting through the Pacific, but I want you to know the score. I want you to know between here and there," he said, pointing at the summit with his balsa swagger stick, "we will have a lot of the battalion killed."

Jack sat silently, listening and taking his last drink of coffee.

"Pierce, the captain and I have observed you. Now, if it had been up to Captain Carlson and me, you'd be in the brig and demoted to private for that shit you pulled on Fuji-san. But Colonel Jones recognized something we didn't, a pair of gigantic brass balls swinging boldly between your legs, and so we've been watching you as squad leader to see if you have the temperament, or shall I say the good judgment, to lead men in combat."

"Well, I appreciate your consideration, sir."

"We've been impressed with you, Pierce. Your leadership during Task Force Kean and how you handled your squad at the Goose's Neck showed damned good judgment, a quality severely lacking at Camp Fuji."

"I understand, sir."

"Listen, Pierce, the captain and I have agreed that you should take a leadership role in this operation against 257. And if anything should happen to Captain Carlson or me, we will give you a field commission to second lieutenant."

"Thank you, sir. But I prefer to stay with my squad. I'm comfortable with the men. However, if the need arises, I'll follow my orders."

"Thank you, sergeant. Now, go back to the bivouac and wake the others. The captain would like to be out of here by 0430."

"Yes, sir."

•   •   •

Three miles into the tapered valley, the war faded away to a passivity not experienced by the men since early autumn in the Japanese Alps. The faint sound of recoilless rifle fire, exploding grenades, and mortar bursts from the battalion's push up the Rat became muted by the vertical green walls rising hundreds of feet from the valley floor. A lively, unexpected stream rolled through the interior of the valley. Its water was indifferent to the war, formless liquid enclosing shiny, marble-colored glass boulders peeking above its surface. And deeper into the valley's interior, the water moved faster and with incredible determination, the sidewalls pressing closer and closer together, placing more pressure upon the stream. It was the first healthy water the soldiers had seen in weeks, and it tasted deliciously cool and fresh, and its smell was sweet and rejuvenating. The men gleamed, hooting and hollering in childish delight while resting at the stream's edge. They made their faces clean and cool with generous, cold-water splashes, drawing untainted liquid into their craving, dehydrated bodies.

Evidence of the displaced villager's prior use of the stream for their earthly and spiritual rituals existed. A footpath meandered along the streambank, but thick, groping, jade-colored foliage began to consume the trail. Ancient stone carvings of the Buddha dotted the valley floor and its low-lying granite walls. Some were just a foot tall, and his deity's features were barely recognizable from a thousand years of weathering. Others were well-preserved, cut from large stone blocks, or chiseled into big, flat, indomitable granite slabs.

In several locations within the stream, villagers had stacked boulders to create shallow wading pools. And fresh Korean Goral goat tracks lay where they sipped the water. A gregarious, round-faced smiling Bodhisattva sat cross-legged atop a ledge overlooking the clear mountain stream at one of the larger, well-formed pools. He'd been chiseled a thousand years before by holy men. Through the decades, the seasons, and the wars, the Buddha showered the passersby with enlightenment: *Do not overlook tiny good actions, thinking they are of no benefit; even tiny drops of water in the end will fill a huge vessel. Do not overlook negative actions merely because they are small; however small a spark may be, it can burn down a haystack as big as a mountain.*

"Sergeant Pierce, how 'bout we break at dis here pool for a quick dip? We can catch up to the rest of the platoon later; it's awful darned peaceful here, ain't it?" Pfc. Lysander Carter suggested above the pleasant melody of moving water and a chorus of delightful chirps from a nesting family of grasshopper warblers.

"Good idea," said Corporal Mike Hesse, removing his meaty hands from his front two pockets. "This is a fine spot for a swim and a cigarette!" He lazily removed his eighty-pound pack from his aching shoulders.

"Hoo wee," Pfc. Willie "Thunderbolt" Johnson called out to the squad, pointing at a ledge overlooking the stream. "Look at that smilin', big ass Buddha lookin' over us. I'm goin' to have a peek. Eugene, can you take a picture? The folks back home aren't goin' to believe this stuff we are seein'."

Jack swung around and hollered at the loafing soldiers. "You all know damned well we can't stop for a dip. The more you think about doing things you can't do, the more miserable you'll feel about not doing 'em. So now, take five minutes for water, a dump, or a cigarette, but then we've gotta get going."

"Heck, sergeant. I stopped dreamin' 'bout ladies, food, and dis brass horn strapped to my pack, which I can't even play no more. Ain't there nothin' a man can think 'bout that gives him pleasure?"

"Sure, Johnson, you can think about safely getting your ass up the Rat. And once the squad is dug in, you can think through tomorrow's flanking attack and how best we will destroy the enemy's positions. And once we've destroyed their positions and reformed into our lines, well, hell, you can start dreaming to your heart's delight about steaks, girls, and jazz—but we can't be daydreaming right now!"

"Heck," Lysander chuckled, "I daydream all damned day 'bout all those things anyways."

Standing behind Lysander, Eugene chuckled at the back and forth and then asked Lysander, "Is it the steak, the girls, or the jazz you dream about most often?"

Snakey Frank Connors, kneeling at the stream, chirped with a nasty grin, "Before I beat my meat, it's the pussy, and after I'm still thinkin' 'bout it."

Lysander chuckled and sneered wickedly back at Snakey Frank. "You are a dirty-minded fool, ain't you, Snakey Frank, always thinkin' 'bout pussy."

The rest of the men removed their packs, unlaced their combat boots, smoked cigarettes, and talked about the girls, steak, and jazz clubs they left behind in Tokyo. Thunderbolt Willie hiked up the ledge to the smiling Buddha, and Eugene snapped a picture for his folks back home. Jack grabbed a smoke, removed his sketch pad, and moved his black pencil across the paper in quick darting movements—up and down, side to side, and again and again. All the while pondering upon the land, stream, heavy canopy of trees, birds, and their perpetual rhythms—patterns—and what is a single man to something so powerful?

Nobody discussed the mission or planned their attack on the North Korean positions. Jack gave the men an extra five minutes, then moved out.

An hour up the trail, Captain Carlson, Lieutenant Somerset, and 1st and 2nd Platoons stood clustered in the shade of a large clump of full-bodied Mountain Ash trees with big groping leaves. Sixty feet away, five wild goats with white-haired necks and muscled legs, pointed tiptoes, and sharp black horns feasted upon a sprawling patch of wild ferns and sweet red raspberries. Beyond the goats, the trail twisted and bent to the right, and here, the men could see the foot of the narrow ridgeline that would deliver them onto the Rat's western flank, five miles west from where the battalion pushed their attack.

"There it is, men, the Point of No Return," Captain Carlson said, looking up at a narrow goat track cut into the skinny ridgeline.

"I can see why they call it that. A man could never get down once he goes up," Pfc. John Meade said, rubbing the tiredness from his eyes.

The calming sound of the fast-moving stream, comfortably secure in the safety of the valley floor, made the men want to stay put. *To hell with this war,* they thought. And one man dispiritingly grumbled, "It's a fuggin suicide mission."

The captain heatedly responded, "A suicide mission is not supporting the men relying upon us to save their lives. Now tighten up your courage!"

Captain Carlson continued, "Gentlemen, this ridgeline will take us back onto Rat Mountain. It's about a three-thousand-foot-long traverse, and we will all need to be damned careful, or it will be our last march. Lieutenant Somerset will be at the head of the column, and I'll be in the middle."

The men removed their packs, lay down their weapons, and took final drinks from the mountain stream before they lined up. Finally, Captain Carlson walked down the line, giving a final round of orders.

"Keep ten feet between you and the man in front of you always! The men in the rear will assist the BAR, machine gun, recoilless rifle, and mortar teams. These men will help with the loads. There will be no talking; walk cautiously and be careful with your footing. Along the spine, focus only on the man in front, and for heaven's sake, do not look down!"

As directed, the men proceeded forward in a single-line formation precisely ten feet apart. The line length was five hundred feet, and its body slithered slowly along the ridge like an unruly green centipede, meandering skyward toward its fate. The heavy weapons men walked in pairs, ten feet apart, their twenty-pound guns carried at their breast, weighing down their arms and making the climb unbearable, as the trail rose sharply. In places, the men kicked the toes of their boots into the soil to form load-bearing steps, grabbed onto trees, and heaved themselves upwards while their eighty-pound packs pulled violently, gravity threatening to throw them off the ridge to their death. In addition, the heavy weapons men had to relay equipment back and forth among their team, causing nerve-racking delays and making the journey even more treacherous.

The column's movement lasted about forty minutes until the centipede's progress suddenly stopped and broke in half. The men asked the troopers ahead, "What the hell is going on up there?" "What's causing the delay?" Word returned that a hundred-foot section of the ridge was just two feet wide, freezing up a machine gunner from 1st Platoon's 2nd Squad. The assistant machine gunner then also panicked, too frightened to turn around and return to safety.

Jack's squad rested two hundred feet below the blockage, just three teams above the last two units at the end of the line. Jack looked to his front, across the sweeping ridgeline, and saw the head of the column moving forward with Lieutenant Somerset in the lead. It appeared to Jack the worst was over for a third of the men, and they would reach the Rat's western flank with another thousand feet of maneuvering. He could see Captain Carlson slowly scrambling down the spine, maneuvering around the stalled men along the trail to the bottleneck. Jack decided to proceed upwards, working around the stalled men to his front to assist the captain. As he moved towards the bottleneck, Captain Carlson sat consoling the machine gunner.

"Specialist Peck, I want you to kneel and slowly place the machine gun on the trail."

"I can't, captain! I'm sick. I can't fuggin breath," the terrified machine gunner croaked in terror.

"Listen, don't think about the crossing. I will get you across this section. You will not have a problem above it."

"But captain, my heart's a jumpin', and I just can't get a good breath. I'm feelin' awful' damned sick, captain. I suppose I'm just scared of heights," the twenty-year-old machine gunner from Lansing, Michigan, moaned before sobbing.

"It's okay, specialist. We all get scared. Don't worry about anything and try to calm yourself; this will all be over soon."

"Thank you, captain. I'm awful damned sorry about the mess I've caused."

Carlson inched his way toward the man. And Jack could see the captain wince with pain as his weight put unadjusted pressure upon his right leg.

"Alright, specialist," the captain said. "I want you to kneel with me, and when we are both kneeling, I want you to lay the machine gun on the trail, and I want you to remove your pack. Can you do that for me?"

The young machine gunner, one of the bravest men in the platoon in the heat of combat, felt his heart slowly stop racing, and his breathing became steadier.

They both bent slowly, and the specialist laid the machine gun down and released his eighty-pound pack onto the trail behind him.

"Okay, that's great, specialist. So now, when we leave here, you will place both hands on my shoulders and look straight ahead. I will lead you across. Can you do that for me?"

"Yes, sir," the young man said. And both men slowly rose to their feet, and Captain John Carlson walked his soldier fifty harrowing feet to safety. But, once across, the young machine gunner dropped on all fours, violently retching, while the other men tried to console him.

"Sergeant Pierce," the captain called across the one-hundred-foot spine, "what the hell are you doing up here? Why are you not with your squad?"

"Captain, I'm real comfortable with heights—I figured you might need a hand."

"Okay, just stay where you're at—I'll grab Peck's pack and the machine gun to clear the trail."

The captain walked back across the ridgeline, again wincing in pain.

"You okay, captain?"

"I'll make it," the captain hollered.

He knelt and pulled Peck's heavy ruck tight against the front of his sturdy chest. Then, looking straight into Jack's sharp, bluish-gray eyes for balance, he slowly raised himself to his feet, carefully maintaining his center of gravity upon the dangerous, twenty-four-inch-wide precipice. Finally, and cautiously, still peering into Jack's eyes, he shifted the ruck out and over the four-hundred-foot ridge and then pulled it onto his right arm, over his shoulder, and finally on his back. Still focusing his attention on Jack's eyes, he moved his left arm back into the shoulder harness and secured the pack tightly to his body.

"Are you good, captain?" Jack hollered.

"Yeah, I'm good. I'll go ahead and grab the machine gun."

"Why don't you let me take it?" Jack hollered in protest.

"No, I got it," the captain yelled back.

With the same focused attention upon Jack's eyes, Captain Carlson bent down with the added weight of the eighty-pound pack to retrieve the heavy weapon.

"Oh, fuck!" the captain suddenly screamed halfway down, in pain.

"Captain!" Jack shouted back to Carlson.

"That hurt like a son of a bitch in my right thigh!"

"Captain, leave the damned machine gun! I'll make my way around Meade and bring it over myself."

"I'm okay!" the captain hollered. And like before, staring into Jack's bluish-gray eyes, he slowly raised himself without the machine gun when, out of the ghostly mountain silence, a sharp *CRACK* exploded across the valley. Jack watched in terror as the captain's face turned ghostly white, and he let out a bloodcurdling scream that echoed from one tapered cliff wall to the other. "Aaah shit, aah shit—my fucking femur's snapped in half—oooh fuck it hurts! My fucking femur's snapped—can you fuggin believe it? Ooh, shit, it hurts like hell!"

The painful screaming ricocheted violently off the valley walls—back and forth and back and forth—and the captain fell backward onto Peck's heavy load, his face becoming blue and white and contorted with pain.

"Jesus Christ!" Jack screamed. "I'm coming to get you, captain!"

"No, you won't!" the captain yelled back to Jack over the terrified face of Private Meade, the young eighteen-year-old second gunner, bawling like a baby on all fours, too frightened to move in either direction.

"Captain, I'll go back and get the medic. I can get some morphine and a splint and fix you all up. Then we'll carry you out!"

"And how will you get me across this ledge without having more men killed?" the captain hollered in agony. "Anyway, there isn't any time for that, sergeant. And the goddamned typhoon is coming."

"Sir, Lieutenant Somerset and the stretcher-bearers are now working their way down here. I'm comin' the fuck over!"

"No, you're not!" the captain screamed in pain. "You will stay right where you are!" He removed his forty-five-caliber pistol from its leather holster and pointed it directly between Jack's two blue eyes.

"You are a goddamned good soldier, Pierce!" the captain moaned. "But that was some shit you pulled on Fuji-san. I never thought I'd see men joyride to the top of a fuggin mountain for sunrise. But damn, that was something to see!" He then moaned again, "My God, this leg hurts something fierce! The men in the company will count on your leadership, Pierce. Lieutenant Somerset is a damned fine officer. Pierce, you help him any way you can!" he hollered in agony.

Blood now soaked through the captain's leggings, and the fractured bone had buckled under the weight of the pack and then punctured the thick fibrous muscle, perforating his thigh and cutting through the skin.

"That damned mortar round must have fractured my femur, and I've been marching all this time. Damned bad luck, Pierce!" the captain cried out. "You tell Somerset to express my love and prayers to my ma and pa. Have him tell 'em I did my best. You boys watch over each other and always be your best. So long, Pierce!" Captain Carlson said before he closed his eyes for the last time.

"Captain!" Jack screamed.

But Captain Carlson rolled himself over the spine and tumbled four hundred feet to his death. His green-clad battered body, still strapped to the pack, lay motionless at the base of a thick wasted pine tree, which arrested his fall just a foot before a field of giant granite boulders.

Screams occurred along the length of the long green centipede, and then it became deathly silent again, except for terrified sobs from a half-dozen men up and down the line.

Jack stood in shock, too shaken to speak or move for what seemed like minutes, unable to remove the vision of the captain's last sorrowful expression and the final painful words of his life — "So long, Pierce!" And then, as if struck by lightning, rage overcame him. He screamed at the world as loud as his lungs would allow, letting humanity know how angry he was. "Fuck you!" he cried, and he screamed again and again until he rested upon all fours, his body tiring and breathing heavily, sobbing from exhaustion. And then he stopped and fell silent, looking out across the spine at the lieutenant, still working his way back across the ridgeline and nearing his position.

Jack stood and wiped the tears from his face, feeling the rage disappear as fast as it had come. "Private Meade, hang in there; I'm comin' over and will help you get across." And he walked across fifty feet to where Meade was crouched.

"John, it's me, Jack—I want you to remove your pack. I'm going to carry it across for you."

"Are you sure, Sarge? I'm sorry," he sobbed.

"It's no problem. I'm comfortable up here; it's like back home in the mountains."

Jack's confidence relaxed the private, and he released the pack and scooted himself forward on all fours. Jack then lifted the man's ruck to his chest, rolled it onto his right shoulder, and swung his left arm through the strap, resting it comfortably upon his shoulder.

"Alright, Meade, can you stand and walk across now?"

"Yes, sir, I was doin' just fine but kinda lost my nerves when Peck got scared and froze up. I started feelin' real dizzy just standing here waitin'," he said, still softly crying.

"That's understandable, and it could've happened to me, too. Now, let's stand up and get the hell out of here. What do ya say?"

Private Meade silently rose to his feet, looking at the lieutenant and the men waiting at the opposite end of the spine. The walk went smoothly and without incident. When he reached the other side, Private Meade sat directly next to the young machine gunner, Peck, who was still sobbing over the humiliation and terrible guilt he felt over the captain's death.

"Son of a bitch, Pierce, what the hell happened out there?" Lieutenant Somerset asked, visibly shaken by the captain's tragic death.

"Captain Carlson's right femur snapped when he knelt bearing Peck's pack. The gook mortar must have fractured his leg at the Goose's Neck, and the wear and tear of the march finally broke it where it did, Sir."

"My God," the lieutenant said, visibly shaken. "And then?"

"I told the captain that we would carry him out. But he refused and pulled his forty-five on me—said there was no time and many more would die if we tried to save him. It was then that he rolled himself off the cliff."

"That's what I figured," the lieutenant said. "He wouldn't risk the operation or more men's lives trying to save himself. I will report this in the after-action report."

"Sir, the captain requested you inform his ma and pa that he loved them and did his job well."

The lieutenant's eyes confirmed that he'd honor the captain's wishes.

•   •   •

Jack led five more men across the spine. He carried each frightened man's pack and weapon, and as Captain Carlson, he pulled the fear-stricken soldiers like boxcars over a trellised bridge to safety. The entire affair delayed the mission by two hours, and four men, even with help, were too terrified to cross. Like the heat-sickened men, they returned to battalion headquarters and filled the reserves for the major thrust against the summit.

Rejoining the Rat's dirty western flank brought the war closer again," making the inevitable danger feel more personal. More men would be violently killed or maimed on the mountain again, just like they were killed and injured during the company's last assault through the

Goose's Neck. The march went straight up, and their breathing became labored in the suffocating heat and humidity, lugging large, uncomfortable loads on their backs.

The opposing armies spared the western flank of Hill 257 from bombardment because they considered it inaccessible to troops and armor. Rat Mountain's western side rose steeply and ruggedly, cut by expansive gorges, making it a precarious route to the summit. The only workable access came from the Point of No Return, and the narrow spine was a death trap and could accommodate only a limited number of troops with light equipment.

Easy Company's thirty-four surviving men from the 1st and 2nd Platoons were now under the command of Lieutenant Somerset. They rucked straight north up the mountain, like a chain gang of green-clad death row inmates, marching without seeing or hearing toward the fighting. They pushed, prodded, slashed, and trudged their way up the mountain's muscled posterior through an unbroken forest of twisting, sharp-needled pine trees and thick, scaly underbrush slicing at their eyes and skin. Then, at dusk, starved mosquitoes arrived with bulging evil eyes in nasty, bloodthirsty packs, attacking faces, arms, and hands—never letting go. The regularly vicious cracks and thuds of exploding ordinance became closer and closer again, testing each man's nerves as he marched towards calamity.

It was approaching nightfall when the soldiers finally arrived at the great chasm that separated the grisly, war-torn northern flank from the unscathed western side. The gorge was far more profound, steeper, and more treacherous than what was visible from the aerial imagery. Still, rudimentary topographic maps informed that a crossing was possible a mile downslope of the North Korean positions, which would require an additional mile of rough trekking straight up the mountain in the coming darkness.

Lieutenant Somerset pulled the men together, pointing up the mountain and shaking his balsa swagger stick straight north. "A mile upslope, the gorge flattens out and will allow for a crossing where we can amass our attack. We will bivouac just below the crossing so the assault can begin at first light."

Still, they couldn't see the battle, but they heard it and smelled it, and the sounds and smells of war hadn't changed, except they were still too distant to listen to the wounded men's pleas.

The emerging darkness forced the soldiers to march fast, without concern for their sore bodies and waning energy. The thick, untrampled underbrush cut and bruised their unprotected skin. Hanging from darkened trees, bow-strung whips and razor-sharp spears poked and scratched at the clamoring men, causing bruised and bleeding limbs.

At 2000, behind schedule and blanketed by near total darkness, the men finally reached their objective, an area to bivouac just below the crossing. They quickly established defensive positions, digging shallow foxholes. Chow was tasteless, always before a battle, and the men passed around a fifth of whiskey, delicious contraband, to calm their weary nerves. Then Operation Red Thunder became visible through the darkness for the first time, like in a scene from Dante's *Inferno*. Bursts of thirty- and fifty-millimeter tracer rounds raced through the night sky in reds, whites, and greens, and the opposing armies traded mortar barrages up and down the mountain, causing earsplitting explosions and spotty fires over the surviving vegetation. And it stunk like burning rubber, the scorched earth belching napalm, like the toxic morning following a drunk's chronic use of alcohol. Meanwhile, Major Johnson's one-hundred-five-millimeter howitzers pulverized the mountain for thirty minutes.

"I want you up at 0300 and in position to cross the gorge by 0400, so we need to be out of here by 0330," Lieutenant Somerset ordered Jack.

"Alright, lieutenant," Jack replied into the darkness.

"Hey, Perkins, gimme another drink of that whiskey," Thunderbolt Willie said, chuckling.

"It's yours," Perkins said, passing the bottle to Thunderbolt.

Thunderbolt took a long drag. "I'm preyin' to Mama this ain't my last drink," he said in a dog-tired drawl.

"Ahh, hell, have another, Thunderbolt. Then, for certain, it's not your last," Perkins offered.

"Thank you, Perkins. You are a really good man," he said, passing the bottle to Eugene.

Eugene took a stiff drink of his contraband, rolling his head back and beginning to sing; the words fell from his mouth like raindrops—deep, sorrowful, light, and surprisingly Irish—dancing in the wind like chimes.

Oh, Danny Boy the pipes, the pipes are calling
From glen to glen and down the mountainside
The summer's gone and all the roses falling
It's you, it's you must go and I must bide.

But come ye back, when summer's in the meadow
Or when the valley's hushed and white with snow
'Tis I'll be here in sunshine or in shadow
Oh, Danny boy, Danny boy, I love you so.

But when ye come, and all the flowers are dying
If I am dead, as dead I may well be
You'll come and find the place where I am lying
And kneel and say an Ave there for me.

And I shall hear, tho' soft you tread above me
And all my grave will warmer, sweeter be
For you will bend and tell me that you love me
And I shall sleep in peace until you come to me.

Afterward, it fell silent and lonely below the dark Korean sky and the flashing of American artillery, except for muzzled sobs from a few men, and each knew what the other was thinking.

"I was rememberin' the captain," one man said, trembling in the darkness, "and his bushy red hair and goddamned big smile. The captain could make a man laugh—always crackin' jokes with that witty Irish humor."

"He fought the Krauts at the Bulge and then rolled himself off a fuggin cliff in Korea. Who in the hell would have figured?"

"It's how this world is, all messed up and crazy."

"He wasn't goin' to risk our lives havin' us try to save him. He knew his luck was up."

"Maybe all our luck is up come tomorrow."

"Ya never know when life's going to run out on you. Be here today and dust tomorrow."

Jack took the bottle of whiskey from Pfc. Carter, the slow-talking pig farmer from Macon, Georgia, and passed it to Perkins.

"When I was a boy," Jack said, "we'd go to the beach with my grandfather and have enormous bonfires. We'd eat and drink until our bellies got rock hard. My grandpa Rufus was a character, always tellin' us boys' stories, and sometimes the same damned one ten times over, but each time we enjoyed it just as much as the first time he said it. I remember him tellin' one of his favorites, both arms flyin' above his head as he would do when he got excited, and everybody laughing. He looked into our boyish eyes, his own becoming deadly serious and hollering above the howl of the wind; he said:

"'The wisest advice I ever received came from an old Union soldier turned Indian fighter. This leathery bastard served under General Crook against the Lakota, and I remember the old man's eyes like yesterday—squinty, bold, the color of rusty sand, and his right lip turned upwards, cracked from the sun. And he said to us, boys:

"'Only a damned fool doesn't spend his money while he's got it. So don't let it sit and get old—enjoy it. Buy yourself a bottle, find a woman, and stay in a fancy hotel. Live your life now while you still got it!'

"I still remember the whole family hootin' and hollerin' and laughin', but I never forget those simple words of advice or my grandpa's face tellin' the story: *Live your life now while you still got it!*"

*   *   *

Darkness infused fear over the mountain at 0200. The sun wouldn't show for a couple more hours, and no man slept for over three, and this was marred by uncertainty, dread, bugs, and rain—the first nasty downfall arriving on the toes of Typhoon Samantha. They awoke with whiskey on their breath and ate without appetites—another tasteless ration of syrupy peaches, crumbly pound cake, and gluey brown beans, leftovers from Iwo Jima.

Before the first light, the troopers continued their scramble up the Rat, concealed by dark gray forest and heavy, razor-sharp underbrush. The going was miserable like the previous night, and they bitched, feeling nauseous and hungry but not hungry enough to eat before the approaching combat. A wet, pasty layer of mud formed beneath their boots from the evening's rain, so they slipped, fell, and stumbled toward the fighting, reopening the raw scabs from the previous day's wounds. The thirty-four remaining men of Easy Company's 1st and 2nd Platoons labored up the western slope until 0400, and then Lieutenant Somerset ordered the column to stop.

Finally, they could see the gorge at dusk and beyond enemy-held terrain. Lieutenant Somerset summoned the squad leaders and described the route to the high ground on the opposite slope. From the current position, the battalion's reserve was visible over two miles away at the mountain's base, a formless colony of tiny red fire ants and plastic toy jeeps seemingly light-years distant from their departure three days before. Between Easy Company's 1st and 2nd Platoons and their battalion's front lines were armed North Koreans, and every man knew the score; there was no turning back.

"Sergeant Pierce, take your squad, move across the gorge to that cluster of four trees at the bottom, and proceed up the opposite slope. Once across emplace covering fire. Signal me when you get to the rim. Now, the rest of you men emplace covering fire to protect their movement."

Jack's squad stretched out fifteen feet, separating each man. The gulch walls flattened to a steep, forty-five-degree slope, and wet chalky soils studded with loose rock, shale, and boulders made it more treacherous. The first to lose his footing, Private Carter tumbled a hundred feet down the vertical wall with his eighty-pound pack and carbine cartwheeling alongside him, a trail of ammunition and gear stretching up and down the slope.

"Halt," Jack ordered. "Perkins and Thunderbolt, get your asses up there and help Carter retrieve his gear."

Pfc. Carter stood from the wreckage and appeared alright, except for a badly mauled right elbow, which took the brunt of the fall with the total weight of his ruck grinding bone against a boulder rock.

"Better be fuggin careful!" Carter hollered, wincing in pain, blood dripping through his shirt sleeve as he remounted his ruck.

The soldiers carefully twisted, turned, and slid down the steep terrain until they arrived at the stand of four trees near the bottom.

"I gotta get me some water, sergeant!" Private Carson hollered.

"Alright, take a minute for water, men, and then we push to the rim, and let's make the water snappy," Jack ordered.

Brittle, ankle-deep shale complicated the final scramble up the last four hundred feet to the opposing rim, demanding three massive steps for every foot of progress and burning the men's thighs as they lugged their heavy loads. Finally, on the opposite side, they collapsed exhausted, falling under the weight of their packs, sticky sweat pouring through filthy green khakis.

Jack observed the forward terrain and couldn't locate any signs of enemy emplacements, so he signaled Lieutenant Somerset to start the crossing.

Lieutenant Somerset's column stretched several hundred feet long like a venomous King Cobra, toting machine guns, carbines, mortars, a recoilless rifle, and grenades. Several more men lost their footing, abandoning a string of expletives, their rifles, and ammo up and down the slope.

Once they'd made it, the men huddled below the rim while the lieutenant surveyed the terrain. It laid out in another finger ridge with a false peak a half-mile upslope and the Rat's true summit another half-mile beyond, obscuring the North Korean positions. And as planned, at 0700 sharp, Colonel Jones's fifteen-minute naval and one-hundred-fifty-five-millimeter artillery preparation commenced, and the entire mountain exploded.

The sudden incoming artillery created monstrous detonations that pinpointed the rough location of the enemy's frontline positions, beginning about a quarter-mile upslope, downslope of the ridgeline, and extending to the summit, where Major Johnson targeted his artillery. "Pierce, push up the ridgeline in attack formation," Lieutenant Somerset ordered. "First Platoon, follow twenty yards behind and provide supporting fire."

Jack slowly maneuvered his six-man squad towards the fighting in a catlike attack formation, walking low to the ground and eying every terrain detail for bunkers, foxholes, booby traps, and snipers. Lieutenant Somerset and the 2nd Platoon remained within the gorge, establishing a base of supporting fire. The six-man assault and fire support teams moved cautiously forward when the artillery ceased firing. A dozen P-51 Mustangs screamed in low, delivering five-hundred-pound napalm barrels, creating a wicked wall of flame and suffocating smoke.

"Blessed mother of Jesus!" Thunderbolt Willie hollered above the terrible roar as the planes broke into the distance, leaving an inferno in their wake.

"I sure feel bad for any man in those flames," Pfc. Carter muttered.

"Quit your fuggin mumblin', nigger, and pay attention for gooks," Pfc. Alfred Carson hollered savagely.

"Shut your fuggin mouth, Carson," Perkins said disgustedly, knowing that Thunderbolt and Carter wouldn't check Carson.

The assault and fire support teams hurried their ascent under the cover of burning napalm. The impending combat surged massive adrenalin waves, producing hyperawareness of any anomalies in the terrain. And secondary senses like the rush of wind or the maddening *crack, crack* from machine gun fire became duller, almost unnoticeable. Therefore, three North Korean soldiers rising above the ridgeline caught the men's attention. Two were skinny, and the third stalky, with thick rubbery arms, and all their faces were young, dirty farmer faces. The lethality of their appearance was unremarkable except for two bolt-action carbines, a Russian burp gun, and a half-dozen stick grenades.

Jack lifted his M1 and pointed it at the lead man's chest. The two soldiers studied each other for the tiniest shard of time that can destroy a man's life. The North Korean was the heavyset one with rubbery arms, carrying the lethal Soviet-made burp gun. He'd dressed in a summer green uniform and cap, equaling Jack's uniform in its uncleanliness. And the man possessed sad brown eyes, the unwitting eyes of the agrarian poor of North Korea, knowing only conflict, labor, and famine.

Jack squeezed the trigger, and the man's chest exploded. Then Pfc. Carter shot the second man in the forehead with his carbine, and the skinny man fell like a rag doll. The third North Korean dropped his rifle, dashing towards the ridge from where he came. Carson and Perkins shot him in the back, and he crumpled to the dirt, paralyzed and dying, only feet from where he had emerged seconds before.

After the surprise encounter with the North Koreans, Jack forcefully waved the rest of the platoon forward. The assault and fire support teams ascended rapidly to the area from where the enemy emerged. Across the mountain, Jack spotted three enemy bunkers several hundred feet downslope holding the North Korean's western flank, firing machine guns onto the advancing American infantry. A dozen charred and mutilated bodies lay in open trenches and scattered about the bunkers, corpses still smoking from the napalm. Lieutenant Somerset set up a pair of light machine guns to cover the bunkers.

"Like before, divide into two assault and fire support squads. Pierce, you will lead the assault teams," Lieutenant Somerset ordered.

"Eugene, you will lead the twelve-man fire support team."

The assault team carried M1 rifles, two BARs, automatic carbines, and grenades. Eugene and his assistant, Pfc. Lenny Tanaka packed M1 rifles equipped with grenade launchers. Close behind, men carried light machine guns, BARs, and automatic carbines.

Jack positioned a BAR man on each flank, the assault line stretching fifty feet, with Jack and Perkins walking point. Privates Lysander Carter, Alfred Carson, and Mike Hesse followed close behind. The fire support squad maneuvered thirty yards back, its weapons packing a similar heavy punch. The teams moved cautiously towards the enemy bunkers, no man talking, only the vicious barking of enemy machine guns firing downslope.

As Jack and Perkins maneuvered closer towards the bunkers, they slid inside a four-foot-deep communication trench littered with bodies still cooking from the napalm, their faces in terrible scowls, and their skin peeling away like beef jerky. Inside, they cat-walked over two charred bodies when, suddenly, a North Korean emerged carrying a burp gun, unaware of the Americans' presence. Jack and Perkins raised their rifles. The North Korean looked up in terror and screamed, but Corporal Mike Hesse shot him in the right eye, blowing a baseball-sized fragment from his skull. More North Koreans streamed from the bunkers, brandishing burp guns and grenades. The assault squad killed four with BAR and M1 fire, sending the others darting inside. Thunderbolt Willie charged the center bunker and tossed two grenades through its slats, destroying the soldiers inside.

The North Koreans reversed their machine gun fire onto the attacking team from the remaining two bunkers. Several other enemy soldiers fled down the slope with burp guns, seeking cover behind the fortified positions. The fire support team and 2nd Platoon's emplaced weapons hit the two bunkers with withering automatic weapons fire to keep the machine guns silent. Still, the North Koreans positioned behind the bunkers tossed grenades onto the attacking team, one detonating between Mike Hesse and Carson. The blast sent shrapnel into Mike Hesse's chest, killing him instantly and knocking Pfc. Carson from his feet.

Eugene directed his M1 rifle at the third bunker and fired a grenade that penetrated the open slat and exploded. North Koreans screamed until Jack and Thunderbolt Willie rushed with grenades, killing the survivors. The North Koreans, hearing the explosions from the downslope side of the bunker, lobbed a volley of grenades at the American side. The support team returned their own, blowing a man's leg off, resulting in more high-pitched screams.

The North Koreans tossed three more grenades, and the third blasted shrapnel into Pfc. Lenny Tanaka's right arm and face. A medic, Pedro Ramirez, ran forward to render help, but a burp gun raked him in the stomach and thigh and he crumpled next to Tanaka.

Screams for medics now intermingled with loud, rowdy bursts of rifle fire, automatic weapons, and thudding grenades.

Meanwhile, the North Koreans inside the second bunker set up a light machine gun inside the communication trench downslope from the bunker, firing bursts into the left flank of the fire support team. Privates Fishman and Dickson died instantly, and a bullet hit Corporal Wilcox, a BAR man, seriously wounding him through the right shoulder. Grenades, machine guns, and automatic rifle fire passed wickedly back and forth with increasing fury.

"Wyan't the gooks throwing grenades on top of us?" Perkins asked, panting and looking wild-eyed and crazy, crouching low in the communications trench.

"They's don't know we is here," Thunderbolt said, panting equally hard and looking terrified.

"Thunderbolt, give Perkins and me your grenades. Then return to the assault team and give the order to retreat to 2nd Platoon's position."

"What about you and Perkins?"

"The gooks don't know we're here. While they're distracted, we'll blow the remaining bunker. When you get back to 2nd Platoon, tell the lieutenant our plan and have him stop the firing long enough so we can rush it."

"Yes, sir," Thunderbolt said, and he slowly cat-walked back down the four-foot-deep trench to the assault team, which had taken cover about a hundred feet away.

Jack and Perkins crept forward within thirty feet of the surviving bunker using the heavy covering fire from the assault team and the 2nd Platoon's firing line along the ridge.

"Okay, let's hold here and wait for the men to withdraw," Jack said.

"How do you wanna attack the bunker?" Perkins asked, sweating, panting, and shivering with fright.

"When 2nd Platoon pauses its firing, we'll charge. Then, once we blow the grenades, we'll maneuver to the opposite side and shoot the gooks downslope from the rear," Jack said.

Jack and Perkins straightened the pins on two grenades and waited as the men executed their withdrawal under the protection of the 2nd Platoon's withering fire from the ridge. Then, with the North Koreans fully occupied, they crawled low inside the trench until they were just twenty feet away. The North Koreans continued their fierce exchange of automatic weapons fire with the 2nd Platoon planted along the ridgeline. "Damn it, wyan't 2nd Platoon stopped firing yet? Maybe Thunderbolt got hit or forgot to give the fuggin order," Perkins said, speaking into the soles of Jack's bloodstained boots, grey brain matter stuck in the treads, inches from Perkins' forehead.

"No, he didn't forget," Jack barked back.

"Then I hope Thunderbolt didn't get killed fallin' back. If he did, nobody will know we are here. Second Platoon will think we're dead!"

"Just wait, and don't panic! We'll work our way back and reengage the bunker if they don't stop shooting, so the guys will know we're alive," Jack whispered loudly.

Just then, the firing from the 2nd Platoon fell silent.

"Go!" Jack ordered.

Both men jumped from the trench and charged the bunker, tossing their grenades through the slits, falling flat and pressing their bodies against its walls. The two grenades exploded loudly inside, and, rising to their knees, they tossed additional grenades over the bunker toward the machine gun firing downslope. After these grenades exploded, they maneuvered to the rear of the bunker to engage the enemy downslope with their M1 rifles.

The North Korean machine gunner slumped over, dead from the grenade blast, but the assistant gunner on the opposite side hastily swung the gun around, spraying the bunker with bullets. Perkins immediately worked to the opposite side, placing the machine gunner into a crossfire. "Now!" Jack hollered, and Perkins and Jack engaged the exposed machine gunner, killing the man with a shot through his neck. Then, with the machine gun silenced, Jack worked cautiously to the trench.

"Perkins, cover me!" Jack hollered.

"I'm fuggin hit," Perkins called back.

"How bad?" Jack screamed, running to check on Perkins, but Perkins was already dead, his hands cradling his intestines.

•   •   •

The first and 2nd Platoons carried their KIA and wounded down the ridgeline to a clump of felled pine trees. The attack upon the bunkers consumed just fifty minutes, but it killed four Americans and wounded another four seriously. Lieutenant Somerset set up a makeshift aid station. Corporal Pedro Ramirez, the tough little medic, joined the dead an hour later from his gunshot wounds.

The fighting now clamped down viciously in thunderous volleys of machine gun fire. Lieutenant Colonel Jones's assault ground into the Goose's Neck, becoming closer to the North Korean's frontal positions. Lieutenant Somerset pulled the surviving men together, pointing to their next objective—the crest of the Rat via its western flank, another half mile up the ridgeline.

"Okay, we will attack the ridgeline to the summit. The battalion's pushing through the Goose right now. Keep pressing forward no matter how heavy the enemy's fire becomes."

The men lay on the dirt or rested upon their knees, just wanting to go the fuck home but thinking only of their survival, meaning every damned gook between them and the Rat's summit needed killing.

"There are twenty-eight left," the lieutenant hollered. "I will take 2nd Platoon and lead the attacking team up the ridgeline. Pierce will take what's left of 1st and provide fire support. I want us separated by thirty yards."

The attack proceeded up the ridgeline, Lieutenant Somerset in the lead. The assault team pushed forward under the cover of the support team, and then the support team went ahead under the cover of the attacking team. Pushing and covering, pushing and covering, moving steadily towards the killing until they reached the false summit at the southwestern end of the ridgeline. It was just 0830. The men awoke only five-and-a-half hours earlier—five-and-a-half hours that killed Perkins, Fishman, Hesse, Dickson, and Ramirez.

Somerset stopped the men under the cover of a rock outcrop to direct the final maneuver. Numerous enemy foxholes littered the area; chewed-up North Korean cigarette butts, trash, fire pits, and human waste scattered about, but no enemy was in the immediate vicinity. Instead, the enemy concentrated every available gun on Colonel Jones's frontal assault teams, oblivious to the flanking maneuver pressing in upon them.

Beyond Somerset's position, the ridgeline rose sharply to a rocky plateau. Then it fell again before rising to the summit a quarter mile upslope, where several enemy soldiers moved about, supplying ammo to machine gunners ripping into the American advance. Beyond the mountain's summit, brewing at the ugly outer edge of the horizon, the sky became dark, heavy, and wicked-looking. The outer bands of Typhoon Samantha raced towards the Rat—dense, towering, vertical cumulonimbus clouds swirling in malicious circles, ready to slap the beast in the face.

Somerset organized the fire support and attack teams behind the rock escarpment. "Take water, extra ammo in your bandoliers, and check your weapons before we push."

The men drank greedily from their canteens, not knowing if it might be their last water in this world. "Same as before, push hard and fast to that plateau," the lieutenant said, pointing his balsa swagger stick to uneven topography marked by three giant boulders one hundred fifty feet from the summit. "Second Platoon will work up to those three boulders and then cover 1st Platoon's advance. You guys ready?"

The men clutched their weapons tightly, some saying their final farewells.

Under the protection of the fire support team, the attacking team sprinted up the ridgeline to the boulders, establishing a defensive position protecting the support team's advance.

The men lay face down on the rough raw back of the Rat, now just one hundred fifty feet from its summit. Some studied its peak, while others simply prayed for their lives. They all breathed hard, sweating salty muck from every pore of their bodies. The suffocating heat and humidity from the approaching typhoon choked their lungs, and their hearts pounded violently, knotting their throats with terror. An unexplainable rush of excitement hurried their breathing. The summit looked blown to hell, ugly up there, and they detested its sight, where trees no longer existed, its sacredness betrayed—ripped away by steel and armament. It existed simply to give one warring army an advantage over the other. The wind now blew violently. It carried the stench of rotting, maggot-infested bodies decaying in the devilish humidity. So terribly inhumane and equally humane was the scene, its blasphemous soul peering upon them, snarling in disgust.

Jack listened to the growl of the violent back-and-forth fighting near the summit, grasping the solid black walnut stalk and the stainless-steel barrel of the M1 with his sweating palms, wrapping his fingers around the rifle with all his strength. Then he lost his whereabouts momentarily, hallucinating he was in the Goose's Neck with the battalion, and its battle unfolded before his eyes. First, he saw it advancing cautiously up the Rat in their attack and support formations. Then entrenched enemy soldiers met them with burning hot Russian lead bullets, mortars, and grenades—blowing them to pieces. "Christ, they must be dying!" he frantically hollered, but like a nightmare, only his ears could hear his cries. Robert, Big Bill Burns, Walter Abbott, Mike Murphy, and the other boys were in the Goose's Neck, and Perkins was already dead! Jack became overcome by delirium and sick in his stomach. Waves of adrenaline washed over him, fueling an uncontrollable panic that got his heart racing. *I gotta go help 'em, I gotta go help 'em, I gotta fucking help 'em,* raced through his mind. But the only way to help was to get to the summit and kill as many gooks as possible before they butchered his friends.

Somerset placed his men into position for the attack, with each soldier fifteen feet behind the man in front. Sergeant Frank Johnson, a solidly built balding alcoholic and combat veteran of New Guinea and the Philippines, readied his M1 and two pineapple grenades. "Lieutenant, let me lead the attack; I wanna be first to shoot the motherfuckers," he volunteered.

"No, Pierce will lead the charge. He's fast and in the best shape. Johnson, you take the middle of the formation, and I'll go last. Okay, the rest follow Pierce, fifteen feet apart."

Jack saw his father's and mother's faces flash before his eyes. Then he and Michiko beneath the shade of the big sprawling tree at the temple grounds in Kamakura. And like a dream, his legs churned violently forward, running, running, running uncontrollably towards the summit. Four others followed, each trooper trying to keep fifteen feet behind the man in front, charging bayonets pointing the way, but Jack was now well ahead of his men, running madly, alone. He heard the *crack, crack, crack* from a machine gun, but kept dashing upslope. A North Korean's short, well-placed bursts hit the fourth and fifth man charging—Pfc. Michaelson in the chest and Corporal Burns in the forehead—who then crumpled lifeless to the dirt. Somerset and

Johnson found the North Korean machine gunner and got him with their M1s.

The men next in line immediately froze up, as if they were heading to the firing squad, a suicide mission.

"Go, goddammit!" Johnson hollered.

And the next man in line charged, and then the next, and the next, fifteen feet apart, some screaming obscenities, until a North Korean gun struck Pfc. Richard Wash in the right foot and thigh. "The gooks got me!" And Walsh crumpled onto Somerset, and the lieutenant pulled him to safety.

Meanwhile, Jack reached the final steep slope below the summit when Sergeant Johnson charged upslope. Jack lay pressed to the earth, panting, trying to catch his breath and clear his mind for his next move. Then, finally, he counted to three and scrambled up the remaining fifty feet of loose rocky shale to a ledge where he could look over at the enemy-occupied terrain on the reverse slope. Three North Koreans sat in a trench encircling their machine gun, firing upon the Americans attacking through the Goose's Neck—*crack, crack!*

The enemy machine gunners lay twenty yards downslope from Jack, unaware that Americans were attacking from the rear. Jack looked over his right shoulder, seeing Johnson and the other men struggling up the last fifty feet, flushed and baffled, surprised they'd live to see the top of the Rat.

Jack ripped the pin from a grenade and tossed it onto the gunners' downslope. He immediately turned left, noticing Johnson's hip firing his M1 Rifle into another machine gun crew to the right before a bullet buckled the World War Two veteran. The bald-headed Sergeant Johnson rolled his damaged body down the slope, yelling encouragement to the men. "Go kill the motherfuckers!"

A savage gun battle ensued as the rest of the attack squad reached the crest and engaged the enemy with automatic weapons and grenades. The men created a firing line overlooking the opposite slope. Lying pressed to the ground, they were within shouting distance of the enemy, hearing the North Koreans barking orders and blowing terrifying whistles. Burp guns hit three men within minutes, and they retreated down the slope where Corporal Lenny Goodman, a twenty-year-old medic from Lincoln, Nebraska, cared for the wounded.

Lieutenant Somerset reached the fighting a few minutes after the first burst of activity and took over the attack. "Conserve your goddamned ammo!" he hollered as he ran along the ridgeline, assembling a coordinated assault. "Get that seventy-five-millimeter recoilless on that fuggin bunker!" The recoilless team responded with two deadly rockets, silencing a machine gun.

A few seconds later, a burst of fire from an enemy burp gun came from the left flank. Jack tossed a grenade just as a shot winged by his left ear. The grenade burst killed the burp gunner, but two other North Koreans ran up the slope, hip-firing at the Americans. Somerset shot one in the stomach with his M1 rifle, and the other crumpled over dead, taking a burst of light machine gun fire.

Jack then started back along the line of riflemen, plugging holes as soldiers became KIA or injured. "Benson and Schmidt, pull ammo from the dead and wounded and distribute it!" he bellowed. The close-in fighting continued, and enemy machine guns redirected their fire away from the Goose's Neck to engage the flanking attack.

Private Perry Simon, a shy-looking nineteen-year-old Jewish kid from Baltimore, Maryland, pulled a grenade at the far right of the line. "There's a mortar crew down there!" he shouted, then tossed the grenade over onto the enemy crew. "That got the sons of bitches!" he hollered before a burst upslope struck him in the back, killing him instantly. Eugene turned his M1 upslope and filled the North Korean full of bullets.

Jack worked back along the line, checking on the men. On the far-left side, Pfc. Hideo Tamura, a rugged, leathery-skinned pineapple farmer from Maui, Hawaii, ran down the ridge, blood spilling over his face from a shrapnel wound. A grenade fragment had cut into his scalp like a lawnmower, leaving a four-inch hairless bloody scrape, and the cut turned his face and neck red. Jack wiped away the blood, bandaged him, and ordered him back on the line. Tamura grinned and sprinted back, engaging the enemy.

Private Lysander Carter fired a BAR onto an enemy machine gunner from the middle of the line. Then, suddenly standing, he hip-fired downslope, hollering for ammo and taunting the enemy, "Come on up, you gooks, and fight like men!"

"Get down on the ground, Carter!" Jack hollered, but Carter screamed, "The fuggin gooks are gonna pay for it!" Carter's good friend, Private Frank Anderson, lay dead, turning the earth red just twenty feet away.

Then an enemy soldier jumped from the opposite side of the ridge, landing on top of Jack, who was stripping a dead man's ammo. The North Korean grabbed Jack by the waist, trying to wrestle him to the ground. Carter charged down the slope, seeing the commotion, screaming profanities at the North Korean. Startled by the screaming, the North Korean turned to see the solid wood butt of Carter's BAR slamming into the side of his head. Carter grabbed ammo from Jack and ran back to the firing line. The back-and-forth fighting continued with more North Koreans running up the ridgeline to meet the flanking attack, but 1st and 2nd repulsed them with heavy automatic rifle fire, grenades, and hand-to-hand combat.

Meanwhile, Lieutenant Somerset repositioned the remaining men to a saddle with a strategic view of the enemy's main firing line, about three hundred feet downslope of the summit. He assigned half the troopers to cover the ridgeline and Jack and the rest to cover the southern flank as the North Koreans attempted to advance upslope to counter the flanking maneuver.

It was now 1030, and from the summit, it seemed that the whole of the Pusan Perimeter erupted into one large firefight. First and 2nd Platoons tossed grenades and fired their weapons downslope at the North Koreans. Meanwhile, the battalion pushed savagely through the Goose's Neck, firing upslope at the entrenched enemy, and the North Koreans fired in both directions. And downslope, Major Johnson lobbed artillery onto the main line of resistance and high over the Rat onto the reverse slope to keep the North Koreans in reserve pinned down. And miles away, the 24th and 25th Divisions engaged the enemy's 6th and 7th Divisions along the Naktong River, making savage thrusts with heavy artillery and Sherman tanks. The offensive bent the North Korean main line of resistance, drawing enemy soldiers from the Rat to reinforce its flank from envelopment.

Jack arranged his team into a firing line overlooking the Goose's Neck and the North Koreans, sandwiched between them and the advancing battalion. He set up a light machine gun and a mortar squad and engaged the North Koreans from their rear. He watched the battalion as it slugged its way upslope, engaging the enemy in a frontal assault with fixed bayonets. The enemy met their charges with machine guns, stick grenades, burp guns, and rifles. Men fell everywhere, dead and injured. Soldiers rendered aid, and snipers and machine gunners picked them off. A cavalcade of smoke, noise, confusion, and blood consumed the battlefield. A sinister scene from the battle of Gettysburg emerged—and then the American assault suddenly stopped.

Seconds later, a succession of giant, beastly lion roars enveloped the entire mountain. Then, traveling at five thousand miles per hour, three barrages of Major Johnson's one-hundred-fifty-five-millimeter howitzer shells screamed up the Rat in a monstrous howl, exploding squarely into the North Korean's fortifications.

The earth shook for minutes, and the Rat belched smoke, dust, rock, blood, and splintered bone. The battalion charged the bunkers with bayonets, shooting from the hip and tossing grenades. Hundreds of North Koreans died in their holes and bunkers. Dozens of others abandoned their positions, and the 1st and 2nd Platoon cut them down from the rear. Jack killed a dozen with his M1—*crack, crack, crack.*

•   •   •

At 1400, the battalion wrested Hill 257 from the North Koreans. The men removed the dead enemy soldiers from their holes and jumped inside. One man leaped into a foxhole to grab a dead gook, and the dead man shot him in the face with a pistol. The discharge ripped off his left cheek. After that, the men's bayonets always confirmed that the North Koreans were dead before taking ownership of their holes.

Colonel Jones ordered Easy Company to remain on the summit and hold the position until the typhoon passed. He called Baker and Charlie Companies off the mountain. The reinforcements from Sasebo began trickling into battalion headquarters. The North Koreans killed fifty-five soldiers from Abel, Baker, Charlie, and the three platoons of Easy Company assaulting through the Goose's Neck, and three times as many were casualties. Machine gun fire killed Big Bill Burns in the Goose's Neck. Robert survived the assault. Easy Company's 1st and 2nd Platoons lost eight more men KIA, pushing to the summit from the western flank. Snakey Frank Conner's right leg was blown off just above the knee, and he was carried off the mountain on a stretcher, screaming profanities. Stretcher-bearers carried away the remaining dead and wounded. Easy Company remained at the summit at just fifty percent of its original strength.

By 1600, Easy Company was alone. Lieutenant Somerset established a defensive line in the shape of a banana moon to cover the approach routes from the northern and western flanks. He placed light machine guns in the center of the line and at the edges to provide interlocking fields of fire and claymore mines within the approach routes. An eighty-one-millimeter mortar squad was on the opposite slope to shell enemy counterattacks. Major Johnson's artillery was on standby for support, and a quick reactionary force was emplaced below the Goose's Neck if needed.

Rain from the approaching typhoon began to fall steadily at 1700. The wind blew harshly across the summit with fifty-mile-per-hour winds, making the soldiers shiver in their drenched uniforms. The men retreated to their holes and tried to stay warm by wrapping themselves tightly in their rubbery ponchos. By 1900, darkness overcame the summit, and the men witnessed brilliant bursts of white lightning toward the storm's center, exploding fantastically in all directions.

By 2000, it became pitch-black, except for thunderous bolts of lightning miles away over the Pacific Ocean. The prior evening, the 1st and 2nd Platoons just arrived in darkness to their final bivouac on the unscarred western flank. They shared whiskey and sang songs that night, still hurting from Captain Carlson and Pfc. Manley's deaths. Jack could still taste the whiskey on his breath when he awoke before sunrise. Five-and-a-half hours later, not even before 0900, Perkins was dead; by now, he'd been dead for over twelve hours.

"Twelve fuggin hours ago, Perkins was alive—still a warm, breathing, living human being just like the rest of us, talkin', laughin', and dreamin'," Jack said to Eugene, feeling sick with sadness. Eugene said nothing, but Jack could hear him sobbing lightly in the rain.

The two men pulled rations from their packs and popped the tins open, trying fruitlessly to keep the rain from spilling into the cold beef stew and wetting the hardtack biscuits. "Some fuggin victory celebration we're havin'," Eugene said with a cracking voice, his legs submerged to his calves in brown, muddy water. "The fuggin foxhole's gonna be overtopped if it keeps raining like this!"

"I'm gonna check on the other men," Jack said.

"Alright, sergeant, but be careful out there," Eugene replied. "Around here, you don't want to walk in the wrong direction."

Jack moved low to the ground, clutching an M1 rifle as he crept from hole to hole. Some men had already abandoned their foxholes to the rising waters and were sitting topside wrapped tightly in their ponchos, one man on watch and the other lying coiled, sleeping in the mud, rain, and wind.

"Our hole is nearly full of water, sergeant; we can't sleep like that."

"You're not supposed to be sleepin', goddammit! So, get your ass back in your foxhole until it's your turn to rest."

"Yes, sir!" And the man rolled back into the muddy hole already filled to his waist.

The wind blew so viciously that Jack thought his poncho might fly from his body at any moment, and at times, he had to crawl to find his way to each foxhole. Finally, after visiting the six men assigned to his squad, he made his way back, where Eugene squatted in the water, sheltering a mud-streaked cigarette.

"You chargin' rent," Jack chuckled, looking down at Eugene, who looked like a bedraggled 1840s New Bedford seaman, dripping with rain and covered by a matted red beard.

"It'll cost you," he said with a sallow grin and red-streaked eyes from his sadness.

"After that cigarette, take your rest. Most of the men are sleeping outside their holes. Then, at 0000, you can have the mansion back," Jack said.

"That's awfully kind of you," Eugene said as he took a last puff of the tasty tobacco, flicking the butt into the stormy darkness. Five minutes later, Eugene lay wrapped tight as a Polish sausage and snoring louder than the angry growl of Typhoon Samantha.

Jack stood in the flooded foxhole and peered into the stormy darkness, with his M1 pointing north like a magnetic compass. The night before, the hole had been dry and occupied by North Koreans. Today, those North Koreans were dead, lying exposed upon the Rat, beastly little rodents, and lazy black flies consuming their lifeless bodies. Perkins was also KIA, Big Bill Burns, too, and Snakey Frank Connors, that kooky son of a bitch, had his right leg blown off just above the knee.

Jack looked outside the foxhole into an unending sea of darkness and thought of Perkins. He smiled, remembering his young, innocent, cowboy face, and he thought over the details of the night when Perkins lost his virginity to Naoko-san, the curvy little Ojo-san whore. "*Holy shit,*" Perkins had said that night more than a year before. "*Look, look, Eugene, do ya see that pretty little Ojo-san? Isn't she somethin' to look at? Goddammit, I do think she wants me, boys. What do you think? For shit-sake, boys, look at her!*" His facial expression melted from tough-faced cattleman to pink flamingo virgin.

Jack felt hot, buttery tears rolling down his cheeks, even as the wind and rain tried to rip them away. He gripped the side of the foxhole, feeling cold, sticky mud squeezing thick and pasty between the palms of his hands, and he began to sob. He must have wept for at least an hour until he was too tired to cry anymore. "*So, where is the common sense in all of this?*" he said angrily, remembering his father's words. "*And for what, Dad? Is this to be our goddamned punishment?*"

Eugene still snored like a boar just a few feet away. The wind and rain had not abated, the foxhole was now full of chilly, dirty brown water, and the stainless-steel barrel of the M1 pointed north toward the North Koreans. *No, it's not just a bad fuckin' dream*, he thought inconsolably. *I am on the Rat, and the Rat is real, and Perkins is dead.*

Jesus, he questioned, *why me? Why us? Why Perkins? But thank God Perkins met that little Ojo-san whore.* "No man should die a virgin," he said to himself, speaking into the thrashing wind and rain. "*She don't use the money on herself; she gives it all to her family*," Perkins had explained to justify his feelings, despite her penchant for wearing fancy new dresses and painting her face with expensive western makeup. Jack chuckled, still crying, remembering how Perkins had once mumbled to him in drunkenness. "*I never did think I could love a gal more than Daniel Boone, but I swear to ya, Jack, I think I love Naoko more than my damned dog*," he had said, and he sincerely meant it!

Jack felt a little better when he considered that at least Perkins had died brave—a true fuggin hero. And that at least he'd gotten to travel to Japan, had tried Japanese food even if he didn't much like it, and had lived on that rustic Wyoming cattle ranch where he'd seen those granite mountains all lit up in "Indian colors." He'd gotten to get drunk on good Kentucky whiskey, gotten himself laid, and fallen in love. He'd experienced that big beautiful sunrise on the top of Mount Fuji...and that was the way it went on the summit of the Rat—peering into the darkness, feeling cold, wet, and sad—repeating these things to himself again, again, and again until he felt a hand on his shoulder. "It's my watch, Jack. You alright?"

"Yeah, I just couldn't stop thinking 'bout Perkins, that's all."

"Yeah," Eugene said, "I fuggin dreamed him during my sleep."

They patted each other on the shoulder—knowing—and then Jack wrapped himself tight as a Polish sausage and fell asleep in the howling wind and rain. It was already past 0030.

•   •   •

The sharp, terrifying shriek of blowing whistles cut through the stormy darkness like a slap in the face. It was exactly 0130. The men didn't want to believe it would happen, not in this fuggin storm; the gooks were supposed to be bogged down in the mud on the mountain's north side. All along the line, men started screaming, "The gooks are coming! The gooks are coming!"

Lieutenant Somerset called for illumination rounds, flares, mortars, and the support of the quick reaction force. The men fired their weapons at hundreds of eerie ghosts swarming across what looked like a fantastic lunar landscape blanketed by sideways rain and howling winds. Jarred awake by the commotion, Jack lay still for a brief second, trying to confirm that he wasn't in a nightmare, but the ferocious barking of Eugene pulling hard against the M1's trigger snapped him into action.

"For heaven's sake, what the hell's going on?" he yelled to Eugene as he leaped inside the watery coffin and fired an M1 rifle.

"The North Koreans blew whistles. They are everywhere, sergeant!"

"Shit," Jack hollered as several claymore mines detonated, skillfully severing legs from some unlucky North Korean attackers.

All along the narrow gray line, Jack could see muzzle flashes and tracers flying up and down the mountain as the battle boiled over into a fury of small-arms fire. "The first wave is meant to extinguish our ammo. The second will pave a trail of dead gook bodies and ammo, which the slimy bastards will use in their third wave to overrun our positions. So only shoot when they get close!" Jack shouted to Eugene, and then he hollered it again to the squad, "Only shoot when they get close!" hoping the men could hear his order above the raging bullets, exploding lightning, wind, and rain.

The back-and-forth firing thundered on, and Jack saw that some foxholes had gone dark along the line. "The fucking gooks have gotten into the lines!" he yelled to Eugene. "Toss grenades!"

Eugene and Jack each tossed a grenade down the slope. The explosions lit the battlefield directly to their front, exposing a half-dozen enemy soldiers crawling on their bellies in the torrential wind and rain, not more than twenty feet away. Eugene and Jack turned their M1s on the incoming enemy and killed them in sharp, semiautomatic bursts.

Meanwhile, Jack heard a rising cacophony of inhumane screams along the line, discerning that these soldiers were engaged in desperate hand-to-hand combat with the enemy.

"Sergeant, I can't sit here any longer and listen to that screaming, I'm going to see if I can help them," Eugene said.

"Be damned careful and fast about it!" Jack yelled. Eugene jumped from the hole and headed up the line toward the screaming. Just one soldier occupied the first foxhole he encountered. "Hey, Ward, it's me, Eugene. I'm going up the line to help. Where's Frank Carson?"

"Carson went up to have a look around."

"Okay, be careful! And the sergeant has ordered only shooting when you see them; conserve your ammo!"

Pfc. Danny Ward shouted out in defiance, "Come and get me, you fuggin gooks!" and sprayed a clip of bullets at several shadowy figures carrying burp guns.

Eugene continued to move in a low crouch towards the screaming. He carried the M1 rifle with a full clip of ammunition and bayonet fixed, oddly comforting in the near-total blackness.

The screams grew louder now, and he could hear the unmistakable cries of Thunderbolt Willie, but he still couldn't see him. So, he kept moving cautiously forward, hunching low to the ground like a prowling gray wolf, when Major Johnson fired three illumination rounds that exploded high above the Rat. The battlefield suddenly became illuminated in a sickly, pale gray glow. Eugene found himself merely forty feet from Thunderbolt Willie, crying out in animalistic screams of rage and terror, fighting for his life as he tried desperately to fend off two North Korean attackers. One had mounted himself atop Willie's back, striking the side of his head with his bare fist, and the other positioned himself to his front, thrusting a bayonet at the black soldier's chest. Pfc. Lysander Carter lay dead next to the hole with a gunshot to the back of the head.

Frank Carson was lying in the mud unnoticed behind a fallen tree, just ten feet from Willie, watching the spectacle unfold. He pointed his M1 Rifle at the unsuspecting North Korean attempting to stab Thunderbolt, and between Carson's teeth rested the six-inch switchblade knife, waiting for Thunderbolt Willie to get killed.

The North Korean thrust his bayonet deep into Thunderbolt's chest before Eugene could raise his rifle to save Willie's life. The bugler let out a horrific scream, louder and more sorrowful than any Bourbon Street toot that had passed through the brass instrument, and then he fell forward, dead, at just nineteen years old. Frank Carson wasted no time shooting the North Korean with the bayonet, and then he leaped forward like a panther at the other North Korean, and in less than three seconds, the man lay dead with Frank Carson's knife stuck into his neck.

Afterward, Carson looked up, startled to see Eugene studying the carnage in disbelief. A sinister smile formed across his ugly face, and he said to Eugene, "You seen what happened?"

"I saw it all. You let Thunderbolt get killed, you bastard!"

"Fuggin good for nothin' niggers and gooks; it serves 'em both right. Don't it?"

Eugene lifted his M1 Rifle, pointing it directly between Frank Carson's beady eyes. "You son of a bitch, you'll pay for this, Carson!" he shouted with hatred. "I don't have time for killin' you now, but I'll get you for this!"

Eugene backed slowly away from Carson, pointing his rifle at his chest until Carson was no longer visible in the vicious rain and darkness. By the time he reached his foxhole, the Americans had taken control of the fight for the line. Well-placed artillery, mortar barrages, and the quick reactionary force had decimated the third wave of attackers, and fierce interlocking fields of fire cut down the North Korean stragglers.

The first light came at 0530. The wind and rain had died down, and everybody stood about in the mud, exhausted, smoking cigarettes and trying to stay warm in their rain-soaked fatigues. North Korean dead littered the battlefield. The new American dead were stacked in a neat row, waiting for litter bearers. Eleven additional men died during the nighttime fighting, and another twenty were wounded. Four men, including Thunderbolt Willie, were killed in hand-to-hand combat.

Jack and Eugene walked up the line, checking on the men. At Privates Ward and Carson's hole, Jack brandished his M1 rifle and pointed it at Frank Carson's chest. "Drop your fuggin weapon and empty your pockets," he demanded. "Eugene, check him for knives."

"Yes, sir," Eugene said, and he patted Carson down and checked deep inside his right foot, where he found the bloodstained switchblade knife used to kill the North Korean.

"Good," Jack said. "Now, Carson, get your ass out of that hole and over to that clearing," he growled, pointing to an area free of debris, dead bodies, and bomb craters.

The other surviving men of the platoon observed the commotion, forming a loose circle around the clearing. "Eugene, tell the men what you saw last night," Jack ordered, pointing his gun at Frank Carson's chest.

"Frank Carson allowed gooks to kill Thunderbolt last night, and he didn't do a damned thing to stop it. I saw it with my own fuggin eyes."

"Now listen up!" Jack hollered. "I will report Carson to Lieutenant Somerset, and I'll do everything possible to ensure that Frank Carson is court-martialed for Willie's killing."

"It's my word against Eugene's," Frank Carson snarled back. "You can't prove nothin' against me! There was only the two of us up there."

"Is that so, Frank?" Jack said. "Your life will be safer in the stockade than in this platoon. If you remain in Easy Company, you won't live through this war."

"Send the bastard over the top!" a soldier hollered, wanting Carson to be forced down the north side of the Rat into the North Korean positions.

"Yeah, leave him for the gooks," several others hollered.

"Men, I'm going up to the CP to report the incident to Lieutenant Somerset. Watch over Carson while I'm gone," Jack said, and then he turned and walked up the line.

The men formed a tighter circle, with Frank standing small and terrified in its center.

"Now's your chance to kill the only witness, Carson," Eugene said savagely, and he entered the circle to face off with the murderer. "You're a rat, Carson! You let Willie get stabbed, and you didn't do a damned thing about it. I should've killed you then, but I'll teach you a lesson—you motherfucker!"

The circle became wider to let the two men have room to maneuver.

"With knives, you nigger lover!" Frank Carson screamed like a maniac.

"With knuckles," Eugene responded calmly. "You deserve my fuggin knuckles bustin' up your ugly face!"

The two men circled each other slowly, fawning jabs and takedowns. Thick, long red hair and an unruly seaman's red beard covered Eugene's face, and he was skinny, wiry, firmly sewn with muscle, and pasted in heavy mud, and if you hadn't known him, you might have thought he was an alcoholic and derelict. But everything about Frank Carson looked mean—his face, tattoos, broken teeth, short stubby arms, and especially his eyes. He looked like the murderer that he was.

They circled like roosters in a cage, waiting for an opportunity to sink their silver claws into the other's neck for the kill. Carson moved first by thrusting himself forward with both fists flailing in a wild, brutal attack at Eugene's face. Eugene deftly stepped to the right of Frank Carson's thrust and hit him with a left-handed counter punch and three blinding rights—the counterstrike smashing into his left eye, the second his right cheek, and the third and fourth finding their mark in the front of his mouth. The sound of Eugene's big round knuckles colliding savagely against bone and teeth was like fresh eggs hitting the side of a concrete building.

Afterward, Frank Carson was placed with the rest of the casualties upon a stretcher and carried off the mountain, where medics treated him for a concussion, a broken eye socket, and six stitches to his lower lip. Later, he would be court-martialed for failing to render assistance in the face of an enemy attack.

The next day, a company of newly arrived men from the division reinforced the battalion. Two days later, the generals abandoned Rat Mountain to North Korean stragglers. Finally, General Douglas MacArthur's landing of Marine and Army forces at Inchon decapitated the North Korean advance. On September 16, 1950, the 8th Army broke out from the Pusan Perimeter, attacking north to Seoul and across the 38th Parallel to Pyongyang and the Chosin Reservoir.

CHAPTER EIGHT
Reflections

I'd spent three weeks with Jack in that pension in March 2003 before returning to Hanoi. Now, telling this story, I recall one night upon my return, an evening I find relevant to the events portrayed here. It was a pleasantly warm Friday evening a week after my arrival. Lan and I leisurely strolled around Hoan Kiem Lake. We weren't the only lovers holding hands; many held hands beneath the Loc Vung trees, which encircle the waters in an envelope of towering greenery. Still, others sat on benches, arms entwined tightly around one another, and the more adventurous kissed, enjoying sparkling night lights reflecting off the lake. I thought, *how much more expressive had this place become since my first trip to Hanoi, a two-week junket from Tokyo in '98, when brownouts were a nightly occurrence.*

Many beautiful women walked the lake that pleasant evening. First a Vietnamese, perhaps twenty-five, with her hair wild black a frizzy—long, unruly, and her cheekbones pronounced, and her spoke of the hill tribes—perhaps the Hmong or Red Dao nea thought. There was also a French woman conversing in that language, walking alongside a rangy-looking Frenchman red beard and wearing a white beanie cap with scented hanging lazily about his neck. The French woman's twenty-four karat gold, and this color matche matched her skin, and she looked slim and sex immediately. Then there was a young Vietnamese couple at a lakeside café, their table close to ours, sipping beer and eating spring rolls overflowing with basil, mint, and cilantro. They resembled Broadway actors, wearing costumes that reminded me of the Parisian Bohemian, beautiful and eloquent. Her face, exquisite in its playfulness, possessed the color of English bath soap, and she had a slender waist, but her breasts were shapely, and I enjoyed the nudge of her nipples against her blouse. He was equally attractive, wearing a silk shirt and a pair of black slacks and smoking a cigarette, projecting strength and confidence in himself and the new Vietnam.

We enjoyed the evening's breeze, sipping beer at this lakeside table, when Lan asked, "Why do you love to stare at the women?"

Taken aback, I responded, "I also love staring at the mountains, sea, and sunsets. I don't tire of looking at beautiful subjects and find beautiful women most enjoyable."

"But don't you find I am also beautiful?" she asked, looking me in the eyes.

"Of course. I often stare at you when you don't know."

"I like that you stare at me," she said, smiling smartly. "But I don't like you when you stare at other women."

"I'm a visual person," I said lamely. "Besides, I thought you'd understand being a visual person yourself. Are we artists not always aware of our surroundings? Don't we need to be inspired to paint, photograph, or write about our subjects?"

"I want to be your subject," she said, no longer smiling, her eyes cold and piercing. "I don't want to walk around the lake holding hands with a stranger who is not there."

"I'm sorry, Lan," I said, taking her hand and examining its delicate features. "If I had a single painting, it would be your eyes, cheeks, nose, and a wisp of your hair, mysterious like an early morning fog rising from the valley floor at Mai Chau in early spring."

She said, "You are very romantic," and added, "when you want to be."

We left the café and walked to the west end of the lake to the Hanoi Opera House, where we sat in oversized lounge chairs, listening to a trio play a perfect rendition of Oscar Peterson. The jazz, the warming effect of a martini, the luxurious lounge chairs, and Lan's snug-fitting black skirt made me hungry and restless. I took my hand and slid it behind her back. She snuggled closer and whispered, "I think you want to relax down there."

That evening, after making love and Lan lying naked, sleeping peacefully under the old metal fan's twirling blades, I thought about what she'd said at the café: "I want to be your subject." *But, good gracious,* I thought, *what have you gotten yourself into, Dane?*

I'd had many lovers—at least six deserving of a frame on a wall: a blonde and blue-eyed nurse at the University of Washington with a voracious appetite for sexual exploration and art; an electric Japanese woman in Tokyo, Sumiko, with short spiked hair, an erotic figure, and a stint as an eccentric dancer. She'd later become a successful attorney, and I'd almost married her before it became too late for me. Also, somewhere in there, I'd lived with a free-spirit Turkish hippie chick in Seattle. She had olive-colored eyes the size of flying saucers and big bouncy breasts she'd smother my face in until I begged for air. Then, trekking Nepal's Annapurna Circuit, another Japanese woman, a deer-like backpacker who adorned herself in Tibetan jewelry, joined me for a blissful three months in India. And finally, in this long list of six, a Jewish American bisexual lesbian. Hannah insisted I take part in lesbian threesomes until "we" became pregnant, and she suffered a nervous breakdown. And the only thing in common was that no relationship lasted more than a year—three hundred sixty-five days— the magic number.

It was like a sickness, this nauseous feeling burrowing deeply into my gut, weighing me down emotionally. "*I want to be your subject.*"

I'd been with Lan for seven months—adored every moment, never tiring of her beauty, bright, pesky, artistic personality, and an honest, unburdened soul. But she was not like me; she didn't have a bunch of frames on the wall.

I slipped, sweating and lizard-like, from the bed, careful not to wake her, donned khaki shorts, and headed straight for the freezer for three solid ice cubes, a slice of lime, and two shots of Bombay Sapphire London Dry Gin. From the verandah, the streets of the Old Quarter were silent. *My favorite time of night*, I thought, and a half-moon settled low over the Quarter so that the old, corrugated metal and red-tiled roofing and fading two- and three-story Chinese and French-inspired facades were visible.

At one far end of Hang Ga Street, I could see a couple of rickety old cyclos and their drivers sleeping inside—caps covering their faces. At the other end, a graying Vietnamese lady wearing black pajamas and a conical hat shuffled up the street in my direction. I noticed she carried two baskets full of lychee, papaya, and rambutan from a bamboo milkmaid's pole twice as wide as she was tall. I imagined this woman in her mid-twenties during the 1972 Christmas bombings of Hanoi, Nixon's Operation Linebacker. And perhaps she had a husband who fought the Americans, my father's generation of men, and he'd died in the war, and now she shuffled along as a childless widow fending for herself.

I could hear birds chirping in the thick drooping canopy trees, a dramatic feature of the Old Quarter. Stray cats and the occasional shaggy dog milled about, searching for scraps of discarded food. And giant gray alley rats, masters of the dark, the Old Quarter's rats—intelligent and shrewd—organized like Little Italy's Mafia bosses.

My brain began to melt from the gin. The gray-haired Vietnamese fruit lady came shuffling by the terrace. I said, "*Bạn là một người phụ nữ xinh đẹp*," meaning, "You are a beautiful woman." She stopped and peered up, squinting as if she'd heard a ghost, and then she smiled, exposing betel nut-stained teeth. "*Bạn là một người mù và ngu ngốc*," she said, meaning, "You are a blind and foolish man."

I laughed and replied, "*Tôi là một người đàn ông ngốc nghếch, nhưng tôi có thể nhìn thấy cũng như một con cú đêm*," or, "I am a foolish man, but I can see as well as a night owl."

The vegetable seller, once a beautiful woman with silken black hair, pearly white teeth, and the lingering memories of her lovers, smiled and patted her heart. I returned her smile and patted my own, and she disappeared into the night.

I slumped into my wicker rocker and lifted my feet upon the verandah's tired railing. The gin tasted good and mixed well with the half-moon, the red-colored roofs, and the singing birds in the canopy trees above. I shut my eyes, feeling the evening breeze sweep my face. I thought of Jack and the old pension in Manila's Ermita district, remembering the cigarettes, the glass-beaded ashtray, the empty coffee mugs, and the deck of cards. For a long time, I played over the story Jack had told me, how he expressed his words, the inner emotions still fresh in his mind after so many years, in the way he described his memories. I tried to recall every detail of his face. The charcoal grayish-blue eyes that saw right through me, the manly contours of his jawline carpeted by rugged gray stubble, the heavy white hair neatly cropped just below his ears, the long-crooked arms and bent fingers warped by time. And I remembered him telling me over Gyoza and beer: "*You never forget their eyes.*"

I still have five more months, I thought to myself, *five months to enjoy Lan's pesky personality before she becomes the "beautiful architect from Hanoi."* I reassured myself that five months was still a very long time, and then I fell asleep. When I awoke, a light mist fell from the sky, the moon barely visible through a hue of soft milky clouds. Shopkeepers began stirring inside their houses, turning on pre-morning lights, striking matches to propane and wood-burning stoves, and making the morning's rice.

I went inside and slipped into bed. Lan's body warmed me, and I took my hand and burrowed it beneath her body, reminding me of her presence. Before sleep came, I noticed the lump in my gut—the anxiety—had passed.

•　　•　　•

During that spring and summer, I spent months researching the Korean War. I bought books, both fiction and nonfiction, highlighting the significant events. I ransacked the internet and libraries for information and watched videos of first-hand accounts from the soldiers who bravely fought there.

I read extensively about the first desperate months of the war when the Army's Occupation Japan troops were rushed from Japan to Korea to block the Communist invasion. The GIs arrived filled with hubris, believing the Communists would retire their weapons once the mighty American Army engaged. The opposite was true. In ferocious battles, the North Koreans attacked the outmanned, undersupplied, outgunned, and undertrained Americans. As a result, thousands of young GIs perished during the first two months of the war, and many more were wounded or taken prisoner.

I read about Task Force Smith, the first American force to fire at the enemy, and its costly attempt to block the North Koreans at Osan. Then I read about the deadly battles that followed: Pyongtaek, Chonan, Chochiwan, Taejon, and Chinju, where the Americans retreated and suffered severe losses; the horrific Hadong Pass ambush of the 3rd Battalion of the 29th Infantry on July 27, 1950; and the many other bloody fights at the Pusan Perimeter during the first three months of the war.

When I read about the battle for Hill 257, "Rat Mountain," my heart stopped. It spilled from the history books, just like Jack had told it. The inexorable heat, the back-and-forth battle for the summit, bloody forays through the Goose's Neck, and finally, the brilliant flanking maneuver up the westerly side of the mountain, culminating in the summit's capture. I read about the typhoon, the dangerous crossing by elements from Easy Company of Carlson's Ridge—so named for the brave captain who died there, his body never recovered. And I read about Lieutenant Somerset's decisive leadership, which the nation's president rewarded with the highest military medal, and the promotion of the tenacious Lieutenant Colonel Jones to colonel by the war's end.

Almost a year after I'd met him, I returned to the cheap pension in Manila's Ermita district. I arrived in the evening in mid-February, having taken a late afternoon flight from Hanoi to Saigon to Taipei and finally to Manila. I turned on the lights to the café, my eyes adjusting to the familiar surroundings, and walked light-footed to the teak stairs, which creaked with a comforting familiarity when I ascended to my second-floor room. The room seemed as I had remembered it: the ceiling fan, the wooden floors, the old bed with soft white sheets and neatly folded towels. I stood and looked out the window at the flickering yellow lights along Mabini Street, grabbed a towel, and walked down the hallway for a refreshingly cold shower.

Lying alone on the soft white sheets, I thought of my Vietnamese girlfriend, Lan, on our first acquaintance at Café Au Loc. I remembered her shining face walking along the tree-lined boulevard fronting the Hotel Sofitel Metropole in the French Quarter. We sat at a corner table by the street next to a bright display of pink orchids. Since that first meeting, a lot had happened in our relationship; our bond became tighter, and that tightness still made me anxious, but I no longer dwelled upon an ending.

When I awoke, I faintly heard the bustle in the pension's kitchen below. I slowly walked to the top of the stairs, gingerly halfway down, pausing to look over the café below. Jack sat at our familiar table, reading the newspaper. Maria placed a tall glass of mango juice to his right, and the glass-beaded ashtray with several butts told me he'd been there for a couple of hours.

I ordered a black Americano, walked to his table, and took a seat. "I've got the cards," he said.

"What are we playing?"

"Split." And then he lit a cigarette, shuffled the deck, and dealt the hands.

We played silently for several minutes as if we'd never stopped. Like some big intermission in the middle of a sweeping epic, the story of a man's life upturned by the pages of history, a deep and unexplainable bond had formed between us.

"I told you a lot," he said. "I've told you things I've told no one else."

"I know," I said.

"You see, that's what life is," he said, drawing upon his cigarette. "One goes to the world's grand museums, observes the great paintings, the masterpieces, sees them, and quickly forgets. Because life is not a painting, it's to be lived and experienced, day after day, in its totality—the mundane, the horrific, the heart-wrenching, the blissful, and the fun. That makes a life—enduring memories, the totality, and chaos of it all."

I looked into his bluish-gray eyes and imagined him as a young man standing atop Mount Fuji with his friends and then atop Rat Mountain a lifetime ago.

"I knew I couldn't make Michiko happy," he finally said. "I went along, but I was numb inside. Then, one spring evening, during the Hanami celebration, I couldn't see the cherry blossoms, and I suddenly realized that the blossoms don't bloom in winter. I overdrank after the war, trying to drown the hurt and my memories. So, I left her without explanation, just promising I would return."

"And did you?"

"Two years later, after I had sobered up and gotten myself together, I tried to find her. I was desperate. I couldn't think of anything else. The feelings, the memories, the guilt, and the love overwhelmed me. My pain became unbearable."

"And did you find her?" I asked him.

"I tried. I returned to Japan. I searched for her. I traveled to her village. She simply vanished."

"And that was it?"

"After all these years, she is just a dream. Sometimes, I don't even know if she was real, but I'll never forget her eyes."

CHAPTER NINE
Cherry Blossoms in Winter

I distinctly remember the emotions that overcame me when the sketchbook arrived. It came without warning, carefully wrapped in transparent plastic bubbles, *The Manila Times*, a yellow parcel envelope, and extra layers of heavy clear tape. Maria Santos, written in fancy letters in the upper left corner, and the pension's return address. I stuffed the parcel into my shoulder bag, zipped my overcoat, and donned a light woolen beanie.

In the misty fog of late winter, the ride from the Hanoi Central Post along Hoan Kiem Lake always charmed me. I liked to take it slow and draw in the flat glassy water, a flock of wild ducks, the bundled-up walkers, tai chi grannies, and the north's sharp breeze against my face. So, my bicycle meandered forward, one push at a time, and without too much effort, toward Café Au Loc. I could smell its flaky hot crusts of baking croissants and sweet French pies, roasting Dalat coffee and cinnamon dolce lattes. Oddly, the weight in my shoulder bag excited me, like the anticipation of a child's Christmas morning.

I took an outside table, comfortable in the north's chilly winter air, peeled back the warm layers of buttery croissant, sweetened it with a dab of strawberry jam, and washed it down with a hot spiced latte. I let the parcel sit on the table until I finished. Then I held it in my hands, felt its weight, peeled back the tape, and exposed its contents—a folded letter in a white unmarked envelope and a sun-faded, leather-bound sketchbook. I opened the book's inner cover and written in thick ink was Jack's full name and the date: April 1949–October 1950. He had never shown the book to me before.

I opened the white envelope and removed the letter. The words were heavy and coarsely written like he had written them after too much coffee and not enough sleep. It read:

Dear Dane,

You will receive this letter after I have departed Manila.

I have told you the details of my life, not that any man's life has more bearing than another's. On the contrary, each man's life is his gift, and he chooses his path uniquely.

You know, I never set down roots, and through my subsequent career in the special forces and the agency, I became the wayfarer my father had once dreamed of becoming. And although this life offered immense purpose and many rousing adventures, it has been lonely.

Following my service in the Korean War, I returned to Japan a very different person from the young man who left. As I told you, Michiko and I resumed our life in the little flat among the rice paddies. I secured a civilian staff job, and she continued her work on the base. Paradise is how I would describe this period—wonderful food, hot showers, a warm bed, and most importantly, no incoming artillery, perilous night patrols, blood, and guts.

During the evenings, Michiko and I loved each other to the sounds of nature until our bodies glistened with our mutual passion. Nothing is so blissful as this shared experience with someone you love. But paradise slowly turned to hell with each passing week. I carried the war on my shoulders, burdened by survivor's guilt and bitterness that my buddies died—the memories, sadness, and rage, and I turned to the bottle to suppress these feelings. Michiko knew all about this, yet she never lost her faith; she understood healing needed to occur. Unfortunately, I lost faith in myself.

I told you that cherry blossoms never bloom in winter, but I never divulged what I had meant. On the third night of the hanami festival, a warm, moonless night in March, the cherry blossoms were at their peak. Michiko, I, and a couple of her close friends secured a blanket beneath one of the grandest trees at Ueno Park. She busily spent the day making delicious bentos, and the night was serene and perfect, except that I destroyed it. Looking back on this evening, I recall that I never saw them once, the beautiful pink sakura. I only remember the anger, the drunken war stories that I hurled in their faces, the threat of smashing one young fellow's skull because he looked at my girl the wrong way, but mainly because I had been there, and he hadn't. And I remember her crying on the bus, not stopping for a second until she finally slept. A week later, I left for America with no explanation except that I would one day see her again.

I don't tell you this story for your pity or for you to feel burdened by the young men who lost their lives in Korea. Instead, I tell you this story so that you may live your life to its fullest potential, that you will seek to leave your mark and be grateful for life.

They have asked me; would you have done it differently with all you know now? How could I? I answer them. It was the defining experience that made me who I am.

I had once had a great love with beautiful eyes, and I had lost her. But I have had an abundant life and will leave it without regrets.

Your friend,

Jack Pierce

P.S. I had read years before in a rather famous American novel that fly-fishing in Burguete, Spain, is Europe's finest. I will mail you once I am there.

•   •   •

I met Johnny at the infamous Apocalypse Now bar that night, feeling especially thirsty for a drink. Johnny and I taught English together in Tokyo during the mid-Nineties. He had ventured into Hanoi during the "early days" when Westerners were trickling back into the country.

In '97, he took his first extended trip when one would stroll through the Old Quarter and around Hoan Kiem Lake and see very few tourists, except for the occasional Russians or returning Vietnam veterans.

Johnny is tall with a long bony nose, angular cheeks, a pointed jaw, and equally long arms with slender fingers. Fortunately, his lanky limbs are in proportion—and with thick black, shoulder-length wavy hair, a mustache, and a goatee—he appears strangely like a modern-day Frank Zappa.

"Fuck, man," Johnny said. "Those were the days, bro! Nobody paid attention to you—you were here, but you weren't here. I would stroll the fuckin' Quarter and be trippin' on the place—bicycles everywhere, hawkers, beggars, motor scooters, black pajamas, and conical hats. And I'll tell you, brother, the chicks in their silk ao dais could tighten your balls."

"Dude, you are such a fuckwit—hey, let's grab another round of drinks," I said. The music blared "Mojo Man" and the place quickly filled with the usual fog of cigarette smoke, hot high-heeled girls looking for a good time, and an eclectic group of Western expats, tourists, and Vietnamese hipsters.

After a long drag on a Tiger Beer, Johnny smiled and said, "I fuckin' love this place, man. I'm never bored like I was back home—that fuckin' daily routine. Here, I'm a million miles from expectations. 'Hey, Johnny,' they say, 'are you doing this or are you doing that? How much are you makin', Johnny? You gotta go, go Johnny go!' Here in the Nam, Johnny does what the fuck Johnny wants to do! This place is alive, man. Bartender, give me another beer!"

"Yeah," I said. "You just like being a foreigner. You can be in the culture, but not. You're an exotic outsider with no responsibility."

"Yes, sir, that's me. Cheers!"

"Hey, Johnny, I wanted to show you this sketchbook," I said, passing him the sketches I received that morning from Jack.

He took the book, thumbing through the pages, stopping and admiring the art. "That's some amazing sketchwork," he said. "Is this the Korean War veteran you are writing about?"

"It is, and I wanted to show you his sketches of Michiko."

"Wow, she's a stunning woman, Dane! I recall you'd said he'd lost contact with her after the war."

"He did, back in late '51. And I just can't stop thinking that Michiko might be alive, and if she is, why did she disappear when he returned to find her?"

"Are you sure you want to stir that nest? The past is the past. People and circumstances change, and someone could get hurt."

"I suppose so, but I already bought a ticket for Tokyo."

"Dude, you never leave a stone unturned, do you!"

"That's where the nuggets are found," I said, smiling.

"You may want to contact your old fling, Sumiko, and see if she'll accompany you. She could be a big help on your treasure hunt."

"I've already emailed her. She's agreed, with reservations."

"And her reservations?"

"That I ought to be careful about stirring the nest. And that we consider making a second go of it."

"Damn, I love that girl. I thought you'd marry her, Dane."

"So did I, but you know my aversion to such frivolous arrangements."

"Hey, speaking of arrangements, do you see that trio of Euro cuties? What do you say, unturned stones?"

"Go for it, bro. I'll watch."

Johnny ventured across the room to three lovely Dutch greener hippie chicks wearing T-shirts with no bras and sipping gin and tonics. Next to the most petite, I watched him glide in, a sexy brunette with rock-hard nipples and a tight round butt. Johnny looked over her shoulder and gave me a wink. He was in for the long haul.

I smiled, walked to the bar, and ordered a whiskey on the rocks. The bourbon went down smoothly with its familiar tints of smoky caramel and quickly warmed my stomach. The music blared, the cigarette smoke burned my eyes, the scene began to tire me, and I was drunk. I gave Johnny the thumbs-up, rolled the booze, and headed for the door.

I made it twenty feet up Hoa Ma Street when a motor scooter zipped alongside.

"Hey, honey, you lookin' for friend? How 'bout some boom-boom tonight?"

I said, "How about giving me a ride to Hang Ga Street?"

"Sure," she said.

We sped into the chaotic night with thousands of other motor scooters, bicycles, and pedestrians. I sat drunk, grasping her tiny waist, wondering what this place would be like in fifteen years when Hyundais and Toyotas would choke the narrow streets.

We zoomed through town, its sidewalks alive with people enjoying the cool evening outside. Families, neighbors, and friends barbequed on small hibachis, games of backgammon and mahjong were played in full throttle, old war veterans shared tea and rice whiskey, and kids played with sparklers and fireworks. Fifteen minutes later, I was naked with Lan—boom-boom, good night.

•   •   •

Something about these flights is always thrilling. That odd space at thirty-two thousand feet, pressed tight against the side of a speeding jetliner, with no escape but a safe landing. *Strange,* I thought, *that we place such dogged trust in technology.* And yet, at cruising altitude, I seemed to do my best work with the lively side of a project awaiting at the arrival gate.

I reached for the red wine in its cheap plastic cup, polished it off, and immediately ordered another from a Japanese flight attendant with cute, dimpled cheeks. Outside, the aircraft's wings began to shake, and the plane started its long slow descent to safety. Fuji-san now filled my window on this cloudless afternoon, and I looked at its snow-covered belly. The sight of the famed mountain roused my adrenaline, and I pondered that decades before, it so excited Jack, Perkins, and Eugene that they climbed to her summit and sang their souls out on the way down. Sometimes, I consider that we don't take stock of those who have done it all before in our race through life.

I shut down my laptop and a seven-day plan to find Michiko or discover what had become of her. Success lay in one slim opportunity: the possible existence of a family-owned *washi* shop in Kakunodate.

Once through customs, the Narita Express swept me like a widget on a Ford assembly line to the Yurakucho Station. From there, I hailed a taxi to the Dai-ichi Hotel. The Dai-ichi placed me at the story's center, in the heart of Ginza and a short walk to where Club Florida would have been. The receptionist assigned me to an upper-floor room, and with the drapes wide open, the sprawling gray mass of Tokyo stretched before me—*All mine for a couple of days!* And I looked out the window to the Imperial Palace, Ueno Park, the five-storied pagoda at Senso Ji, the Sumida River, and Tokyo Tower.

To kick things off, I treated myself to a long hot shower, a cold beer, a juicy cheeseburger with fries and ketchup, and a bottle of Coca-Cola in the hotel lobby. Somehow, I envisioned Jack and the boys eating this meal at the Dai-ichi on one of their romps through town, and I wanted to get into their heads. So, finally, I left the hotel and worked my way across the underground and to the network of streets that Americans once referred to as 5th Street, Utility Avenue, Annex Avenue, Z Avenue, and the Ginza Main Street.

I walked to where Club Florida would have stood in 1949 and then the Club South Pacific, Club New Yorker, Bacchus Club, and Oasis. They were all decades gone, replaced by high-rise office space, condominiums, and ground-floor mixed-use retail with fancy neon signs. And I meandered to the main Ginza Street, one of my favorite streets in the world, and experienced it through their eyes. I imagined walking alongside them now, seeing their expressions and hearing the back-and-forth banter, their seeing the city again, now unrecognizable, but for the occasional landmark.

"Hey, Jack, there's the Kabukiza Theatre! It hasn't changed a bit in sixty years!"

"Well, I'll be damned, Perkins. I recognize that intersection! The Mitsukoshi Department Store and Mikimoto Pearls are still here. This sure as hell brings back memories!"

"Yeah, but wasn't the Lion Beer Hall right across Z Avenue? Well, it sure as hell ain't there now! But, Eugene, we had a good time at that beer hall, didn't we?"

That was how the afternoon went, experiencing the city through their eyes. And they knew that what they saw in the present, in part, was the result of their legacy, the culmination of a terrifically successful military occupation, and the outbreak of a brutal war that checked communist expansion at the 38th Parallel.

•   •   •

I met Sumiko in the hotel lobby for dinner and drinks at seven o'clock. She looked dazzling in a body-hugging black dress, and I unconsciously undressed her, recalling our passionate time together several years before.

"God, you look great, Sumiko, even without the short spiky hair. It seems like ages, and now it feels like yesterday!"

"Are you having second thoughts, Dane? You know, I am single again."

"Single! I thought you were joking. From when?"

"Six months ago. Hiroshi cheated on me. Of course, his secretary, so I'm divorcing him next month."

"Damn, I'm sorry to hear that!"

"No need to feel sorry. It was a well-timed discovery. So anyway, I'm burying myself in the law, and every day is the same—early morning yoga, ten hours at the office, and evenings at the gym."

"Well, it's showing. You look stunning!"

"*Arigato*, Dane-san!"

"And how do you like the law?"

"I like it. It fits my personality. Every case is unique and challenging; I'm learning something new every day."

"Well, you made it! I'm proud of you. And I remember when you nearly quit law school."

"It's an intimidating field for a woman in Japan. It terrified me, but you gave me courage, Dane. Your words infused the American perspective. I'll never forget that."

"And I'll never forget our good times. They're our secret treasures."

She reflected momentarily, staring into my eyes, exposing the remnants of the passion once shared.

"Tell me about Mr. Jack Pierce and Ms. Michiko Okura and how I can assist."

I gave Sumiko the complete backstory and asked if she might search Kakunodate's property, marriage, and death records and then accompany me to the small northern town for the weekend.

"I know I'm asking a lot, but your help would be critical."

"I'd love to go. A diversion is just what Sumiko needs! But there is one condition."

"And the condition?"

"We stay a night at the Tsurunoyu Onsen."

"Delightful! Just like old times!" I replied.

•   •   •

The following evening, we met at a stylish sushi bar in Roppongi.

"I've got some interesting findings," Sumiko said. "The grandfather, Yoshitaro, passed away on February 12, 1970. They listed the cause of death as dementia. The grandmother, Mieko, died from a stroke six years later, on April 11, 1976. The death certificate lists an address in Kakunodate."

"If the family lived in Kakunodate through 1976, why wouldn't Jack have discovered Michiko's grandparents or Kumiko when he returned in '53?"

"Good question."

"How about Michiko or Michiko's sister Kumiko, anything there?"

"Nothing on Michiko. However, I searched the ownership record for the family house, and Kumiko sold it to Mr. Taro Tanaka in 1985. Also, the last recorded taxes paid on the family's washi business were in the same year. Therefore, I assume Kimiko closed the business after selling the house."

"So, Kumiko would have been sixty-five years old in 1985 and in her mid-eighties today. Perhaps she is still alive," I suggested.

"It's possible. I searched the Kakunodate registry and didn't find a death certificate for Kimiko."

"Awesome finds, Sumiko. Now you know why you are indispensable! Tomorrow, our shinkansen departs at 9:00 a.m., and I've reserved an extra night at the *onsen*."

That night, Sumiko and I visited our old Shibuya stomping grounds and retired to my room before midnight. Sumiko showered, and I watched her stroll to her bed, wrapped tightly in a little white towel. Her well-toned body looked fine, and I considered making another pass, but I knew better. I texted Lan the details of the day's events and quickly fell asleep.

We arrived at Kakunodate Station before noon and hailed a taxi to the address listed on the death certificates. The taxi driver took us to the end of a narrow lane and then stopped at a modern, two-story tiled residence. A woman in her mid-forties confirmed she and her husband had purchased the property over fifteen years before. She explained they demolished the historic farm home shortly after and suggested we speak to the Kuge family, a decades-long Kakunodate clan and owners of one of the few remaining original farmhouses further up the street.

Mr. and Mrs. Kuge graciously invited us for tea. We watched the elderly woman bend over the old home's irori fire pit and hang an iron kettle above its flames with long skinny fingers. The fire and hot green tea warmed our bodies, even as snow began falling upon the persimmon trees outside.

"Yes, I grew up in Kakunodate and knew the Okura family, but not too well. I am between Michiko and Kimiko in age, so we were acquaintances, but not school playmates."

"Can you tell us what happened to the Okura family?"

"Kimiko returned to Kakunodate after her grandfather died. She and her grandmother ran the family's *washi* shop for several years, and Kimiko continued the business for several years after her grandmother passed."

"Do you know where Kimiko is now?"

"I don't; it's been almost twenty years since she left Kakunodate."

"How about Michiko? Do you know her whereabouts?"

"I had heard, but I don't remember from whom, that Michiko bore a daughter and later became a teacher. Michiko and Kimiko lived together for many years until Kimiko returned to Kakunodate to care for her mother and the family's business. That's all I know."

"Do you know where Kimiko moved once she sold the house?"

"No, but I believe she wanted to live closer to Michiko. I haven't heard anything for so long."

"Did you ever hear talk about a *gaijin* named Jack? He served in the occupation and would have visited the family's house in November 1949 and again in 1953 to search for Michiko."

"No, nothing at all. Anyway, the Russians detained me in the gulag until 1954. After I returned, I heard nothing of a *gaijin*. Even if there were a *gaijin*, talking about it widely in those days would be taboo."

"Do you know anybody we should speak to who may know about Kimiko or Michiko's whereabouts?"

"Unfortunately, I wasn't that close to them. After the war, I kept to myself and didn't mind other people's business. Our family just survived during those hard years."

We thanked the Kuges and caught a taxi to the town's only nursing home. The small, two-story concrete facility sat next to rice fields with a view of the river and a capacity for sixty residents. We met with the administrator, who suggested we introduce ourselves at the cafeteria during dinner hour. The residents, primarily widows and without caregivers, looked in their eighties and nineties, and I'd have enjoyed more of their time. Still, nobody knew anything that would lead us to Michiko.

• • •

A foot of fluffy white powder on a twenty-degree evening didn't cool the one-hundred-five-degree onsen, nor did it discourage Sumiko and me from tiptoeing naked through a snow-covered forest to submerge ourselves in the river. Instead, the onsen engulfed our goose-bump-riddled bodies like a warm yellow cocoon, and the icy winter wonderland became our delight. We slid like boiling tortoises along the pool's length and settled into a secluded corner below towering, snow-covered spruce, and handsome cedars. Snowflakes fell by the thousands, and the trees grew fluffy, buried in soft white sugar, so we sat naked for an hour, bathing within this warmly lit cocoon.

I thought of Sumiko and the pain she endured from the failure of her marriage, my girlfriend Lan and our relationship, and Jack and Michiko's lost love. But, beyond my journalistic instincts, I suspected other motives drew me to this wild goose chase. Perhaps, in part, regrets over my personal history studded with contentious childhood divorces and short-lived liaisons like the one I'd had with Sumiko.

Back in the room, we sat on the tatami mats warmed by a *kotatsu*, heated bedroll, with a bottle of warm sake. We reviewed what we had learned. Kumiko and her grandparents operated the family business for many more years after Jack's visit in 1949. But if they remained in Kakunodate, why didn't Jack uncover Michiko's whereabouts when he returned?

We also discovered that Kimiko sold the family home and moved in 1985. However, her whereabouts were unknown, and nearly twenty years had passed. As for Michiko, only through decades-old hearsay did we find she may have borne a daughter, opened a washi shop, and become a schoolteacher. If true, these events must have taken place during the 1950s. Thus, Michiko had likely married and started a new life, but that could be anywhere. With the low-hanging fruit harvested, I felt further from Michiko than when we started.

After several cups of sake, we stood from the *Kotatsu* and slid open the sliding window to watch snowflakes fall upon the cedars outside. Cold air rushed in and bit at our faces, and Sumiko turned and pressed herself tightly against my chest. At first, she cried softly, her head upon my shoulder, and then more profoundly, and I understood what she needed—she needed to move on. She wanted somebody to love her.

•　　•　　•

Upon returning to Tokyo, I caught a subway from the Dai-ichi Hotel to the Ikebukuro Station and a connection to Camp Drake. The encampment now served the Japanese Self-Defense Forces, but remnant American facilities remained. Most of these lay in ruins, overgrown by trees and heavy vegetation, eaten away by time and apathy. The area around the camp had also changed. Redevelopment replaced the long seedy strip of manly amusements with faceless, high-rise apartments, including where the Black Cat Bar and the Rex Hotel once stood. On the outskirts of the encampment, used car lots, gas stations, and low-rise commercial sprawl displaced the small truck farms and rice paddies where Michiko and Jack once escaped to their hideaway. Nor did I discover American soldiers moving about the sidewalks, smoking Chesterfields, looking for a joint to shoot pool or find a short-timer.

I walked along the perimeter of the Japanese Self-Defense Force base, peeking through the barbed wire fencing at military vehicles parked inside—Humvees, Bradley Fighting Vehicles, troop transports, and a dozen Sikorsky helicopters emblazoned with the rising sun. I spoke Japanese to a few young soldiers, a restaurant owner, a bartender, and a middle-aged woman walking a dainty white poodle on a ruby-studded leash. Nobody knew the area had once been a significant American military installation during the American occupation. Jack's story seemed dreamlike, except it wasn't because the mystery of Michiko's whereabouts remained unsolved.

I returned to the underground and purchased a ticket to Ginza. That evening, I planned to visit the Golden Gai, a historic neighborhood of small, hole-in-the-wall bars near Shinjuku's illustrious red-light district, popular among occupation soldiers. Perhaps an old-timer would know of Club Florida and the whereabouts of the people who once worked there. I arrived at the Dai-ichi Hotel at 4:30 p.m., took a scalding hot shower, and quickly fell asleep.

At 5:15 p.m., Sumiko called. I picked up the phone in a sleepy daze. "*Moshi, moshi*, hello."

I heard Sumiko shout excitedly through the earphone: "I have her address and found her phone number. She lives in Kamakura!"

"Kamakura, oh my goodness! How did you find her?" I said, now very much awake.

"I received a call from the nursing home in Kakunodate. A younger sister of one resident exchanged New Year's cards with Michiko until 1998. They gave me her address. I then located a telephone number."

"You are incredible, Sumiko!"

"So, what will you do, Dane?"

"We will call her!"

•   •   •

The following morning, on a Wednesday, Sumiko dialed the number. It rang three times, a fourth, a fifth, and a woman named Nanami answered on the sixth. "I'm sorry Michiko isn't available. She'll return in two hours. Can I take a message?"

Sumiko paused. "Yes, my name is Okamoto, Sumiko. I am with Dane Chandler, an American writer, and we would like to speak to Michiko regarding an American soldier she might remember from many years before, Mr. Jack Pierce. Please tell her I'll call again in three hours."

A long silence occurred on the other end.

"*Moshi, moshi*. Are you still there?" Sumiko said.

"Yes, I'm sorry. I'll give Michiko the message."

Sumiko and I gave each other a high-five. "We have to celebrate," Sumiko said. "I can't stand to wait!"

"Let's go to the Tsukiji Fish Market, drink beer, and eat sushi," I suggested.

We bundled into heavy jackets and walked down the bustling Ginza Dori straight for the harbor. During my first year teaching English in Tokyo, Sumiko and I took the same route at least a dozen times for the same purpose. So, I found it odd that several years later, and following many more lovers, we found ourselves not in the least bit disturbed by our prior intimacy.

We meandered through the tightly packed fish market to our favorite sushi vendor. I ordered a tall bottle of Asahi beer, a maguro and nigiri sushi platter, and two steaming hot Japanese rice bowls.

"Like old times, isn't it?" Sumiko said.

"It is. I had a great time. And I couldn't have done it without you, Sumiko."

"It's all I can do. But remember, you gave me the encouragement to complete law school."

"You can accomplish anything you put your mind to."

"Except for marriage."

"You know my opinion," I said, taking a stiff, bitter drink.

"I'm not giving up, Dane. And don't take my outcome, or your parents' divorces, as discouragement. Anyway, tell me about this Vietnamese girl, Lan."

"Amazing—I'm in love."

"So, is there a future?"

"I don't know. My shrink calls it 'commitment syndrome.'"

"Well, Mr. Commitment Syndrome, don't throw a good thing away."

"You sound like Jack. And maybe that's my underlying purpose here in Japan."

•　　•　　•

"*Moshi, moshi.*"

"Is this Ms. Okura, Michiko?"

"Yes, it is. Is this Ms. Okamoto, Sumiko?"

"Yes. Thank you for taking my call. I want to speak to you regarding Mr. Jack Pierce, if you don't mind. Did you know him?"

There was a long pause.

"Why do you ask about my relationship with Mr. Pierce?" Michiko said.

"I think it's best if Mr. Dane Chandler explains this himself. He's Mr. Pierce's acquaintance."

"I'm very sorry to bother you, Ms. Okura," I said. "Do you prefer English or Japanese?"

"English."

"Then receiving a call regarding Jack Pierce must be quite a surprise. But please let me explain."

"Yes."

"A year ago, I met Jack in Manila. He spoke in-depth about his experiences in Japan during the American occupation and the Korean War. After the war, I understand the two of you lost contact."

"Did he ask you to find me?"

"No. Jack doesn't know. But he told me a great deal about your time together. Did you know he tried to find you in 1953 but couldn't?"

"Is he well?"

"He is. Jack said he'd never forgotten your eyes. That your eyes are lovely."

Michiko giggled softly. "He had the most beautiful eyes. I remember them well. Did he marry or have children?"

"No, but he's had a good and adventurous life, if not a lonely one."

"Lonely?"

"Yes, Ms. Okura. I believe you were his one true love. Is it possible, Ms. Okura, that I might travel to Kamakura to meet in person?"

There was another long pause and then some whispers.

"Yes, Mr. Chandler. We would like to meet you."

"Thank you, Ms. Okura. Again, I'm sorry to have disturbed you. I have your address, so is tomorrow afternoon okay?"

"Yes, we will see you then."

The following day, I departed Tokyo Station for Kamakura at 1:00 p.m. I took a taxi from the station to the Tsurugaoka Hachimangu Shrine entrance and then down a narrow side lane to a quaint Japanese home surrounded by a neatly trimmed garden.

An attractive older woman with her hair rolled into a bun answered the door. She introduced herself as Michiko Okura and invited me to a living room overlooking a beautiful Zen Garden, with stands of bamboo, maple trees, azaleas, and a stone path leading to a meditation room with a sitting Buddha inside. She requested I sit, and she poured green tea.

"Please let me introduce my family. This is my daughter, Nanami, and my grandson, Yoshi, and granddaughter, Rie."

"It's very nice to meet you," I said, offering them gifts.

I studied Michiko as she spoke in near-perfect English. Time had shaped her features as water shapes soil, but I saw a woman of great splendor and grace before me.

"Because of the war, I lost my husband, father, mother, and elder brother. So, I didn't see a purpose for living at that time."

And as she spoke, I saw her, a beautiful young woman, boarding the train for Tokyo to find her happiness.

"I worked part-time at a dance hall. That is where Jack and I met. We danced, and I had never felt love so powerful. After he had returned from training near Mount Fuji, we moved into a small house in the countryside outside Camp Drake. We were both so much in love."

And with her memories, the past flashed before me. Michiko, trembling in the rain, waiting at the East Gate, dripping wet, hoping to find Jack. In the mountainous village of Nikko dressed in a beautiful kimono, posing for Jack by the bending red bow of the Shinkyo Bridge. And sobbing in Jack's arms, looking across the flattened landscape of her adolescence, recounting the Tokyo firebombing that took her parents.

"And then the war started, and Jack left for Korea," she said.

"What happened when he returned?" I asked her.

"His face lit up when he saw me. It made my heart burst with happiness. Then we returned to our house by Camp Drake and resumed our life."

"And then?" I asked her.

"One night, I remember Jack shivering uncontrollably in bed like he had a terrible fever. I asked if he was sick, and I tried to comfort him. He said he couldn't forget the horrible moment the captain killed himself and the look of sorrow on his face. 'I tried to help him before he did it,' Jack would say. But I didn't know how to help Jack. He started drinking too much, especially at night, and became increasingly troubled."

"And then?"

"A big incident occurred during the Hanami cherry blossom celebration. First, he acted crazy, almost violent, and it scared me. But then, he said, he needed time to figure things out. And finally, a week later, he returned to America."

"And you never saw him again?"

Michiko began to cry, and so did her daughter, Nanami, and they cried, cried, and cried.

When I saw her, I knew Nanami's father was Jack. Words cannot describe her beauty, even in her early fifties. She'd inherited her mother's large, oval-shaped eyes, her father's angular face, sensual red lips, light brown hair, and the cream-colored skin of the hapa-born child.

Michiko placed a wooden box on the table and opened it.

"When I discovered my pregnancy, I returned to Kakunodate to live with my sister and grandparents. I mailed Jack several letters, but he never responded, and like many others, I felt abandoned. Then Nanami was born in January 1953."

"How long did you stay in Kakunodate?" I asked her.

"Soon after my daughter's birth, I wanted independence, so I moved with Kimiko to Kamakura to open a washi shop. My grandmother and grandfather came to help for several months. Kimiko lived here with me to run the shop until my grandfather passed away, and then she returned to Kakunodate to accompany my mother. When she sold the house in 1985, Kimiko discovered this box in my grandfather's closet."

I opened the wooden box and removed the letters Jack had written. Date-stamped 1952, several letters from logging camps in Forks, Washington, and Sitka, Alaska. Then, date-stamped 1953, there were letters from Tibet and several more from Japan, including Kakunodate. Next, date-stamped 1954 through 1956, San Francisco and Fort Bragg, North Carolina. Then Panama, Italy, Germany, Hong Kong, Taiwan, and Okinawa; and in 1967, '68, and '69, Vietnam. From Subic Bay, Philippines, a final letter date-stamped July 1970.

"I cried for days when I received this shoebox. Jack pleaded for me to contact him, begged for my forgiveness in his letters, and explained that he had returned to Japan to find me. He described how he had searched, returned to my family home in Kakunodate, and sought our mutual friends, but I had disappeared. But incredibly, my grandmother and grandfather were in Kamakura when he returned to my hometown in 1953."

"This is incredible," I said, thumbing through the letters. "Is there a reason your grandparents would hide these letters from you?"

"I don't know why, but it's tormented me for years. I suspect my grandfather didn't trust Jack after he'd left me, and he believed I would leave Japan for America and worried he would miss his granddaughter and only great-grandchildren after losing so much during the war. That is all I can think of. But I am sure my grandmother knew nothing of these letters."

Nanami dried her eyes. "I tried to locate my father for several years, but couldn't discover anything about him."

"Your father became a CIA operative after retiring from the Army's special forces. The government would have protected his identity, and he could have been anywhere in the mid-80s."

I reached into my bag and retrieved the leather sketchbook. "Ms. Okura, Jack gave me this sketchbook. There are many drawings of you inside. There is also a letter he wrote from Kamakura in June 1950. He introduced you to his parents in this letter. I would like you and your daughter to have this."

Michiko took the sketchbook into her hands and brought it to her breast. "I still remember clearly," she said, "him drawing in this book."

"If possible, I would like to meet my father," Nanami said.

•　　•　　•

I checked into the Hotel Rural Loizu at 3:00 p.m. and made a reservation for the two of us for dinner at an outdoor café. I ordered a bottle of red wine, a Spanish Rioja, and it quickly took the edge off the morning's train ride from Madrid and my stewing over how I would break the news to Jack. With the support of the splendid Spanish countryside and the fruity Rioja, I felt alive, unburdened, and wonderful. I couldn't foresee how Jack might respond to my findings, but I felt sure he must know the truth about Michiko, his daughter, grandson, and granddaughter.

I poured myself a second glass of wine, breathing deeply into the sweet blackberry aroma when Jack entered the restaurant wearing a wide-brimmed black Cordovan and sporting a new, silver goatee.

"Alas, we meet again, but this time in Burguete, Spain—what an exciting life it is, my good friend!"

"You look great, Jack! I believe the Spanish trout have treated you generously."

"Very generously, Dane. As a young man, I'd dreamed of fishing Burguete, walking in the footsteps of Hemingway, so here I am."

"So, I will find you in the Green Hills of Africa next year?"

"Oh, I love those green hills, and there is nothing so pleasing as the Serengeti during the great summer migration. But, Dane, I can only stay put in Manila for so long; every year, I take a sabbatical from its chaos and make the world my oyster. And tomorrow, we will fish the River Irati. Perhaps, Dane, you will write a story about this fishing adventure, a tribute to the great American novelist!"

"I shall see, but Jack, I told you I have important news."

"Please tell me you have proposed to this beautiful Vietnamese woman. But first, I must have a smoke."

Jack removed a pack of camels from his breast pocket and struck a match, and then he reached into the same pocket for a fistful of handmade flies. "After your big news, I'll teach you the secrets of each fly so you can catch your limit tomorrow."

"Jack, Michiko is alive. That is the news I came to report. And you are a father. Your daughter's name is Nanami, and there are two grandchildren, Yoshi and Rie."

Jack stared back, his eyes wide open and wild-looking, and I wasn't sure if he would strike me with his fist.

"What? How can you say this, Dane? I searched and found nothing. I sent her letters for almost twenty years and nothing. Are you certain about this, Dane?"

"I'm very much certain. I met Michiko and your daughter."

"Why didn't you tell me you would search for her?"

"There were loose ends to your story in Japan, and I needed to close those gaps. But truly, I expected nothing to come of it."

"So she is not just a dream!"

"No, your Michiko is very much alive and well."

"And did you tell her about my whereabouts?"

"Yes, and they surely want to meet you."

"Then I must leave immediately. Where will I find her?"

"Kamakura."

•　　•　　•

Jack departed the following evening, and I remained in Spain for three weeks, even trying my luck on the River Irati. I then traveled to Paris and hooked up with Lan. On a clear March morning, I proposed with a single, long-stemmed rose and a bright diamond ring atop the Butte Montmartre. The city of Paris stretched before us, she accepted, and our lives became inseparable, offering fresh, infinite possibilities. It had been a long, circuitous journey, but I could now clearly see I wanted to live my life with her.

We returned to Hanoi the third week of April, arriving on a lovely spring morning. I eagerly looked forward to any news that may have come from Jack and his trip to Kamakura. I rode my bicycle to the Central Post. Inside, I retrieved a package and a single card from Japan. I placed them into my shoulder bag and continued to the Café Au Loc.

I took an outside table, the aromatic scent of spring filling my nostrils. I looked across the tree-lined boulevard to watch the cyclo drivers negotiate with European tourists at the Sofitel Metropole. Again, I let my shoulder bag sit on the table until I finished my coffee, and then I opened Jack's package. Inside, wrapped in heavy rubber bands, there were the dozens of letters Jack had written to Michiko, and a single handwritten note. It read:

Dear Dane,

I am writing this letter from a little table on the seashore, where I wrote to my parents many years ago about my new love. Fifty-five years later, I have reunited with her as a happy father of her beautiful daughter, whose age marks the years I was absent from their lives.

Perhaps some would say that our fate was cruel, and maybe this is true, but like the death of Perkins in battle, I've learned to accept the nature of things.

Dane, I do believe in destiny. You have become a central figure in my life and the life of my wife, our daughter, and our grandchildren.

Yes, Michiko and I tied the knot, and my future lies here, in Kamakura, where a young American soldier once dreamed of living his life with this beautiful Japanese woman.

You will find enclosed the letters I had written until 1970, when I determined I could write no more. I look forward to your visiting us in Kamakura, when we may continue our card-playing, and I can fill you in on the many other details of those wildly raucous years.

Yours truly,
Jack Pierce

Next, written on the most exquisite *washi* paper I had ever seen, I opened the letter from his daughter, Nanami.

Dearest Dane,

I hope this letter finds you well.

My father arrived on the afternoon of March 1, a Sunday. I can't explain in writing how excited, scared, and anxious I felt about meeting him. Yet so many unanswered questions remained, and I was terrified that the image I had constructed would collapse once I met him.

In the morning, before he arrived, we busied ourselves preparing. My mother visited the most esteemed beautician in Kamakura, and I bought her a lovely spring dress for the occasion. She looked beautiful!

I thought it best that she and my father have privacy, so I retreated to my childhood room and waited for his arrival. When the taxi came, my heart pounded so furiously that I thought I might die. So I buried my face in a pillow, but I couldn't help myself and opened the door to watch.

My mother stood tall, waiting, and her legs trembled. He knocked, and she feared to move. He knocked again, and she tiptoed to the door and opened it slowly, like a ghost might be on the other side.

I then saw my father for the first time in my life. Neither of them moved. They just stared into each other's eyes for the longest time. I began to cry, and tears were flowing down my cheeks. I watched them. I remembered my mother telling me, a child who looked different from all the others, that she dreamt of carrying his baby, and that baby was me. And on the day he arrived, I finally felt whole for the first time in my life. I saw my face in my father's face, my Japanese and American sides together, and I knew who I was.

"Michiko," he said.

"Hai," she said. And she reached out her hand, and he took it.

They both started to cry, and he took his hands and wiped the tears from her cheeks, and she wiped the tears from him, and she ran her fingers through his gray hair and over the lines upon his face, making sure he was real, and not one of her dreams. And then they embraced and looked at each other's faces again for the longest time, and I could see they were no longer old; he was twenty-one, and she was twenty-four. So, they held each other tight, and they kissed, and they began to dance, and they kissed again, and her steps were better than his, and he danced freely and alive, and she was truly happy for the first time in a very long time, and everything in the world was okay.

Nanami

About the Author

Michael J. Summers is the President of Planning Consultants Hawaii, a land use and community planning consultancy based in Maui, Hawaii. Thus, he "writes" for a living. But more importantly, he is a loving husband and father. Before becoming "serious," Mike spent his late teens and twenties backpacking the world "old school." He worked in Alaska, Hawaii, and Japan, spending dollars on cheap airline tickets, crash pads, and lifelong memories of the fantastic characters, places, and adventures along the way. Mike's unending passion for literature, travel, and nature has significantly influenced his writing.

Mike's debut novel, *Cherry Blossoms in Winter*, is a riveting historical fiction of post-war Japan, a soldier's forbidden love, and the Korean War.

Note from Michael J. Summers

Word-of-mouth is crucial for any author to succeed. If you enjoyed *Cherry Blossoms in Winter*, please leave a review online—anywhere you are able. Even if it's just a sentence or two. It would make all the difference and would be very much appreciated.

Thanks!
Michael J. Summers

We hope you enjoyed reading this title from:

BLACK ROSE
writing™

www.blackrosewriting.com

Subscribe to our mailing list – *The Rosevine* – and receive **FREE** books, daily deals, and stay current with news about upcoming releases and our hottest authors.
Scan the QR code below to sign up.

Already a subscriber? Please accept a sincere thank you for being a fan of Black Rose Writing authors.

View other Black Rose Writing titles at www.blackrosewriting.com/books and use promo code **PRINT** to receive a **20% discount** when purchasing.